Sil...

Chris Ryan

CORONET

First published in Great Britain in 2015 by Coronet
An imprint of Hodder & Stoughton
An Hachette UK company

First published in paperback in 2015

1

A CIP catalogue record for this title is available from the British Library

ISBN 978 1 444 75691 3
Ebook ISBN 978 1 444 77695 9

Typeset in Plantin Light by Hewer Text Uk Ltd, Edinburgh

Printed and bound by Clays Ltd, St Ives Plc

Hodder & Stoughton policy is to use papers that are natural,
renewable and recyclable products and made from wood grown in
sustainable forests. The logging and manufacturing processes
are expected to conform to the environmental regulations
of the country of origin.

Hodder & Stoughton Ltd
Carmelite House
50 Victoria Embankment
London EC4Y 0DZ

www.hodder.co.uk

acknowledgements

To my agent Barbara Levy, publisher Mark Booth, Charlotte Hardman and the rest of the team at Coronet.

one

The voice came down the line like a shiver.

'Avery, thank fuck,' the voice said. 'Arseholes had me on hold for ages. I'm freezing my bollocks off here.'

Avery Chance jerked upright in her chair at MI5 HQ in Thiepval Barracks. She recognized the voice at the other end of the line immediately. John-Joe Kicker was a lieutenant in the Provisional IRA's Internal Security Unit, otherwise known as the Nutting Squad, responsible for monitoring intelligence within the Provos' ranks. Chance had flipped Kicker three months ago. For her, as a novice intelligence officer in the field in Northern Ireland, recruiting a guy like Kicker had been a big deal.

'Joe,' she said. 'Where are you?'

'Backstage with fucking Bono. Where d'ya think?' Kicker said with a snort. It came down the line heavy and fast, like a sudden blast of wind. He went on, 'A phone box on the Falls Road. Listen, I can't stay on for long. Eyes all over the estate.'

Something in his voice alerted Chance. He sounded afraid. But Kicker was an IRA hard man and a convicted murderer, she thought. He'd done his time at Long Kesh. Kicker didn't do fear.

'What's going on?' Chance said.

'Not on the phone. Come and meet me.'

'The line's secure.'

Kicker forced out a laugh, like a one-man audience doing studio cheer. 'Bollocks,' he said. 'This line surely wasn't secure when Martin Sheedy spilled his guts to you. In fact it was so bloody un-secure poor Marty got a pair of bullets in the back of his head for his troubles. I might be betraying my own kind, but I ain't thick.'

Chance leaned back in her chair. 'I'll meet you then. The usual place. Nine o'clock.' She paused. Massaged her brow. 'But you can't keep me in the dark, Joe. I need to know what this is about.'

Kicker was silent for a couple of seconds, then said, 'You know how I said I'd call you if I had something big?'

'That was the deal.'

Another long pause. Chance listened to the line crackling, the wind blasting, police sirens in the background, the machine-like hum of life in east Belfast. Then Kicker took a deep breath and said, 'Well, I'm sitting on something big this time. And if you don't get your arse down here right now, this time tomorrow you'll be picking through a heap of dead soldiers.'

two

Chance was at the RV three minutes early. She hated being late.

She'd bombed up from Lisburn, willing her silver Vauxhall Cavalier to go faster as she threaded her way north up Prince William Road, towards the south-west corner of Belfast. A thin fog had started to spread like a net across the landscape by the time she bounced off the B101 and onto the A501 heading for Andersonstown.

Someone had once told Chance that Belfast was more British than the Queen's Christmas speech and more Irish than a pint of Guinness. That was still true. But times were changing. Bill Clinton had been elected President. Reagan made Irish jokes; Clinton wants to make Irish peace, ran the joke in the tobacco-choked social clubs up and down the province, and there was a kernel of truth in it. Clinton was pushing hard for a ceasefire and wooing Gerry Adams. Closer to home for Chance, the Whitehall rumour mill was working overtime. Whispers abounded that the British and Irish were poised to make a joint declaration on the peace process. Belfast was now divided between those who wanted to hang up their rifles and those who vowed to keep up the armed struggle.

The streets were empty as Chance reached the junction of Andersonstown Road and Suffolk Road. She shunted into Park but kept the engine running and the heater on full blast, the heat caressing her neck and face. She was grateful as outside it was the kind of cold that needled your skin and chipped away at your bones.

The council estate was a bare-knuckled sprawl of mean-looking houses and a parade of shops. Rusted shutters hung like heavy eyelids over the windows of a rundown betting shop and a cab office. A republican flag flew from the roof of every house. Murals on the end walls of the terraces commemorated hunger-strike victims and Palestinian terrorists, vivid splashes of colour amid a sea of grey, while mountains sagged on the horizon like a pair of casually shrugged shoulders. A sign on a nearby building carried a quote from the Old Testament: 'Prepare to Meet Thy God.'

Andersonstown was the kind of place where peelers were dragged from their vehicles and knifed in broad daylight and well-meaning civvies were kneecapped just because they had the wrong surname. Belfast in those days was one of the four Bs, along with Baghdad, Bosnia and Beirut. Places that festered like open wounds. Places the world had left behind.

Chance knew she was taking a big risk arranging the RV in the enemy's back yard. But she figured this was the perfect meeting spot for her source, working on the principle of hiding in plain sight. It would protect her source better than having him march up to the gates of the nearest RUC constabulary with every conspiring Jack and John in west Belfast looking on.

Besides, she got a kick out of the risk. From an early age, when her father walked out on her university lecturer mother to shack up with his PA, Chance had learned that if she wanted to get ahead in life, simply matching her male rivals was simply never going to cut it. She had to be *better* than the men. She had to work harder, longer, and above all smarter. And she had to be prepared to put her neck on the line.

Chance knew that she was not classically attractive. Still,

she had something about her. She was the kind of woman that intrigued men, rather than made them fawn over her. Her cropped brown hair was streaked blonde at the fringe and her small lips parted a little to reveal a prism of pearly-white teeth. She wore a dark suit that accented her hips and disguised her small breasts – the one part of her body that she hated. At sixteen she had been accepted by St Hilda's College, Oxford, to read Philosophy, Politics and Economics. She'd gone on to get a PhD in Logic at the Sorbonne, before joining MI5 at twenty-two.

She was one of the new breed of female fast-trackers: career women ready and able to climb the previously male-only intelligence ladder. Stella Rimington had blazed the trail for her sex in the security services in the late seventies, and her appointment as Director General in 1992 meant that MI5's glass ceiling had been smashed at last. Already the place was filled with highly capable female graduates determined to make the most of the opportunity.

There was just one problem. The men didn't like the fast-trackers.

For the first couple of years in Five, Avery Chance fast-tracked her way to nowhere, real fast. She transferred from one menial desk job to the next, sifting through reams of pointless int. She was an office junior in everything but name. The men had succeeded in pulling the rug from under the female fast-trackers. For a while, Chance considered leaving the service. That was in 1990, when the Cold War was over and MI5 felt more and more like a relic from a bygone age.

Her luck changed on a snow-caked February morning the following year. That day Provisional IRA terrorists parked a van on Horse Guards Avenue and fired three mortar rockets at Downing Street. They failed in their mission to assassinate Prime Minister John Major, but the attack signalled a ramp-up in PIRA's bombing campaign on British soil. Under pressure from a badly shaken government, MI5 was instructed to crush them from the inside. Chance volunteered for assignment to Belfast. A month later she finally got her wish. The fast-tracker was back on track.

She was tasked with identifying PIRA members who might be lured into working for the security forces. Keeping her ear close to the ground, she got to know just about every Mick and Shay north of the border dealing brown to the blacks, or getting some Proddy slag from the Shankhill Road up the duff. The more dark secrets Chance learned, the more leverage she had with potential recruits. Kicker had been her first success. The first of many, she hoped. Like several young women in Five, Chance had adopted a siege mentality towards her male colleagues. She lived and breathed a compulsive desire to better them. The victory the old boys had achieved proved their downfall. In the long term they didn't stop the fast-trackers. They just made them mad.

Two minutes and thirty seconds after she arrived at the RV, a figure slid from the shadows and walked quickly towards the Cav. The guy wore a light-coloured anorak, a dark sweater and grey trousers. He could have been any fucking Jack on his way to get pissed. His face was thin and angular, as if someone had carved out his features with the tip of a blade. His skin was stretched tight across his gaunt cheekbones and a neatly brushed mullet trailed down past the nape of his neck. All things considered, John-Joe Kicker looked like a two-pound shit stuffed into a one-pound bag.

Kicker stopped by the side of the car and rapped his bony knuckles impatiently on the front passenger window. Leaning over, Chance flipped open the door. A blast of chill air bit her nose, slapped her cheeks. Kicker climbed inside, rubbing his hands together like he was trying to get a fire going.

'You must have some brass fucking balls, coming down here,' he said in his clipped west Belfast accent. 'The only peelers you ever see round these parts are behind the wheel of an armoured Landie.' He frowned at the back seat. 'Where's your mate? The posh wanker.'

'Busy,' Chance replied quietly.

It was SOP for all agents to attend meets with sources as a pair. But Charles Grealish, Chance's usual partner, had been promoted, much to her annoyance, since he'd achieved little of note in Belfast. But Grealish was one of the old guard, one of the good old boys. As long as he didn't piss anyone off, he'd smooth his way to the top. And Chance was still awaiting a new partner.

'Were you followed?' she asked.

Kicker laughed deep in his throat. 'Was I fuck.'

'You're sure?'

'I got a taxi to the cemetery and walked the rest of the way here, sticking to the side streets. Just like you told me to do. I took more precautions than a bird on the pill.' Kicker's lips twisted into a bitter smile. 'Don't be forgetting that I've more to lose than you Brits. If the boyos ever find out I've been talking, I'm properly shafted.'

Chance moved the conversation on. 'Tell me what's going on, Joe.'

Kicker shook his head stiffly. 'First things first. After tonight, I want out. I'm done working for you. So before I give you the spread, we need to agree a few details.'

Chance jerked an eyebrow halfway up her forehead. 'What kind of details?'

'I'm talking about my dues, like.' Kicker licked his fingers and counted off a list. 'I want a house. Big, fuck-off garden. Somewhere nice and boring, where nothing ever happens. Like Surrey. A new identity to go with the house. And I want some shekels, too. A little hedge fund, to get me started. I want that in writing and all.'

'You're on a retainer. That's what we pay you for.'

'Bollocks!' Kicker growled, banging his fist on the dashboard. 'You pay me a couple of grand for the information I normally feed you. But this is different. This is top-level shite and I want to be compensated accordingly.'

Chance said nothing. She waited for Kicker to finish his rant. Watched the guy slump back in his seat, his muscles jumping with anger, his head thumping back against the headrest. She patiently waited for the rage to deflate, like a slashed tyre. When Kicker had calmed down, Chance looked him hard in the eye.

'You're done,' she said evenly, 'when I say you're done.'

Kicker opened his mouth but Chance cut him off before he could get a word in. 'The only reason you're here,' she told him, 'meeting with an agent of the British government, is because you were dumb enough to fool around with Victor Costello's wife.'

Kicker flinched at the mention of Costello. With good reason, Chance thought. Costello was the chief of the Nutting Squad. He was also a notorious sadist. He didn't just torture people. He took them on a personal tour of the seven circles of hell. He sewed the severed testicles of informants into their mouths. He cut off eyelids with playschool scissors. As a kid, rumour had it, Costello would tie two cats together by their tails and hang them over a washing line, watching them scratch each other to death.

'You'd better cooperate with me,' Chance continued, 'or tomorrow Costello will open his post and find an envelope full of pictures of you getting real cosy with Caitlin.' She spoke in a delicate but sharp voice. Like a blade slashing silk. Kicker squirmed. Chance paused, milking it. Then she twisted the knife. 'You're a big boy, Joe. I don't need to tell you what Costello would do to you if he found out you were sticking one up his missus.'

Kicker pulled a sour expression. 'You're a bitch.'

'Maybe I am.' Chance's bright blue eyes smiled at him. 'But I'm the bitch who has you by the balls.'

Kicker chewed on the tepid air for a long beat. He clamped his lips and eyes shut and stewed. Chance left him to it and scoped out the estate. The Devlin Social Club stood on the nearest corner. Its windows were boarded up and graffiti scrawled over a poster to the side of the door read: 'BRITS FUCK OFF.' A few old men with too much time and too little money, their hands stuffed in their pockets, miserable faces like picked scabs, shuffled in and out of the place, busily pissing away their Giros.

Kicker popped open his eyes. Chance looked back at him.

'I'll do what I can to help you,' she said. 'But you're going to have to trust me.'

Kicker sighed. 'There's a shipment coming in tomorrow. Eight in the morning. On the Galway coast. I don't know the exact location, on account of the fact Costello ain't telling.'

Chance greeted the news coolly. 'When did you find out about this?'

'Six, seven hours ago?' Kicker shrugged. 'I didn't know anything about it until Costello ordered us all to a meeting. I've been trying to reach you ever since. Jesus, you think I'm holding something back from you?'

'Let's just say some of your tribe have a history of being selective with the truth.'

'Go fuck yourself, Avery. I came to you the minute I heard. Getting hold of int these days ain't easy. Costello is keeping everyone out of the loop. What with all the arrests lately, he's acting paranoid. Everything is on a strictly need-to-know basis, like.'

'What's in the shipment?'

Chance was fully expecting Kicker to reel off the usual shopping list of Semtex, mortars, decommissioned rifles and Second World War pistols, kit that trickled in from East Germany and the former Soviet satellites. But he didn't do that. Instead the Nutting Squad lieutenant sucked in a heavy dose of air and said, 'Stingers.'

Chance felt her blood run cold. Suddenly it seemed freezing in the car.

'Stinger missiles?'

'Aye, and plenty of 'em. We're talking enough to blow a hole in every Brit chopper in the province.'

Chance felt her flesh crawl. The Provos had been trying to get their hands on anti-aircraft weapons for years. They knew that the British relied heavily on Chinook helicopters to resupply several of their bases across Northern Ireland, especially the more remote bases inaccessible by road. Armed with the infrared FIM-92 surface-to-air missile launcher, a single PIRA shooter could down British choppers at the click of a button. Each Chinook represented a critical supply line to the military. Blow them out of the sky and suddenly the situation north of the border would look a lot more hairy.

Another thought burst the bubble Chance was in. 'That's impossible,' she said, shaking her head. 'The FBI has clamped down on the traditional smuggling route from Florida. Of course, the Libyans supplied weapons for a while, but they've gone quiet recently. And we monitor all the major shipping channels. There's no way anyone could smuggle in missiles without our knowing about it.'

Kicker flashed his palms at the agent. 'I'm just telling you the craic, love. Make of it what you will.' He shifted in his seat. After getting comfortable he continued, 'I went to the meeting with the other lads, right. Then Costello starts going on about times being tough. What with all the heat on us from the Brits, you lot infiltrating our ranks, and the shipments from Florida and Libya going Pete Tong.'

'Go on.'

'Then Costello suddenly lights up like the Fourth of July, and says we're gonna turn the tables on the Brits. Says there's a shipment coming in tomorrow, 0800 hours, and we're to cache the consignment down by the border. One of the boyos asks what's in the consignment, and Costello comes right out with it and says, Stingers. The guy looked pleased with himself. Like he'd just landed himself a hot date with that slag from *Baywatch*.'

Chance stared out of the window, and wondered. A new arms smuggling route? Possible, she conceded. The PIRA leaders had been casting their net far and wide in the hunt for new sources of armaments. So far they had met with limited success. Outfits like the PLO and the Colombian FARC were running low on stocks themselves. Certainly those terrorist organizations lacked the means to provide a shipment of Stingers. And no credible nation state would dare flout international sanctions by selling arms to the Provos.

So who's behind the sale? Chance was thinking. 'Where's the shipment coming in?'

'I don't know.'

'You just said you were at the meeting. Don't lie to me, Joe.'

'I ain't lying. We know the when and the what. Costello is keeping the where close to his chest. Eight o'clock in the morning, that's what we were told. We meet Costello at his house. Then a big pile of us Nutting Squad boyos head down to Galway and load the consignment into the back of several trucks. We're to be given maps with the coordinates of weapons caches. New caches, mind – ones that you don't know about.'

Chance looked through the windscreen, soaking up the int.

She saw a wafer-thin middle-aged man emerging from the Devlin Social Club. He was wearing a Boston Red Sox baseball cap and a naff green bomber jacket. The cap's brim shaded his face, so Chance couldn't make out his features. He stopped outside the door, reached into the jacket pocket and plucked a cigarette from a packet. Cupped his shovel-like hands around the trembling flame. Chance noted that his fingers were stitched with colourful tattoos. The man stood in the shadow of the club, sucking on his tab.

The MI5 agent turned back to Kicker. Looked him dead in the cracks of his eyes. 'You have to help me out here, Joe. If what you're saying is true, then the Provisional IRA is about to get its hands on weapons that could derail the peace process for decades. None of us want that, do we?'

'I guess not.' Kicker's voice was soft and thoughtful.

He had a six-month old baby, Chance knew. Name of Mary. PIRA men always turned a little soft when their women started pumping out babies. Chance played on that, gripping Kicker's hand. The human touch. 'You need to give me something more. Something I can go back to my bosses with.' She gently withdrew her hand. 'If they see you're not cooperating, Five will withdraw its protection. Word will get around: Joe turned snitch. All those boyos you passed over to us will be very upset. You don't want little Mary to grow up not knowing her father, now, do you? Of course you don't. You're a good man, Joe. Not a monster, like the others.'

Chance could see her words working their magic. In the periphery of her vision she spotted the guy in the Red Sox cap walking away from the Devlin. Hands stuffed in the pockets of his bomber jacket, chin tucked tight into his chest against the lacerating cold. It was dark and she couldn't make out his face.

Kicker pulled his hand away. Cracked his knuckles and

stared at a spot in the footwell. A small man wrestling with a big problem. Belfast all over. 'This can't be traced back to me,' he said eventually. 'If the RA top brass finds out I've dobbed them in, I'm done for.'

'You have my word.'

A sharp intake of breath, then Kicker said, 'There's this guy.'

'What guy?' A strange thrill ran through Chance at the mention of this new arms smuggler. She was on the verge of uncovering something so big it would blow away her male colleagues. She had a vision of following Rimington all the way to the top.

Kicker dropped his voice so low it could've crawled under the belly of a snake. 'All I know is, the smuggler goes by the name of Colonel Jim. He's like the Father Christmas of the arms trade. Costello reckons he's sitting on enough kit to start World Wars Three, Four and Five and have enough left over for seconds.'

'Where can we find him?'

But Kicker wasn't tuned in. He was facing stiffly forward. Chance followed his gaze. Then she noticed something odd. The man in the Red Sox cap had stopped briefly at the corner of Andersonstown Road and Suffolk Road. He was waving at a pair of headlights thirty metres further south on Andersonstown Road. He hunched his shoulders, looked down at the ground, moved on.

A split second later Chance saw a white Ford Transit surge into view. Speeding directly along Andersonstown Road towards the Cavalier, its growl cutting through the glassy silence. It screeched to a halt ten metres from the Cav, blocking the road.

Then the side doors flew open and four figures in bala-clavas streamed out.

Gunning straight for the Cav.

three

Chance didn't panic. Not at first.

The road behind the Cav was completely clear. She quickly selected Reverse. Figured she could back up north along Andersonstown Road towards the Falls Road and the Westlink, and the sanctuary of Protestant east Belfast.

The four balaclava-clad men swarmed towards the Cav. Provos, without a doubt, she thought, from their Denison camouflage smocks and shapeless, acid-washed jeans right down to their fingerless leather gloves.

'Oh, sweet Jesus, they're coming right for us,' said Kicker, trembling as he spoke, each word sounding like a gasp.

Chance saw the weapons then. All four PIRA men were tooled up. The nearest two gripped AK-47 assault rifles. Their muckers a couple of steps further back were toting Czech-manufactured CZ 75 semi-automatic pistols. They clearly meant business.

Chance said, 'They wouldn't dare open fire. We're in a densely-populated area—'

'That's more Irish than a bottle of Bushmills,' Kicker said, his voice shaking. 'The locals are used to getting shot at by the RUC fellas. Everyone who lives here knows the drill. Look around you.'

Chance glanced up. Kicker was correct, she realized. The

streets had suddenly emptied. A tremor of panic tickled her chest as she put her foot down hard on the pedal, the Cav's engine screaming as she reversed and picked up speed. In seconds the speedo showed thirty kilometres per hour, the steering wheel jerking in Chance's grip, her wrists burning as she fought to keep the car in a straight line. Kicker stared dead ahead. His eyes had widened to poker chips. He had a look on his face like he'd just seen someone rape his mother.

Chance had reversed twenty-five metres when she saw headlights flare up in the rear-view mirror. Her guts squirmed. They were forty metres behind her. Two pairs of them, she realized. Now she could see they belonged to a couple of black cabs, their 'For Hire' signs glowing apricot on the roofs.

'Slow down, for fuck's sake!' Kicker shouted.

But Chance just stared numbly as the headlights swelled in the mirror, her foot still on the accelerator. They're picking up speed, she thought. There's no escape. Fear sank its teeth into her neck. The taxis were racing towards the Cav.

'Stop!' Kicker screamed.

Now Chance snapped out of her stupor and hit the brakes. The Cav wobbled, the rear bumper swerving hard right. The tyres squealed. Then the car stopped in the middle of the road, thirty metres from the Transit, twenty ahead of the taxis. The cabs were still accelerating towards her.

Chance frantically shifted into Drive. The cabs were now just ten metres behind her, their headlights almost whiting out the rear window. Both of them braked at the last moment. And in that same instant Chance yanked the steering wheel hard left and surged forward, steering off the road, towards a grass verge opposite a row of dingy shops. Away from the four gunmen, two now ten metres ahead, the other two just behind, all racing towards the Cav. The speedo was touching fifty now, the engine grinding. Chance still thought she could get away.

Then she spotted the nearest two gunmen drawing their AK-47s level with their shoulders. She heard a roar as the two weapons lit up, flames licking out of their snouts. The gunmen discharged their rounds in simultaneous three-round bursts. The road flashed white, then smoke snorted across Chance's line of vision. For a breathless second she allowed herself to think they had missed. Then the Cav slumped on its axis as a torrent of hot lead punctured both front tyres. A loud hissing filled the air, soon replaced by the whump-whump of rubber bouncing on tarmac. The car jolted to a halt. Chance's seat-belt pulled tight across her chest, squeezing her lungs. A hot pressure exploded inside her skull. Her neck muscles tensed painfully. Beside her Kicker was thrown forward, his head banging against the dash before snapping back.

The gunmen each fired a second time. Six bullets punched holes in the radiator grille and glanced off the bonnet. Smoke filtered out of the grille. The car's alarm shrieked the same insane note, over and over. A single round nicked the wind-screen, fracturing the glass like a pickaxe hitting a block of ice. Chance and Kicker ducked under the dash as a third set of three-round bursts fizzed out of the assault rifles. Six more bullets ripped into the car. Chance closed her eyes. She was sure that she would die.

But the shooting cut out. Just like that. The alarm too. The air was filled instead with the hiss of the radiator, the erratic tapping of the engine. Chance put her fingers to her temples. It felt like someone had drilled holes in the sides of her skull.

She heard shattered glass crunching underfoot. Voices shouting. Coming from her three o'clock. Drawing near to her. Beside her Kicker pawed groggily at the mashed-up bridge of his nose.

Chance cleared her throat. 'Joe,' she said. 'Wake up. We have to leave. *Now!*'

'Gah—'

'Get those cunts out!' a voice spat from outside the car in a bog-Irish accent.

Her door was flung open before Chance could react. A hand thrust into the car and clamped around her right wrist. Meanwhile the second gunman had opened Joe's door, grabbed his neck and was shaking his head from side to side like he was trying to shake a spider out of his hair.

'Oh sweet Jesus no!' Joe moaned in a nasal tone. 'I ain't dying. Not here!'

He wrenched himself free and threw himself out of the car. The gunman grabbed at him but Kicker ducked out of the way and ran screaming towards the grass verge. Chance moved to help him, but the hand gripping her wrist yanked her out of the Cav with such violence that she thought her arm would be ripped from its socket. Helpless, she watched Kicker try to escape. He was staggering as if the left side of his body had been anaesthetized. He was never going to make it. She knew that much. He managed to put four or five metres between himself and the car before the other two gunmen rushed at him from one side. One of them jabbed him in the lower back with the stock of his AK. His mucker booted him to the ground. A short, sharp cry of agony pierced the air. Then there was a flurry of grunts as the tow of them attacked Kicker, the sound of hard wood cracking against bone as both now swung their rifle stocks at him like lumberjacks chopping wood. Kicker raised his hands in a desperate effort to shield his head from the flurry of blows.

Chance turned to face the gunman who had hauled her out of the car.

'You bastard!' she screamed, trying to shake off his fearsome grip.

No response. Then guy was built like a testicle on a pair of stilts, his zipped-up jacket almost bursting open from the thick muscle packed into his torso. His shoulders resembled a couple of rugby balls stuffed into a sack. But his legs were thin and wildly out of proportion to his upper body, and they were bent at the knees, as if straining under the sheer weight they were supporting. His eyes glowered. They were dull and black as a pair of eight balls, and set deep in their sockets.

Stilts gripped a CZ 75 semi-automatic in his right hand. His index finger teased the trigger. Chance found her eyes drawn to the pistol. She stopped struggling to break free when the muzzle was six inches from her face. Strange, being so close to death. Stilts made that feeling realer still, jamming the CZ 75 against her cheek. She shivered as the circle of cold metal dug into her flesh.

'Keep your mouth shut,' he said in a dead-flat voice. 'Scream and I'll fucking put the nut on you right now.' He turned to the gunman at his side. 'Get this slag in the van.'

'What about the peelers, Bill? We'll have woken up the whole neighbourhood. They'll be here any minute.' The second gunman's voice jangled like a bag of rusty washers. He had the awkward demeanour of a kid not yet out of his teens and a scrawny physique to match. Stilts rounded on Skinny, shooting him an evil glare.

'Never mind about the cops. Just get a bloody move on.'

Skinny, clearly scared, nodded quickly. He grabbed Chance and manhandled her towards the Transit. As they hurried along she glanced across her shoulder and saw the other two gunmen scraping Kicker off the ground. His head hung low and from the little she could see of his features, his face had been beaten to a pulp. It looked like a tissue someone had used to staunch a nosebleed. His eyes were closed. Drool spilled down his chin. He appeared to be unconscious. The two gunmen dragged him towards the side of the Transit. Chance swung her head back to Stilts and Skinny. Her mind was racing, still unable to process the past few minutes. This wasn't happening. It couldn't be. Not to her. Not now.

'You're making a big mistake,' she said, her voice high as she strained to keep a lid on the panic rising in her throat. 'I'm a civilian. A government officer, not a soldier. Let me go.'

Stilts looked back at her. There was a cold and impersonal gleam in his eyes and she felt it then – the hatred burning inside him towards her, towards every Brit. 'Just get in the van, bitch.'

Chance opened her mouth to argue again. But Stilts clamped a hand over it and squeezed hard with his filthy-nailed fingers, silencing her. Stilts slid back the side door of the Transit and shoved her in. She let out a gasp as she hit the floor. The inside of the van was a cold void filled with the smell of fresh paint and sawdust. A moment Kicker was dumped beside her. He didn't make a noise. His eyes were clamped shut, his mouth slack. Then Stilts and Skinny climbed in after their victims.

'We did it,' said Skinny, shaking with disbelief. 'Jesus Christ, we did it.'

'We're not out of the woods yet,' said Stilts, pulling the door shut. 'We've still got to get this slut across the border. Keep your guard up, son.'

'Aye, Bill.'

'And stop using my fucking name!'

Chance lay there in the stippled darkness, light trickling through the metal grille between the driver's cab and the rear compartment. Kicker lay sprawled on his front, his features turned to mush, blood bubbling from his nostrils. Everything seemed unreal to the agent. Stilts banged a fist on the grille. A moment later the driver started the engine and as the van pulled away and over to the left, Chance felt her stomach shoot up into her throat.

Stilts turned back to her and booted her in the groin. She lay dry-heaving on the floor, bent double with agony. Skinny looked on as his mate followed up with a right hook to Chance's face. The blow snapped her head back and sent a hot pain shooting down her spine. Her world disintegrated into dim shapes and blunted shadows. The Transit shuddered as it picked up speed. Chance tried to shake her head clear. Her world semi-resolved. She was conscious of Stilts towering over her. Even though he was wearing a balaclava, she could have sworn he was grinning at her.

'Smile, sweetheart,' he said. 'Your wish is about to come true.'

'What wish?' Chance asked anxiously. 'Who are you?'

'We're from the Nutting Squad, love. We're taking you to meet Costello. He wants a word.'

Chance fell silent. Steadied her breathing. Filling her lungs with precious oxygen. She hoped she looked suitably terrified. She watched as Stilts turned away to peer through the grille at the road ahead. Then she took a deep breath and slid her right hand down to her waist. Her movements were subtle and measured. Delicate. Keeping one eye on Stilts and the other on Skinny, she slipped her hand inside her blouse, feeling for the shiny black, matchbox-sized device strapped around her body. Every MI5 agent operating in the field wore one. The black box was the sole reason Chance wasn't completely shitting herself at being abducted by the Nutting Squad. It was her safety net.

Now Chance pressed the panic button on the transponder. In an instant the device transmitted a distress signal on an Ultra-High Frequency back to Thiepval Barracks. It did this by jumping on the REBRO radio-rebroadcast network established across Northern Ireland, transmitting across multiple frequencies and nets to reach its destination. Within seconds the agent's superiors would receive the signal and set a rescue plan in motion. Relief flushing through her system, she let her hand fall away from her blouse just as Stilts spun around.

Chance wore her best frightened face. Smiling on the inside. Now all she had to do was wait.

four

The Transit sped out of Andersonstown. Chance, squatting, couldn't see where they were taking her. But she was aware of Stilts's lustful gaze. With the noise of the engine juddering through her skull, she closed her eyes and repeated a few words to herself, intoning them inwardly like a prayer.

'Everything is going to be OK.'

She had relayed the distress signal. Five had probably already dispatched a rescue unit. They would get to her in time.

'Everything's going to be OK.'

The van stopped shaking. The road smoothed out. There was a buzz of traffic around them. Chance figured they were joining the slipstream of traffic heading out of Belfast. It was a reasonable guess. The Nutting Squad wouldn't want to stick around the North for a moment longer than they had to. Not with a pair of kidnap victims in the back of the van. Too risky. The RUC had stop-and-search powers and enthusiastically employed them. Chance pulled herself upright. Just hang on for a few more minutes, she told herself. She drew comfort from the fact that as soon as the alert was sounded at Lisburn, an RAF Westland Lynx would immediately deploy over Northern Ireland. The helicopter had an electronic listening device programmed to pick up the signal transmitted by her black box. Flying at a height of six hundred metres, staying above cloud cover to avoid being sighted by the Nutting Squad, the Lynx would quickly narrow down the radius of the blip to an area roughly the size of a small street. A signaller based at Lisburn would relay the int on the location over a secure comms line to the ground-based retrieval unit. Then it was simply a matter of waiting for the boots on the ground to establish a Mark One eyeball on the coordinates and locate their target.

Chance decided to try to engage with Stilts. Partly because she remembered her training, and how vital it was to try to humanize herself in the eyes of her abductors. But also because she wanted to tease details out of the guy.

'Where are you taking me?' she asked.

'Don't you worry, darling.' Stilts's voice was trembling with excitement. The guy couldn't wait to get stuck into her. 'Where you're going, none of your Brit mates will ever find you.'

Stilts knelt down beside the agent and slithered a hand between her legs. He grabbed her crotch and squeezed. Chance winced with agony as he whispered into her ear. 'Costello's gonna make you scream. By the time he's done with you, you'll be begging for a quick shot to the head.'

He drew his hand away. 'But you won't get it. No, love. We've got the mother of all tortures planned for you.'

Chance stayed very still. Sweat leaked out of her anus. Stilts glanced away from her, nodded at Skinny.

'Pay attention now, son. This here is an important lesson. When you're dealing with the Brits, you'll have to bear in mind that they're sneaky pricks. Can't be too fucking careful. You hear me?'

Skinny nodded vigorously. 'Gotcha, Bill.'

Stilts shot him a look. Then he turned back to Chance. His eyes were wide, gleaming and hungry. 'Take this slag. A real piece of work. Playing the old sympathy card. Don't believe a word of it. The first thing you do with a bitch like this is take her dignity away.'

'How?'

'Take her clothes off.'

Chance began to panic. If Stilts stripped her naked, he'd discover the transponder. 'You don't have to do this,' she said. 'I can cut you a deal.' She glanced at Skinny. 'Both of you.'

Stilts balled his hand and punched her in the guts. She doubled up in vicious pain, her breath needling her throat, her brain feeling like it was swelling, as if her skull might split open. Tears nudged at the corners of her eyes. She tried backing away and curling herself up into a ball. Stilts merely slugged her again.

'Time to earn your spurs, lad,' he barked at Skinny. 'Strip her.'

Stilts grunted approvingly as the younger man tore off Chance's high-heeled shoes. She thrashed and kicked out wildly, but she knew she was just delaying the inevitable. For her efforts she got a boot to her chest from Stilts and went limp. Now Skinny ripped off her trousers, laughing as he did so, filled with excitement and adrenalin, goaded on by Stilts. He tossed them aside. Stilts gave Chance another couple of swift digs to the head, dazing her. She was dimly conscious of Skinny removing her jacket. Then he tore open her blouse, the buttons scattering across the floor. Suddenly she was down to her knickers and bra.

Then Skinny stopped cold.

There was a terrible silence.

'Hey,' Skinny said at last, his voice a nervous whisper. 'There's something strapped to her waist.'

Stilts dropped to one knee and leaned towards Chance. She flicked her eyes up at him. He stared at the transponder.

Didn't move for several seconds. Skinny backed off. Then Stilts reached down and ripped off the device, snorting angrily behind his balaclava.

'What is it, Bill?' Skinny asked in a whisper.

'Fucking tracking device. This bitch is hot.'

'Maybe we should keep it, Bill? Give it to the engineers, like.'

'Should we bollocks,' Stilts hissed. 'The wankers have probably got a tail on us as we speak. No, I've got a much better idea. Here, get out of my way.'

He tugged open the van door. It was only then – when he tossed the transponder into the tar-black landscape screaming past, along with her trousers and jacket, blouse and shoes – that Chance understood she was in big trouble.

five

2201 hours.

Four kilometres to the north a sleek black Audi Quattro tore through the filmy night as it hunted down the Transit. Belfast was bright in the rear-view mirror, lighting up the sky in oranges and purples, singeing the undersides of the tightly packed clouds. Ahead was a still, perfect blackness, with nothing visible but the faint outlines of trees and a couple of lonely lights on the horizon. The Quattro's headlights raked the narrow road. The three SAS operators in the car hadn't passed another vehicle since turning onto the New Road. They were officially in the middle of nowhere, surrounded by warped fields that resembled swells in a vast black sea.

'Shit,' said the sergeant in the front passenger seat. 'The signal's stopped.' Sergeant Benson Foulbrood glanced at the driver. 'Step on it, man. Before we lose them.'

'Where'd the van stop?' the driver asked, his Scottish accent thick as frozen mud.

'Eight hundred metres west of Silverbridge, on the Newry Road,' Foulbrood grunted back. 'If we pull this one off, I might order the other lads to stop taking the piss and calling you a Jock bastard.'

'Pity,' Jock replied. 'I've grown attached to the name.'

He meant it, too. He was a Dundee lad, and like every kid who'd grown up in that coastal pit, living in the shadow of

Edinburgh and Glasgow, he'd learned not to take shit from anyone, to never back down in a fight. If that's what the other guys in the Regiment considered a bastard, then he was proud to be one. Now Jock upped the speed to a hundred and twenty. In the rear-view mirror a cluster of lights cracked and popped. There were six vehicles in the rescue team: four Regimental Audi Quattros, souped up to the max and kitted out with secure comms units, and two Ford Sierra surveillance cars manned by officers from Special Branch. The vehicles were spread out behind Jock on the single-lane road, with from fifteen to thirty metres between them.

The Audi shuddered as he pushed the turbocharged 2.1-litre engine all the way. The third Blade stewed in the back, clinging on for dear life as they gunned south, on the trail of the Transit.

The three men crammed into the Audi were decked out in civvies, the standard dress code for SAS operators in Northern Ireland: denim jeans, T-shirts and black fleece jackets with roomy pockets on the sleeves. Stashed in their jacket pockets were baseball caps with 'ARMY' emblazoned on the front in case things got noisy. Heckler & Koch HK53 semi-automatic rifles stashed beside the car doors.

They had hit 130k per hour.

'I put us a hundred metres north of Silverbridge,' said Foulbrood. 'Five clicks from the border. Not far now.'

Jock grunted, gripping the wheel hard, like he was trying to choke it to death. 'We can nail the bastards before they move.'

'The signal stopping is bad news,' the Blade in the back seat put in. His voice had the hoarse drone that is unmistakably Mancunian. 'They might have already slotted the agent, mate.'

Jock glowered at him in the rear-view mirror. 'What are you talking about? The Paddy bastards have pulled over to the side of the road. This is our big chance to catch them. *Mate.*'

Foulbrood nodded his agreement with the Manc and
sucked his gums. 'I'm afraid so,' he said. 'The Nutting Squad
have a reputation for executing their victims and dumping
their bodies in ditches. It's very likely they're about to give
Chance the double-tap treatment.'

Manc looked pleased with the mental pat on the back from
Foulbrood and smiled, his lips barely visible beneath his beard.
He got on well with the sergeant, Jock knew. But then again,
he reckoned Manc was the kind of guy who got on well with
anyone higher up the food chain. They were both new recruits
to the Regiment, but only one of them had a first-class degree
in arse-kissing.

'Let's hope you're wrong,' said Jock.

'"Hope" is the right word, mate. The blokes in the Nutting
Squad are sick bastards. If you'd done your research, you'd
know that the odds of the agent surviving are pretty fucking
slim.'

'Well put, man,' said Foulbrood.

Jock banged a fist on the wheel in frustration. He was
twenty-one, with a permanent frown etched across his brow
and a coiled sort of physique, his muscles tight, his veins
twisting up from his forearms to his neck like lengths of taut
rope. His eyes gleamed like polished silver as he focused on
the road ahead.

They were passing through Silverbridge now.

Jock felt his guts tighten into a knot. He was the youngest
Blade in the history of the Regiment, but he figured that
already he knew more about being an operator than the other
two pricks with him. An hour ago he'd been on the Shankhill
Road doing his orientation training, the Regiment equivalent
of the Knowledge, trying to memorize the layout of every
street and every short-cut until he knew the city better than
the back of his hand. Then the distress call had come over the

comms. A minute later the Blades were slingshotting west on the B38 out of Belfast, through Upper Springfield and Hannahstown, touching 130k per southbound along the Moira Road section of the A26. They had taken the third exit at the roundabout, headed south on the B3 towards Bleary, sweeping through the mixed Catholic and Protestant enclaves of Gilford and Scarva before racing towards Newry.

Following the directions relayed from the Lynx, the rescue team were pursuing the Nutting Squad metre by metre. Minute by minute.

But they had been playing catch-up since heading out of Belfast and the van was always one step ahead of them, the captured agent tantalizingly out of reach. By the time the Audi had rushed through Poyntzpass and Goragh and then west on Camlough Road, which led onto the Newry Road stretch of the A25, they were still four kilometres behind the signal.

Jock hated to admit it, but Manc was right. The agent was probably shafted.

The driver hated everything about the guy in the back seat. He'd known him since they took Selection together. Jock had finished first in the hill run, but Manc had stolen the honours on the advanced driving course. The two recruits were polar opposites in just about every way. Jock liked to unwind with a bottle of Johnnie Walker and a flirt with a cheap tart. Manc preferred his pale ales and talking endless bullshit with the ruperts. He didn't rub anyone up the wrong way or pick fights just for the hell of it. And now he was beginning to royally piss the Scot off.

'Take the right,' Foulbrood said as he consulted the map laid out on his lap.

The 1:20,000 laminated map was almost identical to the standard AA map found in petrol stations, with one major difference. This map was divided into colour-coded sections, with numbered red, yellow, green, blue and black sticker dots arranged within each section to identify features of the terrain, like road junctions, or the point where a wooded area met a country road. The comms signaller relayed colour-referenced coordinates to Foulbrood. In the remote event that the Provos were listening in on the chat, they wouldn't have a clue where the Blades were headed.

'Five hundred metres along and we're there,' said Foulbrood.

They were now deep in County Armagh, Bandit Country. The landscape contracted into a knotted mass of trees and grass and bushes, the occasional farm jutting out of the guts of the earth, the horizon gleaming like a knife blade under the brooding sky. The road narrowed, contorted. Took the Audi deeper into the tangled terrain. They were now pissing distance from the border.

Four hundred metres to the signal now.

Darkness swept over the landscape like a cloud of ash. Foulbrood and Manc simultaneously craned their necks as they drew close to the location transmitted by the transponder. They scanned the landscape for any sign of the white Transit van.

Nothing.

Jock felt the dead weight of his secondary weapon, a Browning Hi-Power single-action semi-automatic pistol in a holster on his belt. He had twelve rounds of 9x19mm Parabellum in the ammo clip, plus the round primed in the chamber. He also had an extra thirteen-round clip. The three men's primaries were the HK53s. The cut-down variant of the longer HK33 semi-automatic assault rifle, the HK53 had a barrel 22.2 inches long with the stock collapsed, twelve inches shorter than the HK33's. Although the guns were chambered for the 5.56mm round, they felt and handled more like submachine guns. The HK53 was ideal for close-quarters battle, but less effective at hammering targets from longer range. The team also had grab bags in the boot loaded with flashbangs and supplies: food, including energy snacks, water, para cord, a torch, a box of matches, a Swiss army knife and a first-aid kit.

A hundred metres to the signal now. A clutch of lights from the nearby village of Creggan flickered dimly on the horizon. The middle of nowhere, a land of die-hard Republicans, and they were fifty metres from the target. Jock gritted his teeth, his blood pumping, flesh crawling with a strange thrill. His first proper op in the Regiment since passing Selection. Please, God, I don't want to end up on the losing team.

'Stop the car,' Foulbrood ordered. 'We've reached the signal.'

They steered into the lay-by.

Jock killed the engine and climbed out of the Audi. Bursting out ahead of Manc and Foulbrood, he was scanning the area immediately to the west of the lay-by, the cold scratching at his cheeks, picking at his flesh. Visibility was low and it took a few seconds for his eyes to adjust to the leaden gloom. There was no sign of the Transit. No sign of the Nutting Squad or the MI5 agent. He spied a hedge running along the back of the lay-by. Behind it was a ditch running parallel with the road, the water in it shimmering in the moonlight. Beyond that was a thicket of trees with dense undergrowth below them.

Chance must be in there, he thought.

He steeled his muscles. The ditch was too wide to jump. He would have to wade across it. The cold turned his breath to ice in his throat. Spotting a red light blinking in the undergrowth, he unholstered his Browning HP, gripping it tightly as he jumped down into the ditch.

The water was only ankle-deep. Jock felt the cold through

his trainers, instantly chilling the bones in his feet. He made for the red light, seven metres away. He heard movement at his five o'clock, glanced back, saw Manc storming across the lay-by, then lights behind him as the five other pursuit vehicles screeched to a halt alongside the Audi, the headlamps washing the thicket with pale light.

Jock could now see the source of the flashing red light. A small black box, flecked with mud. He'd seen a transponder before, during briefings. His blood ran cold as he caught sight of something else. A woman's two-piece suit, black and crumpled, on the ground and nearby a pair of high-heeled shoes. A white blouse caught up in a low branch on the far bank of the ditch, the buttons all ripped off the front, the collar and sleeves smeared with blood.

A sick feeling ran through him as he pocketed the transponder, scooped up the clothes and hurried back across the ditch. Foulbrood and Manc were waiting at the lay-by. Manc clocked the bloody blouse and a quizzical look creased his features.

'They must have taken her south,' Jock said to Foulbrood. 'Can't be far. We can still catch them.'

The sergeant squinted at the road ahead and chewed his lip.

'I'm afraid we're too late,' he said, bitterness in his voice. 'I just got off the comms with the watchkeeper. The green army lads were supposed to establish a roadblock at Cullaville. But the reports coming through are stating that our chaps didn't get there in time. They found a burned-out Transit by the side of the road. Plates match the vehicle we've been chasing. Looks like they've already escaped. Sorry, lads. But we're too late. Agent Chance is gone.'

'But they can't have gone far,' Jock countered. 'We can hammer the road south. Keep up the chase. We're getting close. We can't throw in the towel. Not now.'

Foulbrood made a face like someone was removing a splinter from his anus. 'It's a lost cause, man. She'll be dead in a matter of hours. That's if she's lucky. If not, the Nutting Squad will work on her for a few days. They'll take her to a safehouse and torture the crap out of her, get her to give up what she knows. Then they'll kill her. Either way, we're too late.'

Jock shook his head for several seconds. He refused to accept defeat. 'MI5 must have a list of known safehouses used by the Provos. There's sod all around here but a few farms and villages. We can scour the terrain. Raid the safehouses.'

Foulbrood snorted. Shot him a cold look.

'In case you hadn't noticed, we're on the Newry Road. There are just four kilometres of straight tarmac between us and Cullaville. If you'd bothered to study the map of the province, as you were supposed to do for your orientation course, then you'd know that the border is at Cullaville. That means Chance is now in the Republic. The situation is out of our hands.'

Jock simmered. He couldn't leave an MI5 agent behind. That wasn't what being an operator was about. He pushed away at Foulbrood, his anger mounting. 'Why can't we leg it across the border?'

Foulbrood stared at him with ill-concealed rage. 'We can't invade a sovereign country!' he yelled, his eyes bulging. He looked ready to burst. Then he sighed, corked his anger and said, 'I'm just as upset as you are about what's happened. But what's done is done. The best we can hope for is that Avery Chance suffers a quick death. Now get back in the car. That's an order.'

But Jock stood his ground. 'There's an agent whose life is at risk, and you're saying we have to turn around and piss off back to base? That's all bollocks, if you ask me.'

'Nobody asked you,' Foulbrood replied sharply. 'That's why I'm the sergeant and you're at the bottom of the food chain. Deal with it. This is the Regiment, for Christ's sake. We have to play by the rules, man. If you'd studied the Regiment's history you'd know about all the risks of active British servicemen crossing into Ireland.'

Manc glanced at Foulbrood admiringly. 'You mean the Flagstaff Hill incident?' he asked. 'Were you there, Benson?'

That's right, thought the driver. Suck-up!

'Not personally,' Foulbrood said, smiling. 'But I knew the lads who were.'

'What happened at Flagstaff Hill?'

The sergeant shot a withering look at Jock.

'Flagstaff Hill was a diplomatic incident back in '76. Eight Regiment lads were caught red-handed by the Garda sneaking across the border near Cornamucklagh. HMG had to pay a king's ransom to release them. The incident caused huge embarrassment in Whitehall and very nearly triggered a full-blown political crisis. It put both the British and Irish governments in a tremendously difficult position – not that you seem to care about such things – and the last thing we need is another border incident.'

'Then we'll just have to make sure we don't get nabbed.'

'No. That's a risk I cannot accept. Sorry. But we have no choice but to head back to base.'

'I definitely agree with Benson,' Manc chipped in. 'It's over, mate.'

'But she's one of ours.'

'We've taken a big enough risk as it is, heading into Bandit Country. Many of the roads in Armagh are booby-trapped with Semtex, and the locals hate us like the Turks hate Christmas. We chased the signal here. We did everything we could.'

'If it was one of us that'd been taken over the border, we wouldn't just abandon them to some Provo wankers,' Jock snarled at Manc, anger exploding in his chest. 'Maybe you would. But you're just a gutless, boot-licking prick.'

Manc was too stunned by Jock's outburst to reply.

'Back in the car, both of you,' the sergeant thundered. 'Now.'

Jock remained rooted to the spot for a few moments. Looking at the blood-spattered blouse and the transponder. He closed his eyes and remembered why he'd applied to try for the Regiment in the first place. Not to shack up with some girl whose dad owned a farm, or climb the greasy pole to a cosy promotion like Foulbrood. He'd joined because he had grown up on the wrong side of the tracks. His childhood had been spent watching his dad come home shit-faced after a day on the piss and beat the crap out of his mum. As a kid he'd trained hard daily. Boxing, swimming and lifting weights. Preparing for the day when he'd be tough enough to get even with him. The day he turned fourteen, he beat his dad to a bloody pulp. The old man never laid a hand on his mum again. Jock remembered the feeling of euphoria that had flooded through him that day. Of saving an innocent victim and putting down a tyrant. That was why he'd gone into Three Para. Why he'd trained hard to join the elite brotherhood of the Regiment.

And the way he saw it, a woman had been kidnapped and was in the hands of a gang of reckless sociopaths feared by every member of the Provos' rank and file, with a reputation for torture and brutality that even veteran IRA men found hard to stomach. The thought of abandoning the young agent to them made his whole face twist in disgust.

It was only when he opened his eyes that he realized he'd clenched his hands into tight fists, his fingernails digging into his palms. He took a deep breath. Relaxed his face muscles. Nodded slowly at his mates.

'Let's go.'

Foulbrood breathed a sigh of relief. 'We've finally knocked some sense into you.'

Jock sprinted past Foulbrood and Manc, towards the Audi. He dived behind the wheel, his pulse thumping in his neck. He twisted the key in the ignition and the engine roared into life. The two other Blades stood dumbly a couple of metres from the vehicle. They swapped a confused look as the driver reversed out of the lay-by into the road. He hit the brakes, the rear bumper lurching to a halt a cunt hair from one of the Sierras. He spotted Foulbrood foaming at the mouth, screaming at the top of his voice.

'What the fuck are you doing? Stop right—'

Jock wrenched the steering wheel hard right so that the Audi was pointing south on the Newry Road, in the direction of Cullaville. Then he bulleted away from the rescue team. In the rear-view mirror the other men soon shrank to the size of cockroaches, though he could still make out the sergeant shaking his fist at the Audi.

Fuck him, thought Jock. Fuck 'em both.

He was heading for the border.

It took him seven and a half minutes to reach Cullaville. The village was two hundred metres from the border. He rocketed past the local army barracks, its dark observation towers shooting out of the ground to his left and right. The country road wound this way and that before it became a rough dirt track that snaked its way to the border. There was nowhere to cross, Jock realized grimly. Each side of the track was a wooden fence parallel to the track. Running off at right angles to this was a water-filled ditch some fifteen metres wide with a gently rising embankment on either side. Beyond that were fields. In the middle of the track itself stood steel bollards, blocking the way. Three Land Rovers were parked to the right of the track. To the left he noticed the white Ford Transit. The Nutting Squad had burned it. Coal-black smoke frothed out of the twisted metal carcass, oozing into a blacker night.

Fifty metres from the border, the comms unit sparked into life.

'Two One Zulu, turn around immediately. Over,' the signaller broadcast.

Jock said nothing. Thirty metres to the border. From the comms came a series of thuds and crackles, and then another voice blasted down the line.

'Two One Zulu, this is the watchkeeper.' The voice belonged to a fellow Scot. 'You're approaching the border. Turn around this minute before you land us all in the shit. Over.'

'You're a Scottish fella?' Jock asked.

'Aye, Adam Lockie, Falkirk born and bred,' the watchkeeper replied proudly. 'Joined the Argyll and Sutherland Highlanders straight out of Falkirk High School. Started in the infantry, trained up to be a signaller.'

'Why'd you join the army, Lockie?'

There was a pause as the watchkeeper thought for a moment. 'I'm an army son. My ma worked in the canteen at Aldershot. She lost a leg when the Provos bombed the officers' mess in '72.'

'Then you know what those wankers are capable of.'

Silence.

'Listen carefully,' Jock went on. 'There's an MI5 agent who's about to get nutted and I'm not going to abandon her. Tell me to turn around all you want. You're wasting your breath. Over.'

The watchkeeper went quiet for a moment. Twenty metres from the border now. Half a dozen green army squaddies debussed from the Landies and started waving at the driver, gesturing for him to pull over. Jock dropped down to a purring thirty, and that seemed to convince the squaddies that he was doing as he was told.

'Carry over the border and the CO will RTU your arse. Over,' said the watchkeeper.

'Forget about the CO. The Provos got your own mother, now you want to pretend that you're OK with leaving our agent to that scum? Come on, lad. One Scot to another. Help us out and tell me where I can find the target.'

Another blast of frustration crackled down the line. The watchkeeper wrestling with his conscience. Finally the noise died out, and Lockie came back on. 'We had a confirmed sighting of a Mercedes-Benz T1 truck heading south on R179, registration O5-D-70866.'

'Where it's going?'

Ten metres to the border. The bollards loomed across the track.

The watchkeeper said, 'There's only one property any-where near Cullaville. A farm owned by Tom Cleary. Guy's a known Provo sympathizer. We've reason to believe the PIRA uses Cleary's farm as a smuggling base. Shipping cut-price diesel and fags across the border. A quid gets ten says the Nutting Squad have taken the target there.'

'Give us the coordinates.'

'Seven-one-two-three-nine-two-five. Over.'

Jock repeated the coordinates to verify them.

'Roger that.' A pause. 'Two One Zulu?'

'Yeah?'

'Good luck.'

'Roger that. Over and out.'

'Out,' said the watchkeeper.

The radio went silent as the comms cut out. Jock felt his neck muscles stiffen as he approached the bollards. Steering to the right of them, he floored it towards the fence. Eight metres. Now six metres. Four. Two. One.

Bang!

The Audi rammed the fence at seventy, the wooden posts cracking as it burst through and pitched down into the ditch. The car shook like a raging bull. Jock felt his guts slam-dunk into the pit of his stomach. The Audi dipped down then levelled out, cutting across the shallow water, mud splattering the windscreen. The Audi had a five-cylinder engine delivering over 300 bhp, specially rigged for Regiment use. Jock's forearms were trembling with the violent shuddering of the engine. He gripped the wheel tightly as the car ploughed through the water.

Six seconds later he was surging up the far embankment. The grinding and shuddering stopped, and the engine cleared its throat. The embankment levelled out to become a narrow track leading across the fields. Passing over a stone bridge, Jock joined a small metalled road. As he plunged deeper into the borderlands, signs pointed out villages with folklorish names: Blackstaff and Ardkirk, Drumgoose and Kilmurry. The signal on the secure comms unit died.

No going back now, he thought.

He raced towards the farmhouse.

six

Chance heard the cold splash of puddles and the crunching of gravel as the truck came to a halt. But she couldn't see anything. She was crouched in the back, naked and cold, fear almost voiding her bowels. Kicker lay unconscious by her feet. Her anxiety had been increasing with every minute she'd been cooped up in the truck. She had asked Stilts where they were taking her. He'd told her to shut her dirty mouth. And the dread kept on piling on her chest, like rocks, until she couldn't breathe. Not knowing where they were taking her – that was the worst part. She was almost relieved when Stilts said, 'We're here.'

Skinny pulled her up, then booted her out onto the ground. It was like tumbling into an abyss. She landed on all fours and caught her breath, wondering where they were. Chance was a city girl, unfamiliar with the impermeable darkness that shrouded the country at night, and she struggled to get her bearings. She was aware of something cold and wet beneath her, sticky against her bare knees and palms. She squinted at the ground. Mud glistened faintly, a sea of it all around her. The air was cold and still, like her flesh was being pressed against a plate of glass.

A thick stench of manure hung in the air. Stilts hauled Chance to her feet. Slowly she began to discern shapes around her. They had debussed from a Mercedes-Benz T1 truck with a logo on the side that read, 'Cleary's Wholesale Produce'. They had parked at the end of a track that led from the main road, through a battered wooden gate, to a sprawling old farmhouse. This was a crumbling red-brick building with a big chimney, set behind an area of overgrown grass.

'This way,' said Stilts, prodding her at gunpoint down the track.

They walked ten metres beyond the farmhouse. A small tractor was parked beside a gravel path leading from the back of the house, next to a row of farm buildings. Directly in front of Chance stood a barn with bales of hay to the left of it. To her nine o'clock she saw a slurry pit from which a foul stench emanated. A bright-yellow hazard sign warned off intruders.

Skinny broke the silence. 'What if the peelers find something on the van, Bill?'

Stilts grunted. 'Keep saying my name and they'll find something all right. Your thick head on a fucking stake.'

'But—'

'We burned the van. They won't find a thing. Once we're through with this slag, there won't be a thing left of her either. Now stop shitting bricks. Costello sees you acting like that, he'll blow his bloody top.'

Skinny muttered as Stilts shoved Chance towards the barn with the tip of his AK-47. She stumbled along, a numb feeling in her limbs, Stilts's words echoing in her head: '. . . there won't be a thing left of her.' She saw it then. The awful truth. They were going to kill her. She had known it deep down, but now Stilts had given it voice. Made it real. She neared the barn, the sodden ground squelching under her bare feet, her toes now purple from the cold. She glanced forlornly back at the truck. Pictured Kicker sprawled inside, not moving. A bundle of clothes and battered flesh. Hearing a loud creaking, she swung her eyes forward. Skinny was opening one of the barn's double doors, and Stilts thrust her inside.

The floor was strewn with hay, warm and dry. Beneath the high, beamed roof she spotted a hay loft. The air smelled of soil, musty and rich. Like chewing on peat. Silos loaded with fermented grain to her left and to her right a tack room full of bridles and saddles. Then Chance looked straight ahead. Saw a figure standing beside an industrial meat-mincing machine and felt her breath constrict in her slender throat.

The man at the machine was wearing a Red Sox baseball cap.

Oh, shit, she thought.

It was the man from outside the social club in Andersonstown.

Stilts and Skinny elbowed Chance towards a chair opposite Red Sox. Pushed her down into the chair and used plasticuffs to secure her arms behind her back and her ankles to the chair's legs. Chance felt her cheeks burning, sweat boiling on her forehead. She watched Red Sox carefully as he paced around the machine, the baseball cap shading his face from the glare of the lightbulb overhead. He turned to Chance, removed the cap and slicked an intricately tattooed hand through his hair. She got a good look at his face, and her heart did a somersault.

Victor Costello.

The chief of the Nutting Squad looked nothing like he did in the surveillance snaps Chance had seen, the ones circulated by Five in internal field reports. In those long-range black-and-white shots he was a slight and pale presence, like a ghost captured on camera in one of those supernatural magazines. But it was him all right. In the flesh he loomed much larger. He had an angular frame, and his skin was pulled tight across his cheekbones, making his features resemble a latex mask. His eyes were dead, not so much evil as simply not there. He wore a black T-shirt despite the cold. His green bomber jacket was slung over another chair.

Costello cocked his chin at Chance, a sly grin playing across his marbled face. All his teeth were golden, she noticed, the legacy of an ambush by UDA hitmen. The story came back to her now. How the UDA guys had kidnapped him and extracted his teeth one by one. Their fatal mistake had been to leave Costello still breathing. He had exacted a brutal revenge. A month later the hitmen were discovered in an industrial estate, their hands nailed to their arse cheeks and their penises sewn into their mouths.

Stilts and Skinny left the barn. Costello watched them go before turning back to Chance. He gazed at her naked figure from head to toe. The way he screwed up his face, she could tell he didn't like the look of her. There was something in his eyes that made her bones shiver.

'You know who I am, right?' Costello asked. His voice was bare and flat. Like someone had stripped it for parts.

'Victor Costello,' the agent whispered. 'The Man with the Golden Grin.'

That seemed to amuse Costello. That she knew his nickname. He snorted a laugh from his nostrils, then bent down beside Chance, placing his lips close to the smooth skin of her neck.

'You smell something terrible, love. I bet your cunt smells shit and all.'

Chance turned away.

'Look at me,' Costello said.

She was going to die. She hated Costello for it and hurt him the only way she could. 'I would, but the glare from your teeth is blinding me.'

Costello gave her a dig in the ribs with his fingers. Nothing too hard, just a preview of what was on the menu. Chance felt pain flare through her side. She drew in a rapid breath, air grazing her throat like fingernails running down a blackboard. In the same moment Costello clamped his hand around her jaws and forced her to look him in the eye.

'When I tell you to look, bitch, you damn well fucking look.'

Chance struggled to form words. Costello squeezing her jaws shut, her lips bunching up in the middle, his thumb digging into her cheek. 'Please,' she mumbled, overwhelmed by fear. 'Please don't do this.'

'You should have thought about that before, you little slag. Before you hopped on that boat over to *my* country. Flipping *my* people.'

Chance tried to ignore the panic stirring in her stomach. 'If you kill me,' she said, 'every British soldier in the province will be out looking for you. You'll never get away with it.'

Costello laughed.

'We're in Republican territory now, sweetheart. Ain't no one gonna come looking for you here. And if they do, we'll put a cap in them and ain't that the truth.' Costello grinned his golden grin a second time.

Footsteps sounded just outside the barn, followed by a dull scraping as a door was hauled open. Costello stepped back from Chance and glanced at the entrance. Chance twisted her neck in the same direction. Stilts and Skinny, their AK-47 assault rifles slung over their shoulders, dragged Kicker into the barn. They lugged him towards the mincing machine, dumped him at Costello's feet, then stepped back. They unslung their weapons and Skinny stacked them against the nearest wall. Meanwhile Stilts booted Kicker once, enough to stir the guy from his bloodied slumber. Coughing and groaning in agony, Kicker rolled onto his belly. Chance saw that his hands were tied behind his back, the plasticuffs pulled too tight, cutting off the circulation from his bloated, purple fingers.

'You think maybe we killed him?' Skinny said.

'Jesus help me,' said Stilts.

'No, lad,' Costello put in. 'You just gave him a good licking, is all. It takes a surprising amount of effort to kill a man with your bare hands. You have to really put your back into it, and I speak from experience. Now, a gun, on the other hand – killing a man then is a piece of piss. No coincidence that the Brits, a nation of cowards if ever there was one, colonized the fucking world after the invention of the rifle.'

Costello swung his boot into Kicker's ribs.

'Wakey, wakey, Joe,' he hissed.

Kicker squinted at the lightbulb. Then he focused on Costello and instantly jolted, as if someone had attached a pair of jumper clips to his balls and hit the juice. He winced in agony. In the dim light of the truck Chance hadn't noticed the full extent of his injuries. Now she saw that he'd had been beaten to within an inch of his life. His right eyelid was swollen to a hard lump and his nose looked like a piece of gum right after someone had trodden in it. There were several gashes in his jeans where Stilts and his mate had knifed him, presumably for shits and giggles.

'Jesus, look at you, Joe,' said Costello, with a thin smile like a necklace in a pawnshop window, as he towered over Kicker. 'You ain't going to be winning any beauty contests, my son.' He pulled out a cigarette from a packet of Marlboro Reds. Tapped it three times on the packet for good luck. Lit it. He stared at Kicker but spoke in a way that clearly indicated he was talking to Chance.

'You're no doubt wonderin' how we knew this pathetic son of a bitch was squealing.' Costello took a long drag on his tab. He didn't seem to exhale. 'Word of advice, Avery. Next time you try flipping one of our boyos, choose someone less thick than this sack of useless shit.'

Chance frowned. 'Joe confessed to you?'

Costello chuckled meanly. 'No need. I fairly suspected he was shagging Caitlin behind my back. I made that bitch pay all right. Gave her the Costello treatment. Pulled her teeth out one by one with a pair of pliers. I have plenty of experience in the tooth extraction business these days. Could probably open my own practice, come to think of it.'

He chuckled at his own bad joke. Stilts and Skinny felt the compulsion to laugh too. Costello bent down beside Kicker, ruffled his hair.

He said, 'That slag spilled her guts about how Joe was always buying her gifts. Fancy clothes and the like. That got me wondering. A guy like Joe is no good with dough. I mean, he gets fuck all as a lowly lieutenant working for me, and he's too dumb to dabble in the drugs business. There's only one way Joe would've got his hands on a stack of readies, and that's by playing snitch for the Brits. I had my boyos follow him to his meeting. Then I caught him hopping into your car. Bit of good fortune, that. Bagged myself two bastards for the price of one.'

Chance hated him more than she had hated anyone in her entire life, and she shot him the look to go with it. 'Whatever you do to me, it won't make a blind bit of difference. The war is over, Costello. Sinn Fein is negotiating. You're done.'

'Thanks for the offer, love, but I didn't drag you all the way over here to listen to the latest propaganda from Westminster.' Costello stared at the cigarette between his thumb and forefinger. Twirled it. Glanced up at Chance and said, 'Here's my offer. You tell me what other lads you've flipped and I tell the boyos to go easy on you.'

Costello smoked some more and let the offer hang in the air. Chance swallowed hard. She said nothing. Goosebumps crawled like spiders down her arms. All the while Costello was grinning at her, waiting for an answer. Kicker whimpered into the hay on the floor.

'Don't keep us in suspense now,' Costello said.

'I don't have that information,' Chance replied.

'Bullshit!' Costello jabbed a finger at the agent, his yellowed fingernail an inch from her face. She could smell the tobacco on it. 'You're MI5. I know for a fact there's a list of everyone in the IRA who's been flipped, and as an agent you'd have access to that list. And you're going to tell me who's on it, or I'll make you hurt so bad you'll be wishing I'd only ripped your fucking teeth out.'

'I swear I don't know.' Panic choked Chance as she spoke, reducing her voice to a faint scratching sound. The closer she came to death the more scared she was, and the less she could fight it. 'We aren't kept in the loop about sources flipped by other field agents. That's standard agency policy.'

'You're lying. I can fucking smell it on you.'

Chance stayed very quiet. Costello was seething through his nostrils, putting the lid on his temper. 'Here's the craic. I've interviewed hundreds of men, women, even children. And not one of them has failed to spill their guts. Know why?'

Chance shook her head, holding back tears.

Costello grinned again. 'I call it the breaking point. Everyone has one, and there's no one better than me at finding it and smashing it. You can sit there and act tough, but you will break. And with a sheltered little slag like you, it won't take much. A case of pushing the right buttons, is all.'

He dropped to a knee beside Kicker. Skinny grabbed the lieutenant by his greasy hair, lifting his eyes to Costello. Stilts, Chance noticed, had disappeared into one of the barn's smaller rooms. She glanced back at Kicker as Costello blew smoke in the guy's face. A moment later Stilts returned carrying a pair of

aluminium baseball bats in one hand and a blowtorch in the
other.

'You should've kept your dick in your pants, Joe,' said
Costello. 'Think you could get away with knobbing my missus,
eh? Now you're gonna fucking suffer.' He smiled at Chance.
'Pay attention now, sweetheart. This is what's in store for you.'

Patting Kicker on the shoulder, Costello straightened up.
Extinguished the cigarette and grabbed one of the baseball
bats from Stilts, wrapping his fingers around its black polyu-
rethane grip.

'I'm a big fan of baseball.' Costello had a dreamy look in his
eyes as he ran his fingers gently along the bat. 'Frankly I
couldn't give a fuck about Gaelic football and the rest of it.
But baseball, now there's a sport I can relate to. You know why
I love it?'

'Don't do this, Costello,' Kicker groaned.

The Nutting Squad chief appeared not to have heard the
lieutenant. 'It's the crack of a batted ball in an empty stadium.'
He tapped the bat against the palm of his left hand. 'The best
sound in sport, that. The sharp report when the bat strikes the
ball. Beautiful. You know, from a certain point in the stadium,
it sounds a lot like a rifle discharge.'

Kicker's face turned to chalk. His head jerked furiously
from side to side. Skinny pinned him down, pressing his right
knee as hard as he could into the guy's back.

'No!' Kicker screamed as Costello took a swing at him with
the bat and cracked him bang in the guts.

The blow winded Kicker. He grunted, doubled up, rolled
onto his side. Almost immediately Silts started belting him
with the other baseball bat, whacking him on the back and
shoulders, his face shading red with exertion. Costello puffed
out his cheeks, winding up for a big blow. Like he was about
to hit a home run out of the stadium. He took a big swing at

Kicker. There was a distinct metal ping as the aluminium met the side of his head. Kicker crumpled. His eyes rolled up. He went limp and lifeless.

'Wake this idiot up,' Costello demanded, catching his breath.

That was the cue for Stilts to slap a butane cartridge into the blowtorch. He fired up the blowtorch. A bluish flame glowed out of the stainless-steel nozzle. Kicker was still out of it as Stilts drew the flame to his face. The heat burned a hole in his cheek and a squeal escaped his lips, the pain snapping him back into consciousness. His eyes popped open so wide that Chance could almost see the veins at the back. He tried to jerk his head away but Stilts held the flame in place, with Skinny still pinning Kicker to the ground. Now Stilts raised the blowtorch to his one good eye. Kicker instinctively clamped it shut. It made no difference. The flame burned away his eyelid and blazed at his eyeball. He made a gurgling noise in the back of his throat. The sight of the blowtorch toasting his eye hypnotized Chance. Her brain refused to allow her to believe the same horrible pain awaited her. She tried to fight the logic of it. Told herself, Costello wouldn't do that, not to a woman. He'd only do that to one of his own.

Stilts turned off the blowtorch. The flame cut out. Skinny hopped off Kicker's back and dusted himself down. The three Nutting Squad men stood around Kicker, Stilts and Costello laughing as the guy pawed manically at his face, his eyeball oozing from its socket like melted gelatine and slicking down his scalded cheek. His face was a crater of blistered, blackened skin. The raw stench of burned human flesh hit Chance, flooding her nostrils. Skinny was quiet, she noticed. His hands were trembling with fear.

'Stop squealing like a baby, Joe,' said Costello, admiring the handiwork. 'For fuck's sake, kill this prick before he wakes up every peeler from here to Limerick.'

Stilts picked up the baseball bats. He chucked one to Skinny, who wielded it awkwardly. Then the two men rounded on Kicker. He didn't see the attack coming. He was blind in one eye and the other was clamped shut.

'Oh, Jesus! Fuck! Oh God,' Kicker groaned. 'My eye, Costello, my fucking eye . . .'

Costello laughed. Then he turned his smile on its head, into something like a frown.

'Kill him,' he said.

Stilts brought his baseball bat crashing down on Kicker. Skinny followed up with a powerful blow of his own. But Stilts did the lion's share of the work as they belted Kicker for what felt to Chance like a very long time. When they were done, the hay around him was drenched with blood. Bits of gristle, shattered teeth and bone were visible. Kicker was an unrecognizable bundle of bruised flesh. Chance stared at his limp body, a vicious wave of nausea swelling inside her chest and prodding at the back of her throat.

Costello turned back to Chance.

'Who else have you flipped, Avery?'

'I told you, I don't know.'

'Now, you and I both know that's a bag of bollocks. You can tell me what you know, or you can follow the example of Joe here. Choose wisely, darlin'.'

Chance still said nothing. Costello strode over to the MI5 agent, stooped down next to her and whispered into her ear, but it wasn't sweet nothings. 'You ain't as smart as you think, Avery. Saying the war's over and all that. You don't know shit.'

She couldn't help herself from rising to the bait. 'I know you're bringing in Stinger missiles tomorrow.'

That prompted a laugh from Costello. 'That a fact?'

There was a desperation in Chance's voice as she ploughed on, unnerved by Costello's good mood. 'I know where the shipment is coming in. Our assets are mobilizing as we speak. They'll intercept the shipment.'

She didn't know what she was hoping to achieve by telling Costello this. She was stabbing blindly, trying to prompt some kind of a reaction from him. She clung to a grain of hope that maybe he would see that his plan was being derailed, cut his losses and let her go. But even as she spoke, Chance knew she was going to lose. She saw Costello break out the broad smile once more, his gold teeth glowing under the barn lights.

'That's it? That's all you've got?' He laughed heartily. 'Darlin', that ain't even the fucking half of it.'

Chance cursed herself through the pain for allowing her to be abducted by Victor Costello and his crew. The stupidity of it tied her stomach in knots. She looked Costello in the eye. Then she spat at him, sinking to his level at last as she seethed, 'You're a piece of shit, Costello. A relic still playing at soldiers while the rest of the world is moving on.'

Costello coolly wiped away the spit from his cheek. Inspected it in the palm of his hand. 'No, Avery. Don't lump me with those other boyos running around making cooker bombs in their grandmothers' kitchens in Bayswater. I deserve respect. Who managed to score a bunch of Stingers on the black market? Me, that's who. I'm the one who reached out to Colonel Jim. I'm the one who set this whole thing up.'

Chance shook her head at him.

'There's no one called Colonel Jim on our radar.'

'That's because he ain't on your radar.' The hesitation in Costello's eyes had evaporated. He was openly bragging now. 'Colonel Jim is a merc who just so happens to be sitting on a pile of Stingers in Angola. So much for your intelligence-gathering skills. British intelligence? Don't make me laugh. You scum couldn't figure your way out of a wet paper bag.'

Chance felt her heart skip a couple of cold beats. Costello smiled at the puzzled expression on her face.

'Got your attention now, ain't I? No doubt you're wondering how our friend the colonel got his hands on the Stingers. Easy one, that. Reagan sold a bunch of Stingers to the UNITA anti-communist rebels in Angola during the civil war in the late eighties. Luckily for us, the batteries in these beauties are good for five years. So who's the thick one now, Avery? Cos it sure as hell ain't me.'

Chance hung her head low now, utterly deflated. Tears welled in her eyes. Outwitted by an uneducated psychopath. For the first time in a long time, she wanted to cry. Costello tutted at her.

'Hurts, don't it? When someone else has got you by the balls. And you and the rest of the scum in the services are too late. The deal is done. We're getting the Stingers and Colonel Jim gets the twenty million shekels he needs.'

Chance glanced up suddenly, a thought bristling the hairs on the nape of her neck. 'Needs for what?' she asked, her voice cracking.

'You Brits really don't know shit.' Costello grinned, unable to help himself, laying it on thick now and getting a kick out of the obvious despair on his victim's face. 'Colonel Jim needs money to fund his rebel army. That's what he told us, anyhow. He's planning to take over Zaire.'

seven

Costello wheeled away from Chance and nodded at Skinny.

'Give her the Costello Special,' he said.

Skinny hesitated for a beat. His face drained of colour. He glanced nervously at Stilts.

'Do as the man says, lad,' Stilts said to him.

Skinny opened his mouth to protest but Costello cut him off. 'Hurry up with it. I don't have all night.'

'Aye, Victor,' Skinny said as he reached for the blowtorch.

Costello watched Chance the whole time, clicking his tongue. 'It's always the civvies, you see. The ones who think they're tough. Christ, if they only knew. See here, this bitch has grown up differently to you and me. She hasn't seen the things we seen. She doesn't know the limits of suffering. Ain't that the truth, darling?' He winked at Chance, slapped her across the cheek. Dropped his voice. 'Now you're about to find out.'

Skinny fired up the blowtorch. The flame seethed. He paced uncertainly over to Chance, hand shaking, eyes wide with the horror of what he was about to do. He looked almost sorry as he touched the flame to her crotch.

Chance screamed.

The pain was electric, sudden. Unbearable. She instinctively clamped her legs shut. Stilts snapped forward and forced her legs apart. Something shifted inside Skinny as he lowered the blowtorch. Chance saw it. The fear melting in his eyes, replaced by a kind of cruel and savage amusement. He started giggling maniacally. The flame singed her pubic hair. Pain instantly exploded in her synapses, sharp bursts of it stabbing her brain. She puked up into the back of her mouth. Her body convulsed. Skinny was now laughing hysterically. Two, three seconds and then the agony overwhelmed her and she began shaking in her chair, her head jerking left and right, pain shooting like broken needles through her veins and screeching inside her skull.

'Enough!' Costello boomed.

But Skinny kept the blowtorch in place, his victim's screams drowned out by the childlike giggles coming from the gunman as he developed a taste for torture he never knew he had. Chance voided her bowels and bladder. Felt the hot release streaking her legs.

Costello grabbed Skinny, pulled him away and wrenched the blowtorch from his hand. 'Give that here! I said stop, lad, for fuck's sakes. We want to get her to talk, not kill her. Not yet, at least.'

Chance gasped. Something like relief washing over her. Then, with the fetid stench of shit searing her nostrils, she glanced down at her feet. A stinking brown pool spattered the floor between her toes. On the chair, a little puddle of piss stung the insides of her thighs.

'Now, where were we?' Costello asked. He grinned and clicked his fingers. 'That's right. You was about to tell me the list of every treacherous boyo you flipped.'

He folded his arms. Waited.

Chance pressed her lips shut.

'Bollocks to you, then,' he spat, and twisted away from her. He marched up to the meat mincer, a stainless-steel device roughly the size of a large dishwasher, with a funnel at the top for feeding in the meat. The funnel looked big enough to take a cow. At the other end of the machine there was a hole-plate about ten centimetres wide.

Costello pressed a green button on the control panel. The engine whirred into action. Chance felt her emptied bowels seize up at the grinding sounds it produced.

'Please don't do it,' she pleaded. She realized then: Costello had broken her. Tears flooded down her cheeks, mingled with the snot seeping from her nose. 'I swear to God I don't know anything about the list. I'm just a junior officer. I don't have that kind of access, you have to believe me.'

Costello chuckled as he turned back to her. 'You Brits really are something else. I've never met a people who can lie through their teeth like you. Now, you'd best fucking talk, or the lads will shove your arm in there.'

Chance said nothing. Her shoulders collapsed with despair.

'That's what I thought,' Costello said, sighing theatrically. He nodded to Stilts and said, 'Do it.' Then he glanced at Skinny. 'And you can take the barrow and tip the leftovers into the slurry once we're done, like.'

Skinny nodded enthusiastically. He had a feel for it now, rubbing his hands like a kid at Christmas as Stilts approached Chance. Digging a switchblade out of his pocket, he started to slice through the plasticuffs securing Chance's wrists, to release her from the chair.

Stilts had just severed the plasticuffs when both barn doors crashed open.

The sound made him jump out of his bones. He dropped the switchblade. Chance saw the smile rockslide off his face. Then she looked at Skinny, slightly nearer the doors,.

'What the f—?' he began, frozen to the spot.

A cylindrical object – it looked like a black deodorant can

– flew through the opening and bounced to a halt near Skinny's feet. There was a moment of compressed silence broken only by the incessant drone of the meat-mincer. Just enough time for a look of dumb surprise to register on the gunman's face.

Then the flashbang exploded.

eight

Blinding light filled the barn and smoke engulfed the three Provos. They were stunned by the flash and the noise, but it was Skinny who first saw the shadow storming into the barn.

He clocked the rifle in the guy's hands. The HK53 was tucked tight into his right shoulder. His right hand was wrapped around the rear grip, his left under the barrel in front of the mag feed to support his firing stance. Elbows extended, shoulders hunched.

The barrel was pointing directly at Skinny. He turned to leg it. Jock let him have it on the half-turn. Squeezed the trigger and a three-round burst flashed out of the snout. Three quick squirts of smoke and a spark of flame. A metallic roar boomed around the barn. Skinny jerked, then let out a grunt as the three nuggets of hot lead socked him in the chest, ripped through his vitals and spat out of his back. Blood all over the place.

He was still dropping as Jock glided past him and kicked aside the spent flashbang. His movements were controlled and precise as he pushed deeper into the barn, removing himself from the fatal funnel of fire – the point of entry, where an operator faces the greatest likelihood of taking a round. The Blade swept his weapon left to right across the barn, just as he had been trained to do on live-fire exercises during Selection.

Identify your threat. Isolate them. Eliminate them. His right index finger remained tense on the trigger. He was four metres from the barn doors now, and six short of Stilts and Costello.

Jock trained his sights on Stilts. The gunman was bent over beside Chance, coughing and sputtering. The distance between Jock and his target was five metres. In bullet terms, absolute zero. The HK53's effective range was twenty times greater. Jock gave Stilts the good news. Stilts jerked violently as the first round impacted his ankle joint, shredding bone, muscle and connective tissue. The kickback from the discharge raised the weapon half an inch, and the second and third rounds struck marginally higher, slamming into the exposed chest region. Blood fountained from the two bullet holes. Stilts crumpled.

Quickly adjusting his stance, Jock turned towards his ten o'clock. Costello was darting towards the two AK-47s propped against the wooden wall. He had almost grabbed one of them when Jock unleashed a three-round burst, punching holes in the guy. Two of them tore into his upper left leg, the third gashed his stomach. He toppled into the wall.

Jock raced over and in one movement side-footed the weapons away and raised the stock-end of his own. There was a satisfying *crack* as three kilograms of stamped steel slammed down against skull. Costello reeled backwards and dropped to the ground. Boiling with rage, Jock kicked the prone terrorist in the face, landing blow after blow. Then punched him as hard as he could in the midriff. Doubled up in pain, Costello tried to wriggle away. But the SAS man was too quick for him. In a flash he clamped his left hand around Costello's neck and drove his knee into his face. Groaning, the guy went flat on the floor. Jock centred the HK53's sights on him and was about to double-tap him when spotted Chance out of the corner of his eye.

What he saw made him sick to his guts. He lowered the rifle and walked over to the agent. She was in rag order. Her lips were split open, her cheeks smeared with blood, her chin encrusted with vomit. Her eyes were almost closed and resembled a pair of cracked walnut shells. Then he lowered his gaze to her crotch. For a moment he stood very still, barely able to believe the extent of her wound. His face blazed up again with hatred. The veins on his neck twisted in anger. Several seconds passed before he could tear his gaze away from Chance. Then he spun around and pounded back over to Costello.

He was still on the floor. Pawing at his gut wound, blood glistening between his fingers, he was making a keening noise in his throat. Stilts and Skinny were both doing a fucking fine impression of a pair of stiffs.

Jock drew the HK53 level with Costello, dead centre between the eyes.

'You fucking wouldn't.' The Nutting Squad chief spat blood as he spoke. His gold teeth were stained red. 'I'm Victor Costello, you stupid cunt. You can't kill me.'

'Yeah. I can.'

Jock depressed the trigger. Costello jerked. The ground around his body went red. Jock slung his rifle over his shoulder. The engine thrummed aggressively. Jock could see tiny bits of old meat clinging to the hole-plate, sloppy remnants in the wheelbarrow. He picked up Costello's body as easily as if lifting a cardboard box. The man was in the shape of his life – eighty kilograms of honed muscle not yet weathered by all the years spent on the piss and multiple injuries sustained on ops. Jock fed him feet first into the funnel.

The engine rumbled.

The machine vibrated.

Lights on the control panel blinked as if in alarm.

Then the machine began to carve up Costello's legs.

At first there was a mechanical wail. Like a brick cutter slicing through concrete. The engine sputtered. It wasn't designed to pulverize human bones. But it did the job easily enough. Slowly, inch by inch, Jock pushed Costello down into the mincer. Blood gargled in the guy's slack mouth, oozed from his nostrils, streamed out of his ears. His head and shoulders vibrated to the rhythm of the machine.

Then the body jammed at the waist. Jock planted both hands firmly on the top of Costello's head and forced it down. The machine squawked as it chewed up flesh, gristle and bone. Jock walked around it and saw strands of meat spewing out of the hole-plate and dropping into the wheelbarrow. Among the flesh were shards of bone and shredded clothing. The machine trembled as it reduced the skull and brain to a mush.

Soon it had coughed up the last of Costello, and Jock remained where he was, taking a moment to congratulate himself on a job well done.

'Fuck you, you cunt,' he said to the pile in the wheelbarrow.

He stepped back round the machine and flipped the off switch.

Now all was quiet again, he could hear a faint moaning from his three o'clock. He turned to face Chance, who was stirring now. She raised her head and screwed up her eyes at as he picked up his HK53 and hurried towards her. He stopped beside her and knelt down.

'It's all right now, love,' he said. 'Everything's gonna be OK.'

Chance winced.

'Who are you?' she croaked.

'I'm from the Regiment,' Jock replied. 'My name's John Bald.'

nine

Chance watched the SAS operator sling his HK53 over his right shoulder and wrap his arms around her waist. She let him lift her up from the chair. Clung on to him tightly, like she was teetering on the edge of a cliff. Which probably wouldn't have been as difficult as standing up with a vicious pain flaring up between her legs. She stood still for a moment, unable to move, everything hurting all at once. The pain crashed down over her like a wave. Jaws clenched, moaning in her throat, she prayed that the pain would fade out. It did. Then she looked around and a thought pricked at her. She swallowed the acidic dryness in her throat.

'I need to speak to someone from the security services,' she said. 'Immediately. Something big is going down.' A pain flared behind her eyeballs and she shut her eyes for a beat. 'What did you say your name was again?'

'Bald.'

She nodded absently. 'Where's everyone else?'

'Try six kilometres north-east of here. They wouldn't come across the border. Something about sovereign territory and politics. Sounded to me like a bunch of people washing their hands of you.'

'But if the rescue team stayed put, how come you're here?'

Bald ignored the question. He looked Chance hard in the eye.

He said, 'I need you to focus. Apart from the three fuckers who had you in here, are there any other guys in the Nutting Squad? Did you see anyone else hanging around the farm on the way in?'

Chance thought for a few seconds. 'I don't think so.'

'You sure?'

'It was dark, I couldn't see much.' Chance grimaced, the fog clouding her mind began to clear, numbness replaced by hot pain, confusion by rising panic. 'How are we going to get out of here? We're in the middle of a Provo stronghold.'

'The farm's miles from civilization,' said Bald. 'We'll bug out of here and head to the border. By the time their mates realize something is wrong, we'll have been picked up by one of the green army checkpoint crews.'

'Unless the Garda find this mess and put out an alert.'

'I'm going to take care of that.'

Before Chance could ask what he meant, Bald slipped his left arm under her right shoulder and ushered her towards the barn doors. She shuffled awkwardly on the balls of her feet. Like she was treading on broken glass. Her back was slightly bowed and her knees were bent. She hissed with every painful step to the doors. She held on to Bald tightly as he guided her outside and set her down on the ground. She noticed Bald was cradling a bundle of clothes in his arms. He chucked it at her.

'Here. Get dressed.'

It was the threads Kicker had been wearing before the Nutting Squad crew had bashed a hole in his head. Chance smiled weakly at Bald. He slipped her feet into the trousers and pulled them up. The pain came back at her. She puked a little in her mouth.

Bald pulled the sweater, then the anorak, over her head. The arms of both were too long. Bald slipped the trainers onto her feet. They were way too big. But at least the clothes and shoes insulated her from the spiking cold. Almost immediately Chance felt a hot flush of fever work its way through her veins.

'Can you stand on your own?' Bald asked.

Chance hesitated, then nodded. 'I think so.'

'Keep a watch. You spot anyone, you sound the alarm.'

'What's the alarm?' she asked, fighting the burning sensation between her legs.

'Scream.'

'What about you? Where are you going?'

Bald stopped. Half-turned to Chance. There was a silvery glint in his eyes. 'I'm going to take care of the evidence.'

He hurried back into the barn. Chance fluctuated between hot and cold flushes, listening to the clank and grind of industrial machinery coming from inside the building. The noise seemed to go on for ever, an endless cycle of clunks and piercing shrieks. Then there was a brief silence, followed by a sound like something heavy being dragged along. Seconds later Bald crashed out through the doors, shoving a wheelbarrow filled to the brim with a pinkish mess. He nosed it past a mortified Chance and steered towards the slurry pit to the side of the barn. Reaching the edge of the pit, he tipped up the wheelbarrow. He watched as the load was sucked in and disappeared into the stinking pool of animal shit. A broad grin was plastered across his face as he disposed of Victor Costello and his muckers. Congratulating himself on a job well done, he dumped the wheelbarrow and hurried back to Chance.

The agent looked at Bald in horror, speechless. Then she shook her head and for a moment she forgot about the hellish pain between her legs. 'What the hell did you just do?' she said, lingering on each word.

'Getting rid of the mess,' said Bald, nodding over his

shoulder to the slurry pit. He still looked pleased with himself. 'Just like I said. Now, let's get out of here before Costello's other mates rock up.'

Chance did a double-take. The colour drained from her face as she looked from the pit to Bald, her lips trying to form words. 'You idiot,' she said at last, her voice stripped down to the bare bones.

'What are you talking about? The bastards had it coming, after what they did to you.'

'You killed Victor Costello,' Chance almost whispered. 'He was the Provisional IRA's head of intelligence.'

Bald made a face. 'He was a torturing prick.'

Chance stared at Bald. The look in her eyes went a shade darker than black and her face hardened. 'He was also the brains behind a major arms-smuggling deal. We could have taken him in for interrogation.'

'What fucking deal?' Bald asked impatiently, slow-burning at the agent.

'Purchasing Stingers from Angola, via some guy called Colonel Jim. This was the intelligence breakthrough we've been waiting for, and you've just blown it—'

She was cut off by the creak of a door at their six o'clock. Chance turned at the same time as Bald. Both of them looking to the back of the farmhouse ten metres behind them. They saw a figure emerge. An old-timer in a tweed cap, padded wax jacket and wellingtons. He had a shrivelled up face and eyes like a pair of puckered old lips and he was clutching a double-barrelled twelve-bore shotgun.

'Shit,' Bald said. 'Company.'

'What the fuck are you doing?' the farmer barked. 'And where the fuck is Victor?' He snapped the weapon shut. Stopped in his tracks and bared his teeth at Bald. They looked like a row of stubbed-out cigarette butts.

At the same moment Bald unslung his HK53. In response the farmer tucked the stock tight into his right shoulder, peering down the barrel. His bony index finger pulled tight on the trigger. The farmyard lit up with hot, white light as the shotgun jerked up in his grip. A cartridge spat out of the barrel and slammed into one of the open barn doors a metre to the right of Bald and Chance, blowing a hole so big it probably qualified as a local landmark. Splinters showered over them. The farmer swung the shotgun to his left as he zeroed his aim on the pair.

Everything happened in a blur of noise and colour. In that situation, lined up in the sights of a shotgun and with no weapon to hand, a civvie would suffer from sensory overload. But Bald had been trained to process a lot of information lightning fast. He saw the barrel angling towards him, thrust Chance to the ground and rolled forward in the same smooth motion. Bald heard the shotgun boom again. Felt a tunnel of hot air searing above his neck. Heard the twelve-bore round thump into the wall of the barn six inches above his head.

Emerging from his roll into a crouch, Bald raised the HK53 to the farmer as he broke open the shotgun and ejected the spent cases. He was reaching into his jacket pocket for a fresh pair of cartridges when Bald gave him the good news, the semi-automatic flashing, illuminating the gloom. Three spent jackets ejected from the side of the weapon. They dinked to the ground near Bald's right foot at the exact same moment as the farmer dropped clutching his guts and the Scot's hopes of making a stealthy escape went up in smoke.

'Pete – I'm fucking shot!' the farmer rasped. 'For Chrissakes, get these wankers!'

A second guy bolted out of the farmhouse. He had the primary-red cheeks and nose of a lifelong boozer, and was carrying a lot of spare timber on his frame. He wore stained jeans and a sweater, and on top of that was a navy-blue body warmer with a sheepskin collar. In his hands he was clutching a double-barrelled shotgun. His breath frosting in the cold air, he stopped in front of the farmer and saw the blood fountaining out of his guts, his eyes bulging and his cheeks crimson with rage.

'Shoot my fucking brother, will you? Come on, you Brit bastards!'

Bald seized Chance's wrist.

'*Go! Now!*'

He tugged her along the gravel path towards the Audi, parked fifteen metres from the barn, in the shadow of the farmhouse. A quick glance to his three o'clock and he saw the shot man's brother frantically inserting a pair of cartridges into his weapon. Ten metres from the shooter to Bald. Pete took aim and fired off a loose round. Chance jerked as the round walloped into the mud a couple of paces to her left, flinging mud and stones over her. Bald forged on, pulling her along, his face locked in grim determination.

'You ain't running nowhere!' Pete roared after them. 'Costello's mates are on their way. They'll shove it up yer fecking bollocks!'

Bald and Chance ran on. But four metres shy of the Quattro, the agent stumbled and fell to the ground. Bald glanced back along the path. Clocked Pete fifteen metres away, clambering into the John Deere compact tractor standing beside the path. Swinging around and tensing his powerful shoulder muscles, Bald hoisted the agent upright.

'I know you're in a lot of pain,' he said. 'But we need to get out of here – right the fuck now. That prick will have been on the blower to his Provo muckers before he came charging out of the house. They'll slaughter us if we're caught.'

Chance nodded. She struggled on, pushing aside the pain,

compartmentalizing it. When they reached the car Bald yanked open the front passenger door and shoved Chance inside. At the same time a low rumble shook the ground and he looked back and saw Pete starting the tractor. Seconds later it was chugging towards the Audi and picking up speed. Bald figured he had three or four seconds to drive off before the tractor bulldozed the car into scrap metal.

He sighted the tractor's engine down the barrel of the HK53, exhaled and, relaxing his grip slightly on the weapon, fired a three-round burst. The 5.56x45mm NATO bullets glanced hopelessly off the grille of the tractor. Bald may as well have been firing an airsoft rifle. Pete was visible behind the windscreen, shaking his fist angrily at the Blade.

The tractor was now eight metres from Bald's position. Wheeling away, he dived into the driver's seat and started the engine. Seven metres. The tractor bounced through a puddle six metres from the Audi. Bald slid the shift into Reverse and hit the pedal. The wheels churned up gravel as the car began pulling away from the tractor, following the track towards the main road. Four metres between the vehicles. That distance had increased to six metres as Bald slid past the gate and swung out onto the road. Through his side window he saw the tractor rampaging towards him, bouncing as it bombed through the gate. The driver's face was hideously contorted with rage.

Bald nailed the accelerator to the floor.

A moment later the tractor bumped onto the road. Too late. Bald was already arrowing clear of the farm, pushing the Audi hard. In seconds it was tickling 70k per. They were leaving the tractor for dead.

And they were just six kilometres from the border, Bald realized. Six short clicks to freedom. Christ, he'd almost done it. Proved Foulbrood and Manc – Joe Gardner – wrong. He kept his foot to the floor as they raced back along the same narrow country road he'd taken on the way south. After sixty metres the tractor disappeared from view. Finally Chance allowed herself to relax. She breathed out a long sigh of relief, like she'd been saving it up since Bald burst into the barn. They drove on in silence. Bald had put two kilometres between the Audi and the farm when the secure comms unit sparked into life.

'Two One Zulu, come in. Over.'

Bald recognized the voice. It was Lockie, the watchkeeper he'd chatted with earlier.

'Two One Zulu reporting. Over,' Bald said.

'You're in trouble, John. Up to your eyeballs.' The signal was weak, the watchkeeper's voice flecked with white noise. Bald had to ease back to fifty per so he could understand what the guy was saying. 'The top brass are spitting.'

Bald chuckled. 'Fuck 'em. They'll be putting out the bunting when I get back. Guess what' – he cocked an eyebrow at Chance – 'I've got the target.'

A pause. And then, 'She's alive?'

'Aye.'

Another crackling pause. 'What about the Nutting Squad?'

'Gone south.' Bald puffed out his chest with pride. 'They had a bit of an accident in a slurry pit. I'll RV at Blue Nineteen in ten minutes.'

His plan was stupid simple. He would cross back into County Armagh at Cullaville, arriving back at base to a hero's welcome from his Regiment muckers for his daring raid across the border. Cheers and backslaps all round. The lads would be buying him pint after pint at the local boozer after this one. Bald smiled inside at the thought of Joe Gardner watching him head up to Holywood with Chance in tow. He couldn't wait to see the look on his spineless face.

'Do not head to Blue Nineteen. Over.'

Bald angled his head at the comms unit, at first wondering if he'd misheard the watchkeeper. 'What the fuck are you talking about?'

Lockie exhaled noisily. 'That area is a no-go. The Garda and Irish Army Rangers have been alerted to your presence. Checkpoints are being set up along the border. I repeat, you cannot cross at Blue Nineteen.'

'Bollocks!' Bald exclaimed, thumping a fist on the wheel.

'The farmer,' Chance cut in, her voice stricken with pain. 'He must have called the cops. After we ran away.'

Bald remembered the incident at Flagstaff Hill that Foulbrood had told him about. And at once he realized he had taken a big risk going into the Republic. He was a target, simple as that. And prizes didn't get much bigger than an SAS man and an MI5 agent operating on the wrong side of the border. Every copper in Ireland would be on his case within minutes, not to mention the Provo hit squads that would be thirsting for revenge.

'You need to point a way out for us, Lockie,' Bald said. 'We can't be getting arrested.'

'There's an army observation post at Yellow Twenty-Eight.' The watchkeeper read out a list of coordinates, which Bald committed to memory. 'Three kilometres to the west of the OP is a clearing surrounded by woodland. It's dead ground. That's your RV.'

'Roger that.'

'The rescue unit is en route to the RV now. They'll be waiting to pick you up.' The watchkeeper paused. White noise fizzed down the line and Bald strained to make out the voice.

'The RV is for 0000 hours,' the watchkeeper told him. 'Don't be late. Fail to make it on time and you're on your own.'

ten

Bald gunned the Quattro up past ninety as he nailed it along the high-hedged country road. The sound of the engine was matched only by the relentless rush of blood in his ears. He checked in the rear-view mirror that they weren't being followed, then glanced at his cheap plastic Casio watch. Fourteen minutes to the RV.

Piece of fucking piss.

He clenched his jaws. According to the map book, the army watchtower at Yellow Twenty-Eight was situated near the village of Forkhill, due east of Cullaville. Three kilometres up west and south of the watchtower was the woodland clearing.

Bald took a roundabout route to the RV, passing north through Coolcair in County Monaghan, sticking to the back roads as he necked it around Drumboat and Rassan. He figured he was less likely to run into a Garda patrol that way. He'd calculated the distance from the farmhouse to the RV was nine kilometres. He kept to seventy-five, on the good side of the speed limit, as he swung a left at Hackballs Cross and steered north towards Edenkill, and the border.

Less than three kilometres to the RV now.

Beside him Chance was drifting in and out of consciousness. He'd given her a sip of water from a bottle stashed in his grab bag. Her skin was burning hot, despite the freezing temperature. She needed medical attention – fast. Bald tried to think of some way to keep her from drifting off.

'Almost there,' he said. 'We'll be at the border in ten minutes.'

Chance moaned something he didn't understand. She swallowed, bit back on the pain and tried again.

'If I don't make it, you have to tell them—'

She was shivering and sweating, her cropped hair wet and clinging to her forehead. Bald flashed a look at her. Got to keep her focused, a voice in the back of his head said. If she closed her eyes, he knew she wouldn't wake up again. 'Tell them what?'

Chance closed her eyes for a beat, trying to shut out the pain. 'About the attack. I've been hearing rumours of a major attack for months. Something bad.'

'Like Kingsmill or Deal Barracks, you mean?'

'Worse.'

The agent's eyes closed again and stayed clamped shut. Her lips parted and for a moment Bald thought she was gone. Then she opened her eyes and whispered, 'Stingers. They're going to shoot down our helicopters.'

Bald frowned. 'Where the fuck would they get Stingers from? I thought the Firm had all the smuggling routes on lock. And the Paddies I know couldn't smuggle shit out of a dog's arse.'

'There's this guy—' Chance's voice faded, before returning a little stronger. 'I was finally getting close to him. Colonel Jim. Now he's gone.' Bald saw her brow furrow as she said, 'You should have let him live.'

He was apoplectic. 'Costello?'

Chance nodded. 'He knew where the shipment would be landing tomorrow.'

'I did what I had to do,' Bald said flatly, glaring at her.

'Costello and his crew tortured the crap out of you. I don't care what int Costello had, he got what he fucking deserved. End of.'

An uncomfortable silence followed.

Chance pursed her lips as the pain clawed at her again. It felt like someone was peeling off the skin around her crotch with a razor blade. The pain served as a brutal reminder. If the Scottish SAS operator hadn't risked his life to save her, she'd be dead by now. Or maybe not. Maybe Costello and the rest of the Nutting Squad would have kept her alive as long as possible, prolonging her suffering to the bitter end. She wasn't sure what was worse. Then another thought occurred to her and she glanced across at Bald.

'You must have taken a big risk,' she rasped, her lips and throat parched again. 'Crossing the border . . . to rescue me.'

Bald shrugged. They were now one click from the RV. Touching distance to the border. He could see the distant shimmer of lights in Silverbridge, like Chinese lanterns strung across a tar pit. Moments later he spotted several lights up ahead. Perhaps four hundred metres away. A dozen of them. Neon-blue lights pulsing in the gloom. Garda. He hit the brakes hard. Chance jolted forward as the car screeched to a halt.

'Checkpoint,' Bald said, killing his lights. He turned the Audi round and backed up a few metres so that they were facing away from the police cars' lights. 'We'll have to leg it across the border,' he said. 'First I'll burn the car – stop the Provos from getting their mitts on the comms kit.'

'Won't that reveal our position?'

Bald grinned. 'Not if I use it to create a distraction.'

Chance grimaced, then stared ahead at the lights of Silverbridge. 'How far to the RV?'

'Four hundred metres, give or take.'

Chance shook her head. 'I can't walk that far.'

'We don't have a choice. It's this or we get nabbed by the Garda.'

The agent stepped out of the Audi, pain throbbing through her temples. Bald left the engine running and quickly joined her, slinging the grab bag over his shoulder.

'This way. Let's go,' he said.

Bald supported Chance firmly against his left side as they headed away from the road and the checkpoint, pushed through a low hedge and started across a muddy field empty of crops. They moved as fast as her ragged condition allowed, which was not much faster than a crawl. The RV was four hundred metres away and it seemed to take for ever to cross the field. Bald counted their steps, measuring their pace in ten-metre increments. At this rate they were taking twenty seconds to clear ten metres. After a hundred and forty metres, Bald let Chance rest. Then he turned back and trained the HK53 above the hedge at the Audi, centred his sights on the fuel cap and fired a three-round burst. A roar boomed across the land as the bullets penetrated the fuel tank and the Audi burst into flames, sending tongues of fire licking at the sky. In less than a minute Bald could hear sirens bursting into a wailing chorus as Garda cars raced towards the blaze. The explosion would draw every cop in the area, freeing him and Chance up for a clear run on foot to the border.

They pushed on. There was a full moon and Bald had been operating in the dark for several minutes now, long enough for his eyes to make out the watchtower of the RV straight ahead, to the north. It was a rickety scaffold structure with a platform on top. But there was still about 250 metres of field to cross, and it was uphill.

With the HK53 in his right hand, Bald trudged on, guiding

Chance towards the RV. The agent found the going hard. To add to her troubles, the trousers were a thirty-two-inch waist and very loose on her size-eight figure. She had to fasten her right hand around the waistband to stop them dropping to her ankles. Her movements were faltering.

The sky looked like it had been scraped out. Just a flat blackness broken here and there by a tuft of cloud. Bald marched up the slope with renewed energy. Closing in on the border. Visions of the celebrations at Palace Barracks flashed in front of him now. He was looking forward to shoving Gardner's words down his throat.

I'll show that prick what a real Blade is made of.

By his side, Chance was gasping for breath. Sweat slicked down her face and misted in the chill air. The ground was like mulch. With every step Bald could feel his feet sinking into it. At the top of the rise Chance fell to her knees and puked up water. When there was nothing left to throw up she spat out bile. Bald dropped to a knee beside her and grabbed her by the shoulder.

'We have to keep going, love. Almost there.'

He looked ahead and saw how close they were. The RV was a hundred and fifty metres away now. White pills of light flashed from the clearing. Bald counted six pairs of them, all in a line. The rescue unit's headlights.

Three minutes to the RV.

Christ, but they were going to make it.

'Come on,' Bald said, blood pounding in his veins.

Chance rose groggily to her feet. She stumbled on, moaning lightly. Giving it one last push.

They were a hundred and twenty-five metres from the border when it happened.

A staccato crackle ripped through the air. A shaved second later tongues of flame lashed out from the treeline on the edge of the field to the east of Bald's position, ninety metres away. Bullets flew across the field like solid streaks and slapped into the ground eight inches ahead of his feet. Acting on instinct, he dropped to his belly, throwing Chance to the ground, making them both smaller targets for whoever was doing the shooting. He pivoted towards his three o'clock and could make out smoke rising in front of the trees, marking the spot where the rifle shots had come from.

Now Bald sighted them. Half a dozen figures. Denison smocks and jeans and balaclavas. Bursting out from the tree-line and armed with AK-47 assault rifles.

'What's going on?' Chance said, looking frantically to right and left.

'Costello's muckers,' Bald growled as he reached for his HK53. 'They're trying to cut us down before we can leg it across the border.'

Chance went to reply. Another burst of fire erupted, rounds zipping into the ground six inches from her and Bald – nine of them in quick succession. Bald glanced up. In two banks of three, the Provos were rushing towards his position. He quickly worked the angles. The AK-47 had a maximum effective range of four hundred metres on semi-auto. In reduced visibility, around half that. But at eighty metres they'd soon put the drop on him. The second burst had landed closer to him than the first. They were zeroing in. He had to act – now.

Put rounds down on the fuckers, he decided. Give us time to race across the border.

Tensing his muscles, Bald brought his weapon to bear on the advancing gunmen. They were seventy-five metres away as he quickly calculated how many rounds he had left in the clip. Nine rounds expended when he'd ambushed the Nutting Squad at the farm. Three rounds on the farmer, three on his brother in the tractor. And the burst he'd used to blow up the Audi. Eighteen rounds in total. That meant he had twelve rounds left in the thirty-round clip.

He thumbed the fire selector on the left side of the grip assembly. Changed it from the lowest setting, 'F', for burst of fire mode, to the middle setting, 'S', for single fire. Then he lined up the nearest gunman with the lowest notch on the iron sights. Seventy metres. The HK53 felt good in his grip. He depressed the trigger. Loosed off two singles. Nailed the fucker. The guy jerked wildly, as if someone had struck him on the back with a hammer. He did a little dance as the two bullets ripped through his torso. Blood sprayed out of his chest in a bright red spurt, like champagne streaming out of a bottle.

Ten rounds left.

Now Bald swung the assault rifle across his chest in a smooth arc and trained his sights on the gunman two metres to the right of his dead mucker. A quick tug on the trigger and Bald dropped the second guy. Struck him in the throat. The gunman dropped his rifle, blood spurting from his ruptured neck. He stumbled on a couple of paces before his legs gave way. Nine rounds left now. Bald conserved them. The other four gunmen stopped in their tracks and hit the deck, seeking cover before he could take them out too. He'd halted their advance.

'*Go! Go! Go!*' he yelled at Chance as he sprang upright.

But Chance was out of it. Getting up the muddy slope had taken it out of her. She was slipping away. Bald could sense it. He pressed his finger to her neck and felt for a pulse. It was faint, erratic, but she was alive. Breathing hard, he scooped her off the ground, cradled her in his arms and started towards the RV. He had to get to the rescue unit before the gunmen had scraped themselves off the ground and put more rounds down on him. Less than a hundred metres to go, he heard voices yelling at his four o'clock. Glanced past his shoulder and saw the four gunmen getting to their feet. Zeroing their weapons on him.

He looked ahead. Ninety metres from the borders. Sixty seconds.

Keep going!

A clatter of gunfire broke through the sky. Rounds zipped and sliced through the air and whacked into the ground around Bald. Nine bullets throwing up fists of hot dirt, landing so close that he could smell the burnt gunpowder particles flooding his nostrils, taste the hot lead on his tongue. He blinked dirt out of his eyes and looked back at the Provos. They had moved ahead of their two dead mates. Sixty metres from Bald now, AKs raised. He knew it then. They were going to slot him. He wouldn't make it. He would die here, with Chance, seventy metres short of the RV.

Then the ground lit up, like a million paparazzi cameras flashing at once.

At first Bald thought the gunfire had come from the Provos. He half expected hot lead to rip through his vitals. But then he noticed smoke seeping out of the woodland on the far side of the border, from near the vehicles grouped in the clearing. Unseen figures among the trees were putting down rounds, and they weren't aiming at Bald. The guttural cries at his four o'clock told him that much. Bald swung his gaze back to the gunmen. Saw the rounds tearing into the fuckers. All four guys expired in a hail of bullets.

Then the shooting stopped abruptly. Bald looked towards the trees ahead and saw four figures emerge. They were on the Northern Ireland side, brandishing L96A1 rifles. Regiment snipers, he thought. He sank to his knees and laughed as the four men scurried across the border as fast as they could.

They hauled Bald and Chance to their feet and, carrying the agent, rushed them back to safety. A feeling of sheer joy was swirling inside Bald's head.

He was saved.

eleven

At the clearing, lights and figures greeted Bald and Chance. One of the snipers had held back at the treeline, rifle trained on the dead Provos lying in the field, covering the other four Blades in their rescue operation. Now the sniper lowered his rifle and the shadows melted away from his face. Bald felt the joy in his guts harden into a ball of bitterness as he recognized the guy. He had the kind of face you only ever saw hanging around the local Job Centre, bearded and scraggly, and he was grinning smugly at Bald.

'Jesus, John, you look like shit,' Gardner said.

Bald snarled at Manc. Hated to admit it, but Gardner was bang on the money. His chest and legs were caked in wet mud and cow pats. His fingers were smeared with dirt, and dried blood formed a crust on his fingernails. He stank worse than a busload of Chinese peasants.

'Still looking better than your ugly arse,' Bald said.

He brushed past Gardner before he could a get word in, and glanced around the RV, looking for Chance. Wanted to make sure she was OK. Two Ford Sierras and four Audi Quattros were arranged in a ragtag line at a gravel parking lot at one end of the clearing, a short distance from the Ballsmill Road stretch of the A29. There was an ambulance to the left of the Sierras. Bald glimpsed Chance laid out on a stretcher, a pair of medical orderlies hauling her into the back of the ambulance. Next to the vehicle was a gleaming silver BMW 7 Series. Bald started for the ambo, hoping to catch a few words with Chance before they took her to the hospital.

'Wouldn't kill you to thank me,' Gardner said at his back. Bald stopped. Simmered. 'I just saved your bacon, mate. If it hadn't been for me, those Provos would've sent you to the dark side by now.'

Bald turned back to Gardner. Glared at him with barely disguised contempt. 'Fuck off, Joe. Slotting those Paddy bastards was the least you could do after you bailed out on us at the border.'

Gardner looked hurt. 'That's bang out of order, that is. I was just following orders.'

'Bollocks,' Bald spat. 'You were kissing arse.'

'Kissing what, John?'

The voice belonged to Benson Foulbrood and it came from Bald's six o'clock. The Scot spun away from Gardner and looked ahead. Saw Foulbrood standing in front of him, his face full of anger. A second figure was marching purposefully from the Beemer towards the small group. The guy wore a pinstripe suit and fancy cufflinks and was clutching a mobile phone the size of a brick.

Bald flicked his gaze back to Foulbrood as he burst out, 'What the hell were you playing at back there, crossing the border?' The sergeant was spitting mad. 'You disobeyed a direct order.'

Gardner smirked and shook his head, drawing a scowl from Bald.

'I brought Chance back,' Bald said. 'I'm a fucking hero.'

Foulbrood choked on a laugh. 'Don't test my patience, John. If you'd been caught, we'd have all been in the shit. You're damn lucky we got our arses down to the RV. Without us, you'd both be dead, and Whitehall would be shitting its collective pants.'

'You lot were going to leave her to get butchered by Costello and his mates,' Bald hit back, nodding at the ambulance. 'You should be putting me in line for a promotion, not slagging me off.'

'Idiot,' Foulbrood muttered. Then he saw the fury creasing the Scot's features and froze on the spot.

Something inside him snapping, Bald stepped into the sergeant's face. He'd taken enough crap from him and Manc. Risked life and limb crossing the border to rescue Chance. He badly wanted to wipe the smirks off their faces.

'If I'm an idiot, how come I stopped an arms smuggling deal from going down?'

Foulbrood frowned. 'What the hell are you talking about?'

'Costello was trying to import Stingers from some guy goes by the name of Colonel Jim. I turned the bastard into soup. The Provos won't be getting their hands on a bunch of Stingers. Thanks to me, our Chinooks won't be getting blown out of the sky.'

Foulbrood swapped a look with Gardner.

'So you're the one who killed Costello?'

The voice came from his back. Bald spun round and found himself face to face with the man in the pinstriped suit. He was maybe five years older than Bald and at least sixty pounds heavier, sporting a slight paunch and a double chin. A desk jockey, Bald figured from his receding hairline and the harassed look on his face.

'Who the fuck are you?' he said.

'Charles Grealish,' the man said. He spoke in that way all posh people speak: self-important, polite and in a tone laced with mild outrage. 'I was Avery's partner. Now I'm her boss. I came down as soon as I was informed about your reckless behaviour.'

Grealish shook his head, his smooth, sagging cheeks rippling like someone beating dust out of a rug. He glanced at Foulbrood and Gardner in turn.

'Leave us, if you will.'

He watched the two of them fuck off. Then he glowered at Bald.

'You're finished,' he said. 'I'm going to recommend that you're RTU'd at once.'

Bald looked incandescent. 'For killing Costello and stopping an arms smuggling op? Explain that one to the top brass. Chance will back up my story. She told me about Colonel Jim and the Stinger deal.'

'She told you the bare bones. There's more going on here than that small brain of yours could possibly process.'

'I know with Costello out of the picture, the deal isn't going down. You can't RTU me for saving lives.'

Grealish exploded. 'I can do what I fucking like – especially since Costello was working for us.'

Bald felt something like a knife move inside him. Grealish quickly composed his face, but it was too late. The look in his eyes betrayed him, told Bald that the MI5 director had said too much and he knew it. But instead of shutting up, Grealish pressed on, seemingly determined to put the Scot in his place.

'The security services have been aware of Colonel Jim for several months. He's planning a coup d'état against Mobutu's regime in Zaire. Some hare-brained scheme to seize power, install a puppet regime and then milk the billions of dollars Mobutu has extorted.'

'So what the fuck has this got to do with Costello?'

Grealish fought back his rage and continued. 'The Colonel needed money for this enterprise, so hit upon the idea of selling leftover, unregulated stock from the Angolan Civil War to the highest bidder. In this case, the Provisional IRA. Costello was our route to Colonel Jim.'

'Costello was a double agent?' Bald asked, prompting a pitying chuckle from Grealish.

'Don't be so thick, man. Costello was an IRA man through and through. We had him bang to rights on selling cocaine in Belfast. Freelancing in the IRA is an offence punishable by death, a fact Costello was well aware of. He agreed to push through the sale with Colonel Jim and lead us to the shipment. Then we'd detain this Colonel Jim character on terrorism charges and take him to Lisburn for questioning. Then you blundered in with your stupid idealism and scuppered the deal. As I said, you can expect to be RTU'd at the earliest possible convenience.'

Bald felt the blood sink from his head to his toes. He saw it all now. The Brits needing to prop up Mobutu and his anti-communist regime in Zaire. Colonel Jim threatening the balance of power. The security services luring Jim into a trap. And now he had blown it wide apart.

'We can forget about capturing Colonel Jim now,' Grealish added bitterly. 'He won't dare risk selling the Stingers to the Provos once he learns that his one trusted contact, Costello, has been compromised.'

'But I kept the Stingers out of circulation,' Bald protested, feeling the situation spiralling out of control.

'For the immediate future, perhaps. However, the Stingers are still on the market. God only knows where they'll end up. And we'll have to explain this to our American cousins too, who'll no doubt be staggered by our ineptitude. Heads will roll for this one.'

'Starting with yours,' Bald didn't need to add. A thought scratched at him. 'But Costello was going to kill Chance. I saw it with my own eyes. The guy blowtorched her fucking snatch.'

Grealish flashed a curious grin at the operator. 'Costello was the chief of the Nutting Squad. He can't simply change his ways and start going easy on his victims. The Provo leadership would immediately get suspicious.'

Bald looked horrified. 'You were willing to let her die?'

The MI5 director shrugged casually. 'For the ultimate good of the operation. We had to make a call, and we took the same one as we always take. The mission comes first. Other agents have been sacrificed in the national interest. Avery wasn't as stupid as you. She knew the score.'

Bald was speechless.

'Now get out of my sight,' Grealish said.

Bald stood rooted to the spot for a couple of beats, fighting a powerful urge to slog Grealish in the face. Then he brushed past the director. Blood thumping behind his eyeballs, he made for the ambo. Wanting to check up on Chance, hoping she would pull through, that some good would come from this clusterfuck of an op. He found her lying on a trolley. A drip was hooked up to her left arm and an oxygen mask covered her face. Her hair was still sticky with sweat. She saw Bald crouching beside her and pulled off the oxygen mask, her movements slow and heavy as the medication took effect.

'I wanted to say thank you,' she said softly.

Bald waved this away. 'Put a word in with your boss. He's a grade-A cunt.'

Chance rustled up a pained smile, clearly agreeing with him. 'Can I ask you a question?'

Bald nodded. Chance shifted upright, winced.

'Do you have any enemies in the Regiment?' she said.

The question stumped Bald. He thought about Joe Gardner and Benson Foulbrood. The Regiment wasn't short of guys that he had no respect for. Guys who were in it for themselves, didn't give a shit about duty. Guys he didn't trust further than he could piss. But enemies? He didn't think so.

'No,' he said at last. 'Why?'

Chance swallowed hard. 'I was thinking about the gunmen who ambushed us near the RV.'

'What about them?'

Several car doors thudded around the clearing. Bald looked outside. The rescue unit was packing up. Operators and guys from Special Branch folding themselves into the assembled Fords and Audis. Bald glimpsed the two medical orderlies heading back to the ambo.

He looked back to Chance.

'Apart from you and me,' she said, fighting to make herself ahead above the commotion, Bald leaning close to her lips to catch her words, 'the only people who knew about the RV were on the rescue team. And you spoke in code on the comms unit.'

Bald nodded impatiently.

Chance went on. 'So how did the IRA know where we were going to cross the border?'

twelve

A brutal wind blasted across the training compound, buffeting the dozen trainees assembled in a ragged line at the firing range. The silver-haired course instructor looked at them, narrowing his eyes as they fired their AK-47 assault rifles at a bunch of targets downrange, at the other end of a stretch of worn grass. Some of the rounds hit their targets. Most missed. Rage simmered in the instructor's guts with every shot that landed wide of the mark. The indignity of having to train wannabe fighters for PMCs, and military fantasists, gnawed at him. February in rural Poland, grey and cold as a meat locker, a world away from Hereford, and John Bald had hit a new low.

He had been working as an instructor on the Hostile Environment Course for six months. It felt like a long six months. Each week followed the same mind-numbing routine: ferrying candidates from Legnica train station to the compound six kilometres south of town, at the start of a seven-day course teaching basic weapon handling and safety to a collection of retired coppers, security guards and club doormen who needed to get their course certificate before shipping out to the Circuit, where they would earn the big bucks. It should be me on the Circuit, Bald was thinking. I should be the one raking it in – not these pricks. But he had burned his bridges with the Firm, with the Regiment – with his past. Which is why Bald, an ex-SAS legend, had been reduced to asking around Hereford for a job, knocking on doors like some lefty graduate with a shitty 2:2 arts degree from one of those online universities. He'd only got the instructor gig when a former rupert who was a director at Talisman International, a global security company, had taken pity on him.

At first the job didn't seem so bad. But after six months Bald was spitting mad.

Two grand a month, poxy digs at the training compound, crap weather and a job training Walter Mittys in the art of fire-and-manoeuvre. The shame of it flared up in his chest and burned at the back of his throat. Worst of all, Bald had no choice but to suck it up. He'd turned his back on the Firm to work for a Russian oligarch, expecting to get millions in return. But the oligarch had cut him loose and Bald had hung around Corsica for a while, working odd jobs and going out on the piss until his cash ran out and he had been left with no choice but to return to the grim reality of England, broke, disavowed, and a wanted man. Now he was just a figure of fun. The course director took the piss out of him, had him doing the menial tasks like cleaning out the shitter. The candidates mocked him, openly bragging about how much wonga they were going to be earning on the Circuit while Bald remained trapped in a Polish backwater, scrabbling around to make a living, even scrubbing filthy toilets. In short, a laughing stock.

Now he'd had enough.

Anger coursed through his veins as he observed the nearest guy putting down rounds on the targets. This one happened to be the worst on the course, by a fucking mile. Bald could feel his blood boiling as he watched the guy clumsily grip his

AK-47. He looked like a teenager groping a pair of tits for the first time. *And* he had a crap haircut – a cropped Mohican perched atop his round face. Bald watched Mohican fire off several wild rounds at the target, missing with every single one. After the eighth shot missed, Bald exploded.

'That's enough!' he barked, to make himself heard above the crackling reports of the other rifles. 'Lower your weapons, the lot of you!' The gunfire immediately cut out. The trainees lowered their AKs. Bald glared at Mohican. 'There's a beer for anyone who can tell me how many things this cunt is doing wrong.'

Silence across the firing range. Mohican eyeballed the Scot. With his bottom lip sticking out from his round face he looked like an emoticon for a sad face. Bald had figured Mohican for a faker from the moment the guy had arrived at the compound six days ago. Mohican had an overly muscular upper body, the product of years of hammering his system with steroids, his shoulder muscles pumped up like the extended wings of a bat. Bald knew the type well. He was the kind of guy who liked to picture himself a hero but was more concerned with shaping his pecs than saving the world.

Bald pointed out Mohican to the other trainees and said, 'This guy is a classic example of someone who thinks they know how to fire a gun because they've seen Jason Statham do it in the films.'

'That's bang out of order, that is.' Mohican spoke in a Geordie accent so thick it needed subtitles. 'I'm doing it exactly how you showed us, man.'

'Then you must be deaf as well as dumb,' Bald hit back, smiling meanly at Mohican, drawing a chuckle from the others that caused the Geordie to flush red with humiliation. 'Try again, sunshine. And this time try to hit something other than the fucking greenery.'

'Cunt,' Mohican muttered under his breath as he adopted his firing stance again.

Bald folded his arms across his chest and studied the Geordie carefully. The wind picked up now, a scalding cold cutting and thrusting across the compound. Burning the Scot's cheeks, like cold water against raw, peeling skin. Mohican was about to depress the trigger when Bald reached out and stopped him.

'Your firing stance is all wrong,' he said above the buffeting wind. 'For a start, the stock should be tucked firmly into the pocket of your firing shoulder. Gives you a solid firing platform. And you should be forming a V with your thumb and forefinger on the trigger grip.'

'As long as I hit the target, what the fuck does it matter?'

Bald smirked. 'Gripping your weapon like that, you couldn't hit a raghead at a flag-burning contest. I reckon you're the worst trainee I've had on this course. Here, give me that.'

Blood pounding in his veins, Bald snatched the rifle from Mohican.

'What the fuck, man,' the Geordie protested.

Bald's upper lip curled in disgust as he got comfortable with the AK-47. 'One week on this course and you still haven't got the basics nailed down. If you can't shoot a weapon, you won't last ten minutes in Kabul.'

Mohican bristled at the insult. Bald glanced at the other candidates as he stepped forward with his own weapon.

'This is how you fire a gun,' he said.

Adopting the firing stance he'd been taught in the Regiment, Bald kept his shoulder and arm muscles firm but not too tense, a posture engrained in his muscle memory. Now he relaxed his neck, allowing his cheek to fall naturally onto the stock, so the stock weld provided a line of sight through the rear aperture. His eyes focused on the front sight post as he aligned its tip with a bullseye target three hundred metres from his position. Then he exhaled, stilling the air in his throat. As he squeezed the trigger he consciously worked to avoid tensing his muscles, because too much tension would disturb the lay of the rifle. Many inexperienced operators instinctively became rigid at the expectation of a round being discharged, but Bald had fired a tool so many times in his life that it was second nature to him. A simple depression of the trigger, lasting less than a second. Then a tongue of flame lashed out of the snout of the AK-47, accompanied by a deafening roar that boomeranged through the surrounding woodland. A single round of 7.62x39mm lead fizzed downrange, the spent brass jacket spitting out of the ejector in a metallic flash. A faint chink as the round hammered into the centre of the bullseye, the spent jacket dinking on the hard ground. From start to finish, the demonstration of perfect aiming and firing technique had taken twelve seconds. Bald thumbed the fire selector up to the safety setting and thrust the assault rifle back at Mohican.

'That's how a real soldier shoots,' he said. 'A prick like you will never be as good as that.'

'You gonna let him talk to you like that, Derek?' the guy next to Mohican piped up. He also had a Geordie accent, along with the all-over orange tan that only comes out of a spray can.

Spray-Tan and Mohican were best mates. Or maybe lovers, thought Bald. They had been thick as thieves since rocking up at the compound, training together, spotting each other in the gym, mouthing off about how they were going to buy Rolexes and Porsches with the shekels they would be earning on a contract in the Afghan. They were the only two Brits on the course. The rest were Russian, with a few Saffas and Aussies who possessed rudimentary knowledge of how to fire a gun and needed to blow away the cobwebs. At the start of the course Bald had announced a system of fines whereby the trainees were penalized for leaving their rifle beyond arm's reach, even when they went to grab some scoff or make a brew. Ten euros for the first offence, straight into Bald's beer kitty, with the amount increasing for every repeat offence. Mohican and Spray-Tan were joint top of the list.

Now Bald rounded on Spray-Tan, fixing his piercing gaze on the guy.

'I'll talk to you two however I want. I'm the instructor on this course. I've got the credentials. You've got nothing. The fucking Chuckle Brothers have got more skill with a weapon than you.'

Spray-Tan went from orange to red. He took a step towards Bald. 'Show us some fucking respect, man. We used to be in the Paras.'

'Oh yeah?' Bald made a peculiar face at Spray-Tan. His throat tickled with intrigue. 'Which battalion?'

Spray-Tan glanced at his Geordie mucker. There was a definite twitching of his lips as he replied, 'Two Para.'

Bald grinned, smelling blood. 'Is that a fact? I spent three years in Aldershot with the Mob myself, back in the days before I passed Selection.' He paused, grinned, said, 'Jeff Daniels is still the RCM there, isn't he?'

Spray-Tan shifted uneasily. 'Oh, aye, Daniels, that's the guy.'

Bald kept a straight face as he looked at Spray-Tan. Inside him, his blood was bubbling. The Geordies were lying through their teeth and the Scot knew it. But he kept the truth of it to himself. He was sick of the sight of them and needed a beer. Turning away from Spray-Tan, he grunted, 'Class over!'

He nodded at the barracks, some two hundred metres north of the firing range.

'Right, lads. That's the end of the course. I'll be transporting the lot of you back to the train station at 1700 hours. Return to the dorms, pack your shit up and present yourselves for inspection. If I find anyone leaving their digs in a mess, it'll come straight out of your deposit.'

Grumbles all round from the candidates.

Mohican said, 'What about our certificates?'

'Too fucking right,' Spray-Tan chimed. 'We need them to tick the health and safety boxes on our insurance paperwork.'

Bald grinned cruelly at both of them in turn, his ice-cold eyes glinting.

'Waiting for you at the admin office. There's a surprise waiting for you two.'

The Geordies looked quizzically at Bald. Then they trudged off with the other candidates. Bald remained behind to stash the weapons at the adjacent indoor firing range. There were a lot of guns to clear away, all of them the type of weapons candidates would typically encounter on the Circuit: AK-47s, mass-produced, durable and easy to use, and Browning Hi-Power semi-automatic handguns, the standard-issue secondary weapon for most private military companies.

He set to work. The training compound was roughly the size of an out-of-town retail park and had previously been a Polish Army barracks. Talisman, registered in Hereford and running the course, leased it from the Lower Silesian government for a knockdown price. The company had given the buildings a lick of paint but in every other way the compound betrayed signs of its Soviet past, with its uneven brickwork, leaking roofs and gaps where metal downpipes had been ripped out by looters. Bald paid no rent on his digs, but in the winter the dormitory block was freezing and the shower had two settings: boiling hot or ice cold. Jagged mountains squatted on the horizon, a permanent reminder to Bald that he was in the middle of nowhere.

At least he'd compensated for the boredom by getting bang on it with the phys. Long, early-morning runs through the woods enveloping the compound. Afternoon sessions in the gym doing deadlifts, squats and stomach crunches. Giving it maximum effort, Bald had rehabilitated himself. He had also weaned himself off the bottle. From necking a flagon of Johnnie Walker daily, he was now down to nine or ten jars of Tyskie on a Friday night on the piss in Legnica.

That was what Bald called progress.

He worked quickly to stow the weapons in the indoor range. Ran through his plans for the evening. As soon as he'd ferried the candidates back to the train station in the compound minibus, he'd head over to Flannery's expat bar. There was a cold glass of the local brew waiting there for him and a bit of blonde action in the form of a Polish waitress called Danuta. Bald had met her while she was working the tables one night. She was svelte and sweet-voiced and had an arse that could make an Arab burn a Koran. Christ, thought Bald – the things she could do in the sack. He couldn't wait to have another crack at her.

He was still grinning as he stashed away the last AK-47. Then he switched off the lights, turned around and opened the door.

Then Bald froze.

The two Geordies were standing there.

thirteen

The two of them were silent for a long beat. They just stood crowbarred in the doorway, glowering at Bald, their bulky frames blocking out the pale dregs of sunlight. Bald quickly weighed up the situation. They hadn't come to shake his hand and wish him all the best. Their arms were folded across their chests, forearms thick as shotgun chokes, black eyes narrowed in their large faces like slashes in the sides of bulging grain sacks. They looked angry.

Then Mohican stepped forward. Bald noticed that he was gripping a sheet of paper in his right hand. His knuckles were white as chalk and his neck muscles tense as rope. He waved the sheet at Bald.

'Is this some kind of fucking joke, man?'

Bald didn't move. He looked Mohican hard in the eye. The Geordie bristled with savage intent. If he was hoping to intimidate Bald, he was doomed to fail. The Scot had fought raghead terrorists, Chinese militants, Russian hitmen and Israeli assassins. So he wasn't about to be fazed by a couple of Geordies whose concept of extreme violence extended only as far as nutting drunks and dropping minor-league scum in the street.

'I don't know what you're talking about,' he said.

Mohican grunted and thrust the sheet of paper into Bald's face. A checklist ran down the length of the page, listing items like weapon safety, zeroing and cleaning. Next to each item was a score out of ten, with the scores totalled at the bottom of the page. The Geordie tapped this figure.

'Twenty-one out of a hundred, it says here. The bird at the admin office said we've both failed. She wouldn't give us our certificates.'

Bald chuckled easily, enjoying this. 'You should have done better on the tests.'

'Fuck right off.' Mohican's lips twisted like barbed wire. 'You know we need our certificates. The contractors won't let us deploy without having them stamped and signed off.'

Bald flashed a look of fake concern. 'That's too bad.'

Mohican shook his head. 'You know how much those contracts in the Afghan are worth, man? A hundred grand each. Now, we paid good money to come out here. Don't pull this crap on us.'

Bald stared at Mohican and then Spray-Tan, a cold gleam in his steel-grey eyes. 'I failed the pair of you because you're shit. Shooting, cleaning, disassembly, weapon safety, immediate action drills,' he said, ticking off the items on the fingers of his right hand. 'The day I pass a pair of tossers like you is a sad day for humanity. Now piss off out of my sight.'

Mohican chuckled somewhere deep down inside. 'Who the fuck do you think you are, talking to us like that?'

'I'm an SAS hero,' said Bald, puffing out his chest with pride.

Mohican laughed again. '*Ex*-SAS. Aye, you might have been a decent soldier back in the days of black-and-white TV and *Dad's Army*. But now you're just a washed-up old bastard. Face it. The only reason you won't pass us is because you're jealous of us scoring it big-time in the Afghan.'

Bald teased a smile out of his thin lips. His eyes were so narrow they could have sharpened a knife.

'At least I've been there and done it,' he said.

Mohican's features folded in the middle of his face. 'What's that supposed to mean, man?'

'You were never in the Mob,' Bald said firmly. 'There was no Jeff Daniels RCM in 2 Para. I made it up. You're lying through your fucking teeth. You're a couple of amateur thugs playing at soldiers.'

Mohican was rumbled and the look on his face told Bald he knew it. 'Fuck it, what difference does it make? We worked the doors on Quayside for ten years. Hard work, that. We've got the skills for the job.'

Bald laughed again. 'You're pub bouncers. I'm the real deal.'

Spray-Tan stepped into his face and said, 'I've had enough of listening to this bag of bollocks. We're not leaving till you give us our certificates. You're not going to stop us. We're going to fill our boots.'

'The only thing you'll be filling, mate, is dole applications at your local Jobcentre Plus. So long, sunshine. Tell those Geordie slappers up north that John Bald says hello, won't you.'

As Bald shaped to move past the two men, Spray-Tan blocked the door. Mohican stepped closer to the Scot, his face bursting at the seams with rage. 'Don't make me ask you again. Pass us.'

Bald glared at the Geordies. Mentally steeling himself for the fight. He took in a sharp draw of breath, flooding his chest with oxygen and tensing his core muscles. He saw Mohican balling his shovel-like hands into fists. Knew what was coming next.

Bald was ready for the punch even before Mohican threw it.

The Geordie pushed forward on his right foot, dropping his shoulder and launching his fist at Bald in a wide arc somewhere between a hook and an uppercut. But the punch was slow and heavy. All that extra timber Mohican was carrying slowed him down. The guy had the classic body shape of someone who'd spent years bulking up in the gym without ever developing his speed of movement. He wasn't exactly fleet of foot. Bald had been trained to react fast and hard, and now he parried the blow with a quick outward jerk of his left arm, swiping the arm aside with his solid forearm. Bald was fast, effective, surgical. Mohican snarled as his fist collided with thin air.

The Geordie frantically tried to adjust his stance by twisting at the waist. He moved with all the grace and speed of an oil tanker on the turn. By the time Mohican had unloaded his left hook, Bald had already ducked low and avoided the blow. There was just enough time for Mohican to register a look of dumb surprise. Then Bald slugged him in the guts with a quick one-two combo, six months of hard work in the gym paying off as he struck with clinical speed and precision, winding the guy. He unloaded a third punch into the side of his guts, striking him bang on the kidneys. Air rushed out of Mohican's stunned mouth and he reflexively lowered his arms, exposing his face. Bald smelled blood. He struck Mohican clean on the jaw. The Geordie grunted. His head snapped back and Bald landed a devastating blow on the bridge of his nose. Mohican stumbled backwards, his legs wobbling, as if disconnected from his brain. His eyes doing a dance in their sockets. He lost his footing and crashed to the ground just outside the door.

Now Bald spotted Spray-Tan in his peripheral vision. His bowels tightened into a knot as he spied the Geordie gripping something black in his right hand. Spinning fully around, he saw that Spray-Tan had managed to grab a Browning Hi-Power from the weapons cabinet to the left of the door. Spray-Tan trained the handgun on Bald. The Scot stood rooted to the spot. He glimpsed Mohican scrambling away on all fours, groaning nasally.

Then Spray-Tan pulled the trigger.

Nothing happened. There was no shot. Bald grinned. Spray-Tan frowned at the weapon, failing to grasp that he had made a fatal error. The Browning Hi-Power, unlike newer handgun models such as the Glock 19 or the Sig Pro series, featured an external safety catch that locked the trigger seat and the slide. Bald saw the safety latch was in the locked position above the walnut pistol grip. True to his form as the second-worst candidate on the course after his mate, Spray-Tan had forgotten to manually release the safety catch before pointing the gun at the Scot. Now Bald charged at him, intent on punishing him for his mistake.

Spray-Tan ditched the gun, then shaped to block the punch coming his way. Bald got in there first and delivered a brutal fist to the guts, drawing a throated gasp from Spray-Tan. The guy stumbled backwards, clutching his guts, disorientated. In a blur of motion Bald stooped low, scooped up the discarded Browning and let Spray-Tan have it, whipping the pistol at his face. The stainless-steel slider crashed into the Geordie's lower jaw. Spray-Tan shuddered with the impact. Like someone had plugged him into the mains and flicked the switch. He dropped to his knees. Bald whacked him on the side of his skull with the barrel of the Browning. The gun was loaded, the extra weight adding to the impact as the weapon clattered against the guy's temple. Another solid crack with the barrel and now Spray-Tan's legs buckled and he fell sideways, his mouth slackening, his eyes rolling upwards. Bald definitely heard the crunch of his spine as the guy landed on his back.

Bald was about to congratulate himself on a good job when he clocked movement on the edge of his vision. He turned.

Mohican had scraped himself off the floor, and threw his entire weight behind a huge right hook. Bald tried to block the punch. It was like trying to block a two-ton truck with a paper towel. The blow struck Bald in his abdomen. Nausea surged in his chest, constricting his throat. He doubled up in agony, lungs snatching at the air, his brain feeling as if it was swelling inside his skull. Mohican launched a brutal left hook that connected with his jaw. Bald saw white. Pain seared through his skull, stabbing at the backs of his eyeballs. He shook off the grogginess, his Regiment survival instincts kicking in, the lizard part of his brain taking over. He bit back on the pain, smashing the Browning into Mohican's face before he could launch another punch. Then Bald went for a low attack, booting Mohican in the groin. The guy dropped, grunting, his face looking like the arse end of a pig.

Now Bald gave the floored Geordie another boot to the balls for good measure. Then one to the kidneys. Then another. Mohican curled up tight in a desperate attempt to shield himself from the torrent of blows. But Bald wasn't in the mood to stop. Mohican blinked blood out of his eyes, waved his hands at Bald in surrender.

'Please!' Mohican gasped. 'No fucking more. You win.'

Bald wasn't going let the bastard off that easily. He'd had enough of people taking the piss out of him. He didn't see the Geordie lying there. He saw the Russians, the Poles, the Firm, all the guys who'd stabbed him in the back in the Regiment. Rage had been festering in his guts these past few months. Now he gave full vent to it. He was done taking shit. He switched the safety catch on the side of the Browning. Pulled back on the slider smeared with blood and skin from the battering he'd dished out to Spray-Tan. Nestled snug in the chamber was the golden nugget of a round of 9x19mm Parabellum. Bald released the slider. He let it snap back decisively into place. Then he pointed the Browning at Mohican's left kneecap. The guy went wide-eyed with fear.

'Oh, Jesus Christ, no—'

Bald fired. A booming echo filled the indoor firing range as the round exploded from the handgun and smashed into the Geordie's left kneecap. Blood instantly splashed all around, the spent jacket springing out of the side of the Browning, landing in the room behind him, three metres away. Down at his feet Mohican was howling, hands twitching, his face looking like the winner's in a world gurning championship. Bald angled the weapon at the guy's right kneecap and gave him a matching wound. Mohican was in such pain he couldn't even scream. He rolled from side to side, his body convulsing, blood bubbling under his nostrils. Bald just stood there for a short while. Watching Mohican bleed and cry, he felt better about himself than he had done in a long while.

'I've still got it,' he said to himself.

He was conscious of footsteps pounding towards him. Voices frantically shouting. He looked up. Saw one of the other instructors on the course diving at him. The instructor was on top of Bald before he had a chance to react. Moments later a second instructor joined in the fun, tearing the Browning from Bald's grasp. The two men wrestled the ex-Blade to the ground, pinning him down on his front with his hands clasped behind his back. He kept up the struggle until he realized that a third figure had arrived. A grey-haired man, wiry and mean and shrivelled. Talisman's local director.

'You bloody maniac.' The director, another Brit, almost sprayed the words through his nostrils, his teeth so tightly clenched he looked like someone was waxing his crack. He saw Mohican with his pair of bullet-studded kneecaps and looked aghast. Spray-Tan was still out for the count. Blood was spattered on the wall either side of the doorway. The potent smell of burnt gunpowder filled the air.

'The crazy bastard tried to kill us.' Mohican hissed the words out, sweating with the pain. 'He fucking lost it. Chrissakes, get him away from us!'

The director scowled at Bald. 'Is this true, John?'

'Is it fuck,' Bald spat. 'They started it. I was defending myself.'

'By shooting an unarmed candidate in the kneecaps – twice?' The director's arched eyebrows said it all.

Mohican spat out blood. Playing the victim now. 'This mad fucker has been threatening us all week. Ask any of the other lads. They'll back us up.'

The director stared at Bald with such hatred that the Scot felt a cold chill clamp around his neck and shiver down his spine. 'I'm a bloody idiot,' he said. 'The boys at Hereford warned me. They said you were damaged goods. A bloody fool I was, to ignore them. You're going to pay for this. I'll make sure of that.'

The director nodded briskly at the two instructors pinning Bald to the ground.

'Whatever you do, don't let him out of your sight. I'm calling the police.'

Four officers from the local police arrested Bald. They arrived at the compound twelve minutes after the first shot had been fired. Handcuffed Bald and bundled him into the back of an Alfa Romeo decked out in police livery. Then they ferried him to the police station in downtown Legnica. On arrival he was stripped of his keys, cash, wallet, belt and shoelaces and taken to a holding cell with half a dozen neo-Nazis and drunks for company. It wasn't quite the evening's entertainment he'd had in mind.

Three hours later he was hauled to an interrogation room where an immaculately dressed man whose eyes were too far apart introduced himself as Detective Inspector Piotr Kaminski of the Policja Kryminalna. Kaminski spoke English in broken little phrases. But he spoke enough for Bald to grasp the fundamentals. He was in the shit. Up to his neck in the stuff. Facing two counts of grievous bodily harm and a further one of attempted murder for kneecapping Mohican, a charge that could lead to a minimum ten-year sentence.

Kaminski had done his homework on Bald. The guy produced a copy of his medical record and read a few excerpts aloud. He read out the bits about the debilitating migraines Bald had suffered. The repeat prescriptions for amitriptyline to treat post-traumatic stress disorder. The signed doctor's note recommending Bald for psychiatric evaluation. Kaminski laid out his theory: a traumatized ex-SAS operator goes into meltdown and nearly murders two of his trainees in a psychotic rage. Bald himself had to admit, it was a good fit. Then Kaminski looked him in the eye and told him he was finished and that the best thing for him to do was to make a full confession now and avoid the pain and cost of a trial.

Bald told Kaminski to go fuck himself.

He spent the evening getting comfortable with his new family in the holding cell. He was allowed to make one phone call. Was surprised to find he couldn't think of anyone to call except Danuta, his Polish bit. He tried her number. Got her voicemail. Thought about leaving a message. Decided no.

He couldn't sleep. He was furious at himself for how things had turned out. Three years ago he'd been the hero of the Regiment, the toast of Hereford. He'd been all set for a money-spinning career on the Circuit, as a director for one of the prestigious PMCs, perhaps setting up his own outfit. Sell it on to the Yanks for a few million, pocket the proceeds and retire to a beach house in South America. Supermodel girlfriend, beer on tap, live like a king. Now his plans lay in tatters and the only thing he was looking at was a long stretch in a Polish prison.

Kaminski returned for him shortly after midnight. The detective looked bitter about something. It was the look of a man who had been on the cusp of winning a long-odds accumulator at the bookies, only to see it snatched from his grasp.

'Your lawyer,' Kaminski said. 'Is here.'

But I don't have a lawyer, Bald thought.

He managed to keep a straight face as he followed Inspector Kaminski out of the cell. But inside he felt all the pent-up heaviness and weariness of the past twelve hours sliding off his shoulders. Talisman must have sent their lawyer to bail him out. That was it. The company execs back in Hereford had seen sense, realized what a valuable instructor he was and ponied up the cash to get him out of jail.

There was a spring to Bald's step as he arrived at the inter-rogation room. Kaminski opened the door and gestured for him to enter.

A woman was sitting at a table opposite the door, her head bowed and her long, elegant hands resting either side of a substantial case file open in front of her. She had hair the colour of wet sand, cropped short with not a strand out of place. The sleeves of her immaculate white blouse were neatly turned up. She wore a dark blazer and sharply cut trousers. Yes, Bald thought. A lawyer all right.

Then she looked up at Bald and his stomach went hollow. He said nothing for a long beat. Kaminski slammed the door shut, breaking the silence. Then the woman slid out of her chair and smiled sadly.

'Hello, John,' said Avery Chance.

fourteen

0013 hours.

Chance gestured to a chair at the opposite side of the table.

'Please,' she said. She sounded like a therapist inviting Bald to lie on her couch. 'Inspector Kaminski will be along shortly with some refreshments. This could take a while.'

Bald just stood there, his mouth suddenly dry, a strange sensation pulsing behind his eyes. He blinked at Chance, as if not believing she was really here. Her left foot tapped nervously. Her shoes caught his eye – white stilettos with high heels – and then the pulsing in his head exploded into a searing memory, rushing back at him from twenty years ago. Of a pair of mud-spattered high heels lying in a ditch in Northern Ireland a stone's throw from the border with the Republic. They had belonged to Avery Chance. The memories came flooding back then. Of the farm south of the border, the barn where Chance had been held by a bunch of Provos. The putrid stench of burnt flesh. The blood splashed sickeningly across the hay-strewn floor. He remembered the awful rage that had seized him when he'd crashed into the barn to rescue Chance. The blowtorch. The shocking burns to her genitals. The mechanical shriek of the meat-grinding machine as Bald fed her torturers into it.

A long time ago, he thought.

But now, with Chance here next to him, suddenly it didn't

seem so long. And the memory of Northern Ireland snapped his current crisis into sharp focus. Bald recalled that his problems in the Regiment had begun shortly after the Northern Ireland op. He had come close to being RTU'd by the top brass for crossing the border and nearly triggering a diplomatic incident. He'd hung onto his career by a thread, but things were never quite the same afterwards. The other Blades treated him as a liability. The ruperts kept him at arm's length. In despair Bald had turned to the bottle.

That was when he'd lost his way.

An acute pain sank its teeth into Bald. A piercing sound rang in his ears, like a fingernail scraping across the inside of his skull. He touched a hand to his right temple, clamped his eyes shut and slumped into the chair. Chance tilted her head at Bald. Considered him for a couple of seconds.

'What happened to your face?' There was a touch of sympathy in her voice.

'Me and a couple of Geordies had a disagreement,' Bald said.

'Inspector Kaminski told me it was a little more than that,' Chance persisted.

Bald shrugged.

Chance said, 'He told me you almost beat two men to death. One of them is in a coma in hospital. The other one is under the knife. The surgeons are doing what they can to repair his shattered kneecaps. They say he might not walk again. If that's what you call a disagreement I'd hate to see your idea of a heated argument.'

'Save the preaching for the converted, Avery. Why are you here?'

'I came to help you.'

A warm feeling swept through Bald. She had come to repay the favour of rescuing her twenty years ago. 'Thank fuck,' he said. 'What's the plan for getting me out? You'll have to do some serious twisting of Kaminski's arm. That guy is more tightly wound up than a bulldog trying to shit a peach stone.'

Chance bit her lip. 'I'm here on official business.' Her tone had suddenly shifted: clipped and curt, professional. Bald didn't like it.

She went on, 'We've been keeping tabs on you for the past few weeks. Early this afternoon your name was flagged up by Interpol. As soon as we confirmed you were being detained on criminal charges, I caught the first available flight from Heathrow to Wroclaw via Munich. Then I took a cab to this wretched little town. Start to finish, the journey took me just over six hours.' She paused, folded her hands. 'Do you know why I came here as soon as I could?'

Bald shrugged. 'You missed my rugged good looks?'

Chance lifted her eyes to him. They were a faded blue, like ink stains. Almost grey, Bald thought. 'I came here to make you, not so much an offer, more like a lifeline. Six needs you, John.'

The Firm.

Bald had worked as an asset for MI6, reporting to a corrupt agent called Leo Land. Dark thoughts filled his mind. He clenched his fists in rage. 'I should have known,' he growled. 'Should have seen this coming.'

Chance smiled. It was pained and just a little forced. 'As it happens, I'm taking a big risk meeting with you. My boss at Vauxhall would rather feed you to the wolves. It's not the first time I've put my neck on the line to help you.'

Bald frowned. 'What do you mean?'

Chance rolled her eyes. 'Don't tell me it never crossed your mind as to why you weren't RTU'd. Christ, John! You were damaged goods after Northern Ireland. No one wanted anything to do with you. But I campaigned to keep you in the Regiment. If it hadn't been for me, you'd have spent the rest of your military career sweeping barracks and polishing boots.'

For a beat, Bald was too stunned to reply. The migraine flared, the bruises on his knuckles burned. He wondered briefly why she had done it: put her neck on the line for him. But of course, he really knew the answer: because he had saved her. And however badly he had fucked up, that single fact had motivated Chance to stop the top brass hanging him out to dry.

Bald nodded his appreciation. 'Thanks, Avery. But that doesn't change a thing. Six ruined me. I'm not going back.'

'Things are different now. Transparency's the new watch-word.'

Bald grunted. 'Pull away the cover and I bet it's still rotten underneath.'

'It's the truth, John. We've cleared out the dross. I was brought in as part of the new order.' There was a note of pride in her voice now. 'I transferred after 7/7. We'd crushed the IRA. There was nothing left for me to achieve at Five. And anyway I was already spending a lot of time on secondment. I served eighteen months in Karachi, living in a secure com-pound, running and recruiting agents in the Tehrik-i-Taliban. Then they sent me to Oman. Ever been to Muscat? Fifty-degree heat, not a drop of rainfall the whole year. It's like living in an armpit. Then I was appointed to lead the team over-seeing counter-terrorism operations in East Africa.' She winked at Bald. 'Which brings me to my offer.'

Bald nodded. The room was stuffy, there were no windows or air con, and Bald was sweating like a middle-aged tourist on a Delhi bus. He laid his hands flat on the table, ready to listen. He admired Chance's toughness, her willingness to put old loyalties ahead of corporate line-toeing. He watched her reach into her designer handbag and pull out a sealed manila envelope. The agent placed the envelope on the table and slid it towards Bald.

He cocked an eyebrow at her. 'Christ, Avery. If you wanted to give me a Valentine's Day card you could have just popped it in the post.'

Chance smiled. 'In here is a letter from the Polish attorney general, authorizing your immediate release from custody and dropping all charges against you. This letter means you'll be a free man, John.'

Bald stared at the envelope. His lips clamped shut. He needed a way out of his situation, would do anything to avoid going down for a ten-year stretch in the pan. But there was an *if* coming. He could see it forming on her lips.

'I understand you're not happy with how Six treated you in the past', Chance continued. 'I get it. Really, I do. So here's the thing. You can accept the offer, and I show this letter to our friend Inspector Kaminski.'

'What's the alternative?'

Chance took back the envelope and tucked it under the file in front of her. After a deep breath, she lowered her gaze and opened the file at the first page.

'Bald, John Fraser,' she read out loud. 'Born 20 June 1971 at Maryfield Hospital, Dundee, Scotland. Attended St John's Roman Catholic High School in Dundee. Passed Selection to 22 SAS in 1993. May 1995, charged with two counts of assault. Acquitted. August 2000, suspected of executing three prisoners of war during Operation Barras in Sierra Leone. Charges dropped owing to lack of evidence. June 2004, brutally assaults a journalist in a hotel room in Kabul, Afghanistan. December 2009, robs a diamond merchant in Karachi, Pakistan during a counter-terrorism operation. May 2010, reputedly involved in the brutal murder of a police officer during a riot in a favela in Rio de Janeiro, Brazil—'

It was like an invisible hand had reached out and slapped Bald across the face. He saw it then. No one could outrun the

Firm. He was a fool for ever thinking otherwise. He couldn't run away from the Firm any more than he could escape his own shadow.

'I could go on,' said Chance.

'Don't bother. I know where this is going.'

'Do you, John? I'm not reading your case file for shits and giggles. This is serious. Six is looking to bury you after the fiasco with Viktor Klich.'

Bald snarled at the memory of the Russian oligarch he'd been hired to snatch. The mission had gone sideways, and Bald had turned his back on the Firm and ended up working for Klich.

'That wasn't my fault,' he said. 'Leo Land and Danny Cave – they're the bastards you should be going after. Not me.'

Chance leaned across the table. 'I have news for you. Cave lives in China now. Feeds scraps of int to the country's security services. Has a Chinese wife, even speaks Mandarin. He's out of our reach. As for Land, he's off the radar. Fled the country. We think he might be in Cambodia. But you know how it is. Someone's head has to roll. And right now, Six has got you in its sights.'

'What about all that stuff you said about transparency and new brooms?'

'All that is true. But we can't turn over a new leaf without cleaning up our past mistakes. Including you.'

'I'm innocent. Land set me up.'

Chance showed no emotion.

'I want to help,' she said. 'But if you won't agree to the mission, it's out of my hands. Six will begin extradition proceedings against you, on multiple charges of drug trafficking, murder, conspiracy and treason. You're looking at life in prison. No parole. They'll crucify you, John.'

Bald hammered a fist on the table. 'Bastards!'

Chance looked unflustered. 'I'm on your side. Listen to my offer.'

Bald fell quiet for a moment. Rubbing the calluses on his hands. He saw it all now. Chance had come here because she remembered the John Bald of 1993, a twenty-one-year-old lad from Dundee full of idealism and a sense of duty. Before he had opened his eyes to the world, seen its horrors and its lies and been left horribly scarred. Chance had flown to Poland on a hunch that the old John Bald wasn't dead. That she could tease the good out of him. A grim thought struck the Scot that Chance might be his last friend in the world.

She reached across the table and took his hand in hers. 'I don't care for the past. The only thing I care about is getting the job done. And right now I need you.'

These last words sparked a flame of curiosity in Bald. 'Since when did the Firm need me? I'm damaged goods. You said so yourself.'

'Times have changed. The threat of Islamic fundamentalism has changed the way we work. The people at Six are good at all the underhand stuff. Surveillance, chasing paper trails, listening to voicemails. Our brothers and sisters in the CIA indulged in the odd bit of torture, but by and large we steered clear of all that. Whenever we did need to kill somebody, the drones did the work for us. Very effective at bombing Taliban leaders taking tea in their hideaways. Consequently we are overloaded with managerial types. What we lack are old-fashioned assets. Men who can roll up their sleeves and get the job done and who don't give a damn about accountability.'

She meant Bald, and did a thing with her eyes that clearly told him so. He felt a strange thrill crawl through his bones.

'You're the opposite of soft,' Chance went on. 'Those two Geordies you roughed up? Notorious doormen working under a Newcastle gangster called Lee Clayton. Either of them could pulverize most men in a straight fight. You dropped them both. You haven't changed, John. For a while you were out of fashion, I guess. But now—'

Chance spoke with sincerity. Bald heard it in her voice. Felt the truth of it in his guts too. He was a relic. He didn't fuck around on Twitter, didn't have a Facebook account. He never wore skinny jeans or ate probiotic yoghurt, hated words like 'multiculturalism' and 'human rights'. He had been sculpted for war. Still slept with a Glock 19 next to his pillow.

'What's the craic?' he asked.

He saw relief flush through Chance at once. She breathed like she was coming up for air. But as quickly as she dropped her guard she ducked behind it again, composing her face and clearing her throat diplomatically as she closed the folder. A lifetime of caution, thought Bald. Immersed in her profession, fearless when it came to rooting out terrorist cells, but afraid to peek into the shadows of her past.

'What do you recall about Colonel Jim?' Chance asked.

Bald thought for a moment. The name rang a bell. 'The guy who was the arms smuggler in Belfast? Trying to sell Stingers to the Provos?'

Chance nodded. 'He was going to use the proceeds to fund a private militia and launch a coup in Zaire. After you wiped out their Nutting Squad, the Provos pulled the plug on the deal to buy the Stingers. Colonel Jim aborted his coup attempt and went underground.'

'Tragic. But why are you telling me this now?'

There was a glow to her eyes, Bald noted.

'Colonel Jim is back,' she said. 'I need you to find him for me, John. And then I need you to kill him.'

fifteen

Chance let the words hang in the air. Bald was being asked to do again what he knew he did best, and – if he was honest with himself, which wasn't all that often – what he truly lived for: killing.

'Colonel Jim's real name is Kurt Pretorius,' said Chance. 'He acquired the nickname "Colonel Jim" after serving with the Second Paratroop Regiment, French Foreign Legion. Then he became a mercenary. You might call him the founding father of the Circuit.'

Bald frowned. 'Never heard of the guy.'

'He's a British national, but born and raised in Southern Rhodesia, now Zimbabwe. A white supremacist who counts among his friends the late Colonel Gaddafi, Robert Mugabe and the Equatorial Guinea dictator Teodoro Mbasogo.'

Bald puffed out his cheeks. 'With friends like that, you've got to watch your back. Those three bastards have killed more Africans than AIDS.'

Chance shot him a look.

'Pretorius is an Africa junkie,' she said. 'He cut his teeth there after joining the Legion, fighting in various internecine conflicts across the continent. He was injured during the Battle of Kolwezi in Zaire in '78 and medevac'd to the French Bouffard military hospital in Djibouti. There he befriended an officer from the SDECE, France's overseas intelligence agency. The two men stayed in contact after Pretorius was discharged from hospital. He left the Foreign Legion but stayed on in West Africa. The SDECE gave him implicit financial backing to launch a coup d'état against the self-proclaimed Emperor of the Central African Republic, Jean-Bédel Bokassa. That was in 1979.'

'Why would the French leave a military coup to a British ex-Legionnaire? Surely that's the kind of op they'd handle in-house.'

'France has long pursued an underhand policy in Africa. *Françafrique*, they call it. They offer military aid and financial backing to those leaders who best represent French interests, and crush those who oppose them. But removing African dictators from power is a sensitive business, particularly when it backfires. So the French reasoned that it was better to achieve regime change at a distance. They employed Pretorius to get the job done, without the risk of any official involvement by the French state.'

'Like the PMCs today, then,' Bald cut in. 'They go in and get the job done for a big pile of cash and the politicians get to tell the media that they've got no boots on the ground.'

'Exactly.'

There was a grating buzz as the door unlocked and Inspector Kaminski entered the room. Chance pursed her lips while Kaminski shoved a can of Coke and a slice of cheese and tomato pizza in front of Bald. They were the wrong way round: the pizza was cold and the Coke was warm. He washed the scran down anyway, as he hadn't eaten in more than fourteen hours. He raised the Coke to the Inspector. Kaminski shot back a final fuck-you glare. Then he exited the room. Chance watched him go before turning back to Bald.

'I was telling you about Pretorius.'

'Go on.'

'The French decided to pay Pretorius to oust Bokassa after he butchered a hundred schoolchildren for refusing to wear the uniform manufactured at his private factory. Pretorius led a troop of undercover commandos into the country under cover of darkness, secured the main airport early the following morning and by nightfall they had control of the entire country. Bokassa was exiled. Pretorius won.'

'Good for him,' Bald replied drily. 'But what has any of this got to do with you wanting Pretorius dead?'

Chance narrowed her gaze at him. 'You'll need to learn everything about Pretorius, John. What motivates him, his personality, his background. Until you know him better than your own mother. Because he's got more bodyguards than Lindsay Lohan at a court hearing – and the only way to kill Pretorius is to get close to him and win his trust.'

A hot sense of anticipation flooded through Bald. He knew it then. How much he'd missed the game. All those hours beasting himself in the gym – it was like he'd been training for something. He remembered reading somewhere that you had to do something for ten thousand hours before you got to be an expert at it. He hadn't counted the hours but he knew he was an expert at killing. The thought of getting stuck in again gave him a renewed sense of anticipation and he nodded keenly at Chance. She went on.

'After deposing Bokassa, Pretorius began his career as a gun for hire. He helped prop up despotic regimes in Guinea-Bissau, Mauritania, Chad, Burundi, São Tomé and Príncipe. After he tried to unseat Mobutu in Zaire in 1993, Pretorius ran out of money and drifted aimlessly across Africa, a man with grand ambitions but no way to realize them. Until he cropped up in Somalia.'

'What's he doing there?' Bald asked.

'We believe someone has backed him to launch a coup against the transitional government. This would be the same West-friendly alliance we've worked so hard to build from scratch. The situation on the ground is tenuous. Security is provided by a small number of Kenyan and African Union troops. They have restored some semblance of order to the capital, Mogadishu. But much of the land beyond is under the control of al-Shabaab.'

'I've heard of those tossers,' said Bald, polishing off the pizza and the Coke, feeling refreshed and excited and a hell of a lot better about life than he had an hour ago. 'African al-Qaeda.'

Chance nodded.

'Al-Shabaab has a degree of independence from their Arab brethren,' she said, voice rising as she warmed to her subject. She spoke with a passion that impressed Bald. 'Think of them more like a franchise. Like Subway, or Burger King. Al-Shabaab controlled vast swaths of Somalia, from the Puntland province in the north to the port of Kismayo in the south. The Americans are worried about Islamic fundamentalism taking root. So are we. There is a huge diaspora of Somalis with British and American passports, and that is a potential security nightmare. What do you think will happen when they return to their homeland and al-Shabaab is running the show?'

Bald shrugged. 'They put out the bunting and crack open a beer?'

'They'll be radicalized, John. Then they'll carry out attacks against the West. There are a hundred thousand Somalis with British passports. Imagine a hundred, two hundred Boston marathon bombings and Woolwich murders, and you start to get an idea of what we're dealing with. That's why we need this transitional government to thrive.'

'And Pretorius is pissing all over your plans somehow?'

'Pissing would be putting it lightly. Pretorius and his men are seizing villages and launching attacks against key strategic African Union assets across the country. Last month they overran Kenyan forces close to the border. The soldiers were taken hostage, castrated and forced to eat their own testicles. Some had live grenades inserted into their anuses. Others had their skin burnt off. At the same time Pretorius went on a recruitment drive. Child soldiers, John. Some are as young as ten. Plying them with drugs. They're taught to worship Pretorius as a god.'

'Christ!' Bald spluttered. 'And I thought some of the lads in the Regiment were a few French fries short of a Happy Meal.'

'There is method to the madness,' Chance replied. 'There always is with Pretorius. We don't know who is paying him to be there. Perhaps a neighbouring African power with an interest in overthrowing the government. But whoever is backing Pretorius, his actions are undermining our efforts. If he topples the government, it will create a power vacuum, allowing al-Shabaab to thrive.'

'That still doesn't explain why you want *me* to kill Pretorius, and not some other cunt. I'm not exactly on the Firm's Christmas card list, Avery. Why don't the Yanks just take the fucker out with a drone strike?'

Chance acknowledged the truth of that statement with an uncomfortable nod. 'They tried. Someone tipped off Pretorius. He swapped vehicles at the last minute. The drone strike ended up killing four of his foot soldiers. Pretorius fled into the jungle.'

Chance paused and wrung her hands. She wasn't wearing a wedding ring, Bald noted. A woman married to the job. Then he remembered the savage injuries she'd suffered in Northern Ireland and figured that maybe her single-minded focus wasn't entirely a matter of choice. She wouldn't have been able to have kids or even a normal sex life. Not after what the Nutting Squad had done to her.

Then she said, 'Something happened to Pretorius.'

'What do you mean?'

Chance cleared her throat. 'We have eyes on the ground in and around Mogadishu. British Somalis who act as sources. One of them came back to us with a report about Pretorius from within his camp. According to our source, Pretorius experienced what he called an *awakening*.'

'The fuck does that mean?'

'He converted to Islam. He preaches the survival of the fittest, how the strong should rule over the weak. He's set up a training camp to expand his militia. His men call him a genius.'

'A twisted fuck, more like.'

'You need to stop Pretorius, John. His ultimate goal has always been power and satisfying his greed, and he doesn't care who he has to work with to achieve it. But in the end his only allegiance is to himself. Chaos and bloodshed are his trademark – he'll stop at nothing. If he succeeds in overthrowing the government, Somalia will become a crucible of extremism directed against the West. We've invested too much to let that happen.'

Tension simmered under the smooth lines of Chance's face. There was something she wasn't sharing with Bald. He could smell it on her. He thought out loud, 'So the Americans couldn't get to Pretorius, and now they want us to take care of him?'

'Pretorius is one of our own, which somewhat obligates us to take him down. And after Delta Force suffered casualties in Mogadishu in '93, the Americans aren't exactly keen to get their toes wet again. They'd much prefer to handle this one at a distance.'

'Typical Yanks. Create a fucking mess then leave someone else to clean it up.'

Chance laughed cynically. Then she got serious and dropped her voice. 'After what happened – in Northern Ireland – I want to see him burn.'

Bald grinned. 'That makes two of us, Avery.'

Chance straightened her sleeve and the trace of vengeance in her eyes dimmed.

'Your first objective is to find Pretorius,' she said. 'Which won't be as easy. He's protected by his loyal cadre of men. His band of brothers, he calls them. There are rumours that his training camp is somewhere along the River Jubba. But Somalia is a fractured state. There is some semblance of order inside Mogadishu. Outside the city, it's a lawless hole. Pretorius could be hiding anywhere.'

Bald sucked his gums. 'Then how am I supposed to find him?'

'There's a plan.'

'There's always a plan.'

'Not as cute as this one. Pretorius has a trusted lieutenant. Harvey Stegman. He's a former operator with the South African Special Forces Brigade. They met while Stegman was smuggling weapons across the border from Somalia to Kenya. We know from a local handler that Stegman is currently in Mombasa on a recruitment drive. This is why time is critical on this mission. We have one opportunity to get you on board before Stegman returns to Somalia.'

'If Stegman will give me the time of day,' Bald cautioned. 'But he doesn't know me from fucking Adam.'

Chance flashed him a cunning smile. 'We picked up chatter between Stegman and one of his old friends from the Circuit. A guy by the name of Trent Drake. Stegman was fishing for manpower, new recruits to the cause to replace the guys killed in the drone strike. Drake promised to send a couple of guys up to Mombasa. Ex-SBS operators. Needless to say, the guys won't make it. You will be there instead.'

'You want me to impersonate a Special Boat Service fella?'

'Exactly.'

Bald didn't like the sound of that. As an ex-SAS operator, he'd always held a dim view of the SBS. The idea of pretending to be one of them rankled with him. But not enough to put him off the op.

'No problem,' he said.

'I told you it was a cute plan.' Then Chance sat bolt upright and dropped the smile. 'Your partner will assume the identity of the second SBS operator on the team loyal to Pretorius.'

'Partner?' Bald repeated.

Chance nodded sternly. 'Sorry to dent your ego, but this mission is too important to stake everything on you alone, John. His name is Jamie Priest. He's ex-Royal Marines. I'm sure he'll be a valuable addition to the operation.'

'He sounds like a fucking insurance policy.'

Chance shot him a severe look. 'Call it what you will. Priest is accompanying you, so deal with it. Having someone accompany you to the meeting is a condition of your rehabilitation. That's non-negotiable. Those are the words of my boss, by the way.'

Bald leaned back in his chair. He was tempted to argue the point, but the look on her face told him Chance wasn't going to be moved. He pushed his unease aside, figured he could find out a way to ditch Priest once he was in-country.

'We haven't discussed my reward,' he said.

'If you're after money, forget it. We're dealing with crippling cuts at Six, the same as the rest of the country. There's nothing in the pot. Your previous hardly helps your case either.'

He bit back on his anger. Instead he laid on the famous John Bald charm, his Scottish brogue soothing, his smile wide. 'Come on, Avery. Do us a favour. You want me to risk my balls going after Pretorius, fine. I'll do it. But you've got to give me something in return. I'm not asking for millions.'

Chance pouted at him. 'I have something else to offer you. Something better than money.'

'Like what?' Bald asked, intrigued.

'Like, a full-time job at Six.'

A laugh escaped involuntarily from the back of Bald's throat. 'Your bosses would never agree to that.'

'Then you underestimate my powers of persuasion.' And the way her eyes gleamed at Bald told him that she wasn't bullshitting. 'I've already cleared it with my superiors. You'll get sixty grand a year, a company credit card and a car.'

Bald did the eyebrow thing.

'A Beemer?'

Chance smiled, but only with her lips. 'A Toyota Prius, John.'

'Lucky me.'

Bald feigned a smile, trying to mask his disappointment. Admitted to himself that a salaried position with the Firm was a long way from his dream job. It was also a long way from the millions he'd expected to earn working for the Russians. Look how that turned out for you, a voice at the back of his head said. He realized something else too. He was living in a world of lowered expectations. The effect of the recession. People had been forced to downsize their dreams. And maybe Bald would have to downsize a little too, compromise on that dream. He sighed heavily at Chance and nodded.

'OK, Avery. Deal.'

'Good,' Chance replied, her mood suddenly brightening. 'You'll fly out to Kenya this afternoon. There's no time to lose if you're to make your RV with Stegman. The British Consulate in Wroclaw will supply you with the appropriate papers.'

He thought of something else. 'How will I find Priest?'

Chance looked at Bald as if he'd just suggested a three-some.

'You can't miss him. Priest is the biggest guy you've ever seen. Shaven-headed, chest and arms out to *here*. Once you've established contact with him, the two of you will meet with Stegman, secure your places on the team and find Pretorius. Find out who's hired him to operate in Somalia. Then kill him.'

Bald rubbed his jaw. 'You make it sound easy as taking a leak.'

'I won't lie to you, John. Getting close to your quarry is going to be extremely difficult. Pretorius trusts only a few men in his inner circle. He is paranoid, delusional and highly unpredictable. Dangerous. Not least because of all the drugs he consumes. You'll have to earn his trust before you can get close enough to take him down.'

Bald weighed something up. 'Even if it means doing something dodgy?'

Chance closed the file, signalling the end of their meeting. 'You have permission to do whatever it takes to earn his confidence. Within reason, of course.'

'Great. I'll remember that when I'm sat in the back of a police car and wearing a pair of silver bracelets.'

Chance stared at him for a moment. Some kind of expression threatened to crack the ice-cold surface of her face. She buried it, said, 'I don't know the ins and outs of what happened in the past between you and Six. But I've got your back on this one. You have my word.'

'Do you cross your heart and hope to die?'

He got a hard look from Chance as she stood up. 'This isn't

a game. It's vital that we stop Pretorius before he turns Somalia into a lawless hellhole.'

'I'll do the best I can.'

'Then you'd better pray that your best is good enough. Taking down Pretorius isn't just an opportunity for you to turn your life around, John. This might well be the last shot you ever get.'

sixteen

Bald boarded the early-morning flight from Wroclaw to Warsaw. Two hours to the Polish capital, then a connecting flight to Istanbul Ataturk. He landed shortly after 1100 hours with an hour stopover before flying to Kilimanjaro airport in Tanzania. He settled in for the seven-hour flight with a slug glass of Famous Grouse – there was no Johnnie Walker on offer on the flight, to his disappointment – and turned to the farewell present Chance had given him at Wroclaw, a briefing pack running to thirty-nine pages: the life story of Kurt Pretorius.

He had been born in Bulawayo, in what was then Southern Rhodesia, in 1955, the only son of poor white farmers scraping a living from the veldt. His father came from Dutch stock and his mother was a Scot from Glasgow. When Pretorius was nine years old, black workers attacked the family farmstead and butchered his parents. Pretorius survived the attack. He was taken in care by a distant relative in England, in Portsmouth. At a young age Pretorius turned to petty crime and progressed to street robbery. He spent a year in the merchant navy, returned home and one day attacked a West African immigrant in the street, beating him to a bloody pulp. After being cleared by the police, and aching to return to Africa, Pretorius enlisted at the French Foreign Legion barracks in Lille. It proved to be a decision that shaped the rest of his life.

Pretorius was not an outstanding soldier. A report from his commanding officer at the Battle of Kolwezi described him as a reckless and prone to making rash decisions, demonstrating a callous disregard for the life of his comrades. He stood just five feet five inches tall and his all-conquering ambitions led his muckers in the Legion to nickname him 'Napoleon'.

After toppling Bokassa, Pretorius lived a nomadic existence, supporting despots and acting as bodyguard to self-styled dictators. He fathered half a dozen children in four different countries. Eventually the Western intelligence community grew tired of Pretorius and colluded with the enemy to eliminate him. In 1994 he tried to oust Togo's General Gnassingbé Eyadéma from power. On a sweltering hot day in July, he crossed the border from Benin into Togo with a hundred men armed with AK-47s, Glock 19s and hand grenades. They were immediately arrested by lackeys from Eyadéma's security services who had been tipped off by their French counterparts. Pretorius's men were tortured, disembowelled and burned alive in the national football stadium while a marching band played music and showered the crowd with gifts. Meanwhile Pretorius managed to escape back across the border. He fled to Mozambique and disappeared from sight.

Until Somalia.

There was a photograph of Pretorius at the back of the file. It was a poor-quality shot, taken amid the rubble of Mogadishu. He was standing over an al-Shabaab suspect, his boot pressed down on the captured man's back. Pretorius had an angular jaw and leathery skin, a deep frown etched into his brow. His eyes were jet-black and deep as bullet holes. Atop his head he wore a green beret stitched to the right side of which was a bronze insignia depicting a flame rising out of a grenade. Bald recognized it as the distinctive emblem of the French Foreign Legion.

Than Bald looked again at the photograph and felt his stomach churn.

The face staring back at him looked eerily similar to his own.

Bald landed in Mombasa at 1912 hours. Moi International was a cramped 1960s shopping mall masquerading as an airport. Guards toting Uzi submachine guns prowled around the gates in ill-fitting uniforms and cheap sunglasses. Bald breezed past the luggage carousel and made his way down an avenue of garishly lit duty-free and gift stores leading to the arrivals hall. He glanced around the heaving crowd. Chance was right. It took him about three seconds to single out Jamie Priest.

The agent had been telling the truth. Priest *was* the biggest guy Bald had ever seen. His shoulders resembled basketballs stuffed into sacks. The oversized G-Shock watch he wore barely reached around his wrist. His legs looked like they'd been stolen from the colonnades of the Acropolis and his black eyes were pressed deep into their sockets like a pair of copper shirt studs. Compared to Priest, the two Geordies Bald had laid out in Poland were practically midgets.

Bald's second thought was that Chance had made a grave mistake in recruiting Priest. He was easily north of two hundred and fifty pounds. Bald watched the guy lumber over. Thinking, Jesus fucking Christ. The guy looked badly out of shape. In the unforgiving terrain of Somalia, Bald figured he'd be lucky to last five minutes.

Priest was all smiles as he thrust out a hand at Bald. Like a log sliding towards him, thought the Scot. Stretched to his full height, Priest stood a full six inches taller than him.

'Welcome to Mombasa, boss,' he said with a grin.

Bald glared at him. Left the hand unshaken. 'Why the fuck are you calling me boss?'

Priest folded his face into an apology. Even up close his peepers somehow looked too small, Bald thought. 'I didn't mean anything by it. It's just – I've been waiting a long time to meet you. Everyone at the Firm knows your story.'

'Stop calling me boss. Got it? We're not on fucking parade.'

Priest nodded. 'This way, boss.'

Bald quelled his anger. Five seconds around Priest and the guy was already pissing him off with his Cornish accent and his brown-nosing. He almost found himself pining for his dead mucker, Joe Gardner, as he followed Priest, threading his way through the crowd towards the exit.

As they stepped outside, a warm wind immediately fluttered over Bald, drifting in from the highlands and drying the sweat on his back. It looked like they were walking out onto a bowling green. Long stretches of grass, manicured hedges. The terminal resembled a hunting lodge, Bald thought. 'KENYAN AIRWAYS WELCOMES YOU TO MOI INTERNATIONAL,' a sign, lit up in primary red, announced cheerfully on the roof of the building. The night sky was studded with stars. As if someone had fed a De Beers diamond into a wood chipper. Bald followed Priest towards a silver Subaru Forester compact crossover at the short-stay car park.

'Where's the meet with Stegman?' he said.

'The Zanzi Bar, boss. In the old town. The meet's set for 2100 hours, according to the briefing notes I got from Avery. Stegman is expecting two ex-SBS operators. He's going to be getting us instead.'

Bald checked his cheap plastic Casio. 1936 hours. Loads of time to make the RV, he thought. He bundled into the front passenger seat of the Subaru, Priest cramming his enormous frame behind the steering wheel. The guy took off his G-Shock, turned it over and flipped open the back cover. Bald peered at Priest's hands as he scooped out a couple of SIM cards secreted inside the watch. After placing the SIMs on the dashboard, Priest popped open the glove box and fished out a pair of BlackBerry Bolds. Bald scoffed. The Firm still preferred out-of-date BBs over the latest models, allegedly because of the encryption techniques. But Bald figured it was more likely because Whitehall was too skint to upgrade their kit.

He noticed a copy of Kenya's *Star* newspaper on the dash, folded to a photograph of a smiling young blonde woman with bright-blue eyes. Bald tilted his head and skimmed the headline. The report said the woman had been abducted in a suspected pirate kidnapping at a beach resort north of Mombasa.

Priest inserted a SIM into each of the BlackBerries and passed one of the phones to Bald.

'You're to check in with Avery,' he said. 'Verify your whereabouts.'

Bald nodded. Mission protocol. Each of the SIM cards stored the contact details for their handler at the Firm – Avery Chance. With phone-tracking devices easily available over the internet for a couple of hundred pounds, disposing of SIMs was now a standard operational procedure. After a call had been made, the card was to be removed from the phone and destroyed. The idea of using a stash of SIM cards to evade tracking had been pioneered by drug dealers in America in the early 2000s. Now it had gone mainstream.

As Priest drove out of the airport, Bald noticed the temperature inside the car was thirty-six degrees. 'Put on the air con,' he gasped. 'It's fucking boiling in here.'

Priest tapped the a.c. 'It is on, boss.'

Bald scowled at it. 'Piece of junk.'

They headed east, then south along Mombasa Road, the asphalt flanked by rolling plains of savannah grass so parched and brown Bald wondered how anyone had managed to eke a living out of this place. At his twelve o'clock he could see the island city of Mombasa on the other side of the bridge arching over Tudor Creek, brown and white and flat, like a stubbed-out cigarette.

Priest cast an admiring glance at Bald. 'I've followed your career, you know. I know you used to be in the Regiment. I thought about trying out for Selection myself once too.'

Bald grunted. 'Is that a fact?' He turned to Priest, glared at him. 'What were you doing before you joined the Firm?'

Priest grinned. 'I spent three years as a bootneck in the Corps. We've got a lot in common.'

Bald suppressed a smirk. 'Judging by the fucking size of you, we've got nothing in common, mate. You're carrying too much timber for a start. You're going to get crucified in this heat.'

Priest shook his head. 'I'm fitter than most, boss. I was first on the hill runs in the Corps. I've got an oversized heart and lungs. My ticker is twice as big as normal. That's why I'm the size I am.'

'Try telling that to Stegman,' Bald scoffed. 'He's the one in charge of getting us on the team. We've got to convince him that we both know our shit. I've been there, done it and bought the T-shirt, mate. I'm a living legend. What experience have you got?'

Priest thought for a moment. 'After the Corps I served in the Met for four years, made my way up to detective and transferred to the Specialist Crime Directorate, specializing in organized crime. Mainly Russian mafia. My CO in the Marines was always banging on about how I had an eye for numbers. Anyway, I caught the attention of Six and they picked me up soon after. You know how it is.'

Priest remembered something and nudged Bald, grinning broadly. 'If things work out on this op, maybe you'll pass the vetting process, boss. Like I did. Then we'll end up working together full-time.'

'Bollocks to that,' Bald fumed. 'I don't need to pass any fucking vetting process.'

That shut Priest up good and proper, so Bald turned his attention to his BlackBerry. Fired it up, waited for the home screen to appear. Then he tapped open the Contacts tab and thumbed down to the only number stored on the card. 'Dentist,' the name said.

Bald tapped 'Call'.

Chance answered on the third ring. 'Hello?' she said, clipped and curt.

Bald pronounced slowly the security word he'd been given: 'Flamingo.'

Chance's sigh of relief came down the line like a zephyr as the Subaru shot across the Makupa Causeway connecting the mainland to the island. But then she seemed to come over all anxious. 'John, thank God. I've been wearing a trench line into my office waiting for you to touch base. How far are you from the RV with Stegman?'

Bald glanced ahead. The old town sprang up in front of them, a mass of mud shacks and decrepit two-storey housing blocks, their grey frontages scuffed like dirty old sneakers. Behind the maze of derelict and collapsed structures a mountain of rubbish rose over the city, smoke from a trash fire lighting up the night sky and smothering the locals in a filmy smog. Kilindini Harbour was at their three o'clock, the masts of a clutch of boats jutting into the sky above the glistening black sea.

Bald said, 'Closing in on the RV as we speak.'

Chance hissed under her breath. There was a pause and she said something Bald couldn't make out. Then she came back on the line and said, 'Listen carefully, John. We may have a problem.'

Bald tensed up, tightened his grip on the BlackBerry. Anger brewing in his chest, neck muscles tightening. Problems. The Firm. They seemed to go hand in hand.

'What is it?' he snapped. Priest, hearing his tone of voice, slowed the Subaru to 60k per.

Bald listened as Chance took in a sharp draw of breath. Then she said, 'We've just received int from GCHQ. One of our guys picked up chatter between Stegman and Drake a few hours ago. Turns out there's a third recruit to the team. His name is Vincent Dallas.' She paused for a couple of beats. 'Is that name familiar to you, John?'

'No.'

'Well, it should be. Dallas is a regular on the Circuit. According to our files he's worked all over the place. Libya, Zaire, Afghanistan . . . including a job in Baghdad working for the same company as you.'

Bald snorted. His guts tangled themselves into knots. The op was already in danger of going tits up and they hadn't even made the RV with Stegman yet.

Chance went on, 'There's a chance that Dallas might finger you if he sees your face. We can't afford for your cover to be blown. The mission will be dead in the water. You have to take care of him before he has a chance to identify you to Stegman.'

'Shit!' Bald hammered his fist on the dash so hard the Subaru shook. He closed his eyes for a couple of seconds. Suddenly all his old fears and bitter feelings towards the Firm came rushing back at him. Too late to back down now, he thought. Only one thing for it. He popped open his eyes. Took in a deep breath. The air was thick and dry. He sighed.

'Where's he staying, Avery?'

'The Baring Lodge. Across the creek. You'll have to hurry. He'll be leaving for the meet soon.'

'I'll take care of it.'

Bald ended the call. He flipped open the BlackBerry and ripped out the SIM card, his hands trembling with a hot mix of adrenalin and rage as he rolled down the window and tossed the card onto the dirt road. He could feel his hopes of securing a permanent posting with the Firm slipping through his fingers. They had a little over an hour to nail Dallas, dispose of the body and make the RV with Stegman.

Five minutes in Africa, thought Bald, and I'm already having to get my hands dirty.

'What's going on?' Priest asked, interrupting his thoughts.

Bald filled his partner in. Priest listened silently as he steered through the Mombasa slums. Across the other side of the Creek Bald made out a row of gated communities and luxury hotels. Giant billboards were draped over the sides of whitewashed apartment blocks imploring buyers to invest in a strictly white version of paradise. When the Scot had finished explaining the situation, Priest frowned deeply, as if trying to solve a maths problem.

'So what's the plan, boss?' he asked.

'We'll find Dallas. Follow him to the RV. Then we'll fucking do him.'

seventeen

Priest tapped 'Baring Lodge Hotel' into the GPS navigator and followed the directions relayed to him by the honeyed female voice, steering onto Ziwani Road and across the New Nyali Bridge. Bald pointed at the GPS unit.

'Can you get that voice to shut up?' he snapped. 'I'm trying to think here.'

'Sorry, boss.'

They bounced over the bridge and swept past the bay on the other side of the creek. 'That thing is really pissing me off,' said Bald.

Priest shrugged. 'First-world problem.'

Bald shot a look at him. 'What the hell's that supposed to mean?'

'You've never heard the expression, boss? It means something that, you know, is a problem you only get if you're living in the first world. Like, you get stressed when the Wi-Fi at Starbucks goes on the blink, or you're worried about which diamond ring to buy your missus, or—'

Bald raised a hand. Give me strength, he thought. 'I get it. From now on, how about you drop the hip phrases and talk in plain English.'

'Sure, boss.'

They cut down the bay. Several pristine white hotels gazed

out across a palm-treed marina. Bald ignored the view, ignored the GPS, his mind weighing up the angles, figuring out how best to take care of Dallas. He silently cursed Chance. She'd promised a new broom. Instead Bald was quickly learning it was business as usual at the Firm. New faces, same old shit.

Priest arrowed the Subaru down the affluent Links Road. A hundred metres further on, he brought the car to a halt.

'This is the place?' said Bald.

Priest nodded. 'This is the place, boss.'

They had parked fifteen metres due south of a hotel best described as the last word in posh. Whoever had designed it probably considered a night at the Ritz as slumming it. From their vantage point Bald and Priest were out of the eyeline of the staff. Bald craned his neck so he could score a better view. He spied a colonnaded entrance set ten metres back from the road, at the end of a drive lined with marble statues. There was a lavishly planted garden at the front of the hotel, adorned with toothbrush trees and neatly clipped hedges. The hotel itself resembled some aristocrat's country seat, with its ornate roof and elegant frontage. At the main entrance a black valet wearing white gloves and shiny black shoes was smiling attentively at an elderly couple as he ushered them into the lobby. It was all so very English.

'What now, then, boss?' said Priest.

'We wait.'

They didn't have to wait long.

Vincent Dallas emerged from the hotel at 2018 hours. He sported a grey crew-cut and a chinstrap beard and he was decked out in a cream-coloured gilet, beige combats and a wide-brimmed suede safari hat. He looked like he had come straight out of the bush.

Bald noticed him first. Priest was too busy checking a text on his BlackBerry. He hit 'Send', tucked away the phone and looked up, chasing Bald's line of sight. The two men watched Dallas as a valet retrieved his Chinese-manufactured Chery SUV.

Dallas drove away from the hotel and Priest followed at a distance of three cars' length. The Chery raced back across the New Nyali Bridge, then south onto Arab Road, a potholed tongue of tarmac running between dilapidated colonial-era apartments and breeze-block buildings with corrugated-metal roofs. There were no tourists here, Bald noticed. Just the odd woman wearing a colourful kanga and carrying a big bundle on her head. Gaunt-faced old men pushing wagons piled high with jerry cans of potable water.

A hundred metres into Arab Road, Dallas pulled over. Priest eased the Subaru to a halt twelve metres behind him. Most of the buildings lining the road were partially or completely collapsed. They watched Dallas get out of his car and stride towards a two-storey building ten metres ahead. It stood alone, with piles of rubble that were once its neighbours on either side. The paint was peeling and a sign above the battered metal door read, 'WELCOME TO THE ZANZI BAR.'

Bald checked his watch. They had arrived at the RV with fourteen minutes to spare before the meeting. He watched Dallas enter the Zanzi Bar. Then he turned to Priest. 'Right. Let's do him.'

The two men debussed from the Subaru. Bald silently cursed Chance for assigning Priest to the op as they approached the bar. He was too big, too conspicuous, too quick to lick his partner's boots. The Scot made a deal with himself: the first opportunity he got, he would implicate the guy and do whatever it took to get him off the team. He reasoned that he could do a better job flying solo on this op than with Priest around to fuck it up.

As they entered the bar Bald felt the anger flush out of him.

He slipped into training mode. His mind went cold, blocking out negative thoughts and focusing on the task at hand.

Kill Dallas.

Dispose of the body.

Get on the team.

Inside, the Zanzi Bar was a slum. The walls were bare concrete and the multi-coloured mosaic floor had a big crack running across it. Buckets were scattered around the bar, catching water leaking from dark bulges in the ceiling. A cockroach scuttled across the floor. Bob Marley drifted out of the speakers, singing about peace and love and all kinds of other shit that Bald didn't believe in. A projector beamed a live football match onto a wall at the back of the room. Aston Villa versus Liverpool. Slow-motion replays showed a spotty-faced teenage striker with head-to-toe tattoos going down in the box like he'd just taken a shotgun blast to the face. Bald counted half a dozen punters scattered about the joint. Local faces for a strictly local hangout. They looked at him with a mixture of curiosity and hate and Bald had a sneak preview of what it felt like to be the one black guy at UKIP's annual conference. He scanned the bar. Spotted Dallas at the back, heading towards the toilets.

'Follow me,' Bald told Priest.

2048 hours.

Twelve minutes.

At the door of the toilets Bald said, 'Stay here and keep watch. Anyone tries to take a leak, tell them the plumbing's fucked.'

Priest nodded. Bald swept past him and through the door, his heart thumping in the back of his throat. He instantly wrinkled his nose. Someone had dropped a turd bomb in one of the cubicles and the smell of it hung thick in the air. He looked for Dallas. The room was in keeping with the classy décor of the rest of the joint. Three cubicles on the right, two with the doors missing. On the adjoining wall, four filthy urinals, with a wide, frosted-glass window open up above. Cigarette butts and condoms discarded in them. Dallas stood at one of the urinals, shaking the last drops of piss from his cock. Hearing the door crash open, he glanced round. Saw Bald. Zipped himself up. Just a flicker of recognition sparked up in his eyes.

'Jesus, John,' he started. 'Long time no see. What the fuck are you doing here, mate?'

'Paying you a friendly visit.'

There was just enough time for the guy's expression to turn to fear before Bald launched himself at him. The ex-Para was backed against the urinal with nowhere to go. Bald slugged him in the guts. Dallas stumbled to the side, trying to evade another blow. The Scot grabbed him by the upper arms and threw him into the nearest cubicle. His blood was up now. He didn't see Dallas as an old mucker, just an obstacle in the way of the op. Dallas screamed as he stumbled into the cubicle. Now Bald slammed his face into the dividing wall. He groaned, the impact knocking him off his feet. He shoved a hand against the wall to stop himself slipping to the piss-stained floor.

'Christ, what the hell are you doing—?'

Bald cut Dallas off with a vicious blow to the jaw, the guy's head snapping backwards. He followed up with another punch to the stomach. Dallas made a rasping sound, bent double, his hands moving up to clutch his guts as he folded at the waist. His cheeks were shading red and his mouth formed an 'O', his eyes wide with disbelief. He looked like he was trying to shit out a pineapple.

Dallas tried backing away from Bald but he was boxed in. Now Bald reached out and clamped a hand around the back of his head. The guy was too stunned by the first volley of blows to block the move. He made a feeble attempt to wrench his head free, yanking his neck back and forth. Bald slammed his head against the cubicle wall again. His shoulder muscles were pumping now, his biceps and triceps swelling with adrenalin and blood, allowing him to put some serious force into the thrust. There was a dense thud as Dallas connected head-first with the wall, followed by a short, sharp crack, like an axe chopping wood. He howled in agony. A spatter of blood marked the point of impact. Dallas pawed miserably at his face. His nose was bent out of shape and looked like a spoon right after Uri Geller had vigorously rubbed it.

Bald was about to finish his good work when Priest charged into the room and shoved the Scot out of the way before he could block him off. He delivered a quick punch to Dallas's ribs, then clasped a hand around the nape of his neck. Bald looked on as he hoisted the guy's head six inches above the toilet bowl. Inside the bowl was a massive turd nestling among toilet paper. With a violent downward thrust, Priest slammed Dallas's head against the rim of the bowl. His skull cracked against the porcelain with a satisfying dink that gave Bald an immense thrill. Groaning painfully, Dallas grasped the sides of the bowl and tried to steer his head away. He kicked wildly. Bald grabbed his legs.

Now Priest lifted the lid off the cistern and smashed it down on Dallas's head. Blood spattered the porcelain. The Scot heard the pleasing crack of bone, and saw a huge wound in the top of the guy's skull, blood glistening in his hair. Then Priest just pulverized the guy. Even Bald was surprised by the savage show he was putting on as he battered Dallas's head and face with the cistern lid. Blood everywhere. After a third blow Dallas went slack, then voided his bowels and bladder, piss flooding over the tiled floor. His neck muscles spasmed. A fourth blow did the trick and sent him over to the dark side.

Priest kept hitting Dallas with the cistern lid, making a keening sound in his throat, even though the guy was dead. Bald had to haul his partner off him. The two of them took a step back, hunched in the cubicle doorway, snatching at their breath. Priest had absolutely leathered Dallas. There was nothing left of his face. His features had been caved in, his eyes and mouth and nose now a soup of bone and gristle. Bald turned to his partner in disbelief. Priest puffed out his chest with pride.

'I did it, sir.'

'You were supposed to guard the door.'

'I thought you might need a hand.'

'I had it under control.'

Bald glanced at Dallas and exhaled heavily. He turned back to Priest and said, 'You're a fucking animal. We only needed to kill him. We didn't need to turn his face into putty.'

Priest looked upset.

Bald shook his head. 'We have to dispose of the body.'

'What you might call a real-world problem, boss.'

Bald stared at Priest for a long beat, saying nothing.

Then he told him, 'Get round to the back of the building. The other side of that frosted window over there. I'll feed him through to you.' He looked at his watch. 2055 hours. 'Five minutes until Stegman shows. Get a move on, sunshine.'

Priest raced off as fast as a guy his size could move. At the same time Bald slid his hands under Dallas's armpits and fastened his hands arms across his chest. Then he lifted him to his limp feet. The guy weighed a ton. Dead people always did, in Bald's experience. He dragged Dallas out of the cubicle and over to the urinals. Glimpsed his reflection in the mirror on the wall opposite the cubicles. He cut a faintly ridiculous figure. Looked like he was giving a dead guy the Heimlich manoeuvre. Priest called out to say he was outside. Sweat pouring down his back, Bald gave it one big effort and hefted Dallas up, then pushed him head-first through the window.

'Bury him under some of that rubble,' Bald said. He stood on tiptoe and could just see Priest gathering debris from the adjacent collapsed building and then piling it on top of Dallas. It would look just like the heaps of rubble and other shit all around the neighbourhood, and, with the smell of burning rubbish in the air, no one would notice the stench of a dead guy on their own doorstep, thought Bald.

Then he raced over to the washbasin and sluiced the blood off his hands and forearms. 2058 hours. At the door he stopped and surveyed the room. Blood was splattered over the cubicle walls and floor. But it would have to do. There was no time left. But he took a few seconds to compose himself, then stepped out of the toilets.

Outside the door, a man was waiting for him. He had a wiry build and slender shoulders, and his head was shaven. The guy wore cheap shades and a Barack Obama T-shirt that stretched down to his knees. He was so black he looked like a hole. Like a bottomless pit. He grunted at Bald and ripped off his shades, revealing a pair of eyes stark white against his skin, like golf balls that had landed in a tar pit.

Obama grinned at Bald. 'You looking for Harvey Stegman?' He achieved the miraculous feat of making every word sound like a grunt.

Bald mopped sweat from his brow and nodded. 'Yeah. He sent for us. Jimmy Speed,' he said, using the name of the guy he was impersonating. At that moment Priest appeared. 'My mate, Liam Rees,' Bald said.

Obama eyed them both warily.

'Master will see you now,' he said.

eighteen

Bald and Priest followed Obama towards the Zanzi Bar's exit. The projector was now showing a local news channel instead of the Premier League match. A woman's smiling, bright-eyed face filled the screen. Bald recognized her from the article in the *Star* about the pirate kidnapping. The victim ticked all the boxes necessary to warrant a lead story on the TV news. She was young, white, blonde, British. That would've been enough to get the news editors creaming their pants. Nobody cared when a teenage black kid disappeared. That wasn't even news, thought Bald.

Obama caught him looking at the TV and clicked his tongue.

'So many go missing these days,' he said.

'You don't sound too upset,' Bald said.

'And why should I be? These rich people come here looking for paradise while everyone else wallows in filth. They should stay at home, where it is safe and comfortable and there are no abductors.'

'You obviously haven't been to Brixton, mate.'

Obama didn't reply to that. He led them outside and towards a Land Rover parked across the street from the Subaru. Barefoot kids in Barcelona shirts swarmed around them, hawking cheap watches and bottles of water and knackered old mobile phones. Bald brushed the kids aside.

'Where are we going?' he asked Obama.

Obama smiled. His eyes and teeth were like day-glo in the gritty darkness. 'The Zanzi Bar is too open for master. The Americans wish to kill Pretorius and that means anyone who works for him is in danger too. So, the meeting is somewhere a little more secluded than here.'

Bald and Priest looked at each other and shrugged. Then they clambered into the Land Rover. Obama drove them north-west, towards Kilindini Harbour. A hundred metres short of the harbour he turned down a side street and pulled up outside a Portuguese art-deco-style building the colour of wedding cake. He led Bald and Priest through a wrought-iron gate, into the building and up a broad flight of stairs cloaked in shadows. The African, who had an injured leg, limped along a short step ahead. The air was thick as a towel as they reached the first floor. A strong smell of marijuana wafted along the spacious landing. Obama knocked three times at the nearest door. The sound of a woman giggling came from inside the room.

After a pause a voice shouted, 'Enter!'

Obama cracked open the door and ushered Bald and Priest inside. The apartment looked like something off *MTV Cribs*: white marbled floor, white walls, white sofas, white coffee table. Above, chandeliers glittered like oversized Swarovski earrings. The TV fixed to one wall was so big it probably straddled three different time zones. It was tuned in to some too-cool-for-school music station. A bunch of black women in leopard-print bikinis were shaking their booty at a five-foot-nothing guy with corn-rows and a baggy white T-shirt. The TV was in 3-D and to Bald the image looked kind of skewed. To the left of the TV/small nation there was a balcony over-looking the slums of Mombasa in what was either an unfortunate oversight on the part of the architect or a deliberate piece of crass class tourism. Two black women decked out in latex skirts, crop-tops and red platforms the colour of cheap lipstick reclined on one of the two sofas. Their hands were vigorously stroking the inner thighs of the guy stretched out in the middle. His legs were spread so far apart you could smuggle a freight train between them. His eyes were clamped shut as he sucked on a joint and groaned in ecstasy.

'Master,' Obama began, interrupting the guy's pleasure. 'The recruits are here.'

Harvey Stegman opened his eyes and exhaled. The veins on his neck stuck out like hosepipes, his bronze skin was pulled tight across his face and he had a taut physique which suggested that his body fat was in the single digits. He wore a tan-coloured shirt that shrink-wrapped his muscles, and a pair of knee-length khakis.

'You're the blokes my mate Trent Drake sent up for the job?' Stegman asked. He spoke in an Afrikaner accent that took Bald a few moments to decipher. Bald nodded as Stegman ran his eyes over him before turning to Priest. The guy said nothing. Just grunted as he looked them up and down, grinding his teeth so hard Bald could hear the enamel squeak.

Then he burst into a full-blown laugh.

'Bloody hell. Trent has done me up like a kipper this time. Sent me the fucking dregs, hasn't he? You're not a merc,' he said to Bald. 'You should be in a fucking care home.'

The women laughed at that. Bald clenched his jaw. Then a question flashed in Stegman's eyes. 'There's supposed to be one more lad meeting us today. Vincent Dallas. Where the fuck is he?'

Priest and Bald swapped a nervous look. 'No idea, mate,' said Bald. 'We haven't seen him. Isn't that right, Rees?'

'It's the truth,' Priest replied after a pause, like an actor suddenly remembering his lines.

Stegman scratched his crotch. Thoughts whirring and clicking behind his eyes. 'That's weird. Vinnie is never late. Never.' He shook his head. 'No, that's not like Vinnie at all.'

Bald flashed his palms at Stegman. 'Wish I could help you, mate. But we've not seen anyone.'

'If that is true, why was Mr Dallas's car parked outside the Zanzi Bar?'

The question came from Obama. Bald feigned a look of innocence. A tense silence played out in the room. Obama staring at Bald. Bald returning the stare with interest. Stegman rose to his feet and gave Obama a hearty slap on the back, breaking the ice. 'You've already met my son.'

Bald did a double-take. Reset his gaze on Stegman.

'Son?' he repeated.

Stegman grinned. His lips spread apart like a pair of arse cheeks. 'I rescued Eli during a coup in Mauritania a few years back. They still have slavery over there, you know? Darkies enslaving darkies. Mental. I took Eli under my wing. He's like a son to me now. Isn't that right, Eli?'

Eli bowed his head humbly. 'Yes, master . . . and you are like a father to me.'

Stegman ruffled the guy's hair and looked into his eyes. There was an affectionate look in his eyes that told Bald something else was going on here. Maybe the whole father–son thing was a euphemism, he thought. Maybe they had hooked up on Grindr, or whatever it was that gay people did these days.

Stegman turned back to the two Brits. Mean eyes pinballing between them as he spoke. 'Trent tells me you boys are ex-SBS.'

'Aye,' said Bald, remembering the cover story from the briefing pack Chance had given him. 'Ten years in the Boat Service. We fought in the Afghan and Iraq. Completed tours of duty in DR Congo and Gabon too. We've worked as PMCs on the Circuit in Libya and Egypt.'

Stegman pulled a face as he pointed at Priest. He continued addressing Bald. 'You mean to tell me this fat fuck was in the SBS as well?'

Priest swallowed. Bald answered for him. 'Back in the day Liam here was built like a Calvin Klein underwear model. Since we've been out of the Service he's put on a few pounds.'

'A few pounds?' Stegman raised his eyebrow so high it almost hit the ceiling. 'Stick this fella in a boat and it'd sink faster than shares in a Greek bank.'

Bald shrugged and made a what-can-you-do? gesture with his hands. Stegman ground his teeth and stroked his jaw as he thought some more. Finally he said to Priest, 'Well, my boy, Trent recommended you. Which means you're both kosher. But I need to know one thing before I officially welcome you on board. What do the two of you know about training up a militia?'

Bald grinned. British Special Forces were renowned throughout the intelligence and SF communities worldwide for their ability to train up foreign paramilitary and elite units. The Regiment were the kings of this particular line of work and the SBS also dabbled it in from time to time. This was going to be too easy.

'We've trained plenty of lads down the years. We're qualified in weapon handling, first aid and tactical engagement. Give me the men for a month and I can teach them the basics of fire-and-manoeuvre and immediate action. By the time I'm done with them they'll be sharper than any national army unit in Africa.'

The authority in his voice was obvious. Stegman appeared impressed. 'That's good enough for me.' A wave of relief instantly washed over Bald. 'But this doesn't mean you're on the team,' the South African cautioned. 'That's up to Pretorius. All I'm doing is ferrying you boys up there.'

'What else do we have to prove?' Bald asked, his voice tinged with frustration. 'We've got the skills, we're ready to go to work. That's all there is to it.'

Stegman's face clouded. 'Not quite, my friend. Pretorius values loyalty and devotion above all else. You'll have to prove that you're a believer . . . like the rest of us.'

'Believer in what?' Bald asked, amused and intrigued.

'Pretorius is a genius.' Stegman's expression was suddenly rapt. 'He opens your eyes to a whole new way of thinking. He has four hundred men loyal to his cause, each one of them sworn to defend him and the ideals he represents: sacrifice, duty, rejection of the modern world, a return to the way we lived before we became slaves to the fucking machines.'

Seeing the sceptical look on Bald's face, Stegman rolled up his sleeve and lifted his arm to him. The skin on his forearm was lacerated with scars.

'My mark of devotion,' he boasted. 'Pretorius said I couldn't see the light until I cut myself off from my past. So I carved out the tattoo I got while serving with the Recces at Speskop. Hurt like fuck for a month and I almost died from the infection. That's how much I believe in Pretorius.'

Bald didn't know what to say. He'd encountered a few ruperts who inspired utter loyalty in the men under their command, privately educated Sandhurst graduates who thought of themselves as Robin Hood leading their bands of Merry Men into the jaws of danger. Typically the squaddies they commanded were as thick as a shit sandwich and went along with it. But what Stegman was describing was something else entirely. Unease suddenly surged through him. Killing Pretorius, he realized, wasn't simply going to be a matter of chummying up to the guy. He was going to have to buy into this devotional bullshit. And when he did manage to cut him down, hundreds of loyal soldiers were going to be baying for his blood.

'No problem,' he said. 'Give us the chance and we'll prove our loyalty.'

Stegman clapped his hands. 'My ship is moored at the harbour. The *Marlowe*. She'll take us up the coast. Our destination is the River Jubba inlet a couple of kilometres north of Kismayo. If the tides aren't too rough we should reach the river tomorrow morning.'

'Where are we going?' Priest asked.

'The camp that Pretorius established,' Stegman said. 'It's on the banks of the Jubba. Fucking Americans with their Predator drones – means we have to stay well off the radar. That also means while you're based at the camp you will have no contact with the outside world. No mobile phones, no radios, no email. Last thing we need is someone alerting the authorities to Pretorius's whereabouts. If I catch either of you two shits compromising our location I'll personally bury you alive. Got it?'

Priest and Bald nodded simultaneously.

Stegman fished a plastic bag out of his trouser pocket. The bag was filled with what Bald recognized at once as khat leaves. He pressed a wad of leaves into his mouth and it bulged in his cheek.

'We leave immediately,' Stegman said.

'What's the big rush?' Bald asked.

The master and his slave traded wary glances.

'Pirates,' said Eli after a pause. 'Hijacking the supertankers is too dangerous these days, because the American and the British navies patrol the waters. The pirates are getting desperate for money. They have turned to the trade route between Kismayo and Mombasa, looting any vessel they can get their hands on.'

'Why would they attack us, though?' Priest wondered out loud. 'A couple of PMCs. We're not exactly a lucrative target.'

Bald's guts tightened into a knot and he shot a hard look at Priest. He was furious with him for delaying their exit when they had a body dumped nearby with their fingerprints all over it.

Stegman and Eli exchanged a knowing look. 'These are darkie pirates, lad. They're not exactly smart. They see a boat, pound signs flash in front of their eyes. There's been stories of pirates boarding fishing boats, finding fuck-all of value, then executing the crew and burning the boat. We're not taking any chances. The only safe time to make the journey is at night. Coasting it past Kismayo is the dodgy part. Once we reach the Jubba inlet we'll be home and dry.'

'What about Mr Dallas?' Eli asked.

Stegman rolled his tongue around his mouth. 'Screw him. If he can't be bothered to make the meeting, that's his tough shit. He's missed his big chance. We'll have to leave without him.'

Eli grimaced. 'Pretorius will not be pleased, master.'

Stegman grunted. 'We have no choice.' He clicked his fingers. 'Let's go. Smile, boys. Play your cards right, and you'll both be rich beyond your wildest dreams.'

nineteen

They sailed out of Kilindini Harbour thirty-four minutes
later. The moon was bright, a spotlight in an ocean of dark.
Bald stood on the deck of the *Marlowe*, watching the island
city of Mombasa melt into the night, until all that was left was
a faint glow on the horizon, like an afterthought. Unease
weighed like lead in his guts. Stegman made Bald and Priest
chuck their BlackBerries overboard. Priest winked at Bald.
The Scot understood. His partner had the SIMs hidden inside
his G-Shock. But as they headed out to sea a single thought
jarred inside his skull.

There's no going back now, John-Boy.

The boat was a wooden dhow some twelve metres in
length, with a tall prow jutting out above the bow and half a
dozen fenders hanging over the sides of the hull. At the stern
there was a wheelhouse covered by a canopy and, stashed
under the wheel, a Pelican box containing a flare gun. A
strong smell of diesel in the air mixed with the smell of salt-
water spraying off the sides of the boat. The crew was
Stegman, Eli and three other slaves, wearing threadbare
T-shirts and shorts. Stegman referred to them as his children. When he and Priest had arrived at the harbour, Bald
had seen them loading wooden crates from a pallet onto the
deck. Twenty-four crates in total, filled with AK-47 assault

rifles, RPG-7 grenade launchers, hand grenades and ammunition. Supplies for the militia.

They pushed on into the mouth of darkness. Bald touched a hand to his head. A migraine was beginning to grow as they cut through the night, the diesel engine chugging as they motored up the coast at a steady eighteen knots.

To the east, the black swell of the Indian Ocean; to the west, the coastline like the slash of a knife blade. Scattered along it, like pearls ripped from a necklace, the lights of luxury holiday resorts, interspersed with gated communities secure behind electrified fences. They passed the port city of Malindi, a garish sprawl of Portuguese villas and Swahili ruins. Farther north they scraped past exotic islands, white sand glowing purple in the moonlight, paradise gouged out of the misery of Africa. Three hundred kilometres up from Mombasa the lights studding the coastline abruptly vanished, and there was nothing. No beaches, no resorts, no signs of civilization. Just a strip of neglected coast.

They had entered Somali waters.

At first light they swept past Kismayo. In the distance the darkness lifted like a veil to reveal a beach littered with trash and the carcasses of several boats. A swarm of barefoot kids ran along the shore, waving at the *Marlowe* and shrieking. Priest waved back.

Bald felt his migraine worsen as Stegman steered them into the Jubba. The banks were lined with tracts of mangrove trees and thorn bushes silhouetted against the lightening sky. A strikingly green landscape that was a far cry from the dust bowl of Mogadishu.

By the time the sun scudded out of the horizon, Bald felt as if his head would explode. He gripped the gunwale and forced his tensed muscles to relax. Another few hours to the camp. There'd be booze there, surely. A skinful of the hard stuff would put the lid on the pain scraping inside his skull.

Just hold on until then.

And he did, for another thirty minutes, before the migraine overwhelmed him. It was sudden and explosive and he clamped his hands to his head, as if a grenade was about to kick off in there and he was trying to prevent his skull shattering into a million tiny fragments.

Shit! Not this. Not now.

Priest knelt beside him.

'You OK, sir?'

'Fuck it,' Bald spat out a bad taste. 'I'm fine.'

Then he heard a distinctive *click*.

Stegman was standing there, head cocked curiously at Priest. He looked like he had been getting bang on the khat. His eyeballs were bulging in their sockets, his facial muscles twitching frenetically. The wad of khat pressed against his cheek had swollen to the size of a tennis ball. In his right hand he was gripping an M1911 semi-automatic pistol. Pointing the muzzle at a spot between Priest's eyes.

'What did you just fucking call him?' he whispered.

A silence fluttered across the dhow as it moved slowly upriver. Stegman spat his khat wad into the water, flashed a brutal smile at Priest. Bald watched him, fearing for their mission, forgetting about his migraine.

'Nothing,' Priest replied nervously.

'Bollocks! You called this cunt "sir". What the fuck was all that about?'

Priest had no answer. The look on his mug forced a laugh out of Stegman. His index finger teasing the M1911's trigger mechanism. Bald eyed the man rather than the gun. Some sort of paranoid delusion seemed to be gripping the South African. He looked like he hadn't slept in a year.

'Ten years in the business, I never heard one PMC call another one "sir".' Stegman machine-gunned the words, Bald struggling to follow what he was saying. 'Something ain't right with you, boy. Who are you working for?'

Stegman was losing it, Bald realized. Worse, he was losing it with the business end of a pistol six inches from Priest's face. Bald spied Eli and the other three slaves looking on, one inside the wheelhouse, two leaning against it. He stretched a hand out to Stegman.

'Easy, pal. This is a big misunderstanding. Put the tool down and we'll clear it up.'

Stegman rounded menacingly on Bald. His eyes gleamed with intent. Bald stood very still, trying not to think about the damage a .45 ACP round would do to him at point-blank range.

'Let's do that,' Stegman said. 'You tell me who you two are working for, or you'll be scraping your friend's brains off the deck.'

'That cunt?' Bald said, gesturing to Priest. Calling Stegman's bluff. 'He's not my friend. Kill him if you want.'

Priest looked mortified. In the same instant Stegman swung back to him and applied a degree of pressure on the trigger. Priest visibly shrank, went from enormous to just really fucking big as his entire body tensed with fear.

'I'm not even going to count to three,' Stegman rasped. 'I'll shoot your pal here. You're next. The pair of you will be fish food.' The guy was foaming at the mouth, seized by a kind of manic rage.

'I don't know what you're talking about,' Bald said evenly. 'I swear it.'

'Bollocks. First Vinnie goes missing. Now your friend is calling you sir for some fucking reason I can't figure. Your story's got more holes in it than a golf course full of hookers.'

Stegman scowled at Priest. For a cold beat Bald thought the guy was actually going to put a bullet in him, send the fucker south. The Scot was OK with that. The way he saw it, that was one less liability on his hands. Coolly, he studied Stegman, the way his fingers quivered slightly around the pistol grip, the feverish look in his eyes. Bald instinctively tensed his muscles, watching for an opportunity to pounce on Stegman if he was distracted for even a split second. He would grab the tool, use it smash the guy's face in.

Then Eli stepped forward and said, 'You misheard the man, master.'

Everyone turned at once to Eli. Stegman, Priest, Bald. All three looking at him in puzzlement for a few seconds. It was the South African who broke the silence. 'I did?'

Eli shook his head softly. He hobbled over to Stegman. 'Of course, master. He didn't call this man "sir". If he had done, I would have heard it myself. But I heard nothing.'

Stegman hesitated. The tension in his face visibly slackened. 'You're sure?'

'Yes, master.' Eli's voice had slid from its usual mean grunt into a soothing lilt.

Suddenly reassured, Stegman let his right arm fall to his side. The rage drained from him. He ran a hand over Eli's smooth scalp, considering him with affection. 'My child,' he said.

Eli bowed his head. 'I live to serve you, master.'

Priest stepped away from Stegman.

Bald tried to shake the fuzziness out of his head. Could still taste puke on his tongue. His teeth felt like they were covered in fur, his brain like someone had scraped it out with an ice-cream scoop. He watched Stegman stride back towards the wheelhouse. Then, as he turned to Priest, he felt a cold, clammy hand grip his wrist.

Eli's hand. The slave glanced across his shoulder to check his master was out of earshot. Then he said, 'I know what you did.'

'No idea what you're talking about, mate.' Bald trying to shake Eli off, failing. The guy had a surprisingly firm grip.

'Mr Dallas,' Eli said. 'You killed him.'

Bald snorted. 'You don't know shit.'

The smile on Eli's face was thin as spider silk. 'I was watching you from the shadows at the Zanzi Bar, my friend. I saw Mr Dallas enter the toilets. I saw you go in after him. But Mr Dallas never came out. He was a good friend of master. If master learns the truth, you are in big trouble.'

'Not if I break your neck first.'

Eli suppressed a chuckle. He pressed his hands together under his chin as if making a prayer. Bald could swear the guy stood taller now, his hunched shoulders broadening with confidence. 'I have a better idea – a proposal.'

'You must be fucking joking.'

'Not at all. Why else would I stop master from killing you?'

Bald looked Eli hard in the eye. The slave was putting the squeeze on him and he was powerless to do anything about it. A rage coursed through his veins as he said, 'What do you want?'

Eli grinned. 'When we arrive at the camp – when master's back is turned – you are going to help me escape.'

Bald laughed. He was about to tell the guy to fuck off when a droning noise filled the air. It was coming from the rear of the dhow. Bald turned towards the sound. He saw it then. A motorboat. It was fifty metres behind them, surging menacingly down the river, spray hissing either side of its battered bow.

Heading directly at the *Marlowe*.

twenty

Bald counted four guys hunkered down on the deck, two either side of the pilot. All wearing the same gear: black trousers, baggy tunics, faces masked with sunglasses and tartan shemaghs. They were brandishing AK-47s and had bandoliers of two-hundred-round link strapped across their chests. In the early-morning light the assault rifles' barrels glinted like spear points. From fifty metres away the gunmen were bringing their weapons to bear on the crew of the *Marlowe*. The motorboat was rapidly closing in on the dhow, much slower with its heavy cargo. Forty metres between the two vessels. Another forty or fifty seconds, Bald figured, and the motorboat would be level with them.

'Shit!' said Stegman, now coming to his senses. 'Bloody pirates.'

'How the fuck did they find us?' Bald shouted to him. 'I thought you said once we'd entered the Jubba we'd be clear of these pricks?'

'Spotters,' Eli cut in, struggling to make himself heard above the dhow's engine and the incessant drone of the motorboat as it cut through the water behind them. 'The pirates hire gangs of children to monitor the coast around Kismayo. Every time the kids point out a ship, the pirates reward them with a bag of sweets.'

Bald thought back to the kids he'd seen waving on the beach. He remembered Priest waving back to them. Idiot, he thought. He shot a withering glance at the MI6 operator.

'Bastards must have seen us heading for the Jubba and held back,' Stegman said. 'They know these waters better than the fucking Koran. All they had to do was wait for us to steer into the river and bang, they're all over us like flies on shit.'

Then a loud crack ripped through the air.

Thirty metres aft of the dhow, the pirates had opened fire.

Stegman and Eli hit the deck as the first shot hit its target. The slave manning the wheel howled in agony as the bullet severed his spinal column before exiting through his throat. His head tilted back grotesquely, blood spurting out of the exit wound in a hot red flurry and spraying the canopy. His arms fell away from the wheel. The rest of him fell a split second later. Priest looked on, stunned. Bald pushed him down onto the deck as three more shots rang out in a single burst. The calm air was broken by the harsh thwack of rounds chopping up the hull, and by the terrified cries of the slaves wailing for their dead mate. Splintered wood showered onto Bald.

'We need to put down suppressive fire, boss,' Priest said.

'No chance, pal.'

Bald jerked his thumb at the crates stacked up at the bow. 'Those bastards will have the drop on us before we can even crack open the weapons.'

Priest thumped his fist against the deck, exhaling hard.

Bald lifted his head. The motorboat was just twenty metres behind the dhow. Fifteen, perhaps twenty seconds and the pirates would be clambering aboard. He saw the whole clusterfuck unfolding before his eyes. Knew he had to take charge of the situation. Then he remembered something. The Pelican box. He crawled to the wheelhouse but the box was no longer there. Scanning the deck, he spotted it beyond the two slaves, who were cowering face down. It was just three metres from him. He slithered to the box and grabbed it just as three more rounds smacked into the stern. They shredded the wheel-house, ripping holes in the blood-stained canopy and spitting fragments of wood across the deck. Stegman was on his belly near Bald, muttering curses in Afrikaans.

Flipping open the Pelican box, Bald saw the single-shot, twelve-gauge flare gun nestled inside. Four 26.5mm flare rounds lay next to it. Bald slotted one of the rounds into the breech of the gun and snapped it shut as another three-round burst tore up the hull. He waited for the abrupt lull in the gunfire. Then he sprang upright, holding the flare gun in a two-handed grip. With no one at the wheel, the dhow bobbed along, pitching markedly as Bald zeroed in on the pirate boat. Twelve metres to the target. He almost lost his balance as he trained the flare gun on the pilot. Then he gave the guy the good news.

The flare hissed out of the snout in a fist of smoke and fire. There was no accuracy to a flare gun: it was designed purely to sling a round out into the sky. But at a distance of ten metres from his target, Bald didn't need much accuracy. The round did the trick, keyholing the pilot in the upper chest with such force that it spat out of his back and ignited on the motor-boat's deck. One of the pirates stooped to pick up the burning flare and throw it overboard. His arm was instantly engulfed in flames. He gasped in pain and dropped the flare, waving at his mates for help. One of them kicked him overboard as the fire quickly blazed across the deck. He and the other two pirates tried in vain to stamp out the fire.

'*Fucking go!*' Bald boomed.

Stegman picked himself up and ran at a crouch to the bullet-stippled wheelhouse. He grabbed the wheel and cranked up the speed. The *Marlowe* steamed ahead, breaking away from the pirates. Flames were spreading over the motorboat now. Black smoke churned out of its engine and funnelled into the sky. The pirates jumped overboard, wailing for help. None of them could swim. Bald chuckled grimly at their despair as he swung back towards Priest.

'Break out the guns,' he roared. 'We need firepower.'

Priest nodded and spun away, stumbling across the swaying deck to the cargo hold, water sloshing over the gunwale and soaking him. He dropped to one knee beside the nearest crate and wrenched open the lid.

Stegman shouted to his slaves, 'Give the fella a hand, for fuck's sake.'

Bald glanced over his shoulder. They were forty metres ahead of the motorboat now. The fire had pretty much consumed the pirates' vessel. Two of them were fighting over a piece of floating wood. One had pulled a knife and was slashing wildly at his mate as he clung onto the wood with his free hand.

We're getting away, thought Bald.

His relief was cut short by a panicked yell from Stegman.

'Shit!'

Bald spun around. 'What?'

'Look!'

Stegman pointed to the river bank at their eleven o'clock. Ninety metres north of the dhow. Bald chased his line of sight. The bank to the west was a steep incline, and on the top of this, twenty metres above the river, stood a line of acacia trees. Between them ghostly figures were moving about. Ten of them, Bald counted. Wearing the same gear as the guys on the motorboat. And likewise wielding AK-47s. They were taking up positions along the treeline, preparing to put down rounds on the *Marlowe*.

'More pirates,' Stegman hissed. 'The guys on the boat must have radioed ahead to their mates.'

'Master,' Eli said, his voice trembling. 'What are we going to do?'

Stegman's neck muscles tightened. 'Race past them,' he said. 'We're not far from the camp. Seven nautical miles, give or take. If we can just scrape past these bastards we can make it in one piece.'

Bald listened. At the same time his eyes were fixed on the gunmen training their sights on the dhow eighty metres due south of their position. He suddenly realized something and called to Stegman, 'Steer towards the bank.'

Stegman shot him a look like a Turk at a baptism. 'What, and crash into the bank so they can pick us off? You're fucking crazy, man! And you reckoned I was the one chewing too much khat.'

Seventy metres between the *Marlowe* and the ten gunmen, now all in place, their assault rifles trained on the dhow. Bald pointed out a bend in the river a couple of hundred metres ahead. Two boats were just visible there.

'They're lying in wait for us,' he shouted. 'Classic ambush tactics. You have a cut-off group to the back and front, and a main kill group in the middle. The guys on the river bank are the main kill group. They know we're out numbered so we're likely to make a run for it. But if we steam on we'll run into the front cut-off group. The main kill group will swing around the back and trap us.'

Sixty metres to the bank now. Bald saw the slaves scooping out weapons from the crates and laying them out on the deck. He counted four AK-47s and several clips of ammo. Priest unpacked a heftier weapon and glanced at Bald, grinning absurdly. It was a Negev light machine gun, chambered for the 5.56x45mm NATO cartridge and with a cyclic rate of fire of 850 rounds per minute. The kind of tool that could vaporize a man, Bald thought admiringly. Priest unloaded a belt of open-link brass from the same crate and placed it next to the Negev.

'We have to head for the centre,' Bald shouted to Stegman. 'Attack the kill group. If we push them back we can make our way to the RV on foot.'

Eli's eyes widened to poker chips. 'But we'll be steering straight into heavy fire!'

Bald glowered at the slave. 'No two ways about it. We'll sustain some casualties. And we'll lose the cargo on the boat. But it's the only way of getting out ourselves of the shit. If we steam straight on, they're gonna nail us.'

Fifty-five metres.

Stegman nodded firmly at Eli. Nothing sobered up a man like the threat of death. 'He's right. We have no choice.'

A clatter of gunfire erupted. Tongues of flames licked out of the muzzles dotted along the line of acacias and simultaneous three-round bursts fizzed out from the bank like flaming arrows and slapped against the side of the hull. Stegman sank to a crouch as he yanked the wheel hard left. The dhow pitched on its keel and nosed towards the bank at speed, engine growling, water slopping over the sides, washing the blood of the dead slave across the deck. Now a second volley of rounds ripped into the boat, tearing chunks out of the prow. Stegman kept the dhow pointing towards the bank. Gripping the wheel with his left hand, wildly loosing rounds from his M1911 with his right. The river was narrow and Bald saw there was just under twenty metres between the dhow and the bank. But Stegman's aim was poor and even at this short distance his rounds missed their targets, three thumping high into the branches of the trees, three more thudding low into the soil. The gunmen saw the boat surging towards them and started

pepper-potting back, retreating a further ten metres beyond
the treeline, discharging three-round bursts at the *Marlowe*.

The earth moved as the dhow collided with the bank. The
deck shuddered. Bald lost his footing and crashed against the
wheelhouse, pain reverberating through his skull, disorien-
tating him. Like someone had socked him with a bag of span-
ners. There was a powerful tremor as the bow skidded up the
bank. The engine screamed as the propeller scraped the riv-
erbed, churning up sand. Then the boat lurched to a halt.

Bald quickly picked himself up. Shaking his groggy head
clear, he scanned the area immediately ahead of the prow. The
bank rose twenty metres on a steady incline to the treeline,
where toothbrush trees and thorn bushes were mixed in with
the acacias. Beyond the bullet-riddled prow he could pick out
the gunmen. All ten of them. They had finished regrouping
and were some thirty metres from the dhow.

Bald pounded across the deck and, ignoring Priest, grabbed
the Negev. It was heavy – eight kilos of stamped steel and iron
– and he felt the strain in his forearms when he hefted the
weapon up. Like lifting some priceless bronze sculpture. A
belt of 150-round link ammo lay next to the LMG. His hands
working smoothly and with speed, Bald lifted open the feed
tray and inserted the link, snapping the first round into the
groove with the bolt carrier underneath.

'Shit!' Bald glanced back and saw Stegman sucking the air
between his teeth as he pawed at a flesh wound on his forehead. Blood seeped between his fingers, trickled down his
face. 'Banged my head against the fucking wheel—'

Bullets whizzed overhead, a torrent of hot lead zipping
across the prow. Bald slapped the feed tray shut. Then he
tugged on the charging handle on the right side of the Negev,
the belt of open link drooping like a brass tongue from the
feed tray's side. Then he slid back to Stegman.

'We've got to send these pricks south before their mates upriver join the party. We'll take the left flank.' Bald tilted his head at the three slaves. 'Your guys know how to use a tool?'

'They're Somalis. They're practically breastfed on it.'

'OK, you and your men put down suppressive fire on the fuckers.'

'What about you two?'

'We'll break across open ground towards the gunmen and flank them from the left. Once we're in position, you'll attack from the right flank. That way we'll pin them into position and pick them off.'

Stegman nodded. 'Take one of my children with you.'

Eli heard that. He gulped audibly. Bald recognized the sound of fear, having seen enough wet-behind-the-ears squaddies. Priest passed AK-47s to Stegman, Eli and the other two slaves. Gripping his own weapon, he inserted one clip of 7.52x39mm brass into the mag feed on the underside of the barrel and stuffed a second clip into the waistband of his shorts. Nodded at Bald.

The Scot nodded back, then told Stegman, 'On my count, we move.'

From the treeline a cacophony of gunfire crackled through the air, rounds fizzing into the prow of the *Marlowe*. Stegman vaulted over the gunwale and dropped down the right side of the hull. Eli and one of the slaves stumbled after him. Bald saw them take up position on the incline.

'Go!' he barked at Priest and the third slave.

At the same time Stegman roared deliriously to his two men to start putting down rounds on the gunmen. Bald jumped down from the boat after Priest and the other slave. The ground was soft and cushioned his landing.

Gripping the Negev, he led the charge towards the enemy.

twenty-one

The gunmen didn't spot Bald advancing towards them. Not at first. They were pinned down by the rounds coming from Stegman and his slaves. The South African was fulfilling his side of the bargain, concentrating a steady stream of fire on the gunmen from his baseline five metres up the bank from the beached dhow. The rounds powered into the ground several inches short of the gunmen, flinging soil and bits of rock into the air. But the rate of fire was consistent and kept them static, and that was all Bald needed Stegman and his men to do. Isolate the targets while he closed in on the left flank with his own fire team. Adrenalin coursing through him, Bald surged ahead of the other two, filled with a grim determination to finish the job. The pirates had threatened to put the brakes on his RV with Pretorius.

Now they were about to regret ever fucking with him.

He stopped fifteen metres short of the treeline. Four gunmen to the right of the group, farthest from the arc of suppressive fire, had managed to crawl away to cover behind rocks and were returning fire at Stegman. They appeared giddy with excitement, blissfully unaware of Bald unfolding the bipod on the underside of the LMG's stock and sliding to a prone firing stance. His chest were pressed flat against the damp ground, his legs shoulder width apart.

Bald glanced at his six. Priest and the slave were a couple of metres behind. At a signal from Bald the two of them hit the dirt either side of the Scot as he flicked the fire selector on the left side of the pistol grip from the safety position to 'R': semi-automatic. Then he peered down the sights at the rightmost gunman of the four at the rocks. Coolly lined him up between the front post and the rear aperture.

Exhaled.

Fired.

There was zero kickback as he depressed the trigger. Just the bark of the round racing out of the muzzle, the machine-like clang of the Negev's parts sliding back and forth, the sweet kink of the spent jacket flying out of the ejector. It felt good. It felt even better when he saw the gunman's head explode in a vivid shower of brain matter and bone. The gunman dropped. Instantly his three mates swivelled their sights as one towards Bald. He had less than a second to act. He didn't panic. He thumbed the fire selector to automatic and gave the trigger a squeeze, raking the machine gun across the treeline. Bullets pulverized the rocks, throwing up a cloud of dust. The belt link chugged through the feed tray, shells spitting out of the ejector at a ferocious rate. A second gunman did the dead man's dance. Then a third. The fourth dived to the ground.

Seven targets left.

'Displace!' Bald roared.

Priest and the slave shot to their feet and pushed ahead of him towards the treeline. Bald kept up a steady stream of fire at the fourth gunman, hemming him in among the rocks. The suppressive fire suddenly cut out at his three o'clock. He risked a glance at Stegman's team, fourteen metres away. The South African and Eli were reloading, the other slave fumbling with his AK-47. Stoppage, thought Bald. A grim thought hit him. The stoppage had created a fatal lull in the team's suppressive fire. With no rounds being put down on their position for a moment, the six gunmen grouped at the treeline would have a grade-A opportunity to put a bunch of holes in Stegman and his men. Bald grimly adjusted his sights on the Negev, angling the sights towards the targets to the right. Then he pulled the trigger. Didn't have time to aim. Just unleashed a furious burst of lead at the targets. The rounds thumped like invisible fists into the ground. The gunmen scrambled for cover at a scrape a few metres behind the tree-line. Aiming at his back, Bald brassed up another of the fuckers.

Four dead, six to go.

It was only as Bald started to swivel the Negev back towards the lone gunman at the rocks, ten metres ahead of Priest and the slave, that he grasped his own mistake. In putting down rounds at the six enemies at the treeline to protect Stegman's fire team, he'd unwittingly diverted his covering fire from his own men. With no suppressive fire to keep him penned in behind the rocks, the lone gunman now sprang up from cover and targeted Priest and the slave as they advanced up the hill-side. Dread lodged in Bald's throat. He sighted the Negev on the gunman. He was too late. Priest and the slave were exposed. The gunman had time to pick his spot. Three rounds flamed out of the barrel and promptly riddled the slave. The bullets punched holes in his chest, skittered through his lungs and exploded out of his lower back. A scream gurgled in his throat as he dropped like a marionette with its strings cut. Priest immediately threw himself to the ground a metre to the right of the slave as the gunman shrank behind the rock. He left his lower left leg trailing out of cover.

A split second later Bald put rounds down on him. A round tore into the guy's heel. He shrieked in agony, leaning sideways to clutch his wound, removing his head from cover. Bald saw Priest unload a quick burst at him. Three rounds punched the gunman in the face, and Bald saw that he no longer had a lower jaw. His upper teeth were hanging out and Bald could even see the back of his throat, cartilage glistening. Looking at the gunman's body slumped against the rocks, a warm feeling worked through Bald. He was pleased with their work. They'd walloped the four at the rocks, along with one of the others. He hefted the Negev off the ground and raced after Priest, hauling the big man to his feet.

Five dead.

Now he had to take care of the five gunmen grouped at the scrape, four metres ahead of the rocks and fourteen metres away from him and Priest. Stegman's fire team had resumed a stream of suppressive fire, pinning down the five gunmen. Two of these turned their attention to Bald and Priest as they launched up the hillside. They opened fire. Bald and Priest hit the ground eight metres short of the rocks and twelve short of the scrape as a relentless wave of fire chopped and slashed through the treeline. Bald raged inwardly. The five gunmen ahead of them had both angles covered: left flank and right, Bald and Stegman.

Stalemate.

Then a throaty roar went up and Bald glanced over his right shoulder. Eli at his four o'clock. Stegman had been trying to displace to new cover further up the hillside. But the gunmen had the drop on them and the second slave jolted as rounds thwacked into his torso. Eli panicked by his side, throwing himself to the ground as the slave dropped, his body hideously contorted, blood staining the soil black. But with the gunmen preoccupied with the two slaves, Stegman took the opportunity to swing around to the extreme right flank. Rounds ripped up the ground inches from his feet as he reached the treeline. He dropped to a crouch and weaved between the acacia trees as the gunmen swung their rifles towards him and fired. Bullets slapped into bark, showering Stegman in a mist of splinters as he took cover behind a thick clump of acacias fifteen metres due east of the gunmen at the scrape. Bald watched Stegman look over his shoulder, panic flaring up on his face as he realized Eli wasn't by his side. His slave-child was sprawled on the ground further down the hillside. He appeared to still be alive, clutching a trauma wound to his right thigh.

'My son!' Stegman bellowed at the gunmen. 'You shot my fucking son!'

As the gunmen continued to spray the trees surrounding Stegman, Bald spied the two motorboats forming the lead cut-off group along the river. They were heading for the beached dhow, a hundred and eighty metres away. Well within the effective range of the Negev – the LMG was true up to a distance of three hundred metres. But Stegman was in trouble and Bald spotted a chance to take down the gunmen. He turned back to Priest.

'Cover me.'

He got to his feet and pushed up the bank. Heading towards the rock that the last gunman to die had been crouched behind, six metres short of the scrape where the remaining five were gathered. He carted the LMG in a two-handed grip, right hand fastened around the pistol grip, left hand wrapped around the forward handguard as he swept around the rock and dropped to one knee beside it so he could dive behind cover if his plan went sideways. The gunman had their backs turned to him. All five were zeroing their AKs on Stegman, the South African drawing their sting as he shrank behind the acacias, pinned down by an unremitting stream of bullets. One of them saw Bald making his approach. The guy spun round – too late. Bald levelled the Negev with the gunmen and let them have it.

Round after round drowned them in a river of lethal lead, smoke fluting out of the barrel of the Negev. The weapon threatened to overheat in Bald's hands. He kept firing. The gunmen jerked and spasmed. The LMG worked overtime, smoke forming a thin mist in front of him, clouding his line of sight. Heat came off the barrel in thick waves, blowing back into Bald's face. Lead particles and dirt filled the air all around him. He didn't count how many rounds he put down on the five targets. Enough to slot them all in quick succession. Bald saw one guy flop on top of his dead mucker as bullets stitched him. He went on firing. The last guy writhed in agony on the ground and crawled towards him. Screamed something at him in his native tongue. Bald didn't understand what he said, cared even less. He brassed up the last gunman, sent him on a hot date with Muhammad.

After what felt like a long time Bald eased his finger off the trigger.

The gun smoke around him cleared and he had a line of sight down to the bank. The motorboats were a hundred metres from the dhow. If they moved now, he thought, they could get away into the forest before the enemy had a chance to beach and debus. He scuttled down the bank with Priest, racing towards Stegman. A dull ache resonated in his muscles, the stress of combat taking its toll on his body. War. Adrenalin carried you through the heat of it, but once that last round had been discharged the buzz quickly evaporated and you were left feeling all spat out and chewed up. Bald could still hear the roar of the LMG rattling like a tin can in his skull, the blood rushing in his ears. His feet kicked against spent cartridge jackets littering the slope of the bank. He looked down at a sea of gleaming brass.

At the bottom of the bank Bald set down the Negev. Wisps of smoke still drifted off the barrel. More than half of the link had been fed into the chain. Which meant that he'd expended a hundred rounds on the gunmen. As he approached Stegman a thought flashed through his head. The pirates had committed a lot of resources to the ambush. Ten gunmen on the bank, plus the three motorboats. Assuming the two motorboats waiting to finish them off were each carrying the same number of pirates as the first one, that meant twenty-five men in total. Twenty-five guys seemed a lot of manpower to throw at the job on the off-chance that the *Marlowe* was carrying something valuable.

That thought kept niggling at Bald as he drew close to Stegman. The two motorboats were ninety metres away now.

Have to hurry, he told himself. Get out of here before they have a chance to fuck us up.

For a couple of seconds Stegman didn't notice Bald casting a shadow over him. He was busy tending to Eli, wrapping a makeshift tourniquet torn from the dead slave's shirt around his wounded thigh. Eli was bleeding heavily. Beads of sweat glistened on his forehead and he was convulsing with a fever. Tears welled in Stegman's eyes. His hands worked fast to secure the tourniquet. When he'd finished he clasped his hand tightly around Eli's and tenderly stroked his face.

'You'll be OK, my child,' Stegman said softly, stroking Eli's cheek. 'We'll get you to the camp. You'll live, I promise.' Then Stegman took Eli's hand in both of his and the way he did it made Bald think they were more than just master and slave. There was something sexual about it. He felt sick in the pit of his stomach and screwed up his face in disgust.

As Stegman lifted his eyes to Bald, his face hardened. 'You almost killed my son,' he said quietly.

'He's still breathing, isn't he?' Bald replied with fake

sympathy, knowing that Eli had him bang to rights on the Dallas killing. He regretted not killing the slave while he'd had the chance. Swallowing his regret, he nodded at the motorboats steaming downriver towards them.

'What about the cargo?' Stegman asked. 'The guns—'

'Lost cause,' said Bald.

'Shit,' Stegman muttered. He was silent for a moment. Then he gazed up at Bald. 'There's one thing we absolutely must bring with us.'

Bald glanced at the advancing motorboats, now seventy metres from the dhow. At their current speed the pirates would be landing at the bank in less than thirty seconds. He turned back to Stegman and shook his head.

'There's no time.'

'We can't leave it behind. Pretorius will flip out.'

Bald shrugged like he gave a shit. 'Not my problem.'

'It will be when Pretorius finds out you're the one who decided to abandon it.' Stegman licked his lips. His eyes glowed. 'You can forget about getting on the team.'

Bald was burning up inside. Sixty metres between the motorboats and the dhow. 'I'll get it. Just tell me where to find it.'

Stegman grinned. He fished out a key from his pocket, chucked it to Bald. 'It's in the main cargo hold. There's a padlock on the latch. You'll find it inside.'

'There must be tons of shit in the hold. How will I know what I'm looking for?'

That grin again. 'Oh, you'll know when you see it.'

Confused, wiped, out of breath and running out of time, Bald turned away from Stegman and indicated the motorboats to Priest. 'Put down rounds on the pirates. Keep them away from the bank and wait for me here until you displace. Got it?'

'Yes, boss.'

The AK-47 had a theoretical maximum range of eight hundred metres. Theoretical because in practice its effective range was more like half that. Against a rapidly moving target, Bald figured, Priest would be unlikely to nail any of the gunmen on board the two vessels. The best he could hope for was that his partner would put the brakes on their advance and force them to shuttle farther along the river to attempt a landing – buying Bald valuable seconds to retrieve this damn cargo.

Now he sprinted towards the *Marlowe*, wondering what was so important on board the dhow that Stegman refused to leave it behind. He moved quickly, scaling the side of the hull. Priest put down single rounds from his AK-47 on the approaching motorboats as Bald threw open the wooden hatch located midway along the deck and descended the short flight of steps leading down into the cargo hold.

It was gloomy inside the hold. The air was heavy with the scents of spices mingled with the smell of diesel and fish. The hold was roughly the size of a squash court, the ceiling low enough that Bald had to almost bend double to avoid hitting his head against the wooden beams. Squinting, he glanced around. At first he wasn't sure what he was looking for.

Then he saw it.

In the far corner, a pale object was obscured by the iron bars of a cage. Bald took a step closer to the cage, a finger of cold pushing through him.

The woman inside the cage had been bound and gagged and stripped half naked. Her silk bra and knickers were smudged with dirt, her eyes wide with terror and her arms and thighs purple with bruises. Bald stopped in front of the cage, rooted to the spot, feeling draining from his head to his toes. Staring at the woman's face. He had seen her before somewhere. Then he remembered.

She was the abducted woman he'd seen on the news.

twenty-two

The woman in the cage looked up at John Bald and whimpered.

It was hard to see much in the gloom of the cargo hold. A shaft of sunlight shone down through the open hatch at the opposite end of the hold, revealing vague shapes and smudges of grey and brown amid the speckled dark. Bald's eyes slowly adjusted. The woman behind the bars of the cage was blonde, blue-eyed and thirtyish. Her hands were tied behind her back with white plasticuffs; her ankles were cuffed too. Her mouth was gagged and her face was all cut up, like someone had used her cheeks for a game of noughts and crosses. The bruises on her arms and legs looked like eggplants. Blood and snot matted her hair. Her left eye was clamped shut and the lid swollen to the size of a walnut shell.

The woman whimpered again. Remembering the key in his hand, Bald inserted it in the padlock securing the door of the cage and gave it a clockwise twist. The door groaned open. Bald reached in and pulled the rag from the woman's mouth. It was soaked with saliva. And tears maybe?

'I'm not going back,' she said, gasping. 'Please. He'll kill me, just like he did all the others. No, no, I won't go back to him.'

Bald watched her let it all out. Then he said, 'What's your name?'

The woman took a deep breath and closed her eyes. 'Imogen.' She popped her eyes open and looked up at Bald with something like fear. 'He says I'm his favourite, you know.'

'Who?' said Bald.

'Pretorius, of course.'

The name went through Bald like a knife. Kurt Pretorius – the rogue PMC chief he and his partner on the op, Jamie Priest, had been sent to kill. They had been attacked by Somali pirates en route from Mombasa to the camp where Pretorius and his militia had based themselves. In the ensuing firefight Bald had beached the dhow they'd been sailing on and ducked into the hold, where he'd discovered Imogen. Now he had to figure out how to escape the surviving pirates, reach Pretorius's hideout, work his way into his inner circle and secure a place on his PMC team – then slot the bastard before his militia plunged Somalia into chaos.

Kill Pretorius, and Bald could look forward to a full-time career with the Firm. Fail, and his paymasters would send him down for good. Without the Firm – without his handler, Avery Chance, looking out for him – his future looked as bleak as shares in MySpace.

'Pretorius did this to you?' Bald said as he ran his eyes over the woman's purpled lips, the bruises on her cheeks, the clumps of dried blood and dirt in her hair. Ashamed, she turned away.

'Tell me what happened,' said Bald.

Imogen glanced back at him, curious now. 'I haven't seen your face before. At the camp.' She frowned and edged farther into the cage. 'Who are you?'

'A friend,' said Bald. And then: 'What did Pretorius do to you?'

Imogen hesitated. 'He made me his wife.'

'That's why he kidnapped you?'

It was like she hadn't heard him. 'I was his favourite,' she repeated.

More than one, Bald thought. Pretorius has multiple wives. A second thought pricked his skull: if this woman had been married, or whatever, to Pretorius, what was she doing in a cage down in the cargo hold? He wanted to hear her story, get the inside track on Pretorius and the goings-on at his camp. But he also knew he had to bug out of the dhow before the remaining pirates landed and overran their position. He stayed put as Imogen went on.

'His men came in the night. To our villa. We were on our honeymoon. They killed my husband, took me to the camp and Pretorius told me I was his new wife.' The woman's voice dropped to a whisper. 'He warned me, if I ever tried to run away—' She looked pleadingly at Bald, her eyes red-rimmed. 'I can't go back, you see? He'll punish me. Like the others.'

Now he understood why she had been bound and gagged in the cage: she'd tried to escape. Again he thought back to seeing her picture in press and TV reports in Kenya the previous day. At the time he hadn't paid much attention to the story. He remembered a few scant details: the woman had married a Swiss biochemical industrialist at a ceremony that cost somewhere north of a million. Gunmen had snatched her from the island of Kiwayu, a sliver of white sand a few kilometres off the Kenyan coast: paradise hermetically sealed in on all sides by grinding poverty. The news reports had marked a month since her abduction. The police had no leads, although they'd suspected a cross-border raid by Somali kidnappers.

But mostly he remembered her face. In the photographs Imogen had the kind of looks that could make a guy dunk in his fists in a bucket of hot tar: a smile that gleamed like Swarovski, hair like Lana Del Rey, lips parted suggestively in the middle, like she was about to blow you a kiss and break your heart.

The woman in front of Bald was no longer that beauty. Not even close. She had been stripped to her underwear, degraded, humiliated, to the point that every trace of her old life – the one with the gold AmEx and the chauffeur-driven Bentley and the seven-figure wedding – had gone.

'I shouldn't have tried to run,' she said bitterly. 'Foolish of me to think I could ever get away from him.'

Bald searched for some reply to her pain. 'How many wives does Pretorius have?'

'A dozen.' Imogen looked away again. Her entire body seemed to shiver despite the clammy heat of the hold. 'He keeps us in cages. Feeds us like, like – dogs.' She lowered her voice to a whisper. 'I've seen what he does to the others. When they try to escape. He stitches their hands and feet together and buries them alive.'

Bald's jaw clenched tight in anger. The more he heard about Pretorius, the more he realized that the guy's elevator didn't stop at every floor.

'You say you're a friend.' Imogen swallowed painfully and looked Bald hard in the eye. 'Then help me get out of here.'

It's none of your business, the voice at the back of his head told him. Every second he spent here was time wasted. You need to get a move on. Away from the river and the pirates. Imogen saw the cold look in his polished-metal eyes and broke down. Her lips quivered. Tears welled in her open eye.

'Kill me then,' she said in a cracked voice, straightening her back. 'Shoot me. But I won't go back to the camp.'

Bald knew he should leave. But something stopped him from turning his back on Imogen. A memory stabbing at his mind, constricting his throat. Northern Ireland. Twenty years ago. Avery Chance had been a case officer in MI5 back then.

Kidnapped by the Nutting Squad. Stripped naked and tortured in a barn south of the border. Every time he looked at Imogen, he thought about Chance. About how he'd risked everything that night to save her. He'd done some bad stuff in his time. But had he sunk so low he could now walk away from Imogen?

'Kill me,' she implored. 'Do it.'

Bald said nothing.

'Coward,' she said. 'You won't help me. You won't kill me. What kind of man are you?'

Bald looked away and scanned the cargo hold. Found what he was looking for lying on the topmost of a low stack of crates next to the cage. A boat knife. He snatched it up and stepped towards Imogen. She instinctively flinched at the sight of the blade and shrank to the back of the cage, shielding her battered face with her swollen hands. She started to scream. Then he squatted down and slid the blade between her ankles, and with a sharp jerk slashed through the plasticuffs.

Imogen was quiet now.

'Give me your hands,' said Bald.

'You're . . . letting me go?' she asked as he cut through the plastic cord tied around her wrists. She considered her unbound hands with something approaching awe. Bald pointed to the cage door.

'Get out,' he said. 'Now.'

Bald clasped his free hand around her wrist, pulled her up and helped her out of the cage. It took practically zero effort. He owned coats that weighed more than Imogen. Perhaps Pretorius had starved her. Or maybe she hadn't weighed much to begin with. She looked like the kind of woman who spent her days jumping from one celebrity fad diet to the next. He hauled her across the hold and up the wooden steps leading to the main deck. Above her whimpering he could hear the incessant crack of gunfire from beyond the dhow, the waspish drone of motorboat engines in the distance.

'Where are we going?' Imogen asked. 'What's going to happen to me?'

The problem with female hostages: they talked.

'Shut up and keep moving,' he replied, gritting his teeth.

'But you can't—'

Bald shoved Imogen up the steps. Her moans pierced the air as she flopped down on the deck. Bald climbed up after her, emerging to an oppressive heat as thick as a wall. Had to be in the mid-forties. An acrid tang of burnt gunpowder hung in the air, coating his skin like a resin and pasting his T-shirt to his back. He blinked sweat out of his eyes and scanned the river. The dhow had beached bow-first, its tall prow jutting out over the river bank and its stern pointing out to the dull, tea-coloured water. Shielding his eyes from the sun, Bald spotted the pirates: two motorboats seventy metres upriver from the dhow, five men to each boat. Bows slicing through the water and churning up long trails of surf, they were circling. They couldn't venture any closer: Priest was putting down a steady rate of suppressive fire from a clump of rocks three metres along the bank from the dhow. The AK-47 assault rifle looked like a plastic toy in his grip. The sheer size of the guy amazed Bald. Priest was that big, he could have been on show in a Ripley's Believe It Or Not! museum. His shoulders looked like lead weights stacked on either end of a barbell. His neck merged into his back, as if someone had screwed his head on too tight. He unloaded another burst at the motorboats. The rounds fell short and slapped violently into the water.

'Hurry, boss,' Priest called out. 'Can't hold them much longer.'

The pirates returned fire. Priest ducked behind the rocks.

Bullets thwacked into the branches of acacia trees a couple of metres to one side of him. Others chopped up the water nearby.

No time to fuck about. Bald pulled Imogen sharply to her feet and shunted her over the edge of the deck. She let out a cry as she plummeted to the river bank and landed with a light thud. Bald jumped down after her. Spent brass glimmered along the bank like scattered gold. The water around the dhow was stained dark red. The boat itself was studded with bullet holes, the canopy shot through, the fenders severed from their ropes and gently bobbing alongside the hull. Above the dhow, the incline was carpeted with dead pirates.

Got to breeze out of here, Bald thought. Before the pirates catch up with us.

'Jimmy.'

With one hand holding Imogen's wrist, Bald glanced across his other shoulder. A figure stood at his three o'clock. He had the build of a *Men's Health* cover model. His crew-cut hair was so blond it appeared to be on the verge of overheating and his biceps threatened to burst out of his shirt. A wad of khat bulged in one side of his mouth like a clenched fist. Harvey Stegman. A former operator in the South African Special Forces, now the 2iC under Kurt Pretorius.

A black guy lay at his feet, decked out in a knee-length Obama shirt drenched with sweat, a makeshift tourniquet wrapped around his leg to staunch the bleeding from a bullet wound to his thigh. He'd lost a lot of blood despite the tourniquet, judging from his complexion. His pupils were dilated. His face was so pale he looked like Michael Jackson.

'What the fuck took you so long, bro?' said Stegman, narrowing his eyes. 'Where's her plasticuffs?' Bald opened his mouth to reply but the other man cut him off with a wave of his hand. 'Forget it. We're leaving. Right the fuck now. Tell Liam.'

Liam. It took Bald a couple of beats to clear the fog swirling behind his eyes and remember the name his partner was operating under. When Bald and Priest had RV'd with Stegman in Mombasa, they had assumed the identities of a couple of privateers on the Circuit looking for a spot on Pretorius's PMC team. Bald's alias was Jimmy Speed. Priest went by the name of Liam Rees.

Bald turned to head towards his partner. Stegman grinned at Imogen.

'You found the gift for Mr Pretorius, eh?' He clicked his tongue at her. 'Shouldn't have tried to run, sweetheart. Just consider yourself lucky we haven't already gutted you like a fucking pig. You little bitch.'

'Do it then,' Imogen goaded as she took a step closer to Stegman. Bald tightened his grip and held her back. There was surprising strength in her. 'You've had your sick games. You've beaten me, raped me. Why don't you just get it over with and kill me?'

Stegman laughed. 'Because Mr Pretorius likes you, sweetheart. He likes you so much, he gave us orders to bring you back alive. Lucky you, I guess.'

'I won't go,' Imogen said, clapping her free arm to her chest.

'Fine.' Stegman tipped his head towards the motorboats circling on the river. 'Feel free to take your chances with the pirates. They're world famous for their hospitality.' He winked. 'Especially towards pretty young white women.'

Imogen looked at him in horror.

'Animals,' she hissed. 'You're all animals.'

Stegman flashed a smile at her. The veins on his neck bulged. They looked thick enough to abseil down. 'You just keep the compliments flowing, sweetness.'

'Maybe we should cut our losses,' Bald broke in, gesturing

to Imogen. 'Look at the fucking state of her. She's in rag order. She'll only slow us down.'

Stegman flicked his eyes towards Bald, pulling a face like a Greek in a tax office. 'Are you insane? Mr Pretorius explicitly demanded we bring this bitch back with us. If we show up at the camp empty-handed, he'll be furious.'

Bald shrugged. 'That's too bad. But between her and your fucked-up slave there' – he nodded at the black guy on the ground – 'we'll be moving too slow. Those wankers out there on the motorboats will catch up with us before we hit the camp.'

'Don't listen to him, master,' the slave, Eli, said as he tried to sit upright. His voice sounded like someone scraping rust spots off an old car. 'I may be wounded, but I can still walk.'

'We don't have time for this bollocks,' spat Bald. 'We've got to get out of here now. Let's ditch the woman.'

Stegman turned back to Bald and glowered at him. His eyeballs were big and white as gobstoppers. Bald could actually hear the guy grinding his teeth. 'That slimy slit comes with us, Jimmy. End of.'

Bald snorted through his nostrils. At his side, Imogen visibly deflated: shoulders sagging, head hanging low as she came to terms with her fate. Bald wheeled away from her and hurried over to Priest.

'Displace!' he shouted to him, raising his voice above the drumbeat of *ca-racks* as his mucker put down rounds on the pirates. 'Get over here!'

Priest rattled off a final round. Then he shot to his feet and bulldozed his way over to Bald, retreating from the rocks as the two motorboats buzzed about on the river. Priest had surprising speed for someone who was the size of an NFL defensive lineback. Bald scooped the Negev light machine gun off the ground and did a quick weapons check. He'd expended

110 rounds of 5.56x45mm NATO during the pirates' ambush. That left forty rounds of open-link brass hanging out of the feed tray. Not a lot. But enough.

He turned to Priest as the guy caught his breath. 'How many rounds you got?'

'Sixteen in the clip. One spare.'

Bald nodded. Forty-six rounds for Priest – sixteen plus the thirty-round clip. With the forty rounds in the Negev, between them they had eighty-six rounds in total. 'Listen carefully. You're Tail-end Charlie. That means you hang at the rear of the echelon and keep a watch on our six. If the pirates try anything, you give them the good news. Got it?'

'Yes, boss.'

Then Bald wheeled away from Priest and beat a quick path back towards Stegman. The Negev weighed heavily down on his right side. It was big and unwieldy. Like lugging around a car engine. Ahead of him, Stegman wrapped his trunk-like arm around Eli's waist and hefted the slave to his feet. At their twelve o'clock the ground rose steeply towards a clearing littered with rocks and spent brass. Beyond this Bald could see an expanse of savannah, with waves of tall elephant grass brushing against the trunks of acacia and mangrove trees. From a distance came the squawks and shrieks of exotic birds.

Stegman jerked his head towards the savannah.

'Mr Pretorius's camp is this way,' he yelled above the clatter of gunfire as the pirates opened fire on the river bank. Rounds thwacked into the dirt four metres to Bald's left.

'How far?' Bald asked

'Thirteen kilometres.'

'Then we'll have to head into the savannah and try to lose the pirates.'

Stegman nodded. Bald glanced back at the river. The motorboats were scudding fast towards the bank now that

Priest had stopped firing. Fifty metres away. No time to lose. He swung around and started to pound up the slope, pulling Imogen along by her hand. Stegman and Eli had built up a head start and were six metres in front. Priest hurried after Bald and Imogen, four metres back. The firefight had taken its toll on the Scot. His muscles ached. He was badly dehydrated. His head throbbed under the heat and the sweat coursed down his back. Yet he kept up a brutal pace. Thirteen klicks, he reminded himself. In blistering heat. Through an exposed savannah. They were low on ammo and carrying two injured. The pirates had the advantage of speed and numbers.

Crap odds.

They were twelve metres up the incline when Priest said, 'Boss, I think you'd better see this.'

Bald stopped. They had almost reached the clearing. At his side, Imogen was breathing erratically. He did a one-eighty. Saw Priest four metres below them. Giving his back to Bald and pointing out somewhere along the river. The two motor-boats were now twenty metres from the bank. But that wasn't what had alarmed Priest. He was directing Bald to something further north. The water shimmered like loose change under the sun and Bald had to squint to make it out. Then he saw it. Sixty metres upriver. A chill swept through his veins. His blood turned to ice.

Two more motorboats. Racing towards the bank.

Five more pirates on each.

Twenty men in total. All toting AK-47s.

'Shit!' Bald hissed. 'Go!'

He spun back towards the clearing and broke into a hard run.

twenty-three

Skirting the river, they pushed on through the savannah. The sun was so hot it made Bald's teeth sweat, and beads of the stuff ran like candlewax down his spine. Racing through the tall grass brought back memories of training in Belize during Selection. Twenty years ago. Seemed like something from another life. Before Northern Ireland. Before the Regiment's top brass had hung him out to dry, and Bald had turned to the drink, and the migraines began.

Before his life had turned into one big clusterfuck.

He kept looking over his shoulder, like a distance runner gunning down the home straight and checking on his rivals. He saw Priest with his back turned as he stopped to put down single rounds on the pirates. Twenty of the fuckers, thought Bald. Just my luck. He placed the pirates at two hundred metres back. They were moving at a good pace, picking their way through the dead bodies littering the bank and scaling the incline. Slowly but surely catching up. In minutes they'd be on top of Bald and his little group.

The problem was Eli. Bald's fears about Imogen had been misplaced – she moved quickly despite her injuries. The fear of being abducted by a bunch of angry pirates probably had something to do with it, he figured. No, Eli was the one slowing them down. Stegman did his best to hurry him along, as the slave limped frenetically at his side. Bald gritted his teeth. Should've sent Eli south when you had the chance, the voice in his head said. His knackered leg was going to cost them. Big time.

'Keep going,' Bald barked at Imogen. 'Whatever you do, don't stop.'

She nodded quickly. The soles of her bare feet were gashed and bloody from scrambling over the rocks and stones on the climb.

Then a roar thundered at Bald's six o'clock. He looked back to see the pirates putting down rounds on their position. After the roar came the hiss and spit of the bullets as they ripped through bark and thumped into the soil. A hundred and fifty metres separated them now, Bald reckoned. The pirates were steadily closing the gap.

Priest unleashed a three-round burst at them. They dispersed between the acacia trees in what appeared to be a practised manoeuvre, and Bald had to remind himself that he was dealing with a sophisticated enemy. The pirates weren't the usual incompetent local toughs – they had grown up in the blood and bullets of war-torn Somalia. Most of them had been fighting since the day their balls dropped. They had successfully hijacked international shipping routes and repelled attacks from French commandos and US Navy SEALs. They were a formidable enemy.

Bald pushed on. Standard operating procedure when faced with an enemy of overwhelming strength was to execute a tactical withdrawal, bugging out of the killing zone, using every weapon to hand to keep the enemy at bay until neutral ground was reached. But there was one major problem with that SOP: Eli's shattered leg. They were forced to move at a slow pace. He tried to ignore the grim thought taking root in his skull. The one telling him that they'd never escape the pirates in time.

Sixty metres on they saw up ahead an old boat station in a clearing twenty metres up from the river. A dilapidated breeze-block shelter with a corrugated-tin roof and windows like blackened teeth.

By now the pirates were less than a hundred metres behind. Bald knew his group couldn't keep going for much longer. Heat, dehydration, the sheer physical exhaustion of the earlier gun battle – all these were taking their toll. There was a distinct *clink* as Priest emptied the last round from his AK-47. Bald watched him dig out the spare mag from the waistband of his shorts as Eli groaned and keeled over, dropping to the ground beside Stegman.

'It's no good. I can't go on, master,' he said.

Stegman rolled him onto his back. His skin was slick with sweat, his mouth slack. His pupils were the size of bottle caps. Stegman dropped to one knee and took Eli's hand. Bald rolled his eyes. The pair of them looked like they were auditioning for *Brokeback Mountain II*.

'Almost there,' Stegman said softly. Not for the first time, Bald wondered if their relationship was less master–slave and more Elton John–David Furnish. 'One last push, mate,' Stegman urged. 'We have to make it to the camp.'

'I, I can't walk, master. My leg—'

Bald clenched his teeth like he was trying to chew through a lead pipe. 'Leave the cunt.'

Stegman glared at Bald. 'Fuck off, Jimmy. Eli is like a son to me, man. There's no way we're leaving him behind.'

'It's us or him.'

'Then we stay here and fight.'

Bald shook his head. 'There's twenty of them,' he said, jerking his thumb at the pirates, now eighty metres behind them. 'And three of us, not counting Imogen and Stevie Wonder here. We make a stand, they'll rip us to shreds.'

'We're not leaving,' Stegman growled. 'We'll never outrun those kaffir bastards anyway.'

Bald looked away from him. He hated to admit it, but the South African was on the money. Clearly they were in no fit state to escape the pirates on foot. The only option was to stand and fight. It was a long shot, but if they could find a good defensive position, they might hold them off, perhaps inflicting enough casualties to force them on the back foot.

Bald was still weighing up the situation when the pirates opened fire.

He immediately hit the deck. Took Imogen down with him as tongues of flame sparked up amid the trees and bushes. Plumes of smoke fizzled up into the tree canopy. Rounds zipped and flashed through the air – twelve, maybe sixteen, impossible to tell – thumping into the soil a metre to the left of Bald. The voice in the lizard part of his brain took over. You've got to put the brakes on their advance, it told him.

He looked towards the boat station, fifteen metres ahead. The only cover in sight. The building squatted in the middle of an exposed clearing twenty metres wide and thirty long. Dead leaves and rotting bark carpeted the ground around the station, and a gangway of warped planks wound down to the river, where four canoes were moored side by side, partially obscured by drooping reeds. The water gleamed a kind of reddish brown, as if it ran thick with blood.

That's our Alamo, Bald thought.

'The boat station,' he shouted to Priest. 'That's our baseline.' Priest nodded. 'On me. One . . . two—'

On three Bald grabbed Imogen and began hurrying towards the building. A split second later Priest raced up to join them. Stegman and Eli were at Bald's left, the wounded man desperately trying to keep up. Ten metres to the boat station. Then a volley of rounds zipped over his head and thumped into the side of the building. The pirates were closing in. In a flash Bald shoved Imogen aside and transitioned to a kneeling firing stance. He had to put rounds down on the pirates immediately, before his group were on the receiving end of a bellyful of hot lead. He hoisted up the Negev in the same smooth motion and slid his index finger around the trigger mechanism. Then he took aim at the nearest pirate as he broke out of the savannah. The Somali's face was hidden behind a pair of cheap sunglasses and a brightly coloured shemagh.

Forty-five metres away.

Bald depressed the trigger.

The LMG jolted violently in his grip as it dispensed bullets like coins out of a faulty vending machine. Moving parts clanked and thunked. Flames spewed from the nozzle. Empty jackets burped out of the ejector and the pirate spasmed as if someone had plugged him into the national grid. He crumpled.

Thirty-seven rounds of link left.

Four more figures suddenly emerged from between the trees. They raced past the dead man and fired their AK-47s from their hips. Half a dozen rounds landed a few inches short of Bald and Priest, who had dropped to one knee a metre to the right of his partner. At Bald's three o'clock Stegman laid Eli down, then adopted a prone firing stance. Now the three operators put down a stream of continuous fire on the onrushing pirates, while Imogen screamed as she lay face down on the ground beside Bald. Priest brassed up a second target. Stegman nailed a third. Bald struck a fourth pirate and felt a deep burn of satisfaction as three bullets stitched the target's belly. The guy folded in the middle like a penknife.

Thirty-five rounds left.

For the moment they were holding their own. But for every one bad guy they slotted, another three quickly took his place.

Too many, thought Bald. No way can we hold them off. The nearest pirates were less than forty metres away. Four were dead, but that still left sixteen attackers – and they were hopping mad, shouting at Bald as they rushed towards the boat station. An awful realization lodged in his throat – he was going to die here – on this barren strip of land – at the hands of a bunch of Somali scum.

He fought on, unleashing round after round on the fuckers. The Negev shook in his grip. The tongue of link grew shorter and shorter as more rounds were gobbled up into the feed tray and spat out of the muzzle. Five dead now. Fifteen left. He was down to twenty rounds of brass. More pirates surged towards the defensive group. One of them zeroed his AK at Bald. Thirty metres away from his position. He had no time to displace. The muzzles lit up. Three *ca-racks* split the air. Bald ducked as a three-round burst whizzed over his head and pelleted the wall behind him. The rounds were so close that Bald could feel the heat coming off them as they passed.

Now Bald frantically arced the Negev towards the pirate. Down to his last fifteen rounds. Better make them count, he told himself. He fired. The LMG chugged. The rounds strafed the ground in front of the pirate, six inches short of their target, but sufficiently close to force him to dive for cover. Then Bald glimpsed movement at his one o'clock. Spotted three more pirates hurtling towards him, galloping over a fallen tree trunk. He swung the weapon towards the pirates and opened fire. The last few rounds of link disappeared into the feed tray like a python retracting its tongue. Shit! He was out.

The three pirates returned fire. The first four bullets landed short of Bald, flinging soil into the air and showering his face with dirt. The enemy trained their sights on him. Bald knew he was fucked. Felt it in his bones.

'Come on, get it over with, you cunts,' he grunted.

Then a screeching noise pierced the air. Bald felt a cold fear slither down his spine. Screams. High-pitched and childlike. Everyone paused. The next second he glimpsed movement in the periphery of his vision. Coming from his three o'clock – from the mangrove trees twenty metres west of the boat station.

Bald swivelled his gaze towards the treeline to see a bunch of dwarf-sized shadows emerge. Had to be at least twenty-five of them, thought Bald. Soldiers? Hard to tell at this distance. Their figures were shaded black by the tree canopy. They were moving at speed, flitting between the mangrove trees as they sprinted wildly towards the clearing. Moments later they broke clear of the treeline, the shadows lifting from their faces like funeral veils.

They weren't soldiers.

They were children.

For a moment Bald couldn't move. He was transfixed. The children were scrawny-looking and gaunt-faced, with legs skinny as corn stalks and heads totally out of proportion with their slight frames. They looked like a line of coconut shies at a summer fair. Their eyes were like white snooker balls sunk deep into their sockets. Most of the kids seemed to be around twelve or thirteen years old at most. They wore two-sizes-too-big shorts and frayed T-shirts like something out of an Oxfam charity appeal. Crosses were painted on their faces with what appeared to be shea butter. All were armed with AK-47s. Belts of 7.62x39mm link were strapped across their bony shoulders.

'Who are they?' Bald asked.

'Mr Pretorius's children,' Stegman replied, his voice filled with relief. Then his expression darkened. 'Attack dogs, is more like it. The pirates are about to get ripped to shreds.'

Kids against battle-hardened men? Bald doubted it. But then the kids stormed towards the pirates and unleashed their first rounds, taking them totally by surprise. A torrent of bullets ripped through two of the pirates. One guy's shoulder disintegrated in a mist of blood and bone. His mate took a couple of rounds to the face. His lower jaw exploded. Both of them went south as the kids swept down on their position with the kind of rehearsed precision and coordination usually found in elite paramilitary units. Fifteen of the child soldiers broke left and the other fifteen broke right, flanking the pirates and putting down rounds on them from two directions. The pirates were pinned down. Nowhere to hide. They were picked off in short order. One or two tried legging it. The kids slotted them in the back. Bald saw bullets smack into one pirate's head. It snapped back, his brains spattering the guy next to him. Another dropped to his knees, frantically trying to scoop up his emptied bowels and shove them back inside him. The kids kept firing for maybe two minutes. When they had cut down the last of the pirates they began shooting up the dead bodies. This they seemed to think was funny, laughing deliriously as rounds ricocheted off bones and took off chunks of dead flesh.

They're just kids, Bald found himself thinking.

A shout went up. The gunfire instantly cut out, replaced by the eerie stillness that follows a firefight and always reminded Bald of a blanket of fresh snow falling on a city. With the background noise sucked out of the world, every sound was somehow crisper. The gunsmoke cleared. The silence was quickly replaced by cries of help from two of the wounded pirates. At once the child soldiers poured forward and leapt on their fallen enemies with crazed looks in their eyes, baring their teeth and snarling like Rottweilers. One of the kids appeared to be a few years younger than his mates. No older than nine or ten, Bald reckoned. He wore a Manchester City replica shirt with 'TOURÉ' on the back and he gripped a machete with a blade almost as long as his arm. Touré descended with manic glee on the nearest wounded pirate, twenty metres due south of Bald. There was the wet slap as the kid buried his machete in the guy's arm. The pirate howled. Touré giggled. The pirate tried to crawl away. Touré slashed the machete across his back. Then he plunged the blade into his neck. The pirate stilled. Blood disgorged steadily from his throat wound, dark and glistening. Three more kids swarmed over the other surviving pirate and took turns to bash in his skull with blunt rocks. By the time they were through with him, his face resembled a Florida sinkhole.

They're just kids, Bald repeated, out loud this time.

Stegman drew up alongside Bald and heartily slapped him on the back. 'Everything's kif, man,' he said. 'Chill. These kids work for Mr Pretorius.'

'Shouldn't they be playing Xbox or something?'

Stegman laughed. 'Nah, bro. Mr Pretorius trained these kids up himself. Calls them his children. They're the meanest savages on the continent.'

Bald pursed his lips. He didn't know how to feel about that. On the one hand, he was glad that the kids had intervened before the pirates had slotted him. He'd been seconds away from going south. On the other hand, they looked dangerously out of control. He watched them ransack the dead bodies, emptying pockets, hacking off ears and noses as mementoes.

Something puzzled him. He frowned at Stegman. 'How did the kids find us?'

Stegman considered this for a beat, rolling the khat around his mouth and narrowing his gaze on the middle distance. Finally he spat out the damp wad and tipped his head in the direction of the Jubba.

'Mr Pretorius has lookouts positioned up and down the river. In case the Yanks come calling. My guess is one of the kids sighted the kaffirs getting ready to attack us from upriver and sent word back to Mr Pretorius. He would've sent down his children to take care of them. Good job too, eh?' He punched Bald playfully on the shoulder. 'We were a cunt hair away from getting decimated.'

The child soldiers congregated around Imogen, staring at her as if they'd never seen a white woman before. Maybe that wasn't so far from the truth, Bald was thinking. He vaguely recalled what Chance had told him back at the mission briefing in Poland about Pretorius's questionable youth recruitment scheme: snatching children from remote Somali villages and doping them up to their eyeballs, indoctrinating them. Teaching them to believe that he was a god.

Bald pointed to Touré. 'Wasn't that one adopted by Madonna?'

Stegman laughed. The kid took a step towards Imogen and jabbered something in Somali in a deep and snappy voice. She shivered with fear and looked to Bald for help. He turned away, flicking the switch inside his head and shutting off the part of his brain that, well, gave a crap. Bald had an innate cold-bloodedness that had served him well in the SAS. The media liked to portray Blades as selfless heroes who ate courage for breakfast and knew no fear. To Bald's mind, the reality was different. You had to be a ruthless, unforgiving bastard to thrive in the Regiment. Take the glory and fuck everyone else. That should be the Regiment motto.

'The kids'll lead us back to the camp,' Stegman said, helping Eli to his feet. He nodded to Imogen. 'Keep an eye on her, eh? Make sure she doesn't do a runner. Don't want to disappoint Mr Pretorius now, do we?'

The kids led the way. Stegman and Eli followed, with Bald and Imogen a step behind and Priest bringing up the rear.

After ten kilometres of more or less straight tabbing through the savannah they crossed a vine bridge that looked like a prop from an Indiana Jones movie and weaved their way through a further click of dense foliage. Thick thorn bushes nicked their legs. The near-luminous stems of creeper plants trailed across the ground around their feet and the sodden, fragrant smell of the jungle clogged their nostrils. Swaths of the forest had been cut down, leaving behind patches of land scorched white by the sun. Smoke from freshly burned wood hung like a mist and choked the air.

Ten minutes later they entered the camp. Touré went on ahead with Imogen.

At first glance the camp looked like it had been a regular village – before Pretorius and his soldiers had moved in and militarized the area. Ramshackle huts with thatched-reed roofs were arranged in rough columns on either side of a dirt track. In the middle of the camp there was a well where people washed and drank and, apparently, urinated. Probably funded by a charity, thought Bald, built by some blonde twentysome-things from posh universities so they could feel good about themselves. Bony chickens pecked at the dirt. There were ter-mite mounds at the sides of the village, each as tall as a man. Dung beetles scurried across the ground.

They were officially in the middle of nowhere. No wonder the Yanks hadn't been able to slot Pretorius. The guy was so far off the grid he might as well have been on another planet. Bald had the feeling he was guest-starring in one of those charity ads where celebrities pleaded for donations from the public. Any minute now he expected to stumble upon Bono and Bob Geldof. They'd stand next to a dying kid, look solemnly into the camera and promise to make poverty history.

Stegman handed Eli over to a couple of the soldiers, who

carried him over to a hut with a crude red cross sign painted on the door.

Bald and Priest walked on. Then they saw something that made them stop dead in their tracks.

'What the fuck–?' Priest began.

They were staring at a row of metre-tall wooden posts lining the dirt track. A human head had been spiked on top of each post, the eyes closed, the mouths contorted into expressions of mute terror. Bald counted a dozen in total. The freshly glistening blood on the posts and the bloated flesh on each face told him that the heads had only recently been put on display.

Pushing down the fear in his guts until it practically reached his toes, Bald pressed on, Priest alongside him, Stegman now just behind them. There was more. Pairs of severed hands were nailed to the door of each hut. Human skin had been stretched across the windows. In a field to one side of the village, soldiers had set fire to a pile of dismembered torsos. At first Bald had mistaken it for a mound of soil or a rubbish dump. But now he smelled the unmistakable stench of burning flesh. Flies buzzed about his face. The soldiers took turns swigging from a bottle of Jack Daniel's and laughed as the corpses burned. Bald carried on, an awful sense stirring in his bowels that he was about to get sucked into something much darker than he had dared imagine – something it would be impossible to escape from.

'The villagers worship Mr Pretorius,' Stegman said. He spoke in a reverential tone. 'After the Yanks attempted to kill him we set up shop here. In these parts Mr Pretorius is the local mayor, sheriff and priest rolled into one.'

'Does he cure the sick and the blind as well?'

Stegman made a face at Bald like he was sucking on a bag of dicks. 'Pretorius is a prophet. I'm telling you. Wait till you meet him, you'll soon change your mind. You and that fat fucking mate of yours.'

Bald had to tread carefully here. Piss off Stegman and he might shaft his chances of securing a spot on the PMC team. He broke the habit of a lifetime and went for diplomacy instead.

'What makes him so special?'

Stegman puffed out his cheeks. 'Mr Pretorius is a bloody great soldier – the best. The man's deposed half of fucking Africa and he's done it with a fraction of the resources available to the Yanks. More than that, he's a soldier's soldier. Leads from the front.' His eyes burned, his lips trembled with excitement. 'And then there are the stories.'

Bald furrowed his brow. 'What stories?'

Stegman looked apoplectic. 'Don't tell me you haven't heard, bro? Everyone knows the story of Mr Pretorius in Zaire.' Seeing the blank expression on Bald's face, he shook his head. 'He made a pact with the devil, man. The man can't be killed.'

For a moment Bald figured he was joking. Surely a former Special Forces operator didn't believe that a person could be impervious to bullets? He waited for the punchline. None came. After a long silence he realized that the guy was deadly serious.

'This way,' Stegman said, brushing past Bald and a stunned-looking Priest.

They followed him through the village. Everywhere they looked, soldiers were on the move. Hardened veterans in standard-issue green combats and army jackets with the sleeves rolled up, their faces worn and weathered from years spent fighting in unforgiving terrain, busy loading RPG launchers and AK-47s into wooden crates assembled outside one of the huts. Bald saw boxes filled with ammo, Fairbairn-Sykes knives and grenades, Dragunov SVD sniper rifles and Saiga 12-gauge shotguns. Pretty much any weapon he'd ever used in the field. There were stacks of tactical assault vests and ballistic helmets, boxes filled with elbow and knee protectors. Two Dodge Ram pickup trucks were parked in the camp, painted in desert-camo colours.

'How do you think Pretorius acquired all this kit, boss?' Priest asked under his breath as the two operators walked a couple of strides behind Stegman. 'Someone must have paid for it all.'

Bald slowed his pace and lowered his voice. 'Call me "boss" one more time, I'll snap your fucking neck.'

Ahead of Stegman the child warriors whooped and hollered as Touré manhandled Imogen towards a hut in the centre of the village. A pair of guards were stationed outside the hut. At first Imogen resisted. Touré grabbed at a strap of her bra and pulled. It dropped off her shoulder and her left breast popped out. The children screamed with delight, some clutching their ribs in laughter, others making big-breasted motions with their hands and grunting approvingly. She had a good rack on her. Bald enjoyed the view while Imogen screamed in horror and tried to jerk her arm away from Touré. The kid raised his machete above his head, shaping to hack at her, and Imogen squealed, raising her hands to shield her face. With his authority over Imogen established, Touré seized her by the wrist and dragged her towards the hut. The guards swung open the door. Imogen stumbled forward, almost losing her footing, tears streaking down her pallid face, her purpled arm covering her breasts to preserve whatever shred of dignity she had left. Then Touré shoved her inside the hut.

At the same time a fat woman wobbled into view from the next hut along. She looked kind of like Eddie Murphy in *The Nutty Professor*. Arms thick as meat on a kebab skewer, the doughy folds of flesh spilling out of her faded pink dress like meat in an over-stuffed burger. A headscarf was tied across the back of her head. The woman clutched a leather-bound book in one hand and a bag of sweets in the other. Bald recognized the packet. Haribo.

The fat woman called out to the children. Immediately they flocked to her. As she bent down and started dishing out sweets, something weird happened to the child soldiers, Bald noticed: they reverted to being innocent kids. Their dead-eyed looks and menacing body language melted away as the woman made a fuss of them. She pinched Touré's cheek, ruffling his hair and chiding him in a motherly tone of voice. Touré nodded obediently and showed her his palm. She placed a sweet in it, which he greedily gobbled down before giving one of her fat legs a hug. Hard to believe that a short while ago the same kid had hacked a man to pieces. Another kid fetched a stool and the woman eased down onto it – Bald was reminded of a beached whale being airlifted back to sea. She opened the book and began reading to the kids. They were instantly hooked.

'Mama Alice,' said Stegman. 'She looks after the kids.'

'What's the book?' Priest asked.

'Mr Pretorius's writings. His teachings, mostly. He wrote it in prison in Togo after his coup attempt.' He nodded gruffly at Bald. 'You should read it sometime. It's inspiring stuff.'

'I'll add it to my Kindle,' said Bald.

Stegman motioned to him and Priest. 'Follow me,' he said, and set off again.

Bald dumped the empty Negev at his feet. No point lugging it any further. He wiped the sweat from his face – his palms, he noted, were smeared black with grease and dead insects – and trudged after Stegman. Priest held onto his AK-47. After eighty metres the dirt path ended. Ten metres further on stood a low, windowless concrete building with a fence around the perimeter of the plot. In front of it was a long trough filled with slops that were festering in the heat. Bald took it be a pig shed.

'This is you,' said Stegman, gesturing to a hut on the edge of the village.

The hut was clearly the most desirable piece of real estate in the whole place. Built of mud brick instead of the wattle and daub of the others, it was also much bigger: about eight metres long and four wide. Roughly the size of a primary-school classroom.

'What are you waiting for?' Stegman said impatiently. 'Go say hello to Mr Pretorius.'

Bald instinctively tensed up. It came down to this: drop the guy the other side of that door, and all the dark shit that he'd done in the past would be forgotten. One bullet, and a clean break. He took a deep breath, looked at Priest. Nodded.

Then they stepped inside.

twenty-four

It was murky inside the hut. The air, filled with dust, was so heavy Bald felt like he was being smothered with a gym towel. Bars of light poked through the windows. The hut had a dirt floor and was sparsely furnished, with a large clay pot in one corner. Bald took another step and heard something crunch underfoot. He looked down. Red ants the size of .50-cal bullets scurried around his Timberlands.

Then he looked up and set eyes on the man he had been sent to kill.

In the far-left corner of the hut Kurt Pretorius was lying on his back on a crude mattress stuffed with straw. His eyes were shut and his hands rested on his bare chest. He was absolutely still. Like maybe he was meditating. Bald knew from reading his file that Pretorius had been born in Bulawayo in 1955, in what was then Southern Rhodesia. Which put him at fifty-eight years old. The guy in front of him didn't look a day over forty-five. His skin had the texture of papyrus and there wasn't an ounce of fat on his body. Bracelets of human teeth dangled from both wrists. His right ear was missing; Bald vaguely recalled something about it being hacked off during an interrogation in Togo. He had the angular physique and sun-blasted features of a white man who had been spent his whole life in Africa – a man who had stared into the abyss, seen the worst of humanity, and was now utterly indifferent to it.

For a moment Bald toyed with the idea of slotting his quarry right there and then. It'd be easy enough, his inner voice suggested. He could book Pretorius his ticket to the afterlife, leave the hut, double-tap Stegman and bug out of the village before the child soldiers realized that their Great Leader had been killed.

Then Bald spotted the guy next to Pretorius and scrapped the plan.

The man stood guard with his arms folded across his impressive chest. He was a couple of shades darker than the gloom in the hut, his skin glistening like crude oil. He was carrying some serious bulk. He looked like one of those body-building freaks advertising weight-gain products with names like Extreme Gain and Nitro Muscle Max. His pecs were the size of hubcaps, his chest as wide as a forty-gallon drum. He wore a short-sleeved olive-green army-issue shirt and a pair of matching trousers with a large pistol stuffed down the front. Bald recognized the brand by the red strip running down the back of its rubberized grip. A Raging Bull: a large-calibre revolver developed by the Brazilian manufacturer Taurus. It was known in the trade as an elephant gun, because that was all it was good for: killing big game. The Bull had the stopping power of a bazooka and a recoil similar to standing on the San Francisco faultline during an earthquake. In anyone else's hands the sheer power of the weapon rendered it unmanage-able. On this guy it seemed, well, a little on the small side.

'This is Deet,' Pretorius said. His eyes were still closed. 'My chief of security. Deet once ripped the testicles off a fella with his bare hands. The fella in question deserved it, by the way. He betrayed me.'

There was an economy to his voice, every word clipped, his

lips barely moving, as if he wanted to expend as little energy as possible on dialogue.

'Nice name,' said Bald to Deet.

The chief of security just looked at him with his pinhole eyes. There was something inhuman about him, Bald decided. Maybe he was missing his frontal lobe. 'It is from the mosquito repellent,' he said in a slow voice that sounded like a truck reversing up a gravel path. 'Because I swat my enemies. I crush them.'

Just in case Bald wasn't getting it, Deet thrust out an arm and clenched his fist around an imaginary rock.

Then Pretorius opened his eyes and sat upright. He was decked out in a pair of weathered old Palladium boots, olive-green combat trousers and a loose digi-camo jacket, unbuttoned. Now the guy's hands were by his sides, Bald could see several scars lacerating his bare chest. Pretorius studied Bald for a while. His eyes were like jellied eels in a jar. Then he cleared his throat.

'You're late,' he said.

Bald glanced at Priest. 'We ran into some trouble downriver.'

'The pirates. Yes, I heard.' Pretorius picked up a Beretta 92 semi-automatic pistol from the floor beside the mattress and began toying with it, twirling the trigger mechanism around his index finger. 'Still, the sooner you realize it, the better.'

Bald frowned. 'Realize what?'

Pretorius set down the Beretta, stood up and lumbered over to a pot in the corner of the room. Then he unzipped his flies and pissed into it. The hissing and splashing echoed around the hut.

'This place is . . . despicable. The people are ignorant fucks, incapable of honest work, blindly worshipping leaders who promise them the earth. The land is cursed. Disease everywhere.

And the heat ... Christ, the heat. Getting anything done around here takes for ever. Make no mistake, you have arrived in the arsehole of the world.'

Bald scratched his cheek. 'If it's such a crap gig, then why are you here?'

Pretorius shook out the last drops of piss and zipped up. Turned back to Bald. Smiled. 'Simple. Because where others see barbarity and conflict, I see opportunity.' He narrowed his eyes to pencil points. 'What's your name?'

'Jimmy Speed,' said Bald. He pointed to Priest. 'And this is Liam Rees.'

Pretorius shifted his eyes from Bald to Priest and grunted. Bald guessed he didn't like the look of Priest. 'Stegman says you're both ex-SBS operators.'

'That's us,' Priest replied.

'Tell me,' Pretorius said as he swung his gaze swung back to Bald. 'What do you make of the savages?'

'You mean those crazy fucking kids you call soldiers?'

Pretorius laughed. It was a rasping laugh, a short-lived thing that burned in his chest and died in his throat. 'My children? Yes, them. But here's the thing. I've been fighting wars in Africa for more than thirty years. I've spent most of my life living among the natives, no one knows them better than me. And there is only one sure way of breeding loyalty in the savage: fear. You can motivate a white man in a dozen different ways. But the savage only responds to fear.'

He drew closer to Bald. His breath reeked of whisky. Stretched to his full height, Pretorius came up to his chin. Bald didn't normally read too much into these things, but it was obvious to him that the guy suffered from the Little Man Complex. He was practically a walking definition of the term.

Pretorius cocked his head at Bald. 'You doubt me, Jimmy?'

'Where I'm from, you'd wind up in jail for calling someone a savage.'

That seemed to amuse Pretorius. 'Things are different here, as you will no doubt discover. In the West, you have all your rules and regulations. Here, there are no rules. Just the pretence of them. Truth be told, I prefer it that way. Less clutter. Here a man can still make something of himself and answer to no one. But discipline – work – loyalty – these qualities are hard to come by.'

He gave his back to Bald and gazed out of the window.

'One of my children refused to obey my instructions. This was a few months ago. I had to make an example of him to the others, so I had a couple of them place his head between a pair of sticks bound together with rope. Then they twisted the sticks tighter.' Pretorius demonstrated by wrenching both his hands in front of his head in opposite directions. 'It feels like your head is going to explode. Much worse than waterboarding. The child died slowly, of course, and his cries of anguish terrified the others. I made them all watch. After that, no one tried to flee or disobey me.'

He glanced back at Bald. The sunlight caught his face. Wrinkles were cut into his brow like knife marks in a block of wood. Crow's feet were visible either side of his vacant eyes. It was possible that Pretorius had empathy, a soul, whatever you wanted to call it. But somehow Bald doubted it.

'I know how to get loyalty from a savage, Jimmy,' Pretorius said. 'But how do I get loyalty from a man such as yourself?'

Bald shrugged. 'A packet of jelly babies usually does the trick.'

That drew a sharp laugh from Pretorius. Bald could see it rippling from his chest up into his gullet, like a Mexican wave in a football stadium. 'You're familiar with my name?'

'Kurt Pretorius,' Priest said matter-of-factly.

The corners of Pretorius's lips curled up. 'What else?'

'That you're ex-French Foreign Legion. You reached the rank of colonel before retiring on medical grounds. Now you run your own PMC team.'

Bald knew more – knew, for instance, that Pretorius had spent a lifetime launching coups d'état across Africa, that he had gone underground in the early nineties, only to emerge in the cauldron of Somalia, launching attacks against African Union troops and doing his best to destabilize the fragile peace. No one seemed quite sure what his endgame was. Avery Chance's best guess – and the Firm's – was that he intended to topple the transitional government in Mogadishu and turn the country into a security black hole where terrorists could thrive: a breeding ground for Islamic militants with British or American passports, where they could plot attacks on the kind of scale the Tsarnaev brothers could only dream of.

'That's all true,' Pretorius said, 'but there's one thing you should know about me. At heart, I'm an African. I still think of Southern Rhodesia as home, even if that prick Mugabe bled it dry. This is my land. Get this straight: if you want to be on my team, you need to deal with that. Here I'm the king.'

Bald sort of nodded and kept his trap shut, happy to go along with this bollocks as long as it secured them both a spot on the team. Soon as Pretorius gave him the green light, he could begin plotting to wipe out this grandstanding cunt.

'Stegman reckons you saved his life this morning,' Pretorius said, rubbing his jaw. 'When the pirates attacked.'

'Something like that.'

'One of my many talents is that I can tell a lot about someone just by looking at them. And you – you're a tough bastard, Jimmy. Got that stone-cold look in your eyes. Like you'd butcher a family if the mission called for it.'

Bald gave a half-shrug. 'I grew up in Dundee.'

'I need guys like you on the team. So this is the deal. Stegman's vouched for you both. I trust him like I trust my own mother.' He tipped his head at Priest. 'And I guess your mate will do too.'

In the corner of his eye, Bald glimpsed Priest about to burst with excitement, like a dog being patted on the head and told he's a good boy.

'What has Stegman told you about the mission?' Pretorius asked.

It was Priest who answered. 'He mentioned something about training up a militia.'

'Anything else?'

Priest shook his head.

'Training is only half the mission,' said Pretorius. 'You're both ex-SF, which is good, because I have a lot of foot soldiers, but guys with leadership skills, not so much. I need a couple of fellas who know all the tricks of the trade. But I can't let you in on the mission until I know I can trust you both. And I've known you for about as long as it takes for me to have a piss. Do you follow?'

'No worries, mate, we're kosher,' Bald said, doing his best to sound casual.

But Pretorius didn't seem to have heard him. 'In a perfect world I'd get to know you both. Since time is not on our side, I have arranged a test for the two of you. Something that will help you prove your loyalty.'

A cold shot of dread coursed through Bald. 'What kind of test?'

Pretorius waved at the door. 'Follow me.'

The four men left the hut, Pretorius and Deet first. They hung a right, steering off the dirt path and made a beeline for the concrete building Bald had assumed was a pig shed.

Four soldiers were guarding the building. The instant they caught sight of Pretorius it was like they'd set eyes on the Prophet Muhammad. They fell to their knees and bowed their heads. Not to be outdone, two of the soldiers began kissing the ground at his feet in a we're-not-worthy kind of way. Pretorius had a complete hold over his men, Bald realized. He'd seen men worship dictators, but that was different: fake adulation born out of fear of reprisal. This, though – Bald had never seen anything like it.

Pretorius casually waved a hand at them. The guards hurried to their feet and pulled open the gate. Deet and then Pretorius entered, with Bald and Priest a step behind. A vicious smell hung in the air: a foul mix of piss, shit and sweat. Maggots writhed in the fetid liquid in the trough. Pretorius clicked his fingers. As the four guards ducked inside the building, Bald swapped a puzzled look with Priest. The more he wondered about this test, the more anxious he became. Thirty seconds later a line of bedraggled figures shuffled out of the building and staggered towards Bald, the guards hurrying them along by slamming the wooden stocks of their AK-47s against their backs. The ragged figures slumped limply to their knees beside the trough. They were so weak they couldn't lift up their heads. Bald looked at Pretorius.

'Prisoners?'

Pretorius laughed. 'Traitors, Jimmy.'

Bald fought his gag reflex. The stench coming off the men was unbearable.

'These sorry fuckers refuse to renounce their gods and follow me. I killed the rest – you must have seen their heads on the stakes at the other end of the village? These lucky few I have been keeping alive. To draw out their suffering.'

Bald counted thirteen prisoners in total. Most of them were men in their twenties and thirties: a hundred in Somali years.

Three women, a couple of young boys. All the prisoners shared the same dull-eyed look. A few had had limbs amputated and the stumps cauterized with hot tar. Others were missing fingers and toes. Their faces were filled with the silent despair of people who have abandoned all hope. Even Bald felt sorry for these poor cunts.

'What do you want us to do?' he said.

Pretorius grinned. 'Isn't it obvious?'

A leaden feeling sank through Bald as the PMC chief gestured to one of the guards. They picked out one of the prisoners from the group. A child. Six or seven years old. Burn marks were visible down the length of both arms. Flies crawled over his face. The boy was barefoot and half-naked, wearing only a pair of frayed orange shorts. He blinked dumbly at Bald as the guard hauled him forward from the huddle.

Pretorius offered Bald his Beretta.

'Take it, Jimmy,' he said.

Bald didn't want to ask the next question. He did anyway. 'What for?'

Pretorius smiled. 'I want you to kill the boy.'

twenty-five

Bald stood still for a long beat. Like his feet were putting down roots. Hoping that Pretorius might burst into laughter and tell him he was just kidding. But he didn't. The renegade chief of the PMC gang just stood there, right arm extended, the stainless-steel barrel of the Beretta glinting in the sun.

'Take the gun,' Pretorius demanded.

Bald felt his chest tighten. He was bricking it. His bowels tied themselves up into knots. He accepted the Beretta. It felt unusually heavy. The words engraved down the side of the barrel read, 'PIETRO BERETTA – GARDONE, V.T. MADE IN ITALY.' The familiar Beretta logo was embossed on the polymer pistol grip. Three arrows pointing upwards with three rings laid behind. Bald was stalling. He'd done some dark shit in his time – strangled a Royal Navy Wren, killed an MI6 agent he believed was a mole, sold out his former mates in the Regiment. But this . . .

'What are you waiting for? Get it over with.'

Do whatever it takes to earn his confidence. Wasn't that what Avery Chance had told him back in Poland? Only Bald was pretty sure she didn't have in mind slotting a six-year-old. A sharp pain immediately sparked at the side of his head. Like someone was dragging an ice pick across the surface of his brain. He touched a hand to his left temple and clamped his jaw shut. He was caught between the ultimate rock and a hard place. If he killed the boy, Bald would have his blood on his hands for the rest of his life. If he refused, he could forget about winning Pretorius's trust, securing his place on the team and salvaging the op.

Then a shot thunderclapped at his right shoulder, like a tank blasting out a shell, and a bullet struck the boy between his eyes. His neck jerked back, his eyes rolling into the back of his head, hot blood spewing out of the exit wound like champagne from a shaken bottle. The kid swayed on the spot for a second. He dropped like someone had unplugged him from the mains.

Bald turned to his right in horror. He saw Priest with his bulbous fingers wrapped around the grip of his AK-47. Smoke fluted off the barrel. Just then one of the prisoners crawled forward. An old man, all bones and leathered skin, with a face like charred meat on a barbecue grill. The dad, Bald guessed. The old man reached out to the slotted kid with a trembling hand as blood disgorged from his head, forming a slimy pool around his sprawling body. Bald looked on, numb and cold despite the heat, wondering how the fuck his life had come down to this.

Pretorius merely laughed.

'Great stuff, Liam,' he said. Priest beamed with pride. 'Now here's a fella, Jimmy. I like this one. Doesn't piss about. Gets on with it. Good man. Consider yourself on the team.'

He ditched the smile and turned to Bald.

'Now it's your turn.'

Bald almost choked on the muggy air. 'What are you talking about? We've done as you asked. The kid's dead.'

'No, Jimmy. Like I said, the test is for both of you. Liam has fulfilled his side of the bargain. Now you must do the same.' His expression hardened like cement. 'Or you can join the prisoners. Your call.'

The guards dragged the other boy forward. He looked eerily similar to the dead kid. Could have been twins. A village as small as this, they might well have been. He had a prominent scar running down the side of his head. His belly was painfully distended, like someone had pumped him full of gas and forgot to turn it off.

'Kill him,' Pretorius said sternly.

'He's just a kid,' Bald protested.

'This is Africa. No such thing.'

The kid looked at Bald. Bald looked at the kid. The boy's eyes were totally dead. His expression neutral. Either way, he was fucked. If Bald didn't slot him, someone else would. Hadn't Pretorius said he was keeping them alive to prolong their suffering? In a way, by killing him he'd be doing the kid a solid.

So why are you still hesitating to pull the trigger? nagged the voice in his head.

'Do it,' said Pretorius.

Bald went through the motions of killing. He took a deep breath, raised his gun arm until the Beretta was level with his shoulder blade. Tensed his muscles, but not too rigid. Lined up the kid's bulbous head between the front and rear sighting posts on the semi-automatic. He did all this without actually believing he would go through with it. The whole time, the boy didn't so much as blink. Now Bald thumbed the safety lever.

Weird how the kid was looking at him like that.

He found himself pulling the trigger.

The kid was still looking at him as a flame tongued out of the pistol's muzzle and a bullet slammed into his forehead. The kid fell back like a marionette with the strings cut.

A moment passed. Pretorius looked down at the body. So did everyone else – everyone except Bald. He turned away in disgust as one of the female prisoners began to wail at the top of her voice. In that moment Bald hated himself. He hated Pretorius more, for making him do it. He hated the Firm too, for sending him to this dark, ungodly corner of the world. Hated them all.

He tossed the Beretta back to Pretorius. The chief was laughing hysterically. The guards quickly joined in and a chorus of cheers went up above the pained screams of the woman and the moans of the old man. That's when the migraine flared up. Like an assault. Searing pain shot through Bald's brain, as if someone was trying to strike a match against his skull.

God, he needed a drink.

'Good work,' said Pretorius, nodding his approval. 'That's more like it. Took real balls to do that. Now I know you're both golden. And in case either of you ever dares betray me, this footage will find its way to The Hague. You'll be extradited for war crimes in the time it takes the clip to go viral.'

Still smiling, Pretorius gestured towards one of the guards. Bald followed his line of sight. His stomach went hollow as he realized that the guard was holding an Olympus digital camera.

The lens was trained directly on him.

They returned to the hut. Pretorius produced a folding table and three rickety chairs. Deet stood guard at the door, legs wide as a pair of columns, the palm of his right hand resting on the Taurus Raging Bull.

'I've been working towards this goal for ten years,' Pretorius said after placing the Beretta on the table and sitting. 'Now I'm so close I can almost smell it. Like pussy. You two' – he looked from Bald to Priest, gave them both the same steely gaze – 'are going to help me finally achieve my masterpiece. You lucky bastards.'

Bald tried to focus. Fingers scraped along the surface of his skull. Nausea tickled the back of his throat. The migraines were getting worse. He prayed that Pretorius had some booze knocking about the place. The soldiers he'd seen earlier, the ones burning the dismembered bodies, swigging from a bottle of Jack. That would do nicely, he thought. Maybe now they were officially on the team, Pretorius would crack open a bottle of Johnnie Walker Black Label. But the migraines were so bad, Bald would've settled for mouthwash.

Pretorius said, 'We pull this one off, we're going to live like kings.'

'How d'you figure that?' asked Bald.

A broad grin flashed across the chief's face. Something wild glowed behind his eyes that reminded the Scot of a tele-vangelist. Pretorius signalled to Deet. 'The whisky, my man. For my new friends.'

Deet nodded and left the hut. For a split second Bald con-sidered killing Pretorius, now that they had some alone time. The thought evaporated almost as soon as it entered his head. If he tried it right now, Deet and his loyal followers would slot him before they could make their escape. Priest too, although Bald couldn't give two fucks about his partner. Besides, he'd worked up a serious thirst. He needed that drink.

'Ten years,' Pretorius began. 'That's how long I was black-balled from the Circuit. After Zaire, this was. Back in '93. A lifetime ago. I'll level with you: Zaire really messed my shit up. I had nothing.' He screwed up his face and shook his head. 'Ten fucking years.'

Bald shifted in his seat. A thought prodded him and he cast his mind back to the horror of Belfast twenty long years ago. Back when he'd been the newest recruit to the Regiment, alongside his old mate Joe Gardner, and Pretorius was a weapons smuggler who went by the name of Colonel Jim. The guy had been conspiring to sell Stinger missiles to the IRA in order to fund a coup in what was then Zaire and is now the Democratic Republic of Congo. Bald had played his part in wrecking the plan. Now Joe was dead and Bald was hanging in there in the tenth round, taking the blows, riding the hurt. And Kurt Pretorius was a despot living in the remote jungle, feeding off deluded visions of himself. Sometimes you just had to take a step back and realize that in the end nobody got to win.

Still no sign of that drink. His mouth was drier than a nun's gusset.

'What did you do after Zaire?' he said.

'Drifted, mostly. I worked for one tin-pot African dictator after another.' Pretorius cracked his knuckles, trying to put the lid on his rage. 'I worked as a bodyguard for a warlord in Swaziland, a guy who owned a fleet of Porsches and a penthouse in New York. I had a stint as a security adviser to Museveni in Uganda. Shit, I even helped stamp out a rebel uprising in Liberia. We were kitted out with technicals, FN assault rifles and Milkor MGLs. The rebels were indigenous nut-jobs armed with sticks and fucking stones. That's what I was reduced to, Jimmy. Me, a legend of the Circuit. Gunning down Bible-bashers for a few pennies.'

The door flew open. Deet had returned, clutching a bottle of scotch. Bald perked up. Then he made out the label and died a little on the inside. Famous Grouse. Ah, well. Maybe they'd break out the expensive shit after the op.

Deet placed three chipped glasses on the table and resumed his day job of blocking doors. Pretorius poured a generous measure into each glass. Drops splashed onto the table, glowing like liquid gold in the sunlight. Bald eyed his glass thirstily as Pretorius continued.

'People are forever giving advice. You want my advice, don't listen to any of it. Advice is bullshit recycled as knowledge by smug bastards who somehow made it to old age. The only thing anyone ever told me worth a crap was this: the people who really get somewhere in life, they're the ones who crawl through a river of shit. The ones who smell of roses – they're the liars and the losers.'

'You should put that down on paper,' said Bald. 'Turn it into a self-help manual.'

'I already have,' Pretorius smiled. 'I'll make sure Deet gives you a copy of my teachings.' He handed a glass each to Bald and Priest. Raised his own. 'A toast. To swimming through the shit.'

They clinked glasses. Bald took a long swig of Grouse. It scorched the back of his throat and a warm feeling immediately flowed like honey through his veins. He smacked his lips. Pretorius necked his shot and slammed his glass down on the table.

'Gentlemen,' he said, 'we are going to launch a coup. Succeed, and I promise you we'll be so rich we'll make the sheikhs look cheaper than crack whores. Are you in?'

A dark feeling stirred inside Bald. Might have been the Grouse going straight to his head on an empty stomach. But the idea of getting minted after years of being short-changed by the Firm ignited a spark in him, reawakening dark thoughts he'd tried to keep buried – ever since the shoot-out in Antibes six months ago and his run-in with the Russian oligarch, Viktor Klich.

'Aye,' he said without looking at Priest. 'We're in. What's the target?'

Pretorius smiled. 'The Comoro Islands.'

twenty-six

Something like a knife moved through Bald. He stayed very still. Suddenly everything made sense: the weapons crates, the militia Pretorius had put together, the Dodge Rams – all of it essential kit for regime-change enthusiasts. Avery Chance had speculated that the coup might be in Somalia, which made sense, because the transitional government was weak and Pretorius had assembled his militia in-country. But the Comoro Islands? Bald had never even heard of them. He knocked back the rest of his drink. Despite the whisky burning a hole in his guts, the migraine was getting worse. A drilling pain that screeched in his ears and swelled inside his skull. His head felt like it would explode. He hastily poured himself another shot.

'You're familiar with the Comoros?' Pretorius asked.

'Geography,' Bald shrugged. 'I never gave much of a fuck about it in school.'

'It's an archipelago about three hundred kilometres east of Mozambique,' Priest put in.

Bald glared at his arse-licking partner. At the same time Pretorius got up from his chair and walked over to a metal box near the bed and came back with two maps. After moving the Grouse to one side he spread one of them out on the table. He tapped his finger on a group of islands slap bang in the middle of the Indian Ocean, nestled between the much larger island of Madagascar and the east coast of Africa. Bald craned his neck for a closer look. The Comoros were just a blip.

'There are three main islands. Grande Comore, Mohéli and Anjouan. Total population eight hundred thousand. The Comoros declared independence from France in 1975. Since then there have been more than twenty attempted coups. Now it's our turn.'

He drummed his fingers on the edge of the table and his eyes darted from Bald to Priest like a pair of hockey pucks sliding across a rink. Something about his expression told Bald that they were still on probation. That this whole set-up – even the coup itself – was somehow a test. Strange thought, but there it was.

'You want us to take over a bunch of islands?' Bald asked.

'Not any old islands, Jimmy. Paradise!'

Bald scratched the nape of his neck. 'We can't just stroll in and boot out the government. Even with our expertise, a country that size is bound to have its own standing army, cops, the works.'

Pretorius stared at him. A smile tickled the corners of his lips.

'The newly elected president, Mustapha Khalifa, has made drastic cuts to the budget. Currently the force on the Comoros amounts to a few hundred poorly trained cops and five hundred members of the Comoros Defence Force. There's a reserve force, part-time soldiers, but they shouldn't pose a threat.'

'What about outside help?' Priest piped up. 'A move like this, we're bound to piss off the neighbours.'

Pretorius conceded the point with a slight nod of his head. 'The French maintain a garrison of Foreign Legion troops on the nearby island of Mayotte. But if we move quickly and with precision, we'll have secured the Comoros before they can send in reinforcements.'

'How quick are we talking?' Bald asked.

'Twenty-four hours.'

'Doesn't give us much margin for error.'

'The way I've planned this operation, we won't need it. As we speak a small detachment of men based down in Kismayo and led by an old friend of mine from the Legion are preparing to head out on Zodiac boats. They'll land under cover of darkness at an inlet near Chindini, on the south coast of Grande Comore. Then they'll arrest the general in command of the Comoros Defence Force and persuade him to order his men to stand down. That paves the way for our role.'

'Which is what, exactly?' Priest asked.

Pretorius snatched away the map. Underneath it was the other one, showing Mogadishu and the surrounding terrain of the Lower Shebelle region. Bald started to relax a little. The booze was kicking in, reducing the migraine to a faint throb. He reached for the bottle and helped himself to shot number three as Pretorius pointed to an airfield fifty kilometres south of the Somali capital.

'This is the K50 Airport. The UN operates a humanitarian aid service from Nairobi twice a week, using a Hercules C-130 transport. We'll seize the Herc, load men and equipment via the tailgate. We'll land on a dirt road south of Moroni. That's the beauty of a Herc: you can land it practically anywhere. Once we're in-country the men from Kismayo will RV with us. We'll get the lads kitted out with kit from the Herc, and split them into separate strike teams, launching simultaneous attacks on the local airport, radio station and government offices. By that point the security forces will be under our control. We'll have command of the airwaves, the borders and the military. No one will be able to stop us.'

'When do we attack?' said Bald.

Pretorius topped up his glass. '0500 hours. We'll RV outside the airport at 0400 hours. That should give Deet and his co-pilot, Liam here, enough time to sneak past the guards and board the Hercules.'

Priest flashed a panicked look at Bald. 'Co-pilot?'

Silence hung between the three men like meat from a butcher's hook. Pretorius gave Priest a funny look. 'You *do* have a pilot's licence, right? Stegman told me that was the case. Why else do you think I hired you?'

With that Pretorius made the bottoms-up sign and tipped the whisky down his throat.

Fly a plane? Chance hadn't mentioned anything about that in the mission briefing. But there was no way they could back out now – not having come this far. Bald nodded at Priest in a way that said, 'Everything's cool.'

Pretorius went on, 'Once Liam and Deet have the Herc primed for take-off, the rest of the team will board. Start to finish, the op should take twenty minutes. All things being equal, we'll land on Grande Comore at dawn.'

Bald had a hard time imagining Deet piloting a Herc; the guy looked more likely to crush it. 'I don't get it. Why base yourself in Somalia if you're planning to take over a country halfway across the ocean?'

'I didn't come here to plot a coup. The Americans reached out to me. They needed my expertise to combat the growing influence of al-Shabaab.'

Bald sat up straight. Al-Shabaab: 'The Youth'. East Africa's local Al-Qaeda franchise, only with fewer theological blow-hards and more garden-variety psychopaths. Their foot sol-diers numbered several thousand; their favourite pastimes included stoning women to death and amputating the hands of suspected thieves. Until recently they had controlled much of the south of the country. Joint-combat ops between AMISOM – the African Union Mission in Somalia, supported by Kenya troops – and private security contractors, guys like Pretorius, had pushed al-Shabaab out of the cities and into the hinterland.

Bald helped himself to another slug of Grouse. Stuff was starting to grow on him. Or maybe it just tasted better after a hard tab through blisteringly hot jungle.

Pretorius snorted out a laugh.

'It's almost funny. For years the CIA and the MoD turned a blind eye to al-Shabaab wreaking havoc across east Africa, slaughtering thousands and indoctrinating fuck knows how many people. Then some skinnies assault a shopping centre, a few Westerners die and next thing you know, al-Shabaab's a big deal. Crushing them becomes the number-one security priority. But the Yanks being slippery bastards, they wanted al-Shabaab taken down without getting their hands dirty. No boots on the ground. It's Libya and Syria all over again.'

'They still remember *Black Hawk Down*,' said Priest.

Pretorius nodded. 'So they turned to me.'

A troubling thought pricked at Bald. His mouth suddenly felt very dry. Avery Chance had lied to him. The way she'd painted it, no one in the intelligence services had a clue why Pretorius had rocked up in Somalia. But then the Firm had previous on selling Bald lies. No surprises there, then. He just expected better from Avery.

'Why did they hire you?' he said. 'The Americans must have a hundred former operators on speed dial. Guys who don't come with baggage.'

'But none who have deep experience of fighting African wars. They needed someone who could command the local clan fighters, train up a militia and drive al-Shabaab back to whatever fucking hole they crawled out of.'

It was the fifth slug of Grouse that did the trick. Bald tipped it down his gullet, finally submerging the migraine behind a dense cloud of fog. The warm feeling spread through his veins; he didn't even care about Priest giving him the evil eye for hoarding the booze. Ah, drinking: one of the few things Bald was any good at.

'The shit I've seen,' Pretorius added, 'you wouldn't even believe. Soldiers slashing open the bellies of pregnant women and smashing their babies against trees. Generals marching into battle butt-naked, their bodies smeared with the blood of their enemies. Out here there are people who believe if they rape a new-born they'll be cured of AIDS.'

'Sounds like Dundee on a Friday night,' said Bald.

Pretorius's eyes went dark and very small. 'I spent eight months in Somalia working for the Americans. Doing their dirty work. And then it happened.' A smile played across his face like someone slashing open a sack of grain. 'My awakening.'

'Awakening?' Priest echoed.

It was as if Pretorius hadn't heard the question. His eyes were distant. 'I remember the day clearly. A small village twenty klicks north of Kismayo. We had int that the villagers were hiding senior figures in al-Shabaab. It was a trap. We walked right fucking into it.' He gripped his glass, fuming through his nostrils. 'Al-Shabaab attackers flooded into the village. Half my men died. An RPG came right at me. Hit me here.' He thumped his hand against his chest. 'Fucker didn't go off. Can you believe that? Bounced right off me and died in the dirt.' He swallowed the rest of his whisky.

Bald stared at the bottom of his glass. Gears grinding inside his head. He'd heard one or two reports from Afghanistan of RPGs failing to detonate on impact. Something to do with the grenades needing to travel a minimum distance in order to prime the explosive charge inside the head. But it was a rare occurrence.

'That's when the local doctor came over. Said he'd never seen anything like it and declared it a miracle. Said I must be a god.' There was a dangerous gleam in his eyes, thought Bald – like the tip of a blade catching the light. 'Soon the whole village worshipped me. That's when I knew. I'd always believed I was destined for great things, but now I had the proof.'

He leaned across the table. His voice dropped like a spanner down a mineshaft.

'In this life you're either the exposed neck or the teeth sinking into it. Eight hundred million people get up each day in the West and go to work and never realize that they're slaves to their own fears. But here's the thing: only a chosen few have the opportunity not to live under the heel of others. I saw my opportunity. And I took it. I retreated into the camp with a few men, Stegman and Deet among them.'

'Must have pissed off the Yanks,' said Bald. 'Turning your back on them like that.'

Pretorius chuckled, as if laughing at some private joke. 'As soon as my paymasters realized I'd gone AWOL, they sent in the drones. The Americans are nothing if not predictable. They nailed the camp and killed a few of my followers. As luck would have it, I wasn't there at the time. After the strike we went off the grid and set up shop here. Every day more disciples arrived. Men and children who'd read my teachings and wanted to join my cause.'

'And what cause is that?' This was from Priest.

'Renewal.' Pretorius motioned to Deet. A fire blazed in his eyes. His features were strict and taut, like animal hide pulled over a drumhead. 'This world of ours, it's failed the niggers just as much as it's failed you or me. You want to go on playing the same old game, Jimmy? Sticking to the rules? Look where it's got you.' He pressed his palms down on the table and looked the Scot hard in the eye. 'Join me in the Comoros. We'll be gods walking among men. Everything we've ever wished for – riches, women, power – it will all be ours.'

Bald said, 'Stealing a Herc isn't going to be easy. It's not like we can just smuggle it out without anyone noticing.'

'There will be some, shall we say, token resistance. I've had guys OP'ing the airport for the past six weeks. Getting a Mark One eyeball on the kind of force we're up against. The place has round-the-clock guards. Twelve guys in total.'

'It could get noisy.'

'That's where you come in. You'll lead the frontal assault on the six sangars guarding the airport. We'll have the element of surprise and overwhelming force.'

'What about getting our guys on the Herc?'

'There are two security guards posted at the front of the terminal building. I've arranged for a couple of prostitutes to pay them a visit in the early hours. So Liam and Deet should be able to sneak through security without raising the alarm. Once they've given us the all clear, our main force will load onto the Herc. By the time any reinforcements show up, we'll be long gone.'

Bald grinned. 'When do we leave?

'2100 hours. The airport's a seven-hour drive north of here. I'll be riding in the lead vehicle with Deet. You'll follow in the second Dodge. Harvey and Eli will be right behind you. The rest of the team will follow in a train of Hiluxes.'

'What about the kids?' Priest asked. 'They're coming with?'

Bald detected a slight twitch on the face of the PMC chief. 'I love my children dearly, but stealth ops aren't their thing. They'll stay here and keep the camp secure, look after the prisoners until I send for them. Here.' Pretorius nodded at the Grouse. 'Since you like it so much, Jimmy. Keep the bottle.'

Pretorius stood up, signalling the end of the meeting. Sunlight, bleaching the camp white, blinded the two operators as they passed Deet and exited the hut. The ground was so hot Bald could feel it burning his feet through his boots. In the middle of the village the child soldiers had gathered by the well and were playing a game. Tag. Mama Alice stood to one side of the group, her deep yet lyrical voice rising above their wild shrieks of laughter. Bald watch the underage killers running around in circles, tagging each other, and wondered how much weirder this day could possibly get.

'We're in the shit, boss,' said Priest.

Bald turned to him. 'What makes you think that?'

'Flying a plane?' Priest puffed out his cheeks. 'What are we gonna do when it comes to the op? Soon as I step into the cockpit, we're rumbled. Pretorius will know we're not the guys he sent for.'

'We'll figure something out. Worst-case scenario, you'll have to wing it.'

Priest looked at Bald, his dumb eyes wide, jaw slack with disbelief. 'Pretend to fly a Herc?'

Bald glanced at him and shrugged. 'What choice do we have?'

Priest said nothing to that. He looked away from his partner, scratching his cheek as he frowned at the kids. 'Why the Comoros, anyway? Why not launch a coup here, or somewhere else on the mainland?'

'Fuck knows, mate. Maybe it's the easiest target.'

Priest was about to reply when Eli hobbled over, supported by a wooden crutch. The slave sported a clean dressing on his trauma wound. The Obama shirt was gone and he sported a fresh olive-green T-shirt and faded beige shorts. Some of the colour had returned to his face. He looked a little less shitty. Michael Jackson on a good day.

'You're still alive,' Bald said with fake concern. 'Fucking shame, that.' He nodded at the crutch. 'I guess your injury rules you out of the op.'

'Of course not,' Eli snorted. 'Where master goes, I go.' He looked over his shoulder to make sure no one was listening. Then he went on, 'Besides, you still have to fulfil our deal.'

Bald laughed. 'Bollocks. We're on the team now. You can take your deal and shove it.'

'Perhaps you forgot the arrangement we made on the boat. You agreed to help me escape master, remember? And in return I won't tell Mr Pretorius that you and your friend' – he tipped his head towards Priest – 'killed Vincent Dallas.'

Bald chewed on the air. Vincent Dallas. He and Priest had battered the guy to death in the toilet of a bar moments before he could reveal Bald's true identity to Stegman and blow their cover story. But Eli had witnessed the attack. The Scot hated to admit it, but the slave had him by the balls.

'I've given this some thought,' Eli said. 'And here's what you're going to do. I want you to kill master.'

Bald did a spit-take. 'No chance.'

Eli shot him a cold look.

'Once master is dead, I'm a free man.' He took a step closer to Bald. 'You're going to do it or I'll make sure that Mr Pretorius finds out the truth.'

'Know what'd be easier?' Bald stepped into Eli's face. 'Killing you.'

'Do that,' Eli replied, holding his gaze, 'and master will have you thrown off the team.'

He'd called Bald's bluff and both men knew it. The slave smiled the kind of thin smile that could slice a watermelon in two. Bald resisted a powerful urge to punch him in the groin.

He went on: 'We land on Grande Comore tomorrow morning. I know that Mr Pretorius has ordered master to lead the attack on the radio station. You will both volunteer to go with him. Once you're alone – you'll kill him.'

Then Eli wheeled away and shuffled along the dirt track. Bald watched him go. Blood simmering, the migraine thumping relentlessly away inside his skull. So much for self-medicating. He balled his hands into angry fists. First Pretorius had dropped the pilot bombshell on them. Now Eli was threatening to shaft the mission. He was in the mother of all tight spots, and as the sun beat down on him he figured it was only a matter of time before the op went sideways.

twenty-seven

2058 hours.

They rolled out of the camp under cover of darkness. Half a dozen vehicles riding in a loose train, the two Dodge Rams out in front followed by four Toyota Hilux rust buckets, paintwork scraped off like the foil on a scratchcard, dirt crusted on the windscreens, soldiers jostling for space on the flatbeds next to the weapons crates, worn tyres churning loose soil and coughing up thick plumes of dust that blazed white in the electric glow of the headlights. Twenty-six guys in total. Enough men to infiltrate an airport and steal a Herc? Maybe, thought Bald as he steered down the mud track leading northeast out of the village. In the bad old days after the fall of Siad Barre, tribal warlords had regularly seized Mogadishu's airport in order to 'tax' the aid shipments landing there. But with the transitional government asserting its control over the city and surrounding area, Bald figured a meatier presence might be waiting for them at the airport. His stomach muscles contracted.

At 1815 hours the sun had burned itself out on the horizon, its cigar glow replaced by a night sky thick as a river of ash. Now Bald could see only a short distance ahead of him as he steered the Dodge off the mud track and onto the rutted main road. The lead Dodge motored along four metres ahead of him at a steady eighty kilometres per hour, its lights slicing like steel blades through the flat dark. Pretorius and Deet were in the lead Dodge, Stegman and Eli in the Hilux behind Bald. The convoy would ride the main road south for ten kilometres until they hit the town of Jilib. Then travel north and east along the main coastal road for three hundred kilometres. If everything went according to plan, they'd arrive at the airport around 0400 hours.

Beyond the lead Dodge lay an impenetrable black void which even the quartz sheen of the moon seemed unable to illuminate. Bald fiddled with the air-con unit. Christ, it was hot. And sticky. Dusk had brought respite from the unrelenting glare of the sun, but at night the air had taken on the consistency of melted tar. He'd tried opening the windows but that simply brought a rush of hot air into the cab, making it feel like he was putting his head into a blast furnace. So he gritted his teeth and stuck it out with the feeble a.c. Next to him Priest was sweating like a Brazilian on a Tube train.

Imogen brooded in the back seat. The only one of Pretorius's wives to be dragged along for the journey to Grande Comore. Which got Bald thinking. She was the chief's favourite – she'd said so herself when he rescued her from the dhow, and now Pretorius insisted on taking her on the coup. Had to be a good reason for that. He would have quizzed her, but she was giving Bald the silent treatment and even his famous charm couldn't break through that icy exterior. She stared blankly out of the window, indifferent to where they were going, not even bothering to acknowledge Bald and Priest. She looked good, though. Or at least better than she had done in the cage. Mama Alice had cleaned her up a bit, made her look presentable. She now wore a shapeless black shawl around her body, with a brightly coloured hijab wrapped about her head. The sight of her breasts lingered in Bald's memory. In different circumstances, he would definitely have been tempted to have a crack at her.

He drove with his left hand, swigged from the bottle of Famous Grouse with his right. He'd downed half of it already. Going into an op half-cut ranked as pretty fucking dumb even by his standards, but he consoled himself with the fact that he didn't have a choice. The migraines were excruciating. Horrific images swirled inside his skull – the child soldiers hacking up the Somali pirates; the kid he'd slotted lying in a pool of his own blood. No matter how much whisky he downed, he couldn't shift that last mental image. He remembered squeezing the Beretta, the look of mute horror on the kid's face. Pretorius had done this to him. And yet there was something about the PMC chief that reminded Bald of himself: his fearlessness, his charisma. Pretorius wasn't afraid to cut down anyone who got in his way, and if he could skim a little cream off the top along the way then, hey. But there was more to it than that, Bald knew. Pretorius had his eye on the grand prize. Money, power, the five-star lifestyle: all the things Bald craved.

Focus on the mission, he told himself. Killing Pretorius was the reason the Firm had sent him to Kenya in the first place. But slotting the chief had proved impossible so far. The problem was one of timing. At the camp he could have observed Pretorius from afar for a day or two, monitored his routine, worked out the best time to plan his attack and given the guy the double-tap while no one was looking. Job done. But now they were on the move, preparing to enter a combat situation. When things got noisy he would be too busy trying to stay alive to worry about taking down Pretorius. Which meant he'd have to wait until they landed in the Comoros to slot him. And by then it might be too late. The islands might already have fallen into his hands. The Firm would blame Bald, naturally. He'd take the fall, his last shot at a clean break flushed down the toilet.

So maybe you don't kill Pretorius, he reasoned. Maybe you

go along with it. How much do you owe the Firm anyway? After the way they hung you out to dry?

Bald tried to put the lid on that voice. He was conflicted. It sounded crazy when he thought about it. When you laid out the promises he'd made to Avery Chance to keep his nose clean and the threat hanging over him from the Firm. But there it was, all the same. The voice had been quiet to begin with. A soft tickle at the back of his mind. With every passing moment in the camp it had grown louder and louder, until it became a deafening pulse between his temples, distinct from the migraines. Is this really what you want? the voice asked. Truthfully, Bald was no longer sure. He had been, once. But not now.

There was the problem of Eli, too. Didn't matter if he slotted Pretorius or joined forces with him – if the slave spilled his guts to Stegman, Bald was fucked either way. Part of him wondered whether he ought to be concentrating his efforts on killing Eli rather than Pretorius. A pleasing thought. But at the same time, Eli clung to Stegman like flies to shit, and Bald was up against the same problem he had with Pretorius: how to get the guy alone long enough to send him south.

All of this weighed heavily on his mind as he drove through the night. He wasn't aware of how much time had passed but at some point the convoy passed Jilib and steered onto the motorway, or what was left of it. The motorway carried the scars of decades of civil war. Craters swallowed up entire sections of tarmac and the Dodge nosedived then pitched sharply up as they hit a major hole in the road, temporarily jolting Bald out of his drunken stupor. Then Priest's voice cut through the silence.

'What's the plan?'

Bald checked the rear-view mirror. Imogen was sound asleep. 'Still working on it,' he replied.

He was steaming, slurring his words. He was on the Grouse big time. It was the only way to keep the lid on the migraines. He could feel them lurking under the surface. Ready to sink their claws into his cranium the moment he sobered up. He took another hefty swig.

'Boss,' Priest said after a beat. 'We have to take him down. Pretorius, I mean. Before we get on that plane. Otherwise the op is dead in the water.' He pursed his lips. 'We're running out of time.'

'That's going to be tricky.' Bald stared at the road. At the blackness. Like they were heading into the mouth of a cave. 'Deet follows him everywhere.'

Priest considered this. 'We have to warn Avery, then. Give her the heads-up. What do you think?'

He waited for an answer. Bald said nothing. The thrum of the engine filled the silence. Priest said, 'We're helping someone take over a foreign country. We've got to do something.'

Bald shot his partner an angry glance. 'We had to toss our BlackBerrys into the water outside Mombasa, remember? We've got no way of contacting the Firm. If we get the chance, we call in and give them the int. Until then we stick to the plan. Got it?'

Uncertainty flickered across Priest's face for a moment. Then he nodded and looked ahead at the scarred road, apparently happy with the new plan. Bald had just bought himself some time. He still didn't know what he was going to do. Kill Pretorius and wipe the slate clean with the Firm? Or shake hands with the devil and instigate a coup d'état in some forgotten colonial atoll? He drove in silence, steering through a war zone, alone with his whisky-soaked thoughts, his mind returning to the promise Pretorius had made to him at the camp.

'We pull this one off, Jimmy, we're going to live like kings.'

★

At 0349 hours the K50 Airport slowly disgorged from the horizon, an indigo smudge against the night sky. Four hundred metres due south of it the convoy slowed to fifty per and Bald ran his eyes over the airport. From this distance he could make out a few basic details. The K50 was strictly functional: it made Luton Airport look like a six-star Dubai skyrise. There was a single terminal building, a two-storey, whitewashed concrete block with an aircraft hangar to the left and a radio control tower to the right. A hulking black mass rested on the runway: the Hercules C-130. Its vertical stabilizer jutted out of the dark roots of the earth like a shark's tail in open water, navigation lights on the wingtips pulsing red and yellow. As they drew nearer, Bald tried to reach deep inside himself and feel bad about nicking a plane that was used to deliver vital aid to a famine-hit people, but honestly, he didn't feel a thing.

About three hundred metres from the airport, Bald glanced to his right. Two kilometres due east the crests of waves flashed like knives out on the Indian Ocean, before fizzling out in the enveloping blackness. Impossible to tell where the sea ended and land began. Six metres ahead of Bald, the lead Dodge went dark as Pretorius and Deet suddenly killed the lights and veered off the main road, lurching onto the scrub desert at their nine o'clock. Bald switched off his lights and followed them. So did the four pickups at his six. Imogen stirred as Bald wound the Dodge down to thirty per and lurched across rocky terrain. The soldiers in the pickups to the rear cut out the chatter. The only sound Bald could hear was the soft crackle and pop of the tyres rolling over loose stones. That and the furious rush of blood in his ears.

You're here now, John. What's it going to be? Pretorius, or the money?

Pretorius and Deet came to a halt two hundred metres due

west of the airport. Bald stopped a couple of metres behind their pickup. Priest looked at him and said, 'What now?'

'Now we go to work.'

The operators debussed. Priest helped Imogen out. The Toyotas stopped in a rough semicircle around the two Dodges. Soldiers hopped off the flatbeds. Drivers climbed out of the cabs and stretched their stiff legs. Bald sucked in a lungful of toasted air. Better. He'd laid off the booze for the last stretch of the journey, pulled himself back from the brink. Adrenalin had done the rest of the work, sobering him up and squashing the migraines. Now he was ready. He looked at his watch.

0353 hours.

Almost time.

Everyone automatically entered silent mode. Stegman lugged two black gym bags out of his Hilux and dumped them at his feet. Wiping sweat from his brow, Bald leaned in for a closer look as Stegman unzipped the first bag to reveal a pile of Vertex EVX-530 two-way digital radios nestled inside. He began distributing them to the guys on the team. Each walkie-talkie came with a tactical headset equipped with soft-hook earpieces designed to pick up the slightest transmission and boom microphones attached to the lapel clips. Bald clipped his radio to the waistband of his combats and connected his earpiece to the handset.

'The comms packs are pre-tuned to the same VHF frequency,' Stegman said quietly to the group. 'Stay in contact at all times, but keep chatter to an absolute minimum.'

He unzipped the second bag and dug out some xGen Pro Digital NightVision monoculars, which he handed to Pretorius and Deet.

Now Pretorius spoke. 'This is the last time I'll run through the plan, so listen hard. Right now, the guards are having some fun time with the local talent. With the guards distracted,

Liam and Deet will be able to enter the main terminal and reach the Herc without being detected, then once aboard run the pre-flight checks.' A thought occurred to Pretorius and he turned to Priest. 'How long do you need?'

Priest gulped loudly. 'Uh, I'm guessing, thirty, maybe thirty-five—'

Deet cut in. 'We've got to check the three main tank boost pumps on the fuel system, the APU bleed air leak, electrical systems, the brakes and nose-wheel steering systems. Shouldn't take more than twenty minutes, max.'

'You've got fifteen. Whatever corners you can cut, do it.'

Deet nodded and glared at Priest. They set off in the direction of the terminal building, Priest glancing back helplessly at Bald. Fuck that prick, Bald thought. If he was found out, the guy was on his own. Bald would deny knowing anything about the guy. He watched his partner go, maybe for the last time. The two men shrank to the size of insects and quickly melted into the darkness.

Then Pretorius addressed the twenty-two other guys. 'We'll move into position and wait for their signal. Soon as we get it, that's our cue to move in. We'll divide into separate fireteams and ambush the sangars simultaneously. Six sangars – that equals four guys on each team. Stegman will organize you into fireteams. You go in hard, spray anyone who moves. Fuckers won't know what's hit 'em.'

A chorus of grunts rose up from the soldiers around Bald.

'Jimmy, you're with me on the sixth team. We'll attack the sangar closest to the tailgate. Once we've broken through we'll help put out any fires at the remaining sangars.' Pretorius pointed out two hefty black guys to Bald's left. 'Goodluck, Moses – you're on our team. Stegman?'

'Yes, Mr Pretorius.'

'Look after my wife. Take good care of her.'

'Of course, Mr Pretorius.'

Bald said, 'I need a piece.'

Pretorius flashed him a broad grin and cocked his head at one of the Toyota pickups. 'There's a stack of Colt Commandos in the crates loaded on the back. Fill your boots.'

Bald paced over to the pickup and grabbed a Colt CAR-15 Commando semi-automatic rifle from the nearest crate. He smiled on the inside. The weapon felt familiar in his grip. He'd first used a Colt Commando in the early days of his career in the Regiment, putting down rounds on the range at the Brecon Beacons. It was reliable as fuck, effective up to a range of three hundred metres and, unlike most women, it had never let Bald down. He snatched two extra mags. With a fresh clip inserted into the mag feed on the underside of the weapon and twenty rounds per clip, Bald had sixty rounds in total. He stuffed the two spare clips into his back pockets and trudged after Pretorius. Goodluck and Moses, the two other guys on their fireteam, were at his nine o'clock. Indian Ocean surf flashing at his three, the airport at his twelve. Stegman, Eli and the other eighteen soldiers who made up the remaining five fireteams at his back. Imogen stumbled along beside the South African. She lifted her head wearily and made eye contact with Bald for a second, shot him a look of hate so pure you could bottle it and sell it at Whole Foods. It wasn't the first time a woman had looked that way at him. Wouldn't be the last either.

He was a hundred and eighty metres from the sangar guarding the main gate when Deet's voice crackled over the comms. 'We're in.'

Bald tensed his muscles. Stilled his breath.

This is it.

He still didn't know what he was going to do. The prospect of taking over the Comoros appealed to Bald. But if he walked away from the Firm, his life would be over. He'd have to go underground, sticking to the shadows, hopping from one fallen state to the next – much like Pretorius. And before any of that, he had to find a way of dealing with Eli. An irresistible weight pressed down on him, like two big sacks of sand weighing on his shoulders. He shook his head clear. Focus, John. The Colt Commando felt reassuring in his grip.

A hundred and fifty metres from the main gate, Pretorius knelt down and examined the Herc through the xGen Pro viewfinder. Bald chased his line of sight as his eyes gradually adjusted to the dark.

'There she is,' Pretorius said. 'Sixty million dollars' worth of transport craft. In a little over twenty minutes it's going to be ours.' He flashed a grin at Bald. 'Makes you feel good to be alive, eh?'

Whatever else Pretorius might be, Bald had to admit the guy had a pair of brass balls on him. The plan had all the hallmarks of a Regiment op. It was bold, surgical, and mad as fuck. And Pretorius had won his grudging respect. He was a leader of men. Not a rupert kissing arse and climbing up the greasy pole, but a man who led from the front. A soldier's soldier, as Stegman had put it. As the minutes counted down to the assault, Bald found himself thinking of another great warrior: his old mucker Joe Gardner.

Lights flickered from within the terminal building. The asphalt runway was riddled with potholes and ran for maybe five hundred metres on an east–west axis, with the terminal building to the north and Bald and Pretorius approaching from the south. A row of concrete anti-blast blocks flanked the runway on each side. On the north side Bald spied a 'technical' – African-speak for a battered pickup converted into a gunwagon. This one had a Browning M2 heavy machine gun mounted on the flatbed. The other five sangars were strategically located around the airfield, offering full-spectrum security: two sangars were sited on the southern side of the runway, with one at the runway's eastern fringe and a fourth west of the Herc. The fifth sangar protected the terminal building.

Bald watched. And waited. Tiny black flies the size of specks of dust flitted about his face – thousands of them. Sandflies. Evil fuckers. He'd witnessed the effects of sandfly fever up close. A mate had come down with it during an op in Sierra Leone, bitten during a tab through the jungle. Next thing he knew, the guy was shitting water and pissing blood, his skin turning black. He ended up spending three months on a drip in Selly Oak. Bald swatted the flies away and waited some more.

At 0414 hours the comms unit crackled into life.

'All set,' said Deet.

Pretorius sprang to his feet, motioning to Bald, Goodluck and Moses.

'That's it, let's go!' he barked as he sprinted towards the main gate.

Bald immediately gave chase, blood pounding in his veins. His breathing seemed impossibly loud. He hurried along a metre behind Pretorius. Goodluck and Moses jogging at his side. A hundred and twenty metres to the sangar now. He slowed his stride and tucked the rifle's stock against his shoulder, index finger tense on the trigger, ready to give the guards operating the sangar a bellyful of brass. Around him the other five fireteams were sweeping towards the remaining sangars. Stegman kept Imogen close beside him.

A hundred metres to the sangar defending the main gate. Lights from the terminal building bathed the runway in an apricot glow. Bald noticed that the tailgate on the Herc was in the lowered position. He could see the incandescent fizz of the cargo bay's lights from within the fuselage. Must have landed not long ago, he thought. The letters 'UN' were painted on the vertical rudder.

Eighty metres from the sangar, Pretorius stopped. Bald wondered why for a moment. Then he saw it too, and instantly sobered up.

'What the fuck—?'

The sangar had been abandoned.

Pretorius and Bald stood side by side on the spot for a beat. Then Pretorius walked on ahead of Bald. Approaching the sangar. Bald scanned the airport. The other fireteams had closed in on their designated sangars. Every one of them was unmanned. HMGs appeared to have been removed in a hurry, with the tripods and brass link left behind. Bald joined Pretorius at the sangar, rifle at his side, and scratched the back of his neck as he tried to figure out what was going on.

'Oh, shit,' Goodluck said. 'Look!'

Bald and Pretorius swapped a look. They simultaneously looked at Goodluck. The guy pointed out something at their six o'clock. Coming from the direction of the main road. Bald chased his line of sight and felt a cold dread sink its claws into his guts. He counted a dozen pairs of headlights shimmering in the distance, white as aspirins. He couldn't calculate how far away they were, not in this dark. But the lights were getting bigger. Second by second. They swerved past the parked Rams and Hiluxes and swelled to the size of distant moons. The growl of engines carried like animal noises through the desert night air. In the next moment twelve Land Rovers percolated out of the darkness, rear tyres spewing out clouds of dust the colour of charcoal ash. A long line of them. They all screeched to a halt sixty metres due south of the sangar guarding the main gate.

Doors thudded open. Operators jumped out of the Landies. White guys, Bald noticed. Four operators to a vehicle.

Forty-eight guys. They were all kitted out in tactical combat gear, armed with FN SCAR assault rifles identifiable by their khaki-coloured stocks and the Picatinny rail systems on top of the chamber. A leaden feeling plunged through Bald and a grim realization hit him like a fist to the guts.

They had walked straight into a trap.

twenty-eight

0416 hours.

There was a lapse of maybe a second between the Landies' doors slamming and the operators firing the first shots. Their SCARs lit up in a staccato sequence. Gases squirted out of the barrel snouts. Flames erupted and the ground at their feet lit up as if someone had just thrown a load of firecrackers. Bullets zipped across the night sky, a shrill clang sounding as they ricocheted off the concrete and landed wide of their targets, along with the distinctive clink of spent jackets tumbling to the ground.

'Get behind cover!' Bald roared as he spun away from the operators and scrabbled towards the hessian sandbags amassed at the sangar.

Pretorius displaced in the same instant. The two men scrambled behind the sangar as the operators unleashed a second volley of 5.56x45mm NATO rounds, which thudded into the sandbags. A few more rounds thwacked into the asphalt either side of the sangar. There was a wet slap as a bullet pierced Goodluck's throat. He pirouetted on the spot, blood gushing out of the hole before he slumped to the ground. Moses rushed past his dying mate as several bullets sparked against the concrete, eight of them landing in a close grouping. As he dived behind cover, another grouping spattered the sandbags in a chorus of dull slaps.

'Who the fuck are these guys?' Bald shouted above the throated screams of soldiers being cut down at the other sangars. A couple of stray rounds ripped into Goodluck's lifeless body.

Pretorius said, 'I reckon it must be the Americans working with AMISOM.' He cursed under his breath in French. 'Cowboys. They're not supposed to be on patrol in this area.'

'Then what the fuck are they doing here?'

'They must have known about the attack. Lured us into a trap so they wouldn't have to fight us on open ground.' Pretorius thumped a fist against his thigh and worked his features in a scowl. 'Someone betrayed me.'

The cowboys were getting closer. Bullets peppered the top sandbags inches above Bald's head. Ten, eleven, twelve rounds thumped into them in quick succession. A round zipped above the sandbags and grazed Moses's cheek. He fell back, clasping a hand to his face. Bald ducked low and hunched his shoulders. He turned to Pretorius. 'We've got to get to the Herc before the cowboys overrun us.'

'I agree,' Pretorius shouted above the blunt, mechanical hammering of rounds being discharged. 'But if we make a run for it, there's no way we'll reach the Herc in time. The Yanks will wipe the floor with us.' He scanned the terrain. 'There must be some other way.'

The rifle reports were growing louder. The cowboys were closing in. There was a break in the firing and Bald risked a glance above the sangar, mind frantically racing as he tried to think of a way out of the shit. They were splitting into six groups, eight guys to a team, pepper-potting towards the individual sangars. Four guys in each group concentrating fire on the sangars while their muckers kept their eyes fixed to their SCARs, waiting for the moment their clips emptied before taking their turn to blitz the sangars with hot lead. Bald counted four dead soldiers. The rest of the team were hunkered behind cover, loosing off rounds whenever the opportunity presented. He spied Stegman's fireteam at the sangar next to the Herc at the edge of the runway, forty metres to his left. Eli crouched behind cover, Imogen curled up in a ball, eyes clamped shut, her body rigid with fear.

Thirty metres from Bald to the cowboys approaching his sangar. Levelling his Colt Commando, he sprayed a three-round burst at them. He missed by a mile, but sent the cowboys scuttling behind the anti-blast blocks twenty-five metres short of the sangar. He unleashed another burst. This time his aim was truer and the rounds spattered against the blocks, throwing up puffs of concrete dust into the humid air. He dropped to a crouch as the cowboys returned fire. A ferocious stream of fire peppered the sangar, shredding the sandbags.

'Twenty metres, master!' Moses yelled, pawing his cheek, blood oozing between his fingers. 'We can't hold them off much longer.'

Four guys down. Minus Deet and Priest in the Herc cockpit, that left twenty soldiers against a force more than twice that number. Crap odds. They were stuck. If they made a run for it, the Yanks would cut them down. But if they'd stayed put, the Americans could bide their time, keep them pinned down until their ammo reserves ran dry, and then move in for the kill. Unless—

Pretorius beat him to it. 'Look,' he said. 'Over there.'

He was pointing towards the other side of the runway. Bald chased his line of sight. Herc at his two o'clock, at a distance of twenty metres. Terminal thirty metres away at his twelve. Then he saw it too: the technical parked next to the terminal building. The one with the HMG mounted on the flatbed. Pretorius said, 'If we can get to the technical, one of us can use the .50-cal.'

'I was just thinking the same thing,' said Bald. A wicked grin creased his features. 'It packs enough punch to put the drop on the cowboys. Gives us a chance to board the Herc by the tailgate.'

Pretorius grinned. 'Last one on the plane buys the beers.'

'Deal.'

Pretorius turned to Moses. The guy fired a burst at the cowboys, seemingly oblivious to the blood seeping out of the wound to his cheek. He slid down behind cover as the PMC chief spoke. 'Here's the plan. Me and Jimmy will make a run for the technical. On my count, you'll put down covering fire. Now, you keep your finger tight on that trigger until you're out of ammo, no matter what they throw at you. Got it?'

Moses nodded dutifully. 'Yes, master.'

Then Pretorius plugged a finger in his left ear and reached out to Deet via the boom mike attached to his earpiece. 'We're getting the fuck out of here,' he said sharply. 'What's your status?'

Deet's voice crackled over the comms: 'We have a problem.' A pause. 'It's Liam, sir. He's out of his depth.'

Pretorius frowned. Bald felt his chest muscles constrict as an invisible band pulled tighten around him. Priest had been rumbled, surely? He sensed the op hanging in the balance. Tried to act casual as he waited for Pretorius to respond.

'"Out of his depth." The fuck does that mean?'

Another pause. Static hissed and fizzed down the line. Difficult to hear anything above the incessant crack of gunfire, the screams of dying men. 'Liam says he has no experience of flying a Herc.'

No response from Pretorius.

Deet went on, 'I can handle the take-off by myself, sir. But it's going to take time. Everything will have to be done manually.'

Pretorius stiffened his jaw and glanced at Bald. Weird. The guy's face showed no flicker of surprise about Priest blagging it. Something moved inside Bald. He knows, he thought. He knows about Liam.

Maybe he knows about me too.

'Whatever you need to do to get us airborne,' Pretorius told Deet, 'do it.'

'Yes, sir.'

The PMC chief swung back to Bald. The soldiers occupying the sangar at the eastern end of the runway began to retreat under a hail of lead. They were almost out of time. Another minute, Bald figured, and the cowboys would have seized the airport.

Pretorius said, 'You ready, Jimmy?'

Bald grinned. 'Does Dolly Parton sleep on her back?'

A rush of excitement hit Bald – the hot thrill of going into a combat with a brother-in-arms. He hadn't felt it since the days he'd fought alongside Joe Gardner in the Afghan. He'd forgotten how good it felt. That sense of being unstoppable. 'Gods walking among men,' Pretorius had said. He was a born soldier, thought Bald. Would've made a first-class operator in the Regiment. He watched the chief fill his lungs before shouting across his shoulder at Moses. 'Covering fire!'

The soldier sprang up from behind the sangar and brought his Colt Commando to bear on the cowboys. A crack thundered across the runway as he discharged the first shot, a glimmer of white light illuminated the sandbags and Pretorius roared, 'Now!' as he bolted forward.

Then Bald started to sprint towards the technical.

twenty-nine

Bald raced after Pretorius. Muscles pumping, sweat gushing down his back, his breathing ragged as he tucked his head close to his chest. Gunfire erupted at his six o'clock. Rounds flecked the ground a few inches to his left. He kept running. Twenty-five metres to the technical. Another grouping of shots landed at his six. Close. He ran on, the shrill shriek of the bullets cannoning off the asphalt piercing his ears. A short stride ahead of him Pretorius zigzagged towards the vehicle as another flurry of rounds landed wide of their target.

Twenty metres to the technical.

Don't stop, the voice in Bald's head urged.

Fifteen metres to go. Bald glanced past his shoulder and clocked Moses fifteen metres back at the sangar, elbows propped like a spider's legs on the sandbags as he fired round after round at the cowboys. Smoke seethed out of the rifle's muzzle, accompanied by a steady rhythm of retorts. Sounded like the sky was cracking its knuckles. The cowboys were pinned down behind the anti-blast blocks. Then Bald heard a metallic *clack* and a cold wave hit him as he realized Moses was out of ammo. In the next instant the cowboys sprang up from cover with their SCARs drawn and Bald swung his gaze north.

'GET THE FUCK DOWN!'

He dived at Pretorius, tackling him to the ground as bullets zipped past the spot where he'd just been standing and slammed into the side of the technical, throwing up sparks, sounding like a bunch of hammers banging against a lead pipe. Pretorius glanced at the technical; then at Bald. The look on his face was a mixture of shock and disbelief – the look of a man who had been inches from death. He struggled to form words. Bald rolled off him and rapidly arced his Colt Commando towards the cowboys. He let off a wild three-round burst in the hope of buying a precious second or two. It worked: the cowboys scattered. Now Bald wheeled around and dashed towards the technical, Pretorius scraping himself off the ground to his left.

'I'll drive in a circuit,' Pretorius said as he tugged at the door on the driver's side of the technical.

'Roger that.' Bald caught his breath. 'Keep the speed steady. That way I'll have a chance of nailing as many of the fuckers as possible.'

Pretorius clambered inside the cab as Bald vaulted up on to the flatbed and got to grips with the Browning. He knew the basics – he'd handled one several times with the Regiment. A quick weapons check revealed that the last user had kindly inserted the end of a link of ammo into the feed tray: .50 BMG calibre. An absolute beast of a round capable of vaporizing a human-sized target at a range of up to a thousand metres. Had to be at least three hundred rounds stacked in the ammo crate. The Browning rested on an M3 mount. Bald hooked around to the back plate on the HMG and pulled on the bolt release, manually cocking the weapon. There was a loud *ker-thunk* as the link shunted through the closed feed tray and the first round shunted into the firing position inside the chamber. Now Bald clasped both hands around the spade handle grips located on either side of the back plate, both thumbs resting on the butterfly trigger mechanism. Finally he was in business.

Pretorius flipped down the sun visor and the keys tumbled into his lap. He cranked up the ignition. The engine sputtered into life, the tyres screeched as he put his foot to the pedal. They accelerated towards the sangar at the eastern end of the runway, travelling in the opposite direction from the way the Herc pointed, skimming around the runway's edge. The two remaining soldiers at the sangar were fleeing across the asphalt. They had no choice. They were coming under heavy fire from the eight cowboys, who had broken out from the cover of the anti-blast blocks and were now charging towards the sangar. Sixty metres from the technical to the cowboys. Bald brought the .50-cal in a steady arc towards the sangar. Lined up the targets with the sights, front and rear, straining to keep the Browning trained on them as the technical bumped over a deep pothole.'

Then he let rip.

The perforated barrel lit up. Bald felt the recoil shaking in his bones, juddering through his muscles. It was like clinging on to a pneumatic drill. The muzzle flashed repeatedly, lighting up the asphalt as three rounds pelted out of the barrel and streaked through the air like fireflies. The force of the recoil drove the bolt back and shanked another round of .50 BMG link into the feed tray. Spent jackets belched out of the T-ejector located at the right side of the receiver. The first three rounds smacked into the cowboys as they neared the sangar. Two of them vanished in a cloud of blood and gristle. A third guy jackknifed. The other cowboys stumbled forward, chopping their strides in a desperate attempt to reach the cover of the sangar. Bald unloaded two more rounds, pulverizing the back of a fleeing cowboy's head. His skull exploded like he'd put a hand grenade in his mouth and pulled the pin. Blood everywhere. His decapitated body rolled limply away.

'Circle the sangar!' Bald bellowed above the jarring engine.

'On it,' Pretorius roared back.

They were eight or nine metres beyond the sangar now. Pretorius hit the brakes and the technical canted as he swerved to the left, turning so that they were facing the sangar head-on. He accelerated towards the sangar at the side of the runway and parallel to the Herc. Stegman shoved Eli face down on the asphalt next to Imogen as Bald thumbed the butterfly trigger and pummelled the five cowboys charging the sangar. The cowboys had no chance. Their bodies jerked and jittered with the impact of the hot lead. Limbs exploded. Torsos were ripped in half. The cowboys were taking a trip to the dark side by the time Bald relaxed his thumb on the trigger and arced the Browning towards the next targets, at the sangar next to the Herc, sixty metres ahead.

He was starting to think that he and Pretorius made a good team.

'Everyone on board the Herc!' Pretorius ordered over the comms. 'NOW!'

At once the soldiers began dashing across the asphalt towards the lowered ramp. Moses led the charge. The cowboys directed their sights towards the technical. Bullets peppered the cab. Bald let them have it. Easy. By the time he was finished, the cowboys had more holes in them than a bunch of hookers on a golf course.

Sixteen cowboys down. Thirty-two to go.

They'd levelled the odds. But there was still a way to go before they could kick back and crack open the Stella. Pretorius kept his foot to the pedal as they streaked past the Herc, all thirty metres of her, and raced towards the next sangar being overrun by the cowboys, twenty metres beyond the plane's nose cone. At the same time a mechanical whine sounded as Priest and Deet fired up the Herc's turboprop engines. The noise crescendoed to a droning peal and the rightmost of the four propellers started to whirr.

'Keep going!' Bald thundered as he swung the Browning towards the next targets. Brass jackets rolled around the flatbed like loose change. The cowboys at the third sangar were still getting their shit together as Bald unleashed a flurry of rounds on their position. Three of them did the dead man's dance. Another took a round to his arm. The .50-cal bullet shattered his elbow; his forearm dangled like a loose thread. Their cries were drowned by the drone of the Herc's engines. The remaining two cowboys scarpered back towards the Landies, sixty metres outside the airport. The soldiers, who had been on the retreat, smelled blood. They brassed up the cowboys before they could reach the vehicles. As they were cut down, one after the other, the cowboys' wretched cries carried across the pre-dawn sky.

Good work. Half the cowboys were now dead or wounded. The surviving twenty-four were spread out across the other three sangars. Bald looked past his shoulder as Pretorius angled the technical towards the fourth sangar a hundred metres past the Herc. The rest of the soldiers hurried towards the loading ramp. No sign of Stegman. He was still at the sangar next to the Herc alongside Eli and Imogen, providing covering fire for the other soldiers. A second four-bladed propeller began to spin – slowly at first, then faster, until it became a blurred circle. The Herc was almost primed for take-off.

Bald faced forward. They were forty metres from the fourth sangar. The cowboys attacking sangars four, five and six had given up trying to take down the soldiers and concentrated their fire on the technical. But Pretorius weaved this way and that, slaloming across the asphalt, dodging bullets and impressing Bald. He wasn't just a first-rate warrior – he had some serious driving skills. Rounds zipped either side of the cab and ricocheted off the flatbed's sides. Bald kept his cool and put the drop on the cowboys at sangar number four with a devastating arc of .50-cal gunfire. He severed one guy in half at the waist. Reduced another to a rag of blood and bones. The cowboys were on the back foot.

We're winning! Bald thought.

He missed that feeling. It was a long time since he'd last experienced it.

Deet's voice hissed over the comms. 'Thirty seconds to take-off. Hurry it up!'

Pretorius slammed on the brakes and fishhooked around the front of the Herc so that they were heading towards its rear. All four propellers were now spinning. Bald turned his attention to the cowboys at the fifth and sixth sangars and opened fire. His wrists were burning from locking the Browning on target while Pretorius skated and skidded across the runway. One sangar left – the one next to the terminal. Pretorius raced towards it as the Herc began to slowly taxi along the runway, the drone of its engines blasting across the carnage-strewn airport. The last soldiers piled into the back of the Herc. Bald saw Stegman and Eli making a break for it, sprinting towards the plane, Stegman shouldering Imogen, with Eli hobbling after them.

Drop these last cowboys, Bald told himself, then we're home and dry—

CA-RACK!

A loud bang was followed by a sharp hiss as a bullet punctured the front wheel. The technical dipped to the left and swerved out of control, yanking Bald away from the HMG and throwing him off the flatbed. He landed on the ground with a jarring crunch; it felt like his jaw had slammed into the roof of his skull. Sharp pains fired down his left side. His head felt like someone had dropped a piano on it. Every nerve ending in his body screamed. The haze cleared from his head and he saw a cowboy storming towards him. SCAR muzzle trained on his chest. A cold fear clamped around his neck. He had no time to react. The cowboy had him in his sights.

He waited to die.

Then a blur of motion shot across the asphalt. The cowboy paused for the slightest moment as Bald watched a pair of headlights paint halos on his chest. The cowboy turned to his right just in time to see the technical arrowing towards him. The front bumper slammed into his midriff and cut him down. He rolled like a rag doll under the wheels as the vehicle bounced over him before screeching to a halt next to Bald. The driver's door flew open. Pretorius jumped out and offered Bald his hand.

'Now I've saved your life, how about we get out of here and get rich?'

Bald hesitated for a beat. Then he took the hand. Fuck Priest. Fuck the op. And fuck the Firm. He owed them nothing. People said money didn't make you happy, but that was a lie preached by sad cunts who didn't have a pot to piss in. The truth is, money opens doors. Money buys you respect, women, friends. Money buys you better teeth and a longer life expectancy. When you got down to it, it was money that got people elected president and featured on the front of *Forbes* magazine. Bald figured it was time he started looking out for number one.

'Let's get bang on it,' he said as he climbed to his feet.

The cowboys at the final sangar sprayed rounds at the technical. Pretorius hit the ground. Bald crouched by the front wheel as rounds pinballed through the vehicle and starred the windscreen. Ten metres short of the Herc, Eli collapsed. His cries for help were drowned out by the gunfire. Stegman hauled Imogen on board the plane with his back to his slave, unaware of the fact that he'd fallen.

They had only a few seconds left to board the Herc. Bald had to act now. Or never. He sprang onto the balls of his feet, reached into the cab and grabbed the Colt Commando lying across the front passenger seat. He let off a burst at the cowboys, but his aim was way off and the targets quickly shrank behind the sandbags. Didn't matter. He'd bought himself a second or three. That was all he needed. At the same time Pretorius picked himself off the ground and leapt up onto the flatbed – exposing himself to enemy fire.

'What the *fuck* are you doing?' Bald barked.

'Dismounting the .50-cal. We can't board with it mounted. It's too high, we'll crash against the cargo ceiling. Cover me.'

'Shit!' Bald hissed. They were taking too long. The Herc was going to leave without them. Too late now. Gritting his teeth, he sprang up from cover and put down a second burst on the cowboys while Pretorius pulled out the pin securing the HMG to its mount. The gun toppled onto the floor of the flatbed like Saddam's statue. In his peripheral vision Bald saw Eli struggling to his feet. Ten metres to the Herc. The soldiers were crammed inside the cargo hold, the uninjured tending to the wounded. No one had spotted the slave sprawled on the ground to the rear of the plane. Bald sensed his opportunity.

Now Pretorius jumped down off the flatbed and dived into the front passenger seat. Meanwhile Bald gave the cowboys a third burst of good news before climbing behind the steering wheel. A pair of spider-web cracks decorated the windscreen. Glass shards sprinkled the dashboard. To the right of the technical, twelve metres away at his three o'clock, the surviving cowboys were manoeuvring out from behind the sixth sangar.

Bald shifted into Reverse. Pedal to the floor. The technical groaned as it backed away from the sangar. The speedometer needle registered ten per. Then fifteen. The tyres squealed.

The eight cowboys at the sangar switched their weapons to fully automatic and unleashed continuous bursts at the reversing technical. Rounds blitzed the bodywork. There was a sound like a bag of coins spilling on the ground as the front passenger-side window shattered. Pretorius ducked forward. A round embedded itself in the side of his seat.

'Hit the throttle,' Bald said over the comms. 'But hold the brakes. We're on our way.'

The Herc's engines now reached a deafening roar, obliterating the wounded cowboys' howls of agony and the steady thrum of the technical. Bald looked over his shoulder and lined up the vehicle with the ramp. Eli rolled onto his back and waved frantically at him to stop. Bald kept going. With the front wheel fucked, the technical threatened to veer to the side of the ramp and he had to fight hard to keep it in a roughly straight line. Ten metres. Then five. Eli stopped waving.

There was a look of dumb horror on the slave's face as the rear bumper hit him. He was sucked under the technical and Bald heard a brief scream and then a satisfying crunch as the wheels crushed him. Pretorius shot him a look.

'What the fuck was that?'

Bald said nothing. He smiled on the inside. Take that, you prick. That's what you get for screwing with me. The technical lurched again as Eli passed under the front wheels and his lacerated body rolled to a halt in the middle of the runway. Pretorius couldn't see him – his side of the windscreen was obscured by cracked glass. Pleased with his work, Bald continued to reverse. There was a jolt as the technical bumped up the ramp and into the cargo hold. Behind the vehicle the soldiers hurriedly cleared a path, carting the wounded to the rear of the hold. Bald ejected from the cab, hit the intercom fixed next to the ramp.

'GO! GO! GO!!' he roared.

From somewhere behind the technical Stegman screamed, 'My fucking son!'

The Herc catapulted forward. There was a grating sound like a dentist's drill as the ramp drew up and the plane gained speed. Every fitting shook. Bald planted a firm hand on the padded fuselage to steady himself. He glimpsed the cowboys shrinking from view, taking random shots as the Herc scorched across the desert. Then a jolt, and suddenly they were climbing. Only then did Bald breathe a sigh of relief.

He wiped his sopping brow. He needed a drink. Then he remembered he'd left the Grouse in the Dodge. Cursing himself, he scanned the hold. It was twelve metres long, a shade over three metres wide and roughly the same height. He counted twelve soldiers aside from himself, Pretorius and Stegman. Fifteen all told. That meant they'd suffered nine KIA on the ground. Eight, Bald corrected himself, remembering that he'd taken care of Eli personally. He smiled briefly at the image of his limp body rolling on the asphalt.

No one said a word. There was just the whirr of the engines and the faint hum of the air-con pressurizing the compartment. Cold air wafted Bald, turning the beads of his sweat on his face to drops of ice. He spotted Imogen hunched up in a corner, her knees pulled tight to her chin, her eyes carrying the same thousand-yard stare Bald had seen on the vacant faces of a hundred squaddies after getting their first taste of war.

Stegman marched up to Bald. His face was twisted into a hideous knot of rage. His jaw muscles twitched. He was spitting mad. 'You cunt,' he said. 'You killed him. My son. He's fucking dead.'

'What's this?' said Pretorius.

'Eli?' Stegman rasped, jabbing a finger at Bald. 'This prick ran over him.'

Bald feigned a look of ignorance. He was good at those. He'd had plenty of practice down the years. 'No idea what you're talking about, mate,' he said. 'I was focused on getting us out of the shit.'

'Bollocks. I saw it with my own eyes. Eli was crying out for help. You drove over him.'

Bald went to protest. Then he felt the icy tip of a muzzle pressing against the nape of his neck.

'Turn around,' Pretorius said.

Bald raised his hands slowly and said, 'I didn't kill him.'

'I don't care.'

Bald did a one-eighty. Came face to face with Pretorius. The PMC chief was training the Beretta on a spot between his eyes, breathing heavily through his nostrils. A wicked smile teased his face.

'Liam told us everything,' he went on. 'We know you're working for Six, Jimmy. Or should I say . . . John. You led the Americans here. And now you're going to pay. The minute we step off the plane, you're a dead man.'

thirty

The Hercules C-130 landed with a shudder and a screech. In his fold-up seat in the rear cargo compartment John Bald bucked forward as the transport plane rumbled along the ground, rattling and shaking violently. The militia team gripped their seat belts in grim silence. Kurt Pretorius, the leader of this rogue band, stared ahead calmly, not moving a muscle. There was a final jolt as the Herc braked. Then the engine noise reduced to a faint hum. The men breathed a collective sigh of relief as Bald sat there and grimaced. Riding in the back of a Herc was just as crap as Bald remembered it from his days in the Regiment. Like being inside a tin can someone had kicked down the street.

There was a sense of tension in the plane. Bald could feel it, mixed in with the sweat and the stench of diesel and kerosene wafting in from the four turboprops. Three hours ago the soldiers had loaded onto the back of the Herc at an airfield near Mogadishu and travelled 1500 kilometres south along the east coast of Africa, to a small cluster of islands north of Madagascar and east of Mozambique: the Union of the Comoros. The Comoros was an unlikely paradise, thought Bald. The people were dirt poor and the islands themselves were starved of natural resources. But the President had a habit of embezzling foreign aid, the government was weak and the military poorly trained. If you were going to launch a coup, the Comoros was the place to do it. Which is exactly what Kurt Pretorius was about to do. He operated on the principle of high risk, high reward. And, Bald reflected, rewards didn't come much higher than this.

'This is it, gentlemen,' said Pretorius. 'Grande Comore. Capital of the Comoro Islands. No turning back now. We're about to make history.'

The men whooped and hollered with delight, no doubt already thinking of the money that would be coming their way once they'd ousted the President and seized control of the entire country. Pretorius remained perfectly still as he fixed his gaze on Bald, his teeth gleaming in the semi-dark of the compartment.

'Pity you won't be joining us, John,' he said. He kept the Beretta 92 semi-automatic trained on Bald. 'But then that's what you get for trying to stab me in the back. Now get up. It's time for you to die.'

'Fuck you,' said Bald.

A smile flickered across Pretorius's face. 'You've got that the wrong way round. You, in fact, are the one who's fucked. There are street hookers in Thailand less fucked than you.'

A hot rage swept through Bald's veins and he tensed his fists, turning his knuckles white. Much as he hated to admit it, Pretorius was right. Two hours ago everything had been looking rosy. The Scot and his partner on the op, Jamie Priest, had been ordered by the Firm to infiltrate Pretorius's militia under assumed identities. Their mission: kill Pretorius, to prevent him wreaking havoc in Somalia and turning the country into a terrorist safe haven. Instead Bald had joined forces with Pretorius and signed up to his plan to stage a coup in the Comoros, tempted by the thought of being richer than Bernie Madoff before the cops moved in. Everything had been going smoothly – until Priest decided to spill his guts. Sold him down the river. Now Pretorius knew that Bald was working for the Firm. He was truly shafted.

A series of mechanical whirrs and clanks echoed through the cargo compartment as the rear loading ramp lowered. Light seeped through the crack, colouring in Pretorius's face: his lips thin as a knife slash, the knot of flesh where his right ear had been severed, the deep grooves carved into his weathered complexion. Bald remembered the promise Pretorius had made to him shortly after they'd boarded the Herc back in Somalia.

'The minute we step off the plane, you're a dead man.'

The ramp hit the ground with a dense thud. Pretorius shouted an order to his men in French and one by one they leapt up from their seats and marched down the ramp. The last soldier to bounce out of the Herc dragged a dishevelled blonde woman with him. She wore a black shawl and a colourful hijab – and on her face a look of sheer terror. Bald had almost forgotten about Imogen after having a gun pulled him on during the flight. But seeing her now got him thinking. Pretorius had several wives – his name for the group of white women he kidnapped and kept prisoner at his camp in Somalia, using them as his sexual playthings – but he'd only brought Imogen to the Comoros. Why?

But Bald had no time to worry about this. The soldier yanked Imogen off the ramp and fanned out across the ground with the rest of his mates. Now only Bald and Pretorius were left in the plane.

'We could have made quite a team,' Pretorius said. 'You, a hero of the SAS. Me, a living legend of the Circuit. Fighting side by side, ruling these islands together – all the money we'd ever need – the natives at our beck and call. Now you won't get to enjoy any of that. Pity.'

'Bag of bollocks,' said Bald, trying it on. 'I'm not working for the Firm.'

Pretorius laughed as he gave a sad shake of his head. 'You're a great soldier. One of the best even. But you can't lie for shit. Do you really think I'd take two strangers onto my team without properly vetting them? I knew that my enemies would try to kill me again, once they realized the drone strike had failed. They needed me out of the picture. So they sent you.'

Bald clenched his jaw. 'Priest is lying, for fuck's sake. Trying to set me up.'

'Save your breath. I know the truth, John. He already told me chapter and verse. About how you roped him into your plan to impersonate a couple of guys looking to join my team. You planned to work your way into my inner circle, didn't you? And when nobody was looking, you were going to take me down. *Pow.*' He formed his hand into a pistol and made a shooting motion at Bald. He half-smiled. 'Got a pair of brass balls on you, I'll give you that. Now on your feet.'

Bald trudged down the loading ramp. There was a heavy feeling in his legs, as if someone had strapped lead weights to his ankles. His mouth was dry. His clothes were soaked through with sweat. Mice scampered about in his stomach. Bald wasn't scared of dying. He'd seen enough men go south in the field to have become hardened to it. No, what pissed him off was the fact that his mucker had sold him out He'd survived gun battles with the Pakistani Taliban, shootouts in Brazilian favelas, the Russian mafia. It wasn't supposed to end like this – fucked over by an overweight ex-cop on the MI6 payroll. The indignity of it burned a hole in his chest.

'Hurry up,' Pretorius snapped at his back. 'I've got a country to take over.'

Bald stepped off the ramp. The air was moist and heavy: a sponge dunked in water. They had landed on a dirt road in a clearing amid dense forest. Long brown grass rustled, buffeted by the cool morning breeze picking up on the ocean. Six VW Amarok pickup trucks were parked in a row alongside the runway. To the north loomed Mount Karthala, its volcanic cap hidden under a cobwebbed morning mist. Pockets of stunted trees and scrub bushes were scattered along its slopes, interspersed with patches of hardened magma. South of the volcano, scattered along the coastline, Bald could see small towns with their mix of colonial buildings and mosques. Nine or ten kilometres distant, he guessed. The dirt road continued for a hundred metres east of the Herc, where it merged with a bigger, potholed road that snaked towards the coast.

Pretorius narrowed his eyes to scan the clearing.

'Where the fuck is the second detachment?' he said to nobody. 'Our brothers should be here by now. They were due to land on the south coast an hour ago.' Then he shook his head, glanced at Bald. Grinned. 'No matter. In a few hours I'll be ruling this country and you'll be maggot feed.'

Bald bit on his anger. Kept his mouth shut.

'You know what happened to the last man who betrayed me?' The way Pretorius said it sounded less like a question and more like a threat. 'I had his hands and feet chopped off. Then I had his feet sewn to his arms, his hands surgically attached to his legs.' He smiled faintly at the memory. 'The sepsis claimed him – eventually. If I told you how long the man lasted, you wouldn't believe me.'

Bald knew it then. *Nothing I can say will change his mind. He's going to slot me and there's not a fucking thing I can do about it.*

Pretorius glanced across his shoulder at the two men exiting the Herc's cockpit. One guy was pale as milk. The other had skin dark as the mouth of a cave.

'You two,' Pretorius called out. 'Over here. Give me a hand.'

The white guy, Priest, exchanged a look with the black guy, Deet – Pretorius's personal bodyguard. The pair of them marched down the dirt road towards Bald, moving with the exaggerated gait of bodybuilders, their torsos twisting at the hips as their weight shifted with each stride, arms dangling out at the sides like wrecking balls hanging from a couple of cranes. Pretorius forced Bald down onto his knees.

This is it, the Scot thought.

This is where I die.

'I'll make it quick,' Pretorius said. 'A double-tap to the head. One last favour, from one warrior to another. What do you say?'

Bald said nothing. He looked at Priest with obvious hate. Then Pretorius spun away from Bald and thrust the Beretta at his partner, eyes beaming. 'Here,' he said. 'Do the honours.'

Priest looked surprised. His tiny eyes flickered with uncertainty as he stared at the pistol and for a moment Bald allowed himself to think that he wouldn't go through with it. That he didn't have the guts to slot one of his own tribe. But then Priest reached out and wrapped his fingers around the stippled grip, and Bald felt an intense pressure building in his chest. He was going to do it, then.

'I'm sorry, boss.'

'Fuck you.'

Bald swung his gaze back to Pretorius. 'Let this prick kill me and you'll be making an enemy of every lad who used to be in the Regiment. Blades look out for their own. They'll hunt you down.'

Pretorius raised an eyebrow. 'You really expect me to believe that? You're John Bald. Nah, no one's going to shed a tear over you. In fact, I'd put good money on the boys in Hereford having a piss-up to celebrate when they hear you've copped it.'

The leaden mass in Bald's chest now plunged into his guts. In desperation he scanned the horizon, as if an escape route would present itself. None did. He was out of options. Out of time. Out of everything. For a moment he wondered if they'd bury him in a shallow grave, or perhaps leave him by the side of the road for feral dogs to feast on and children to poke with sticks. Ultimately, it didn't matter. He'd still be dead, and Priest and Pretorius would be as rich as fuck.

Priest drew the Beretta level with Bald. 'No hard feelings, boss.'

'Get it over with.'

Fear knotted his bowels. Nausea lodged like a ball in his throat. He forced the fear down to the pit of his guts and waited to die.

thirty-one

He kept waiting. A moment passed. Then two. He closed his eyes and waited for the bark of the Beretta. Its sudden jerk. The white-hot flash of the muzzle. The brief spasm of pain he'd feel as the cartridge bored through his cranium. And then the blackness of forever.

Still nothing happened.

His stomach muscles were clenched so tight they could've cracked walnuts. Then a sound reached his ears. The familiar *click* of the hammer against the firing pin of an unloaded weapon. Again. *Click*. A soldier in the field dreaded that sound. It meant you were out of ammo, that there would be a lull in your gunfire that the enemy could fatally exploit. But to Bald, on his knees and facing the business end of a pistol, it was the sweetest noise in the world.

Click-click.

'What the fuck . . . ?' Priest began.

Bald opened his eyes. He saw Priest fumbling with the Beretta with his paddle-like hands, pointlessly pulling the trigger and getting the same result. Pretorius stood to one side of the guy and looked like he was about to explode with laughter. His lips were pressed tight but they trembled at the corners and he swapped a knowing look with Deet. As if the two men were sharing a private joke. Bald stayed where he was, knees anchored to the dirt road, a tingling sensation drumming like fingertips on his temples. What the fuck was going on?

'Bastard's empty,' Priest muttered. He pulled back the slider and offered the pistol to Pretorius as if to prove that it hadn't misfired because of laughable incompetence. Bald craned his neck for a better look. There was a hollow black groove where a round should have been chambered.

'Here,' Pretorius said. 'Allow me.'

He snatched the Beretta from Priest and thumbed the magazine release button on the right side of the grip. He caught the empty mag as it slid out of the feed on the underside of the grip and tossed it aside. Priest looked on as Pretorius produced a fresh clip from the waistband of his trousers. This one was fully loaded: a round of 9x19mm Parabellum brass gleamed at the brim. He inserted it and pulled back the slider all the way. Then he released it. There was a *ker-crack* as the slider crashed forward and shunted the top bullet from the mag into the chamber.

Then Pretorius did a funny thing. He didn't hand the weapon back. Instead he manually cocked the hammer. Priest blinked at the loaded gun in his hand.

'A word of advice, Jamie.'

Priest frowned. 'What's that?'

'Next time you try to frame someone, think up a better cover story.'

Pretorius raised the loaded Beretta to Priest's forehead. The guy had just enough time to register a look of dumb surprise. Then Pretorius pulled the trigger.

There was a sound like a carburettor backfiring as a bullet spewed out of the muzzle and struck Priest between his eyes. His head tilted back. There was no look on his face now. Mostly because he didn't have a face left. Brain matter went everywhere. Blood spurted out of the back of his head in hot arcs. His arms went limp at his sides. Then he dropped. Like a sack of oats someone had chucked out of a tenth-floor window.

For a long beat nobody spoke. There was only the steady pump of blood out of Priest, the distant squawks of birds frightened by the gunshot. Bald wiped the blood from his eyes. Priest's blood, he reminded himself. Warm drops of it traced veins down his cheeks. He felt relieved, confused. Then Pretorius laughed. Deet joined in. Canned laughter in a blood-soaked nightmare. After a few seconds Pretorius quietened down and wiped away the tears with the blackened palm of his gun hand.

'Did you see the look on that idiot's face?' he said with a snigger. 'Fucking priceless, that.'

Bald clenched his fists. He was getting tired of Pretorius and his mind games. Tired of people messing with his head. He watched the blood spill out of his partner and seep into the earth.

'You understand why I had to do that, John? I had to be sure you weren't working for MI6.'

Raw anger coursed through Bald. 'Wait a minute. You mean, you knew Priest was with the Firm all along?'

Pretorius smiled at Bald but offered no reply. Instead he nodded at Deet. 'Show him.'

Nodding dutifully, Deet dropped to one knee beside Priest, careful to avoid the blood rapidly pooling around the dead operator's hefty frame. Then he reached down to the bottom of Priest's right trouser leg and pulled it up to the knee. Bald's blood froze as he stared at the bracelet clamped around his mucker's ankle. It was a steel band half an inch wide with some kind of transmitting device strapped to it. Bald looked at Pretorius, as if seeking an explanation.

'What you're looking at is a GPS bracelet,' Pretorius said. 'It allows a person to be traced anywhere in the world to an accuracy of roughly eight metres. I've seen a few of them. High-value targets occasionally wear them in the field in Somalia. To protect against K&R attempts.'

Bald nodded dimly. His brain rewound three hours, to the assault on the airport outside Mogadishu, when they had nicked the Herc in order to smuggle men and kit across the Indian Ocean and RV with the second detachment landing by boat to the south. Things hadn't gone to plan. Big surprise.

'The Yanks were tracking this sack of shit every step of the way,' Pretorius said, tapping Priest with his foot the way a driver might kick a dog he's just hit. 'That's how they were able to ambush us at the airfield.'

Bald realized something else. The Firm had lied to him. His handler had mentioned nothing about Priest wearing a tracker. 'That fat prick,' he muttered. 'He fucking played me . . .'

'You and me both.'

Bald pulled a face. A thought prodded him. Like a finger jabbing him repeatedly in the chest. 'But if you knew Priest was spying for the Firm, why did you pull the gun on me?'

'You understand why I had to do that, John? Why I had to kill Priest? He was an asset. Working for MI6. After all, you and Priest did come as a team. And you lied to me about your name. But, I must admit, I had my doubts.' He kind of smiled. 'No offence, but the chiefs in Whitehall would never employ an old bastard like you.'

'None taken,' Bald replied, masking the relief flushing through his body. Thinking to himself, I'm off the hook.

'Besides,' Pretorius continued, 'if you really *were* working for Six, you'd have spilled your guts when your friend had a gun to your head. But you didn't fess up. You got down on your knees and prepared to face your death and you didn't break.' He punched Bald lightly on the shoulder. 'You're one of us now.'

Bald rustled up an uneasy smile. Still, he wondered about Priest wearing that GPS tracker. Why hadn't Avery Chance given him the heads-up? He weighed it up some more and decided that he didn't give a shit. He was alive, Priest was out of the equation. Cut past the crap, that was all that mattered.

His anger slowly drained from his head to his feet, until all that was left was a pang of bitterness. Not at Pretorius, but at the Firm. Four days ago Avery Chance had sat him down and fed him a load of crap about clean slates and transparency – a brave new era for MI6. But she'd kept him in the dark about Priest. Fuck knows what else she had been lying to him about. It was the same old rules at Vauxhall, Bald realized. The same old deceits.

Pretorius noticed his sour mood and pounced on it. 'I need to know that you're still with us.' His voice was charged like a current. 'Because if you're not, then we have a problem.'

Bald hesitated. Earlier, siding with Pretorius had seemed like the ultimate no-brainer. Take over a country, get rich, get your end away with an endless supply of beautiful women. Suddenly he wasn't so sure. Normally that kind of offer appealed to Bald – to his instincts. But the way Pretorius had fucked with him gave him pause for thought. *If I go along, maybe he'll pull a gun on me again. Maybe next time there'll be a bullet in it.* Second-guessing Pretorius was a dangerous business. The guy gave nothing away. So you never knew quite where you stood with him. Or where his loyalties really lay.

You have no choice, countered the voice in Bald's head. *Time to face facts. Priest is dead. You're out of contact with the Firm. Turn your back on Pretorius now, you're a dead man. You've got to go along with him.*

'You want to be rich, don't you?' Pretorius smiled at Bald. His lips twitched with excitement. 'This is our moment. Let's seize it.'

Bald was waiting for the inevitable second voice to spring up. The one that would argue he had a duty to stick to the mission. That he couldn't cut out the Firm now. Not this time, not having been given the chance of a fresh start and a job for life with them. That, somehow, he owed Avery. He waited for the voice but it never came. There was only the murmur of a migraine brewing inside his skull. Meanwhile the blood flowing out of the back of his partner's skull had reduced to a faint trickle.

And yeah, he did want to be rich. Seventeen years in the Regiment, getting maimed and shot at for peanuts – he figured the world owed him. Big time. The truth was, being poor didn't suit Bald as a lifestyle choice. He liked his whisky triple-distilled, he preferred high-class hookers and he liked his cars to have 'super' tagged on the front. That's why he'd ended up despising his best friend from the SAS, Joe Gardner. Joe was too humble, too grateful for the things he had, never realized he was being fed crumbs. The way Bald saw it, life was one big fucking landgrab. You took what you wanted, and if you had to elbow a few people out of the way to get what you wanted, tough shit.

Pretorius rested a hand on Bald's shoulder and looked him hard in the eye.

'I saw how well you fought against the Yanks back at the airfield. You're a mad, brilliant fucking soldier. You and me' – he slung an arm round Bald – 'we're blood brothers. We're not young men any more. And that's a good thing. We've seen how the world really works. How it chews people up and spits them out. You know, as I do, that the world owes us. This, truly, is what we were born to do.'

That voice again. You've gone too far now. There's no going back. Not after this.

In the back of his head he realized that if the coup failed, he could expect no mercy from Avery Chance and her bosses. They would crucify him for this act of betrayal. Then again, he reasoned, they might punish him anyway. After all, he had ignored the Firm's instructions to kill Pretorius. Instead he'd taken part in an ambush, stolen a Herc and was now about to participate in the takeover of a sovereign nation.

'Well, John?' Pretorius asked. 'Have you made up your mind?'

thirty-two

Bald was about to open his mouth in reply when a shout came from behind him. Pretorius stared past his shoulder, his pupils pricked with anticipation. Bald turned and spotted a group of shadowed figures breaking across the clearing from the treeline a hundred and fifty metres to the south. Twelve of them. His stomach muscles pulled tight like tensed rope and for a second he feared that they were about to be ambushed by the local security forces. But then the dozen men pulled clear of the shadows cast by the jungle canopy and Bald saw that they were decked out in the same kit as the soldiers beside the Herc: digi-camo trousers, olive-green T-shirts, polished black boots. They were also equipped with the same Colt Commando semi-automatic rifles. Behind him, Pretorius breathed a sigh of relief.

'At last,' he said. 'Our brothers have arrived.'

The second detachment pushed across the open ground and approached the Herc. They were led by a gaunt white guy with about as much meat on him as a kebab stick. He approached Pretorius, gave a half-hearted salute. His face was heavily drawn, his cheeks sunk deep like footprints in mud. His nose looked like a dog had chewed on it. Bald looked at the guy and thought, Eric Cantona on a hunger strike. The eleven black soldiers stopped in a line behind him and formed a quiet, hulking mass.

'You're late,' Pretorius said tersely.

'We got held up,' Cantona replied in a soft voice with a slight accent. French, Bald thought. Or maybe Belgian. 'Things got noisy.'

'How do you mean?' Pretorius asked.

Cantona rubbed his unkempt jaw. There was a sullen weariness to the man. As if he'd seen it all. His expression was totally devoid of emotion. 'The General,' he said with a shrug. 'He had company.'

Then he gave his back to Pretorius and snapped his fingers. The soldiers parted down the middle and one of the men at the rear booted three bedraggled figures to the front. The men were a miserable sight, their hands bound behind their backs, black masking tape pulled across their mouths. One look at them told Bald they were officers. They were dressed in white trousers and matching short-sleeved shirts with green epaulettes decorated with two golden stars. Their uniforms were smeared with blood and dirt. The guy in the middle had ten years on the other two. He wore a pair of Ray-Ban Aviators. He had a large paunch and a toothbrush moustache. A ton of military decorations dangled from the left breast of his jacket. Cantona gestured grandly to him.

'Mr Pretorius,' he said. 'May I introduce you to General Hatem Ben Said, Chief of Staff of the Comoro Islands Defence Force. General, Mr Kurt Pretorius. The man who will be your next ruler.'

The General snorted. Cantona scratched his cheek, then jerked his head in the direction of the south coast.

'We made our way to the General's house after landing at the inlet,' he said. 'As per your orders. Turns out he was having himself a late-night party with his subordinates. Poker, prostitutes, vodka.' Bald felt thirsty at the mention of booze. He made a mental note: be sure to root through the President's office once they've gate-crashed the palace. The guy was bound to have a collection of fine whisky gathering dust somewhere.

'And these men, Girard?' Pretorius asked, pointing to the officers either side of the General.

'His subordinates.'

'Casualties?'

'None.' Girard grinned. 'Unless you count the prostitutes. We couldn't leave any witnesses.' He flashed a puzzled look at the Herc, scratched his chin. 'Where are the supplies we discussed?'

'We were ambushed at the airfield. Barely got out of there alive. Had to leave all the kit behind. RPGs, grenades, sniper rifles, ammo – the works.'

Girard looked unsure. 'But our men are carrying less than a full clip each.'

'Then you'll have to ration your ammo and take what you can from any guards you drop. Once the initial attack is complete, we can resupply with the weaponry stored at the army barracks.' Girard went to protest but Pretorius cut him off with a brusque wave of his hand. 'Don't test my patience, Girard. We're going ahead with the mission. We've come too far to give up now. Understood?'

Girard dropped his eyes to his feet. '*Oui*, Mr Pretorius.'

Pretorius nodded approvingly. 'I want to speak with the General,' he said.

Girard sort of shrugged with his pinched shoulders as if to say, whatever. Then he bent down and ripped the tape off the General's mouth. The man let out a sharp scream, his face burning. 'Bitches!' he roared, spitting uncontrollably as he spoke. Tiny drops flecked Bald. 'Untie me. I command it!'

Pretorius put a finger to his lips to shush him. Then he

trained the Beretta on a spot between the General's eyes. 'General Ben Said.'

'What?'

'I'm the one in charge now,' Pretorius replied calmly. 'I give the orders, not you.'

The General went very still. Breath trapped in his chest. Eyes pasted to Pretorius. His face folding in the middle like a hand making a fist. 'Who the fuck are you?'

'Me?' Pretorius arched his eyebrows and pulled a face. 'I'm the guy who just landed some thirty armed and highly trained soldiers in your backyard without anyone knowing about it. I'm the guy who is about to seize control of your country. So don't go pissing me off.'

The General listened to this, shaking his head furiously. 'Bullshit. I have five hundred men under my command. Once they hear what you're doing, they will crush you.'

'Not if you side with us.' Pretorius smiled.

'What the fuck are you talking about?'

'Publicly denounce the President and tell your men that you will be supporting our side in the coup d'état. Tell them' – Pretorius made a grandiose gesture with his right hand – 'we represent a new dawn for the people of the Comoros. Tell them we'll increase their pay – whatever. The main thing is, once President Khalifa hears that you've turned against him, he'll have no choice but to surrender.'

The General almost choked on his own spittle. His facial muscles were knotted with rage. 'Never,' he said. 'President Khalifa is like a brother to me. I will never betray him. Now let me—'

There was a deafening crack as the gun in Pretorius's hand lit up and a round smashed into the General's forehead. The officers beside him flinched, blood splashing their uniforms as their comrade jerked backwards and dropped to the ground.

'I told you not to piss me off,' Pretorius said as he lowered the Beretta. He fired another shot into the General. His body jolted like someone was using a defibrillator on him.

Pretorius is speaking to dead people now, Bald thought.

For several seconds nobody said a word. Then Pretorius trained his pistol on the officer on the left. He was a short guy, stocky build, chest as deep as a fridge. He was shaven-headed, with a gold chain round his neck and big, round eyes like drops of oil in a glass of milk. His mouth was filled with so much gold he could probably open a bank. The man stared blankly at Pretorius, who said, 'You. Name.'

'Colonel Abdul Rashidi.' The officer's voice was like cement pouring from a mixer. Pretorius nodded briskly.

'Here's the deal, Colonel. You've got two choices and about one second to make them. You can take charge of the military, throw your support behind me. Or you can join your general in the afterlife.'

The Colonel took less than a second to make up his mind. 'Fuck it,' he said. He shot a withering look at his dead superior. 'Rashidi hated him anyway. Piece of shit took bribes but kept many people out of the loop.'

Pretorius nodded at the third officer. 'This man is your new subordinate. Here's what's going to happen. Two of my guys will escort you to the barracks. You'll round up your men, explain that the General has stood down and you're now in charge. Order the soldiers to put down their weapons until further notice. They're to remain on standby. We'll need them after we take down the President.'

Bald felt a hot thrill in his bones. This was what he was born to do, he thought. Fighting dirty wars in the grim corners of the earth, one of a handful of men with guns and the determination to win through on a mission of impossible odds. Taking over a foreign country was bold, reckless – borderline insane.

It was exactly how they did things in the Regiment. He was loving every minute of it.

'Girard, take your guys and head for the airport, north of Moroni. The twelve of you should be enough to deal with the guards and secure the airport.'

'Yes, Mr Pretorius.'

'The airport's closely guarded and you can expect to meet some stern resistance. Meanwhile the rest of us will sweep into the city, then we'll split into two teams. One team of six guys will seize the radio station.'

'What about us?' Bald asked.

Pretorius grinned. 'We'll be going for the President. He's based at the Palais de Beit-Salam, at the northern tip of the city. We fight our way inside and give the President an ulti-matum: stand down with immediate effect and go into exile. Or die.'

Colonel Rashidi thought of something. 'President Khalifa has a loyal cadre of bodyguards,' he said. 'They're trained by French Special Forces. They follow him at all times. They won't give in.'

'Then they can die a glorious death alongside their beloved leader. Doesn't matter. Once all three targets are secured and the President executed, nothing can stop us. The Colonel's men will sweep through the city, neutralizing any last pockets of resistance. Within twenty-four hours, the entire island will be on lockdown.'

The Colonel frowned. 'It's really going to be that easy?'

'Not easy.' Pretorius fixed him with an icy glare. 'Taking over the country – any country – is going to be dangerous and laden with risk. All we know for sure is that the President is a control freak. There is no infrastructure of government here. It's just one guy. Anywhere else, we'd be dealing with a far wider spread of targets. That means the odds are a little better in our favour. Even so, there's a fair chance it could turn into a clusterfuck. But no one ever got rich playing it safe.'

This seemed to satisfy the Colonel, who shifted uneasily on his feet. 'Who becomes President?' he asked. 'You?'

'Don't be so stupid. A white foreigner declaring himself President of an independent country in the Indian Ocean is not only against the local constitution, it'll attract the attention of Western governments. Attention we could do without. No, we need a Comorian national as President. A face to present to the outside world. Someone who's pliable. A yes man.'

'Who do you have in mind?'

'There's an academic who's been living in exile in Madagascar. We'll fly him over once the island is secure and install him as President. Naturally,' said Pretorius, grinning, 'the real power will rest with us. We'll be de facto rulers.'

Rashidi pursed his lips. His pupils receded to pinpoints. 'What's in it for Rashidi?'

Bald rolled his eyes. The guy had an annoying habit of referring to himself in the third person. Like he was some kind of rap superstar. Pretorius shot the Colonel a dark look and for a moment Bald thought he might send him the same way as the General.

'You'll receive an appropriate cut,' Pretorius said with a sigh. He smiled thinly as he added, 'And you get to live.'

The Colonel said nothing. His face was blank. His range of emotional expression was about equal to a slab of granite. Then he cocked his head at a figure among the group of soldiers and said, 'Rashidi wants her.'

Pretorius turned to follow his line of sight. So did Bald. Pretorius cocked an eyebrow at the Colonel as he wheeled back around. 'That whore?'

Rashidi nodded. 'Give Rashidi the bitch, maybe we have deal.'

There was a long pause as the PMC chief weighed it up.

Staring at the Colonel the whole time. Finally he beckoned to the soldier keeping a hold on Imogen. 'Hand her over,' he said. Turning back to Rashidi, he added, 'Don't take your eyes off this one. She has a bad habit of escaping.'

Imogen tried to wrestle free as the soldier manhandled her towards Rashidi. The Colonel rubbed his hands expectantly. Wrapping an arm around Imogen's shoulder, he began to tenderly stroke her cheek with a bony, scarred finger. 'OK. Now we golden.'

Pretorius turned away in disgust and muttered to Girard, 'Move out immediately. The airport is thirteen klicks north of the city, so you'll need a head start.' Girard nodded. Pretorius glanced at the Colonel. 'You'll head out now as well.'

There was a murmur of approval from the soldiers at the prospect of finally getting stuck in. Twelve out of the twenty-eight men – Girard and his team detailed to take the airport – climbed aboard two of the Amaroks. Two of Pretorius's men ushered Colonel Rashidi and his subordinate into a third pickup. The Colonel stopped and snatched the Ray-Bans from the General's dead body, slipped them on. Imogen sat between the Comorian officers in the rear seat. She looked back at Bald and shot him one last look of utter contempt. He seemed to be getting a lot of those lately.

The turbocharged diesel engines growled as the three trucks fired up and began trundling down the dirt road leading east from the clearing. The Amaroks picked up speed, the tyres coughing up dirt. With that, fourteen soldiers were gone. That left the same number of men at the RV.

One of these pounded angrily over to Pretorius. A muscular figure with biceps the size of boulders and a jaw that looked as if it had been chiselled out of marble. Harvey Stegman pressed a fresh wad of khat into his mouth and glowered at Bald with undisguised hatred. Then he turned to Pretorius.

'What's the deal with this cunt? I thought we were sup-posed to be slotting him?'

Pretorius folded his arms across his chest. 'A misunder-standing. John is with us now.'

Stegman's eyes threatened to explode out of their sockets. 'This bastard ran over Eli. He was like a fucking son to me. He killed him and you're just gonna let him get away with that?'

'Things have changed,' Pretorius replied coolly.

'Bollocks!' Stegman chewed furiously on his khat. 'I saw him kill Eli with my own eyes. If you're not gonna do it, I'll do him myself.'

He went to raise his Colt Commando at Bald. Pretorius shot forward, slapped the palm of his hand on the receiver and lowered the rifle with surprising force.

'We lost nine good men when the Yanks ambushed us,' he said firmly as he stared daggers at his 2iC. 'That's left us low on numbers. We need every man we can get for the assault. John is on the team. Deal with it.'

Stegman paused for a couple of seconds. Then he pursed his lips and grudgingly nodded. 'Yes, Mr Pretorius.'

'Good.' Pretorius straightened his back. 'Get the men ready to move out.'

The South African spun away. As he brushed past Bald he whispered, 'This isn't over. Once the island is taken, you're dead. I fucking promise.'

'But the anticipation is killing me.'

'Fuck you, bro.' Stegman spat out his khat and ground it under the heel of his boot. Then he strode towards the soldiers grouped by the remaining three Amaroks. Looking back, he shot Bald a final fuck-you. The Scot shrugged inside, turned back to Pretorius and watched him drop to one knee beside Priest. Something had caught the PMC chief's eye. He picked up a spent shell case glinting dully near the pooled blood, and held it up to the sun.

'Do you know where the name Parabellum comes from, John?'

'Never gave it a second thought.'

'It's from the Latin. *Si vis pacem, para bellum.* "If you seek peace, prepare for war."' Pretorius swung his eyes towards Bald. 'You know what I like about a bullet? It has the power to change the world. Forget laser-guided bombs and drones and nuclear warheads. None of those things has changed the direction of history. But a bullet . . .' His face flushed red with hatred. 'I remember the day like it was yesterday. I was nine years old when the niggers invaded our farm. Know what that's like, John? To have some darkie hold a gun to your head while they rape your mother – while they make your father watch? To see your old man screaming as they cut his balls off with a machete. I've spent almost fifty years waging wars. Fighting to restore the world to its natural order. Now I'm going to paint my masterpiece. Today. Here. On this island.'

Bald saw it then. For Pretorius, this wasn't about the money. It had never been about the money. It was personal. What had he said back at the jungle camp? 'In this life you're either the exposed neck or the teeth sinking into it.' Pretorius had spent his life as the neck. Now he planned to turn the tables. Bald saw that now. And he wouldn't stop until every last drop of blood had been spilled.

Pretorius tossed the case aside. Dusted himself down and stretched to his full height. Looked at Bald.

'Now,' he said. 'Let's go to war.'

thirty-three

The landing RV was thirty-five kilometres due south and east of Moroni, the capital of Grande Comore, and the journey north took the three pickups along a stretch of worn tarmac flanked by thick walls of mangroves and coconut palms. Shafts of sunlight poked like spear tips through the canopy. Bald was behind the steering wheel of the lead pickup, Pretorius beside him in the front. Deet was somehow crammed into the back seat with Stegman. With six soldiers jammed into the second pickup and a further four guys in the third pickup. Six men would seize the radio station, while the others, under Pretorius, would take the palace. Bald hoped to fuck that was going to be enough manpower.

As they headed west the coast gradually slid out of the horizon. The shoreline was black and angry. Grey clouds pressed down over the Indian Ocean, carrying the threat of hard rain. Waves swelled on the water, absorbing energy before hurling themselves at the shore and pounding the rocks. A tropical storm was brewing.

With the speedometer showing 130 kilometres per hour, the pickup juddered violently as they bounced over potholes deep as bomb craters. Bald gripped the steering wheel, his stomach knotted with tension.

This is it, he thought. It's about to get noisy.

A Colt Commando rested on his lap. They were short of equipment and ammo. Bald himself had only had two clips of 5.56x45mm ammo – forty rounds in total – to see him through the attack. Something else was bothering him, though, besides the lack of kit. How Pretorius had managed to fund his coup? There were the stacks of equipment and weapons he'd seen back at the camp in Somalia. Then there were the six pickups waiting for them at the RV, the Zodiac boats used by the second detachment to land on the island. Where was the money coming from? He thought that Pretorius might have paid for the op himself, but dismissed the idea almost immediately. Pretorius had been blackballed by the Circuit for years. He wouldn't have access to the kind of readies needed for such a large-scale op.

Bald closed his eyes for a micro-second. He was physically and mentally wiped. It had been, what, four days since he'd had a proper night's kip or a decent meal? A snatched hour of sleep here and there, coupled with a refuelling process that had consisted of knocking back a bottle of Famous Grouse. He was running on fumes. He wouldn't be able to last much longer. Just see this through, the voice in his head urged. Whatever it takes to get through today.

His eyes opened wide at the angry trill of a mobile. Pretorius fished the phone out of the pocket of his trousers, a rugged-looking thing in a hard shell. A JCB Toughphone Sitemaster. That old saying about owners looking like their dogs? Nowadays that was true for people and their phones, thought Bald. The JCB was like Pretorius. Durable, military-certified and hard as nails. Pretorius checked the screen, and Bald caught sight of the caller ID.

Charles Grealish.

He did a double-take, panic flushing through his body. Grealish. Christ. He hadn't heard that name in twenty years. Not since the botched job in Northern Ireland when he'd rescued Avery Chance from the Nutting Squad. Back then Grealish had been the director of operations for MI5 in the province. He'd threatened to have Bald RTU'd from the Regiment after ignoring orders, guaranteeing himself a place for life in the Scot's black book of people who had it coming.

Bald touched a hand to his temple. His migraine had flared up again. Brutally this time. What the fuck did Grealish have to do with Pretorius? Ghosts from the past screamed in his ears. Pretorius must have seen the confusion written large across his face, because he explained, 'Grealish, he's my business partner.'

'Partner?' Bald repeated. His lips were numb.

Pretorius nodded. 'He used to be a big deal in Whitehall. He had some, ah, personal problems. A jumped-before-he-was-pushed deal. Our paths crossed on the Circuit, and he's been funding me ever since.'

The phone vibrated, demanding to be answered. Pretorius continued.

'It's a useful arrangement. Grealish supplies me with the means to eject governments. After the dust has settled, he swoops in and secures favourable contracts for real estate at rock-bottom prices.'

Bald said, 'That's why he's fronting the cash for the Comoros?'

Pretorius nodded. 'Soon as I take over, he'll show up with a bunch of contracts stuffed in his briefcase, all waiting just for signatures.'

'But I thought the island was dirt-poor.'

Pretorius rolled his eyes. 'Think about it, John. Grealish takes the land, develops a bunch of luxury hotels and beach resorts. Then all he has to do is wait for the country to settle down and the tourists to show up. Fast forward a few years and he's sitting on a bunch of resorts each worth millions.'

Bald took all this in and tried to compose his features as Pretorius finally took the call. A voice crackled at the other end of the line. Bald tried hard but with the noise of the engine he couldn't make out what was being said. Then the line went quiet.

'We're in,' Pretorius replied.

He paused again. It was Grealish's turn to speak. Bald glanced at the dashboard. The built-in GPS navigation system put them a kilometre south of Moroni. Which meant there were four minutes to go until it all kicked off.

After a few seconds Pretorius said, 'We took a good few casualties back at the airfield. But it could have been worse. If it hadn't been for one of the new guys, we'd never have made it out of there alive. You should be thanking him, not me.'

Grealish said something. This was driving Bald mad. He made an extra effort to cut out the background noise, focus on his voice. No good. Pretorius had the Sitemaster pressed tight to his ear.

'John Bald,' he said. 'Why?'

Grealish said something else. There was a cold pause as Pretorius listened to what the former MI5 man had to say. Then he glanced quickly at Bald. His expression was passive, so Bald couldn't get a reading on it. Does he know? he wondered. Has Grealish told him I'm working for the Firm? Maybe, he thought, Grealish is out of the loop, doesn't know a thing about my mission. But no. The old-boy network was a permanent feature of Whitehall, former directors talking in low voices with their successors in the gentlemen's clubs of St James's. Bald tensed up, acutely aware that his life hung in the balance. No one said a word for several seconds.

'I'll be in touch,' Pretorius said at last. 'When this thing is over.'

He killed the call, shoved the Sitemaster back into his

pocket. Stared impassively at the road. If Grealish had spilled
the beans, Pretorius wasn't showing any sign of it. Maybe he
doesn't know, thought Bald. And then they were rolling into
town and there was no more time to worry.

They travelled north on Boulevard Karthala, passing dilapidated slums. The roads were narrow and unpaved and Bald
had to slow to ninety per. The town was a warren of ramshackle huts and crumbling mosques whose minarets jutted
above a sea of corrugated-metal roofs. Plastic bin bags filled
with rubbish were piled high at the side of the road.

The locals took little notice of them at first. They were a
mix of African and Arab and Malay. Some were dark-skinned
with heavy features; others' faces were more chiselled, with
skin the colour of tea, the centuries of foreign conquest evident in their blood. Toothless old men rocked back and forth
on rickety wooden chairs outside slum dwellings. Women
trudged past the pickups, some lugging wicker baskets filled
with mangoes, others carrying bunches of bananas on their
heads. Barefoot children in rags played tag in the streets. A
normal person might see this and feel guilty. But Bald looked
at the grinding poverty around him and just felt glad to be the
'three Ws': white, Western and working.

A shout went up from the side of the road. Bald swung his
gaze across. Saw a kid in a ragged pair of shorts pointing at
Stegman and Deet in the back, their rifle barrels visible through
the side window. 'Gun, gun, gun!' the kid yelled, sounding the
alarm. People immediately stopped what they were doing. Kids
fled indoors at the call of their anxious mothers, abandoning
their worn footballs. Women ditched their baskets of fruit,
spilling mangoes across the road which were then crushed by
the pickups. It was like watching a well-rehearsed fire drill. To
Bald it seemed as if the people had lived through enough coups
and didn't want any part of it. Better to stay indoors and wait

for the dust to settle than get caught in the crossfire. Fair play
– if he was in their shoes and saw a bunch of armed men roll
into town, he'd be thinking the same thing.

By the time the Amaroks were half a click south of the Palais
de Beit-Salam, the streets were virtually deserted.

'Pull over,' Pretorius said.

Bald hit the brakes. The two other drivers pulled up a couple
of metres to his rear. Six metres ahead of the convoy stood a
rundown three-storey building with the words 'Office de la
Radio et de la TÉlÉvision des Comores' emblazoned above
the door. Pretorius gripped the Beretta 92 in his lap and
turned to Bald.

'Ready?'

'As I'll ever be.'

Pretorius grinned. 'We'll debus here.'

Bald slid out from behind the wheel. A blast of salty air hit
him like a slap from a jilted lover. The air was greased with the
smell of damp rock and the stench of rotten fish. Pretorius
hopped out and a moment later Deet and Stegman joined
them. The ten soldiers debussed from the two other pickups:
six from the second, four from the third. Clips were inserted
into mag feeds, sights were adjusted. Equipment checked.
Bald felt a hot wave of adrenalin rush through his veins. He
was never more alive than in the last few seconds prior to an
op. He was in a heightened mental state, everything was
somehow sharper – as if he was wearing a pair of hi-def
glasses. He filled his lungs. No going back now. It was do or
die. And that was just the way Bald liked it. At his side,
Pretorius exuded an almost supernatural calm.

Six soldiers beelined towards the radio station. Pretorius
broke into a jog and the remainder of his team – Bald, Stegman,
Deet and the four soldiers from the third pickup – pushed
north towards the Palais de Beit-Salam. Eight men with rifles

in their hands and blood on their minds. There was an eerie quiet in the streets, thought Bald as he ran after Pretorius, a dull ache in his leg muscles as if they had been wrapped in barbed wire. There were no vehicles on the roads, he noticed. No kids playing in the streets. There was only the whoosh of breeze fluttering across the island, the rustle of palm leaves. It seemed as if the entire city was holding its breath. The few locals in sight ducked into their houses or darted into alleyways leading deep into the slum districts. It was almost as if they sensed what was about to go down.

They had run for just ten metres when Bald heard men shouting at his six. He looked back over his shoulder. Saw two security guards charging out of the radio station to confront the soldiers, reaching for their holstered pistols. They walked straight into a hail of bullets. The militiamen opened fire simultaneously. Half a dozen rounds belched from their rifles in a staccato burst and cut down the guards. Blood sprayed through the air in dizzying arcs and splashed the glass doors of the building. Spent shell cases cascaded on the tarmac. There was a clatter as the two pistols dropped to the ground. The guards quickly joined them.

It's begun, thought Bald.

'John! Get a move on, for fuck's sakes.'

He spun around. Pretorius and his gang had upped the pace and were twenty metres ahead of him. Bald sprinted after them, the shrill shattering of glass and the crack of rifle rounds sounding at his back, every nerve ending in his body screaming with pain and exhaustion.

Three hundred metres to the north Bald could see a left turn off Boulevard Karthala with a petrol station on the corner. The palace was just sixty metres down that road. Almost there, Bald told himself. Keep going a little longer.

He heard a woman shrieking close by. He glanced back at the

radio station and saw the soldiers herding employees out of the reception area and forcing them to their knees in the street. One of the soldiers was dragging a heavily pregnant woman out into the street. She tried to break free of his grip. In a fit of rage the soldier booted the woman in the small of her back and sent her tumbling to the ground. She tried to crawl away but the soldier kicked her onto her back and raised his rifle's stock above his head as if preparing to smash her face in. The woman instinctively lifted her hands to protect her head. But he brought the stock crashing down on her bump, and the woman bent double in agony, her terrified screams echoing through the street. Then the soldier started stomping on her belly in a frenzied attack, as if he was trying to put out a bush fire. After the third or fourth blow, the woman stopped screaming and her arms fell limp by her side. Blood oozed out from between her legs.

Pretorius was losing the plot and they hadn't even ousted the government yet, thought Bald.

And he's taking you down with him.

He tried to shrug off the thought and pushed on. Two hundred and fifty metres to the petrol station now. Almost there. He buried the pain and the doubts swirling behind his eyeballs and upped the pace. Gunshots and wails chorused in the distance behind him. Bald kept his eyes fixed ahead. A semi-naked child no older than three or four years old stood abandoned at the side of the road, tears streaming down his face as he cried out for his mother. Bald ignored him too. Focused solely on the mission, and the riches that would be waiting for him at the other end. He drew alongside Pretorius. Two hundred metres to the petrol station.

'This is what it feels like to be alive,' Pretorius said grandly. 'Whoever said one man can't change the world was full of shit. Give me a bunch of savages, a stack of Colt Commandos and a couple of technicals, I'm invincible.'

Bald gulped for air. His chest was burning. Sweat slicked down his forehead and stung his eyes. Pretorius wasn't even short of breath.

'Slotting civvies,' Bald gasped. 'What the fuck for?'

'A necessary evil, John. Today we put the fear of god into the natives. Tomorrow every man, woman and child on this island will be worshipping us. Gods among men.'

Bald was flagging. He couldn't keep up the pace. Pretorius breezed ahead. A hundred and fifty metres to the petrol station. At that instant a beggar jumped out in front of Bald. A shrivelled old man with a face like petrified wood. He cupped his bony hands in front of his chin, his eyes pleading. The rest of the soldiers were racing ahead. Bald slammed the butt of his Colt Commando into the beggar's stomach. The old man jackknifed. Air escaped from his slack mouth like a punctured tyre. Bald elbowed him aside and ran on.

Pretorius suddenly halted. So did the rest of the team. A sound carried across the street. Bald heard it clearly above the distant cracks of gunfire to the south. The distinct roar of an engine being revved, the nails-on-a-chalkboard screech of rubber on tarmac. Bald caught up with the soldiers as a car surged into view from the road to the left of the petrol station. The road leading to the palace. The car was a Lincoln, the kind of stretched-out, jet-black motor used to ferry presidents around at G8 summits. Must be doing 120 k per, Bald figured. The Lincoln slowed momentarily as it hung a left at the petrol station. Then it started bulleting away northwards down the main road.

'Shit!' said Pretorius. Bald glanced at him. His eyes were small as knife points. His lips barely parted as he spoke. 'That's the President's car. He's getting away.'

thirty-four

At that speed, Bald knew the Lincoln would be three hundred metres clear of their position in another two seconds max. Three hundred metres was the threshold of the maximum effective range of the Colt Commando. Which meant he had two or three seconds to save the op. Bald was able to process all this information instantly because he possessed superior military intelligence – an ability to shut out physical and mental stress, process the situation and formulate a plan on the spot. It was why he'd been able to survive brutal firefights in some of the most desperate corners of the world. And now it was why he brought his rifle to bear a split second ahead of the other soldiers, tucking the stock tight to his right shoulder and wrapping his hand around the rubberized grip. With his left hand clasping the STANAG clip on the underside of the receiver and his cheek resting on the receiver, Bald filled his muscles with oxygen and sighted the Lincoln through the rear aperture and front sighting post. Two hundred and eighty metres. Almost out of range. He focused on the left-rear tyre. Squeezed the trigger.

A white-hot flame licked out of the barrel. He felt the kick of the recoil. His eyes were locked on the Lincoln. He saw sparks flying as a round ricocheted off the number plate.

Fuck!

Three hundred metres.

You're losing him.

The Lincoln was shrinking from view. Bald didn't panic. It was a natural thing, panic, and in the Regiment you learned to shut out emotions. To compartmentalize them. You cordoned off a space in the back of your brain and shoved all your thoughts and anxieties into it. You listened only to the feeling in your muscles, the instinct in your guts and the training voice inside your head. Everything else was just white noise. He calmly lowered his aim a quarter of an inch and zeroed the sights on the tyre.

Distance, three hundred and forty metres.

It was worse than a long shot. At this range, it was barely even a shot.

He pulled the trigger anyway. A second shot exploded out of the barrel. There was a momentary pause as Bald feared he had missed again. And then he saw the Lincoln sagging on its left side and veering towards the side of the road. He'd struck it. He put the celebrations on ice and swivelled his weapon across to the other tyre. Gave the trigger another satisfying pull. The tyre exploded. The Lincoln swerved to the right, then the left, as the driver fought to regain control. Then it banked sharply again to the right and crashed into an office building beyond the petrol station, the front of the car crumpling like an empty Coke can being stamped on. Smoke puffed out from under the twisted bonnet. Bald lowered his Colt Commando, a warm feeling flowing through his body.

Still fucking got it.

'NOW!' Pretorius roared. 'GO! GO! GO!'

There was no time to lose. They raced towards the Lincoln, Pretorius in the lead, Bald matching him stride for stride now. Adrenalin was rushing through his bloodstream, pumping fresh blood into his weary legs. Less than three hundred metres from the grand prize. All they had to do was seize the President and force him to resign – then the country would be theirs.

Three of the Lincoln's doors flipped open. Bodyguards clambered out: two from the front, one from the rear. They were dressed as if they had gone to Bodyguard University, from their broad shoulders and black tie, white shirt combos right down to the earpieces snaking down their trunk-like necks. And they were wielding Uzi submachine guns. The guy who'd debussed from the rear dived back inside the vehicle while his two mates crouched by the front wheel and started putting rounds down on Pretorius's men. As bullets struck the road a metre ahead of him and glanced off the tarmac in a furious stream of lead, Pretorius darted for cover at the side of an ancient mosque on the left side of the road. Bald scrambled after him, along with Stegman and Deet. The four soldiers supporting them ducked to the side of a battered shop directly opposite the mosque.

The bodyguards opened fire again. Bald could feel the stopping power of the bullets in the way they quickly tore chunks out of the front of the shop. He lost count of the number of rounds discharged. The gunfire cut out. Silence blanketed the street like crisp snow. Stegman dropped to a knee and took aim. Then the others followed suit. The silence was shredded. Bullets pummelled the Lincoln. Round after incessant round, like a bunch of hammers raining down on a lead pipe. Bald glanced around the corner. Saw the bodyguards slide behind the Lincoln as bullets bounced off the bodywork and spider-webbed the rear window. There was a lull in the gunfire.

Bald shouted to Pretorius, 'I don't see the President. Where the fuck is he?'

Pretorius peeked out from behind cover. 'I count only three doors open. He must still be in the back seat. Direct your aim away from the car. Repeat, away from the car.'

Bald nodded. Any rounds that fully pierced the bodywork would ricochet violently through the car, potentially killing the President.

'Me and Harvey will give covering fire,' Pretorius said. 'You and Deet close in on the Lincoln, spring the President out of there. Ready?'

'Let's do it.'

Pretorius did a three-count. On three Bald and Deet broke out from cover with Pretorius and Stegman covering them at their seven o'clock. Keeping his chin tucked low to his chest, Bald scudded towards the petrol station. It was eighty metres away; the Lincoln a hundred and twenty metres further on. The pace they were going at, they'd get hammered before they even made it to the petrol station. Then Bodyguards Two and Three shot up and discharged their Uzis at the two soldiers darting towards them. Bald instinctively hit the deck. Deet landed at his nine. There were so many rounds raining down on his position that the ground around Bald seemed to crackle like fat in a frying pan. But they missed the target. The first problem with Uzis: they were notoriously inaccurate at ranges over a hundred metres.

Now Bald shifted to a kneeling firing stance, thumbing the fire selector from single shot to burst as he sighted Bodyguard One. The trigger felt good when he squeezed it, and a violent three-round burst hammered into the wheelbase, forcing Bodyguard One to crouch behind cover once more. At the same time Bodyguards Two and Three sighted their Uzis on Bald and unleashed a couple of quick bursts. Jackets spat out of the ejectors like coins from a fruit machine after hitting the jackpot. Rounds pelleted the ground six or seven inches ahead of the Scot. Deet unloaded a quick burst in return. The rounds missed but the bodyguards disappeared. Bald looked to his rear just in time to see Pretorius and Stegman bursting out of cover and breaking across exposed ground. Across the road, the four backup soldiers scuttled forward from the shop and moved into position behind a beat-up old Nissan Micra ten metres ahead and to the right.

Bald swung back to his twelve as Bodyguard Three put down six quick rounds on him. They landed short. In the next instant Bodyguards One and Two made a run for the petrol station. Why are they turning back towards us, Bald wondered, instead of getting as far away as possible? Didn't make any sense. They were headed straight for trouble. Then he spotted a third man sandwiched between the two BGs. He wore dark shalwar trousers with a white kameez tunic over the top and a threadbare grey jacket. A round white Muslim prayer cap sat atop his head, decorated in green and gold.

'That's him!' Pretorius shouted above the hollow echo and clang of gunfire as he drew alongside Bald and Deet. 'That's the President. I knew it.'

Up ahead Bodyguard Three raced after his comrades towards the petrol station, firing from the hip as he ran, keeping his attackers pinned down. Then he stopped. Dropped to one knee and fumbled with his Uzi. Just by observing the guy Bald knew he'd emptied his clip. The second problem with Uzis: they went through magazines like celebrities through coke. Now Bald brought his Colt Commando to bear. Sighted the bodyguard. Fired. His aim was true. It was better than true. It was gospel. It was the Ferrari of aims. Three bullets thudded into the guy's neck. He fell away and died a lonely death in the middle of the road, pawing dumbly at his throat as blood fountained out of his trauma wound in a hot gush. From a certain angle it appeared as if he was vomiting blood.

Bald took a weird satisfaction from sending the guy over to the dark side. A powerful sense of achievement. It was something only those who had been in a kill-or-be-killed situation could relate to – the preservation of your own life by the taking of someone else's.

Bodyguards One and Two and the President had sought refuge behind three rusty old petrol pumps. Bald had a moment of dread that a round could hit the pumps and the petrol station would go up in flames. But then he noticed the weeds poking up through the concrete, the boarded-up windows, the vines hanging from the roof, and quickly realized that the place had been disused for a long time.

Pretorius got to his feet and shook Bald by the shoulder. His blood was up. Victory burned in his eyes.

'Bastards are trapped,' he said. 'Let's finish the job.'

'Fucking aye.'

Bald sprang to his feet and pushed on, Pretorius in front. Deet and Stegman were putting down rounds on the pumps. Bullets blitzed the forecourt and struck the concrete pillars supporting the building. Fifty metres to the petrol station now. As he ran he worked out the number of rounds he'd expended so far. Eleven. That left him with nine in the clip. Plus the spare mag, twenty-nine rounds. Bald was forty-four metres from the petrol station when the bodyguards, realizing they were outnumbered and outgunned, were panicked into action. Wild sprays of 9mm cartridges thumped into the advancing party. There was a howl of pain as one of the soldiers breaking clear of the Nissan took a pair of bullets to the groin. He slumped to the ground, screaming at the top of his voice, hands clamped over the leaking wound.

Bald and Pretorius were forty metres from the petrol station now. Bodyguard Two reloaded and brassed up a second soldier at the Nissan. Two of the support soldiers were now dead. We're down to six now, Bald thought. Those bodyguards are starting to take the piss.

Thirty-five metres away, Bodyguard Two turned his attention to Bald, arcing his sights across ninety degrees. The Uzi zeroed on Bald. The Scot dived to the ground. Then Pretorius shot to his feet and gave two quick pulls on the Beretta's trigger. The semi-automatic pistol barked. Two bullets smacked into the nape of the bodyguard's neck. His head snapped back; his arms jerked. He fell away as if somebody had taken a pair of garden shears to marionette strings. Pretorius lowered his pistol and pumped a fist in the air in celebration.

'*Yessssss!*'

Seeing the tide of men swarming towards him, Bodyguard One panicked and turned to flee. He didn't get far. Bald calmly lined the guy up with his Colt Commando and depressed the trigger. A three-round burst slammed into his spine. He jerked. Then he dropped. All three bodyguards had been wiped out. There was still no sign of the President, which meant he must be cowering behind the pumps.

Bald sprinted towards the petrol station. Pretorius powered a stride ahead of him, unable to contain his glee.

'We've got him pinned down, John. There's no escape. The President's ours.'

Bald felt his heart beating like a snare drum. His muscles were juiced. He lived for this. Scraping by, keeping his head down, taking crap from the boss – that had never been John Bald's way. He'd been programmed by the Regiment into a hard-as-fuck killing machine who sought comfort in the cold grip of a weapon and the look of raw fear in the eyes of his enemies. Not for him civvie street, with its slippery truths and half-hearted promises. Bald had forged his personality in the certainty of conflict, the black and white of life and death. In

Pretorius, he'd found a kindred spirit. Finally he was back to doing what he did best: getting stuck in, fighting wars, slotting scum. It felt good to be back.

Pretorius slowed as he hit the forecourt. Stepped around the dead bodyguards, feet brushing aside spent niner jackets. The acrid smell of gunpowder wafted through the air. He reached the pumps.

'Shit!' he said.

Bald caught up with him. 'What is it?'

The President wasn't there.

'Where is he?' Bald asked.

Pretorius didn't reply. Bald followed his gaze. Down the road leading from the palace to the corner of the main road. The road the Lincoln had scudded down. Bald spotted a figure in a grey jacket and a turban hat shuffling down that road. The President.

Hurrying back towards the palace.

thirty-five

They chased after the President. Big drops of rain spattered the road as the dark clouds that had massed out over the ocean began rolling inland. In the distance Bald could hear abrupt gunshots, the faint screams of terrified civvies. By the sounds of it the attack on the radio station was going to plan. Now they just had to corner the President. He was forty metres ahead, lumbering towards the palace.

'Got to stop him,' said Pretorius at Bald's three o'clock. Deet was running behind him, with Stegman and the two backup soldiers.

'What does it matter?' Bald replied between thirsty gulps of air. 'He's not going anywhere.'

'If the President retreats inside the palace compound, he'll barricade himself in. We'll have to fight our way to him. It'll take time. Time we don't have. The longer the President is still in power, the harder it'll be to unseat him.'

Bald pushed on. Chest heaving. Heart thumping. Eighty metres ahead stood the palace, within a compound surrounded by a two-metre-high concrete wall. Above the gates there was a battered sign, like a in a Wild West frontier town. 'PALAIS DE BEIT-SALAM,' it read in colourful lettering. A sentry box stood at one side but there was nobody home. The gates were still open.

The sight of the palace sent a strange thrill running through Bald. They were going to do it, after all. He licked his lips with anticipation and powered on towards the President. He was so close to the money now he could almost smell it.

The President tripped on a crack in the pavement and fell on his face. Thirty metres from him now, Bald sighted the President down the barrel of his rifle as he struggled to his feet. He was half a second away from depressing the Colt trigger and watching the back of the President's head explode when Pretorius thrust a hand out in front of the rifle barrel and blocked his view.

'No, John! We take the President alive,' he said. 'Unless you're happy being piss-poor.'

'The fuck do you mean?'

'All the millions Khalifa has siphoned off international aid packages – we need to know where he's stashed it. Account numbers, passwords, assets. Without that stuff we'll just be rulers of a Third World slum.'

Gritting his teeth, Bald reluctantly lowered his weapon. Pretorius had a point, he admitted. The Comoros had no natural resources to speak of; the islanders weren't sitting on big oil reserves or mines overflowing with diamonds. The only money coming in was in the shape of relief aid from the international community. No doubt the President-slash-dictator took a kickback from each financial aid package and diverted the money into a secretive offshore account. Bald had seen for himself how guys like Khalifa milked the system. The luxury shops of Geneva were filled with former Third World dictators who were sitting on vast retirement funds courtesy of the IMF or the World Bank. If Bald got his hands on that kind of cash, he could truly live like a king.

Ahead of him, the President stumbled on. Twenty metres from the gates now.

'Any news from Girard?' Pretorius called out to Stegman.

'Not a word, Mr Pretorius,' the South African replied breathlessly.

Pretorius growled deep in his throat. 'What's taking him so fucking long? Girard should have seized the airport by now.'

No response. Bald sensed the mission slipping away from them. First the President legging it towards his compound. Now this business of the delay in the airport attack. He was pissed off. He hadn't come all this way – killed a child in cold blood, been shot at and threatened – only to fall at the last hurdle. From somewhere deep inside, Bald found his second wind. He sprinted past Pretorius towards the palace gates, his hands chopping by his sides, legs kicking out aggressively like a runner on the home straight, the veins on his neck bulging like tensed rope. He closed in on the President as he ducked through the gates.

Bald was twelve metres behind his quarry as he himself raced into the compound. Through the middle of a lawn, some forty metres wide by twenty deep and broken up by palm trees, a stone-paved path led to steps at the front of the palace. The building itself was a drab whitewashed affair, tackily decorated with ornamental stonework and with a solid-looking walnut door intricately studded with gold, as the main entrance. At the foot of the steps, the Comorian national flag fluttered in the cool, damp breeze, the metal snag hooks clinking against the aluminium flagpole. Below the steps a Mitsubishi Triton pickup was parked, its bodywork painted in the livery of the Comoros Defence Force and on its flatbed a Soviet-manufactured NSV heavy machine gun mounted on a pintle tripod. For a moment Bald slowed his stride, wondering what the fuck an army pickup was doing here.

The President was just six metres ahead of Bald, lumbering

the steps. Bald reached him in three big strides. Launched himself at him, wrapping his arms around his waist and rugby-tackling him to the ground. The President let out a pained groan as he hit the deck.

Bald pinned him to the ground until Pretorius and the rest of the team had joined him and he was satisfied there was nowhere for the President to run. Then he jumped to his feet, keeping his eyes on him. The man was clutching his windpipe and coughing violently as he rolled onto his back. Catching his breath, he looked up and warily surveyed the faces of the six men stood in a circle above him. Lighter-skinned than many of the locals Bald had seen, he had features that were distinctly Arabic. His eyes were small and black as prayer beads, his nose wide at the nostrils and slightly hooked. The white cap had tumbled from his head, revealing cropped grey hair. His hands trembled. On his face was a look of numb horror.

'Who' – the President struggled to form words, his lips quivering uncontrollably – 'who are you?'

Pretorius dropped to one knee. Grinning at the President, he said, 'I'm the man who just evicted you from office. I'm calling the shots now.'

Defiance flared in the other man's eyes. 'Impossible. I am the President of the Comoros, the Commander in Chief of the Defence Force. My men will never stand for this act of aggression. As a matter of fact, they'll be here any minute.' He folded his arms triumphantly across his chest. 'I've already sent a message to my General.'

'General Ben Said is dead,' Pretorius replied flatly. 'I've installed Colonel Rashidi as the new chief of staff. My forces have seized the radio station and are in the process of securing Prince Said Ibrahim airport.' He said all this in a matter-of-fact tone, as if reading the small print on a contract. 'It's over, my friend. The country belongs to me now. You can surrender, or die. Choose wisely.'

The fire in the President's eyes petered out. He gulped loudly.

'Why are you doing this?' he whispered.

'Because I can,' Pretorius replied in that same toneless voice. 'Because I have the will to do it, and the means, and in this life that's all you need. Now, here's the thing. You're going to cooperate and if you're lucky, I might let you live. Or you can play hard and suffer a long and painful death. Not like your friend General Ben Said. He took a bullet to the head. *Bang* – nice and easy. So what's it going to be?'

The President swallowed hard. 'What do you want to know?'

'Where you keep your money.'

The President looked blankly at the soldiers. 'Money?' Then he understood, and spat out a cruel laugh. 'You fucking idiots.' His lips were cracked and flecked with spittle. 'I don't have a pot to piss in. They took it all away from me. Froze my assets.'

'Who?' Pretorius growled.

'Who'd you think?' The President sat upright. Knees pressed to the ground, his voice bolder now. 'The Americans.'

Stegman took a step towards the President. 'You're lying.'

The President looked outraged. 'It's the truth. I swear I have nothing. I am but the humble reflection of my poor countrymen.'

Stegman choked on his khat. He turned to Pretorius, his eyebrows arched. 'You're not seriously buying this shit? He's lying through his teeth.'

Pretorius said nothing. He calmly bent down and drew the Beretta pistol next to the President so that the receiver was level with his ear. Then he fired a shot. The bullet pinged off the stone steps. The President squealed in pain, rolling away as he pressed a hand to his ear. Pretorius stood upright, trained the Beretta on his forehead and said, 'You have three seconds to start telling the truth.'

'OK, OK!' The President pleaded through gritted teeth. He took his hand away from his ear and waved both hands in surrender. His ear was bright-red and stinging. 'I'll tell you – but please don't kill me.'

Pretorius hardened his expression. 'You were saying about the money.'

The President pursed his lips. His eyes shifted left and right. Pretorius shoved the Beretta against his face, the end of the muzzle digging hard into the plump folds of his cheek.

'It's in my office,' the President said anxiously. 'I keep everything in a safe there.' Noticing the sceptical looks on his captors' faces, he added quickly, 'This is the Comoros, not Wall Street. The money is not safe in any bank account. I give you the code. Just let me go, eh?' He looked desperately from Pretorius to Bald. His eyes lit up. 'Fifty million US dollars. Cash. All yours.'

Pretorius stared at the President for a moment. Gears grinding inside his head. Then he nodded. 'OK. In your office. *Now.*' He turned to the two support soldiers. 'Keep watch at the door.'

The President stumbled to his feet and started to climb the steps. Deet hit them ahead of him and swung open the door, his arms like a couple of battering rams. Pretorius nudged the President along with the pistol at his back. Close behind, Bald glanced back and saw Stegman shooting him a look like a Turk at a christening. Anxiety sank like teeth into Bald's guts just then. He remembered the promise Stegman had made back at the RV. 'This isn't over. Once the island is taken, you're dead.'

Killing Eli had been a necessity. The slave had had dirt on Bald and threatened to expose his identity. But by squashing one problem, Bald had created another for himself. Given the amount of khat chewed and the psychotic rages he was prone to, there was little doubt in Bald's mind that Stegman would make good on his threat at the first opportunity. Unless Bald killed him first. The idea came out of nowhere, and caught him by surprise. But there it was, all the same. The more he thought about it, the more he liked it. A pre-emptive strike, attacking Stegman when he least expected it, double-tapping the junkie fuck in the back of the head. The idea appealed to Bald, to his dark instincts. It was simply a matter of watching his back and waiting for the opportunity to present itself. Meanwhile he refocused on the mission.

The four men swept through the palace while the other remained on guard. Inside, the two-star theme continued. The floor was shiny marble, like something out of a Mr Muscle ad. The lobby was full of tacky decorations and potted plants. Mundane landscape paintings hung from the walls. At the far end glass doors led out to a garden the size of four tennis courts and bordered by exotic plants and marble busts on plinths. At one side of the doors a staircase led to the upper floor.

Bald scanned the lobby. Two doors to the left, two to the right. The President led the way towards the first one on the left. He turned the chunky knob and stepped inside the room. Pretorius and Bald followed.

They found themselves in the President's office. It looked like the office of a small-claims lawyer. The walls were magnolia and lined with framed photographic portraits. Overhead an ornate ceiling fan whirred loudly. To the right stood a large, glass-fronted case full of leather-bound books. To one side of the window the Comorian flag draped from a pole, more colours on it than a float at a Gay Pride parade. In front of the window there was a large oak desk with a bronze engraved nameplate that said, 'LE PRÉSIDENT'.

Bald instantly recognized the man sitting behind the desk.

thirty-six

Colonel Rashidi sat with his hands folded in front of him, Ray-Bans wrapped around his face. He was flanked by four soldiers, two either side of the desk. Thickset men decked out in woodland camo uniforms and armed with FN FAL automatic battle rifles. The *clack-clack* of rounds being chambered into rifles filled the air as the four soldiers loaded, then trained their rifles on Bald and Pretorius. Both men stood perfectly still. Nobody said a word for what seemed like a minute but was in fact no more than a few seconds. The rain beat down in a relentless dull hiss. For a long moment it was the only sound in the world, raindrops hitting at the window, tracing veins down the glass like melted gelatine.

Colonel Rashidi rose and strode confidently around to the front of the desk. He flashed a gold-toothed grin at Pretorius. His hefty frame threatened to burst out of his muddied white uniform. He snapped off his shades and looked the PMC chief hard in the eye.

'Your guns,' the Colonel said. 'Lose them.'

Bald glanced at Pretorius. The guy looked like he was chewing gravel. The skin was pulled tight on his face, the air hissing through his flared nostrils. His jaw was visibly clenched. If Bald cupped his hand to his ear, he could probably hear the grating of his teeth. Footsteps sounded at his back. He turned to see two more soldiers nudging Stegman and Deet into the office at gunpoint. They stopped behind Bald and Pretorius, with the two support soldiers alongside them. The Colonel's men had obviously been lying in wait inside the palace and had quickly rounded up the militiamen as soon as they were trapped. At least that explained why they hadn't met any resistance once they'd breached the palace compound, Bald thought.

'So good of you to join us,' the Colonel said. He flicked his gaze back to Bald and Pretorius. 'Now, don't make me ask twice. Drop your weapons, or my men will kill you all.'

In a rapid motion Pretorius pulled the President close to him, the Beretta pressed tight against his cheek. 'Anyone takes a shot, I blow his fucking brains out.'

The Colonel grinned. His cool, relaxed demeanour suggested a man totally in control of the situation. 'Rashidi is taking over the country now. And he is glad that you bring brother President back to his loving embrace. He was hiding from me. We feared we had lost him. Now you have returned him, truly this is a sign from Allah. He means for Rashidi to be king.'

The President shook his head. Not an easy thing to do when a pistol muzzle is digging into your cheek. 'But, brother Rashidi – you must spare me. Look, I brought these men to you. At the very least, I deserve your mercy.'

It was then that Bald understood what had happened. In a last desperate throw of the dice, the President had led Pretorius and his gang to Rashidi. Hoping that the Colonel would express his gratitude by sparing his life. Judging from the mean look on Rashidi's face, the plan had backfired.

'We will discuss your – ah, future – later, brother Khalifa. First Rashidi must take care of these dogs.'

Pushing the Beretta harder against the President's face,

Pretorius rasped, 'You're shit without me, Rashidi. I control the islands. I'm the one in charge – I run this ship.'

The Colonel appeared nonplussed. He calmly tucked the Ray-Bans into his top pocket and smiled faintly. 'There are five hundred armed men on their way to the palace who would disagree with you.'

Pretorius went as white as a chalk cliff.

'That's right,' the Colonel continued. He perched himself on the edge of the desk, rolling the palm of his hand over the contents of a gold-trimmed cigar box. 'The Defence Force is under Rashidi's command now. You do as Rashidi says. Like the game Simon Says. I tell you jump, you jump.' The smile on his lips spread up to his ears. 'I tell you die – you die.'

'We had a deal.'

'*Had*,' said Rashidi, tapping the side of his nose. 'Not *have*. See. Rashidi masters English, and it is not even his first language. I think I will make good President, yes? Now, hand over brother Khalifa and surrender your weapons.'

Pretorius shook his head, less out of disagreement than out of pure disbelief.

'But my men – they were supposed to accompany you to the barracks.'

'This is true. Is also true Rashidi had a change of heart.' He plucked a cigar from the box and rolled it around in his hands. 'I asked myself: "Rashidi, why you work for these white dogs and help them take over your country? Why you getting this much"' – he pinched an inch of air between his thumb and forefinger – '"when you could be getting all this?"' He swept his arm broadly across his chest.

Then the Colonel turned back to Pretorius. His smile was like a Rottweiler baring its teeth. If a Rottweiler decided to get its teeth capped with gold. 'It is a very convincing argument.

So I told myself, "I will take it all instead, and cut you and your friends out of the equation." And here we are.'

'What happened to my men?' Pretorius said coldly. 'The soldiers who escorted you to the barracks, where are they?'

'Dead,' the Colonel replied simply. 'Dead, dead, dead.' He said this in a cheerful tone of voice. 'My men, they follow my orders very good. I told them, "Rip these men to pieces." So, your men died like dogs. Soon your men at the airport will be dead too. Then I came here to install myself as the new leader. Rashidi wants to execute brother Khalifa live on TV, so all the people can see who is the new boss. But the President was hiding, like the coward piece of shit he is.'

'At least I'm not a traitor.' The President shook a fist at the Colonel. He was foaming at the mouth, beside himself with rage as the dark realization sank in that leading Pretorius into this trap wasn't enough to save his life. 'How dare you stab me in the back! After all I did for you and the General.'

'Loyalty has a price, brother Khalifa. Sadly for you, you did not pay enough to buy Rashidi's. The General's, yes. But General Ben Said is dead. Gone away. Now there is only Rashidi.' He turned back to Pretorius. 'No more games. Put down the gun and give me the President.'

'Let us go, then,' Bald cut in. 'That's the deal. We give you the President, you get to chop him up or whatever floats your boat, and we'll be on our merry way.'

The Colonel chuckled easily. He sniffed the cigar, inhaled the aroma deeply. Closed his eyes and sighed. Bald glared at him. In the corner of his eye he could see the President looking anxiously from Pretorius to the Colonel, his breathing shallow and erratic.

Then the Colonel walked back around the desk. 'Look.' He nodded at the window. Bald could see across the lawn to the palace gates, and beyond them, Rue de la Corniche running north-south. On the left side of the road a row of Arabic-style buildings were arranged like tombstones. On the west side was the harbour, where dozens of weathered fishing vessels and rust-bucket trawlers were moored between volcanic rock jetties. In the middle of the road a convoy of military trucks was heading directly for the palace. Renault GBC 180s, all-terrain heavy cargo trucks painted in woodland camo colours. Had to be at least fifteen of them, thought Bald. The line of trucks caterpillared all the way down the road. He turned back to the Colonel, face blackening with rage.

'You're outnumbered five hundred to six,' the Colonel went on as he paced back in front of the desk to jab Bald in the chest with the butt end of the cigar. 'Here there isn't no fucking negotiation.' His accent slipped into French as he grew impatient. 'This is Rashidi telling you what to do.'

'Fuck that for a bag of dicks,' Stegman piped up. The Colonel turned to the 2iC as he went on. 'If we hand you the President, what's to stop your boys from putting a bunch of holes in our heads?'

For a beat, the Colonel looked at him. 'Nothing,' he said. 'Rashidi has already decided you must die.'

'This cunt is bluffing,' said Bald. 'If he wanted to slot us, he would've done it already.'

'Wrong,' the Colonel countered. 'Rashidi prefers to keep you alive. For the time being. Then, tomorrow, we hold a big celebration in the main square. Everyone is invited. People will drink and cheer. Then I will show them what happens to anyone who dares try to fuck with Rashidi. My men will put you on a stage and beat the shit out of you. Then they will stab and burn and shoot you. It will be a big party. After, we tie your feet together and hang your bodies from the lampposts. People will be free to spit on you, piss in your faces, cut off your testicles. Whatever they want. Everyone happy.' He pushed out his bottom lip and traced a fake tear down his face. 'Except you. All of you. Very sad.'

Bald fought an urge to smash the Colonel in the face. At his side the President began to rock back and forth, his eyes glued shut as he quietly intoned prayers.

'Hand over the President,' said the Colonel.

Pretorius simmered. The knuckles on his gun hand were white, Bald noticed. 'You won't get away with this.'

As he spoke he kept the Beretta trained on the President, drawing him closer by clasping his left hand around his shoulder. Pretorius glanced at Bald. There was a cold glint in his eyes, like a crescent moon on a chilly night. Bald understood instantly what Pretorius was planning to do. A hot feeling pulsed in his veins and he steeled his muscles as he looked back to Rashidi, the survival part of his mind working the angles. The Colonel was standing in front of the desk with the four soldiers two metres behind him at either end of it. Throw in the two soldiers in the doorway and there was no margin for error. They had one chance to get this right.

The Colonel tightened his face like a screw going into a hole. 'Now, please. The President.'

Stegman stepped forward. 'Don't do it, Mr Pretorius. Don't let him win.'

'It is too late,' the Colonel grunted. 'Already too late the moment you met Rashidi.'

All eyes turned to Pretorius. He paused, readying himself. One last draw of breath. And then he said, 'You want the President? Here!'

Pretorius shoved the President at the Colonel.

Bald knew what was coming next. Knew from the mad light in Pretorius's eyes. And knew because, if he'd been the one holding a gun to the President's head, he would have done the same thing. Pretorius was one step ahead of the

Colonel and his soldiers. Everything happened very fast. The President staggered forwards, arms waving frantically as he lost his balance. The Colonel jumped back in surprise. But he couldn't get out of the way in time. The President crashed into the Colonel and sent him flying backwards onto the desk. The Colonel instinctively grabbed the President by both arms to stop himself landing flat on his back. Still on the balls of his toes, Pretorius shot forward, raising the Beretta and training it on the two soldiers to the left of the desk. One of them discharged a round in a panic. There was a strangely soft thud and the Colonel grunted as the bullet hit him in the back on his way down, piercing his vitals. He jerked like someone had attached a pair of jumper cables to his balls. Pretorius shot twice at the two soldiers. The bullets thumped into the midriff of one of them. His arms dropped like hammers. The rest of him quickly followed. His lifeless body hit the floor with a wet slap, like a sack of wet cement dumped out of a window. Pretorius swivelled his aim towards the second soldier.

Bald reacted in the same instant. Years of hard living and drinking had dulled his reactions, but the old sharpness was still there, buried deep in his bones, engraved into his fast-twitch muscle fibres. A good operator was like a professional sportsman; the sharpness might dull in injury or retirement, but the innate ability was still there. Now Bald harnessed it, sinking to a crouch as the two soldiers to the right of the desk fired at him. One round whizzed over his head and thwacked into the wall. The echo of the shot was still ringing in Bald's ears as he raised the Colt Commando, sighted the nearest of the two soldiers and let rip. The guy spasmed as three bullets punched into him in a pleasing rhythm. *Whump-whump-whump*. Immediately he swung the rifle across and brassed the last soldier, his body pirouetting violently on the spot as the rounds corkscrewed through his vitals. The four guards lay sprawled in two piles at either end of the desk.

Then Bald remembered the two guards in the doorway. He spun around just in time to see Deet almost single-handedly overpowering them, with a little help from Stegman and the two support soldiers. Deet had a giant arm wrapped around the throat of one of the men, while Stegman tried to wrestle the FN FAL rifle free from his desperate grip. The second guy had already been taken care of. He was on his back, his face bloody. Then Bald noticed that he was still alive and reaching for his holstered pistol. Bald set his weapon sights on the prone guard and pulled the trigger. Sent him the same way as his muckers had gone: south. Six rounds left in the clip now.

In the next instant Stegman finally tore the rifle from the other guard. Now Deet shoved him back into the doorway, allowing Stegman to unleash a volley of hot lead that almost cut the guy clean in half. His arms flailed this way and that as his rifle fell from his grasp. He slumped against the door, clutching his belly, his head hanging low, as if he was bowing his head in prayer. The polished wood glistened with fresh blood. Then everything went very still.

The firefight had lasted six or seven seconds. The air was suddenly thick with the smell of blood and gunpowder. Bald loved that smell. It told him that he'd survived. A steely determination gripped him then. He wasn't going to die. Not here. Not today.

He swung back to see Pretorius towering over the Colonel as he lay sprawled on his back on the President's desk.

'Cross me, you fucking animal!'

The Colonel was in rag order. Blood leaked from a rough hole in his chest the size of a coat button, soaking his jacket. His eyes danced in their sockets. Bald detected a flopping sound in his chest. He was grasping at life the way a drowning man clings to a piece of wood, making a wheezing sound in his throat with each strained in-breath.

'Look at me,' Pretorius said.

Ignoring him, the Colonel reached with a trembling hand down to his breast pocket. He pulled out the Ray-Bans and went to slip them on his face. Pretorius intervened, snatching the shades from him and tossing them aside.

He said again, 'Look at me, you dead fuck.'

The Colonel swallowed painfully, sweat flowing down his face and pain racking his body. Slowly he lifted his eyes to Pretorius, the muscles of his face twitching, blood sloshing around his mouth, dribbling out of the corners. Then he did a strange thing. He began laughing. It wasn't recognisably a laugh, but a gurgled, almost inhuman cackle.

'What's so funny?' Pretorius snarled. He was spitting mad and this only seemed to make the Colonel laugh harder despite his injuries.

Pretorius snapped. Lost it. He snatched up the President's nameplate and went to town on the Colonel, smashing one end against his face in a mad flurry of blows. The Colonel groaned as the bronze slab cracked his nose. He raised a limp hand in a futile attempt to shield his face but Pretorius brushed his arm aside and lamped him on the jaw, and there was a sharp crack like a piece of wood snapping in half as his jaw shattered. The Colonel gasped in agony. He tried to roll out of the way but Pretorius smashed the makeshift weapon against his face like he was hammering nails into a piece of timber. The Colonel stopped grunting. Pretorius stood upright, ditched the nameplate and admired his handiwork.

'Who's laughing now, eh?' he said, panting with effort, his eyes blazing with cruel intent. Then, much louder: 'I said, who's fucking laughing now?'

The Colonel couldn't reply. Mostly because he didn't have a mouth. His face resembled a Florida sinkhole. Through this mess of gristle and bone, he was making a grating, hissing noise as if he was sucking soup through a straw. Blood formed a lake under his corpulent torso. He wasn't fully dead – not yet anyway. Bald gave it four or five minutes – if the guy was lucky. Longer if he wasn't. Beside him the President rolled around on the floor, desperately patting himself down to make sure he hadn't taken a bullet. Pretorius clasped a hand around his arm and hauled him up. The President stood limp and distant, his eyes fixed on the dead Colonel, the colour draining from his face like dirty water from a sink.

Then one of the support soldiers called out to Pretorius, 'Sir, we have a problem.'

'What is it?' Pretorius snapped.

The soldier pointed at the window.

Pretorius spun around and gazed outside. Bald joined him and they watched as a convoy of military trucks parked up outside the gates. Fifteen soldiers piled out from the back of the nearest truck, each man clutching his FN FAL rifle and looking like he meant business. Bald counted another fifteen emerging from the second truck. Thought, if there were an equal number of soldiers in the back of each truck, then that meant . . .

An icy dread percolated down his spine.

Hundreds of soldiers, he realized.

Hurrying straight for the palace.

thirty-seven

0936 hours.

Stegman shook his head and stared out of the window. 'But the Colonel's dead. They've nothing to fight for.'

'They don't know that,' Pretorius replied. 'All they know is there's been a bunch of shots fired in the compound, and their new President is sat right here.'

'What if they find out the Colonel's dead?' Bald asked.

Pretorius shook his head. 'Won't work. It'll piss off the foot soldiers and convince the 2iC, whoever the fuck that is, that the path is open to the Presidency. All he's got to do is takes us out of the picture and the top job is his for the taking.'

'What are we gonna do?' Stegman asked.

'This,' Pretorius replied.

Without a moment's hesitation he smashed the glass with the grip of his pistol as the first wave of soldiers rushed through the gates. He traced the nearest soldier's path across the compound with the Beretta and fired once.

Bald put the distance from the window to the gates at twenty-five metres. The shot nicked the ground in front of the soldier farthest from the gates. Bald raised his rifle; so did Stegman. They squeezed off a couple of three-round bursts. Their aim was rushed and the bullets zipped high and wide of their targets, but the soldiers ducked anyway, fearing for their lives, their poor training evident in the way they beat a hasty retreat, backtracking towards the compound walls either side of the gates in order to remove themselves from the line of fire.

Now Bald unleashed another burst at the truck. The rounds hammered into the grille. The driver panicked and scurried from the cab, joining his muckers behind the wall. The suppressive fire had bought them an extra second or two; no more than that. The second wave of fifteen soldiers had by now flooded out from the back of the truck immediately behind the lead vehicle and were sweeping towards the compound. Nine or ten seconds, thought Bald. That's how long he figured they had until the soldiers regrouped and attacked in strength.

'Spread out,' Pretorius said, turning away from the window. 'Harvey, you set up shop here. Deet, head to the other side of the building, find a good vantage point. John, you're with me. We establish a baseline at the main door. The door is our red line. Whatever happens, we don't let anyone reach the palace itself.'

Stegman shook his head. 'Mr Pretorius, there's too many of them. They'll keep coming at us until they get through. We can't hold out for ever.'

Pretorius clicked his tongue. But he said nothing. He stared at a spot on the wall, wilfully ignoring Stegman and the rest of the team. As if he refused to consider the bleak truth staring him in the face. That there was no hope, no glimmer of survival. The odds didn't allow for the possibility of victory. They would die here, all of them, and Pretorius refused to accept it.

'Loot those soldiers,' he said brutally at last. 'Rifles, secondary weapons, grenades. Whatever you can get your hands on.'

The President looked on as the men hurriedly snatched weapons and kit from the six guards they had killed in his office. He shivered, then glanced up at Pretorius.

'What about me?'

Grinning, Pretorius replied, 'You stay no more than a metre from me at all times. I catch you trying to run, I put a bullet in that slimy skull of yours.'

Four of the team flooded out of the office, leaving Stegman and one of the other backup soldiers manning the window in the President's office, putting down rounds on the gates. Deet and the second support soldier shuttled off down the opposite corridor to find a similar vantage point, while Bald and Pretorius sprinted down the lobby with the President in tow. They rushed outside through the main door and quickly established a baseline on the steps to confront the enemy. Right on cue two soldiers bolted around the compound wall and scurried through the gates. Bullets skipped up around their feet as Stegman put down rounds on them. Bald coolly switched to single shot and showed the South African how it was done, discharging a pair of rounds. He hit the jackpot with both. Bullet number one thumped into the head of the soldier on the left. Bullet number two pencilled his mucker through the throat. He made a gargling sound in his throat as he tried to staunch the wound with his bare hands. A third guy ran to his mates' aid, firing wildly from the hip as he moved. His firing stance was tragically bad. His aim was all over the place. The rounds struck somewhere east of the palace door. Pretorius punished him with a single shot to the guts. The guy didn't die like they did in the movies. He writhed in agony on the ground, legs kicking out as he screamed for help. Pretorius chief gave him another ball of lead to the chest. The guy stilled. Bald figured that the Comorians would have seen their mates taking hits as soon as they moved through the gates and had second thoughts about wading into the compound. But more and more soldiers were grouping outside the compound walls now – he could see them assembling by the trucks lining Rue de la Corniche. Bald counted sixty, seventy of them. Hundreds more were lying in wait, itching to give the guys dug in at the compound the good news.

An advance unit of thirty Comorian soldiers hooked around the military truck and advanced towards the gates thirty metres from Bald. Fifteen soldiers dropped to kneeling firing positions and targeted their FN FALs at the palace door while their mates advanced. Basic fire-and-movement tactics. But efficient.

'GET DOWN!' Pretorius roared, hurling the President face-down as the soldiers opened fire.

Hot smoke seethed out of their rifle barrels. A dozen cracks thundered across the rain-soaked garden. Bullets sprayed the steps and chewed up the door. A round flew over Bald and missed him by no more than an inch, the heat grazing his scalp. There was a sound at his six like a bag of coins being dropped from a great height as the bullet struck a window, and then he heard Deet call out, 'Man down! Man down!' They were five now. The chances of escaping from the palace with their lives dwindled further.

The Comorian soldiers fire-and-moved forward again. In seconds they'd reach the gates. Bald grimly assessed the situation. Then he sprang to his feet, gesturing to Pretorius as he tipped his head in the direction of the Triton.

'Cover me,' he bellowed above the incessant hammer of gunfire. 'I'll get on the HMG. Brass these wankers up.'

Pretorius grinned. 'We make it out of here alive, I'm buying the first round.'

'I'll drink to that.'

Pretorius put the brakes on the advancing soldiers with a steady stream of bullets. Bald raced towards the Triton. Nine metres. Piece of piss. His stomach muscles contracted and a chill ran down his back despite the clammy heat, bristling the hairs on the nape of his neck as he sprinted done the steps and towards the pickup. As an SAS operator he'd fought plenty of engagements against enemies with superior numbers and firepower, but nothing like this. He remembered the stories of an old trooper pissing away his retirement fund in his local boozer in Hereford – Bald in twenty years, if he lived that long – a guy with a haggard face and shoulders like a couple of breeze blocks who'd been at the Battle of Mirbat, in Oman, back in 1972. A handful of Regiment operators had repelled wave after wave of attacks from three hundred militiamen. Only, this was worse, thought Bald. Like Mirbat times ten. He knew he was going to have to call on all his training and expertise if he was going to stand a chance of coming out the other end in one piece.

He blocked out the anxiety gnawing at his guts and looked up at the gates sixteen metres away. Six more soldiers darted inside. Four of them were swiftly cut down in the vicious criss-cross of arced gunfire coming from the firing positions at the opposite corners of the palace. That still left two guys dispersing either side of the gates. They spotted Bald racing to the NSV, dropped to a prone firing stance, sighted their weapons on him and unleashed a quick one-two. The distance was minimal but Bald was moving fast, his chin tucked in tight, and the bullets slapped into the grass at his six o'clock. More rounds slapped into the front wall of the palace, throwing up great fists of concrete. Four metres to the Triton now. The remaining two soldiers aimed at Bald and it looked like he wasn't going to make it. Then Pretorius unloaded from the steps and cut down the pair of them down.

'Nail the fuckers!' he shouted. 'NOW!'

Bald leapt onto the back of the Triton. A soldier beyond the gates, fifty metres back, shot up the cab as Bald got to grips with the NSV. It was a Soviet-era gun, one that he'd operated once or twice during foreign weapons drills. He knew it took the 12.7x108mm cartridge, a slightly larger bullet than the standard .50-cal used by Western HMGs. The NSV had the stopping power of a cruise missile. The mechanisms were almost identical to the .50-cal he was used to. A long line of link coiled up from the ammo box to the feed unit via the right-hand side. He located the firing controls on the mount. These took the form of a pistol grip fixed to the cradle of the tripod, which had already been adjusted so that the barrel was high enough to fire over the side of the Triton. Bald flipped the safety and thumbed the fire selector to single shot.

Good to go.

At his three o'clock Pretorius was coming under sustained heavy fire from the two prone soldiers. Bald pivoted the NSV towards the soldiers as they opened fire again, peppering the door and keeping Pretorius pinned down. Then Bald rested the sights on the soldiers. Filled his muscles with air, and fired.

The first rounds thundered out of the NSV's muzzle and cut the soldier in half. His torso went one way, his legs the other. His entrails spooled out on the ground in a long, greasy trail. Bald actually heard the man scream above the discharge roaring in his ears – a guttural wail, like foxes mating, which filled the ex-SAS man with a perverse joy. He angled the HMG slightly to the right, gave another short pump of the trigger. The second soldier exploded. Turned to relish. Nothing left of him but fractured bones and shredded skin. Spent jackets the size of Red Bull cans burped out of the ejector tube on the right side of the receiver, showering the flatbed.

A group of five soldiers swept through the gates, caught sight of their vaporized mates and displaced. Bald lined up a third soldier and gave him the gift of hot lead. His head toppled off his shoulders like a skittle knocked over by a bowling ball. His headless torso slumped to the ground as his mates fled for cover. Bald unloaded a round at a fourth man. The round struck low, blasted his leg below the ankle to dust. He crumpled. Bald corrected his aim. Pulled the trigger. Felt the killing power of the NSV in the heavy recoil, in the way the round scudded through the air and thumped into the soldier.

'Fucking take it!' he muttered.

Bodies littered the area around the gates. But dozens more soldiers were disgorging from the trucks. They were moving forward and working in distinct two-man teams: one man putting down rounds while the other displaced and established a baseline closer to the target. Then the second guy went into covering fire mode to allow his mucker to catch up with him. The nearest soldiers were just eighteen metres short of the gates, so forty-three metres from the door of the palace. Almost on top of them. Half a dozen of them were now putting rounds down. Bald pivoted the NSV towards the gates and let them have it, but the soldiers were already sliding back behind the wall of the compound and the rounds thumped uselessly into the tarmac as the soldiers joined their comrades grouped behind the perimeter wall. More soldiers were gathering outside the gates now, and the awful realization struck Bald that very soon they would have the palace surrounded. There would be no way out then. He cursed his luck.

Soldiers began darting out of cover, loosing off ragged shots and scurrying back behind the wall, all in the blink of an eye. Pretorius shouted to Bald above the incessant din, 'Stop them, John, for fuck's sake!'

Switching the NSV from single shot to semi-automatic, Bald swung the weapon a few degrees to the right of the gates, so that the iron sights were lined up with a section of the wall to the immediate west of the sentry post – roughly at the point where the Comorian soldiers had found cover. Three-quarters of a metre of concrete stood between them and Bald. He pressed the trigger on the pistol grip. Kept it pressed for a few seconds as five rounds torpedoed out of the muzzle in a searing burst of smoke and thunder and slammed into the wall of the compound. The 12.7x108mm cartridge could punch a hole in an armoured tank and made short work of the wall, each round smashing home like a fist into a bowl of flour, clawing away at the concrete.

The sixth round broke through the twisted metal rods and exited the other side of the wall. A hideous scream carried across the compound as the round slashed through the chest of a soldier hunkered down on the other side. Bald unleashed three more shots at the wall, increasing the size of the hole until it was roughly a metre wide and forcing the soldiers to displace. Meanwhile Stegman and the backup soldier in their firing position at the window to the President's office, and Deet at the other end of the palace, were nailing anyone who tried slipping through the gates. Bodies were piling up in the compound now. At least twenty of them, sprawled, limbs spread, mouths slack, eyes heavy-lidded with that look of mute horror Bald had seen on a hundred dead men in a dozen different war zones.

The rain continued to fall.

The soldiers kept coming.

Bald kept firing. Out of the corner of his eye he saw that Stegman, Pretorius and Deet were making short work of it, bullets tracing white-hot streaks across the garden, ripping into palm trees and throwing up great clumps of dirt into the air, slicing and dicing the soldiers like vegetables in a blender, and for a moment the Scot dared to think that they might hold out.

But an instant later the bleak truth twisted viciously through his guts. They were running out of time. The plan had hinged on taking control of the Comoros with lightning precision and speed: there was a French Foreign Legion garrison based on the neighbouring island of Mayotte, some five hundred men, and once the first shot had been fired the alarm would have been raised. Securing the Comoros before the Foreign Legion could deploy and augment the Defence Force troops was vital to the success of the op. Bald guessed they had an hour max.

And then?

Then didn't bear thinking about.

At that moment one of the military trucks sputtered into life and sledded towards the gates.

The truck abruptly picked up speed. Dozens of soldiers gathered behind the vehicle and Bald understood immediately what was happening. They were going to use it as a battering ram. The dread realization clawed at him as the truck trundled towards the gates. Forty metres away. Now thirty. Bald flicked the selector on the NSV back to single shot as he lined up the sights with the windscreen. Squeezed the trigger. The truck was close enough for Bald to see the brains squirt out of the back of the driver's head, spattering the cab as the round hit the bullseye. He discharged two more rounds at the truck's bonnet. The bullets worked their magic, piercing the hood and crippling the engine. The crippled truck skidded to a halt just inside the gates, smoke spitting out of the grille, the engine sounding a death note.

No sooner had the truck stopped than soldiers began swarming behind it. Now they had a beachhead established inside the compound. Bald unleashed six rounds at the truck, hoping they would pinball through the chassis and strike down one or two of the soldiers hunched behind it. But it was desperation stuff. The floodgates had opened. Soldiers swarmed into the compound, fanning out to the flanks and establishing a baseline across the length of the garden. Bald realized they were being overrun. Nothing he could fucking do about it. Bullets spattered the Triton in a ferocious cacophony. Above it the Scot heard a throaty cry at his five o'clock. He glanced back at the door. Saw Pretorius drop to one knee, clutching his left shoulder, blood seeping between the fingers on his right hand.

'Inside!' Pretorius cried, staggering to his feet. 'Fucking go!'

After unloading two final rounds from the NSV, its muzzle red-hot now, Bald vaulted off the flatbed and hit the ground running. He bombed up the steps and reached the door as Deet emerged from the lobby. Deet chucked him an FN FAL rifle liberated from one of the dead soldiers inside the palace and helped Pretorius to his feet under an unrelenting hail of lead.

Bald swung around to face the enemy as he grappled with the FAL. He had no experience of the FN variant, but he'd used the L1A1 Self-Loading Rifle derivative manufactured by the British Army plenty of times on the Circuit. The only difference between the SLR and the FN FAL was the muzzle. The assemblies were basically identical and his hands automatically felt for the grip and operated the trigger mechanism without his even having to think about it. The three-round burst shot up a soldier tearing towards the steps. He fell back as if he'd slipped on black ice.

Deet followed up with a quick burst from his secondary weapon, the Taurus Raging Bull wrist-breaker. Shot a soldier in the groin. The guy made an 'O' with his mouth and shivered speechlessly, as if stunned by the pain. He gaped down at his disintegrated manhood. Stringy threads of his balls dangled between his legs. The man cupped his hands to them and sank to his knees.

Deet took a bullet to the ankle as he led Pretorius and the President back inside the building. He didn't stop. Kept moving. Bald emptied a last three-round burst at the soldiers swarming over the compound. Stegman was waiting in the lobby. He pulled the firing pin from a grenade and tossed it through the crack in the door into the crowd of soldiers advancing towards them. Then he slammed the door shut. Frantic shouts from outside were quickly followed by an earth-shuddering thud as the grenade detonated. Fragments showered like hailstones against the door. Quiet descended on the garden. It wouldn't last for long, Bald knew. No sign of the other backup. Guy must have taken a hit during the firefight, he guessed.

Pretorius rounded on the President. 'You must know a way out of here.'

The President shook his head nervously. Pretorius gripped him by the throat and thrust the pistol muzzle into his face. In the back of his head Bald knew they were running out of time. Any second now a bunch of soldiers would come crashing through the door.

'Think again,' Pretorius said. 'If we don't kill you, the Colonel's men will.'

'My helicopter,' the President replied hastily, pointing to the stairs at the back of the lobby. 'It's on the roof. A Eurocopter. I use it to fly to my hunting lodge in Mozambique.'

'Why didn't you take the chopper when you fled earlier?'

'The Colonel killed my pilot when his men attacked. I don't know how to fly myself.'

Pretorius looked to Deet. 'Can you fly that thing?'

Deet thought for a moment. 'A Eurocopter?' He shrugged. 'No problem.'

'Then let's go.'

Pretorius turned back to the President. 'How long to get to Mozambique?'

'Less than an hour.'

Shouts came from outside, getting louder as the soldiers neared the door. 'Move,' Pretorius said, starting to bundle the President towards the stairs, twelve metres away. He glanced at Bald, then Stegman. 'Cover us. Once the chopper's ready to go, make your way to the rooftop.'

'Roger that,' Bald said.

Pretorius moved freely, seemingly oblivious to the blood pouring out of the trauma wound on his left shoulder. His camo jacket was soaked through. Bald watched Pretorius, Deet and the President disappear from view as they hurried up the stairs. Then he swung back to Stegman – and found himself staring down the barrel of a Colt Commando.

Stegman said, 'This is where you and me part ways, sunshine.'

Bald stood his ground. A quick glance at the palace door ten metres back. The shouts were super-loud now. The soldiers were practically breathing down their necks. Seconds to spare until they blitzed through the door. Bald slid his eyes back to Stegman, his mind racing. Trying to think of something – anything – to stop the South African from blasting a hole in his face.

'You can't kill me,' he said.

Stegman smirked. 'The fuck I can't.'

'I'm with the Firm,' Bald said slowly and clearly.

It worked. Stegman didn't blow his brains out. He kept his finger on the trigger but the smirk disintegrated and in the next moment he pulled three faces for the price of one: disbelief, puzzlement, curiosity. Then he shook his head fiercely. 'Bullshit. If that was true, Mr Pretorius would've killed you back at the RV. The other one, Priest: he was with the Brits.'

'I sold your boss a lie,' Bald pressed on, his voice wired with urgency. 'I'm working for the Firm. They sent me here to take out Pretorius. He's out of control. If you kill me, you'll be automatically bumped to the top of the Firm's most wanted list. That's cast-iron, that.'

Stegman shook his head again. Firmly this time. 'This can't be true,' he said. His voice was distant now. 'You can't be with Six. My handler would've told me.'

'Handler?'

Stegman tensed his grip on the rifle. 'I'm with the Company.'

Something like a fist slogged Bald in the guts. The cold sensation on his neck turned to ice, stabbing his flesh and needling his spine. He was dimly conscious of soldiers congregating at the door, his heart thumping like a fist against his chest wall as if in tune with the footsteps.

The Company. He means the CIA.

Stegman is CIA.

thirty-eight

The door flew open and four soldiers crashed into the lobby. Bald put his confusion on ice and centred his FAL rifle on them. Stegman did a one-eighty, dropped to a knee and hefted up his rifle in a swift but controlled blur. The two men each let off a three-round burst and hosed down the soldiers with a hot spray of 7.62x51mm lead. They went down in a big pile in front of the open door. Bald squeezed off another burst and a fifth soldier fell in the doorway, screaming as he reached down to his shattered ankle. Stegman finished the guy off with a neat burst to the head. His brains splashed across the magnolia wall. Bald heard the heavy clomp of boots on stone as more soldiers raced up the steps.

'We have to fall back,' Stegman said.

'To the chopper,' Bald said. 'I'll lead, you cover.'

'Long as you don't put a bullet in me.' Only half-joking.

Cunt, thought Bald as Stegman fired another three-round burst through the doorway, forcing the soldiers back into cover. As Bald wheeled away from the door he heard the sound of breaking glass coming from the rooms to east and west of the lobby. The soldiers were storming the palace from every conceivable angle now, intending to attack Bald and Stegman on three separate fronts. If that happened, it'd all be over. Bald pounded across the lobby with renewed energy and determination. He glanced back at Stegman as he emptied another burst at the doorway and launched up the stairs. Suddenly the air was filled with a terrific *whup-whup-whup*, accompanied by a high-pitched drone. The Euro copter's engine was firing up.

'Hurry,' Stegman boomed. 'We don't have much time.'

Bald looked back. Stegman was a metre behind him. Fifteen metres back a soldier steamed through the front door and immediately lost his footing on the puddle of blood greasing the floor. Bald let him have it with a quick burst, put the brakes on the Comorians' advance. Then he spun around and hurried to the first-floor landing. Reached it in four long, quick strides. Stegman unloaded a final burst, sending four soldiers dispersing around the lobby in search of cover. He cleared the last two treads and joined Bald as more soldiers flooded into the lobby from the rooms to either side.

Turning on his heel, Bald darted down the corridor, past a conference room, making for a door at the end of the corridor, twelve metres ahead. The door had been left open and a gloomy staircase led up to the roof. He kept up the pace, conscious of the noise of soldiers amassing on the floor below. He and Stegman had a head start on them, and he hoped to fuck it would be enough to allow him to get on the chopper and bug the hell out of this bloody island.

Stegman hurried along at his shoulder. Bald said without looking at him, 'You can't be with the CIA. You're not even American, for fuck's sake.'

'The Company recruited me,' Stegman replied. His face was covered in sweat. 'A case officer met me in Jo'burg. Told me they needed a local asset to do the job, someone who could pass themselves off as a PMC. By then I'd been out of the game for a few years, but when this case officer told me about the rand on offer, I jumped at the chance.'

Bald flashed Stegman a quizzical look. 'They ordered you to kill Pretorius too?' Thinking, why would the CIA and MI6 both send assets into the field to take the guy down, and not tell each other about it?

Six metres from the stairs, Stegman said, 'That was the original plan.'

Bald shot him a look. 'But the mission got fucked up,' Stegman went on. 'Pretorius kidnapped the case officer. I couldn't get rid of Pretorius until I secured her release.'

Her. Unease tightened like a noose around Bald's chest. He couldn't breathe. He couldn't feel his legs. He looked at Stegman. 'Imogen?'

Stegman nodded.

'But back in Kenya – on the boat – you abducted Imogen.'

'I had . . . no choice,' Stegman replied falteringly. 'If I didn't bring her back to the camp – if I went back empty-handed – Pretorius would've booted me off the team. And then I'd have no chance of completing the mission. We agreed she'd play along until I had the chance to nail the bastard.'

Three metres to the stairs. Voices sounded close at their six o'clock. The soldiers were climbing the first staircase. Stegman said, 'This is what we're gonna do. First, we shut Pretorius down. Then we'll find Imogen.' He paused. Glowered at Bald. 'And then you owe me an explanation for why you killed Eli.'

Bald tried to mask his panic. 'Your partner?'

'An old friend. He was also on the Company payroll.'

Shit. Bald had a big problem. If Stegman really was working for the CIA, then that meant he was in a position to fatally compromise Bald. All the stuff about siding with Pretorius and turning his back on the Firm, he could explain away as a means to an end. He'd just told Pretorius what he wanted to hear in order to win his confidence and get close enough to kill him.

Bald's mind was made up as they approached the stairs.

He waved Stegman ahead. 'You first.'

The agent swept past him and hit the first tread. At the same time Bald hiked up his rifle so that the muzzle was pointed at the middle of Stegman's back and gave a deft pull of the trigger. Momentarily the grainy stairwell lit up white. Stegman jolted as if he'd been struck from behind with a sledgehammer. He lost his balance and fell to his left, his back slapping wetly against the wall. His face registered shock as his legs gave way and he tumbled to the foot of the stairs. He reached for the Colt Commando; Bald kicked it away. Stegman looked up at him with blood in his mouth and a neat hole in his chest, a look of animal hatred in his eyes.

'Cunt!' Stegman rasped, blood gurgling in his throat. 'Son of a cunting bitch.'

'Don't blame me,' said Bald. 'Blame self-preservation.'

He stepped over the agent and raced to the door at the top of the stairs. He hit the bar and emerged onto the roof. The chopper was a lightweight Eurocopter AS350. Deet was manning the controls. The engine droned, the rotor blades spun superfast. Pretorius was seated in the back, one hand gripping the pistol trained on the President, the other stemming the blood from his shoulder wound. Bald dashed towards the chopper. He climbed in and slumped into the seat next to Pretorius. The PMC chief looked across to the door leading onto the roof and his brow furrowed.

'Where's Harvey?' he said icily.

'Took a hit to the chest,' Bald replied. 'Nothing I could do for him.'

Pretorius pounded his thigh in frustration. 'Get us out of here,' he said to Deet. 'Off this fucking island.'

The drone of the engine picked up, sounded like a hive of angry hornets. The blades whirred. There was a lurch as the chopper pitched forward and left the ground. Then they were rising above the roof at 8.5 metres per second. The maximum effective range of the FN FAL was four hundred metres. It would take the Eurocopter forty-five seconds to climb beyond firing range. They were forty metres off the ground. Still another three hundred and sixty metres until they were safe.

The door to the stairs flew open. Stegman staggered out, his upper body glistening with blood, his clothes flapping in the strong downdraught from the chopper. He lifted his head to the Eurocopter, shook a fist of raw rage at Bald. He was still shaking it when the first soldier stepped out onto the roof and put a round in his chest. Stegman jolted. His arm lowered slowly, involuntarily. The Eurocopter was now a hundred metres above the palace. Then a hundred and twenty.

Nine more soldiers fanned out across the roof. They formed a semicircle around Stegman and began emptying rounds into him. Bullets ripped into his limbs and torso, blasting away muscle and bone and tearing off strips of skin. Blood gushed from a dozen exit wounds. Stegman jerked with the impact of each round but somehow remained standing. The Eurocopter was three hundred and fifty metres above the palace by the time the gunfire cut out, the soldiers exchanging looks of disbelief at how Stegman was still on his feet. His bullet-riddled body swayed on the spot, blood pooling between his legs, his face knotted with anguish. At last one of the soldiers stepped forward and capped him with a shot to the back of the head.

The Eurocopter climbed to four hundred metres above the palace. Some of the soldiers turned their attention from Stegman and started taking pot-shots at the chopper. But it was too high now, and their bullets went well wide of the fuselage. Bald glanced down as Stegman and the soldiers surrounding his body shrank to the size of insects. Then to specks. At last the chopper pitched forward and shot off towards the harbour. Bald breathed a sigh of relief. Yes, he was wicked and callous and cold-blooded. But he had been shaped that way by the world around him. The way he saw it, he was simply giving back what the world had given to him. He saw nothing wrong with what he'd done, because he'd witnessed – and done – much worse in the line of duty. It was no excuse. But Bald wasn't a man who bothered with excuses. He just did what he had to do in order to survive.

'This should have been mine,' said Pretorius. He stared at the compound as it shrank into the middle distance. He took a deep breath and snorted, as if expelling his resentment through his nostrils. Then a thought flashed across his features and he turned to the President.

'Why would a coward like you own a hunting lodge on the mainland? You don't even know how to fire a gun.'

'I – I like the hunt,' the President said fakely.

Pretorius jerked forward in his seat, grabbed the President by his collar and thrust his head out of the window. The prayer cap was whipped off his head by the sharp wind and drifted down towards the Indian Ocean.

'The truth, my friend. Or you get to see what it's like to freefall without a parachute.'

The President flapped his arms manically. 'No! Please!'

Pretorius shunted him further forward so that his upper body was outside the cabin door, his head nearly level with the landing skids.

'Shit!' he screamed above the battering wind, the steady whoosh of the blades, the mechanical whine of the engine. 'OK, OK. I – I keep my money there. All fifty million of it. US dollars. Cash.' He added shrilly, 'It's all yours! Take it.'

Pretorius yanked the President back into the cabin, releasing his grip on his shirt collar. The President fell back in his seat, soothing his neck as he tried to steady his frantic breathing.

Pretorius turned to Bald and grinned. 'What do you say, John? How about the President compensates us for our losses?'

Bald grinned. 'Aye, I'm up for that.'

He smiled to himself as he gazed west out of the cabin window. Out on the horizon there were no clouds. Sunlight glimmered on the sea like a band of gold. Fifty million. He rolled the number around his mouth with his tongue. Not bad. Split three ways, it worked out to a shade under seventeen million each. Pocket shrapnel compared to the money they would have made if they had taken control of the Comoros. But still, a good whack. Enough to get Bald started on that dream of a new life far away from the Firm. He'd made the right call, then. Joining forces with Pretorius, slotting Priest and Stegman. He tried to ignore the migraine nudging at his skull – faint tremors that pulsated through his brain and scratched at the backs of his eyeballs – and turned his thoughts to Mozambique and the prospect of getting seriously minted.

1053 hours.

The President was spot-on. The flight from Moroni to the hunting lodge on Mozambique's east coast took exactly fifty-three minutes. The Eurocopter had a range in excess of 650 kilometres and a cruise speed of 132 knots, equivalent to 244 kilometres an hour. As they neared their destination Deet pitched the chopper into a gentle descent and they swept across the Quirimbas archipelago, paradise islands scattered along the coastline. The Quirimbas National Park straddled the Mozambique coast, a hundred-kilometre stretch of lowland forest and savannah running north to south. The Eurocopter began its descent over the middle of a flat, rugged plain north of the national park, tall elephant grass rippling in a golden wave under the steady thrum of the chopper's blades. The engine receded to a gentle hum.

'This is the place,' said Deet.

Pretorius grabbed the President and shoved him out of the cabin door. He fell onto all fours on the baked earth. Bald, then Pretorius, followed him out as Deet clambered out of the cockpit and established his bearings. Forest to the north. Giant inselbergs rose out of the plain to the west, granite fortresses towering over the wild. Elephant grass whispered in the cool late-morning breeze. At the edge of the plain lay a shallow lake, and the hunting lodge stood at the water's edge. A porch on stilts afforded a view of the lake. At the back a wooden table and four chairs stood in the shade. It was a good place to stash money, thought Bald. The area was deserted, as far from civilization as you could get. Dundee minus the concrete. It'd take days to journey here by foot from the nearest township. Somewhere in the distance, a lion roared.

The four men waded through the tall grass towards the lodge. As they reached the door the President took some keys from his pocket and fiddled with a series of locks. Clacks and clangs, then he tugged the door open. It groaned on its hinges as first Pretorius, then the President, stepped inside. Bald and Deet followed them.

The lodge was the kind of place that gives animal activists douche chills. Hunting trophies hung from the walls: antelope horns, the stuffed heads of rhinos and buffalo. There was enough ivory on display to keep the piano business going for years. The sofa was covered in a genuine leopard skin. The rug was a bear skin. Practically every ornament and decoration in the lodge had been an animal. The table was made from bones. Horns and tusks were used as drinking vessels. There was a black-and-white photograph on the wall – inherited from a previous owner, Bald figured – of a plump white man in a waistcoat and breeches with a bushy moustache standing proudly over a lion, an old Winchester repeating rifle propped against his shoulder as he posed in front of the slain beast. In one corner of the main room was a bar, with bottles lined up on a shelf behind it. Johnnie Walker Red Label, Bowmore, Talisker. Bald licked his lips. He'd hit the jackpot.

Pretorius said, 'Where's the money?'

The President said, 'It's buried. Outside. I'll show you.'

Pretorius flicked his eyes to Deet. 'Grab a shovel.'

Deet nodded dutifully and stepped into a utility room piled high with equipment. He pulled a shovel out of the clutter and the President led him out to the back yard. Soon the distant chirping of grasshoppers was replaced with the thunk of a shovel cutting into the scorched earth. Bald could hear Deet grunting as he heaped up the soil. Pretorius eased himself down on the sofa. Bald made for the bar. Jesus, he was parched. His tongue was like sandpaper, pasted to the roof of his mouth, his teeth covered in fur.

'You know, it's funny,' Pretorius said.

Bald reached for the Johnnie Walker. 'What is? Because this whole op has been one big bag of laughs.'

Pretorius sniggered. 'I'm talking about the traitor in our midst. Priest, he seemed to fit the bill. The GPS bracelet he wore, the fact he couldn't pilot a plane. I'd convinced myself he was the guy. But it appears I was wrong.'

Bald wasn't really tuned in. He was too busy unscrewing the cap and raising the bottle to his thirsty lips. He was about to neck his first swig when he caught sight of the Beretta pointed at his face. He stilled. Bottle mouth pressed to his lips, the honeyed scent of whisky teasing his nostrils, so close he could almost taste the good stuff. He turned real slow to face Pretorius. There was a peculiar glower to his eyes and his lips were curled in a twisted smile.

He said, 'The traitor has been staring me in the face all along.'

For a beat Bald couldn't speak. A numb feeling slithered down his spine, spreading to his guts and limbs. His right arm had lowered the bottle and he hadn't even realized it. A savage pain fired through his temples. The migraine. Shit, it was back. He gripped the bottle, his right hand trembling like an alcoholic going cold turkey.

'I know you're working for MI6,' Pretorius added.

'Bullshit.' But his voice didn't sound convincing to Bald, let alone Pretorius. The migraine pounded viciously between his temples, a searing pain that seemed to graze his cranium. He sucked his teeth, gripping the edge of the bar with his free hand to steady himself. Questions surged through his mind, amplifying the sharp throbbing in his head. Pretorius stood up from the sofa, took a few steps towards Bald.

'No point lying, John. He told me everything. On the phone. En route to Moroni.'

'Who?' Bald muttered.

'Grealish.'

As he said this, Pretorius shuffled closer to Bald, his brow stippled with sweat. He looked weak from the loss of blood. Bald remembered now. The name on the JCB Sitemaster screen. The conversation. Pretorius telling Grealish the name of his new mucker on the team, John Bald. Pretorius drew nearer to him. The Beretta muzzle eyefucking him.

'As soon as I mentioned your name, Grealish gave me the heads-up. Told me that you were tight with Six. That a former colleague of his, some jumped-up bitch, had hired you to find and kill me.'

Bald shook his head. Coupled with the migraine, it felt like a rack of snooker balls was sliding around his head, crashing against the sides of his skull, splintering his thoughts. He tried to focus. 'Grealish must have got his wires crossed. Priest was the guy they sent. For fuck's sake, you saw the GPS tracker he was wearing.'

'I thought about that. Grealish told me he personally requested Priest be included on the strike team.'

'Why?'

'So he could keep an eye on you.' Pretorius chuckled. 'Why else do you think, you idiot? Grealish is forever boasting about his ability to pull strings in Whitehall. He said that once he learned you were being dispatched, he decided to put his own man on the team. Someone he could trust. Someone who could stop you before you carried out the mission.'

That's why Priest sold me out to Pretorius, thought Bald. To take me out of the picture. He now understood why Avery Chance hadn't told him about Priest wearing a tracker: because she hadn't known herself. Grealish had gone behind her back, used his black book of contacts and secured Priest a place on the team. A favour from an old mate, no doubt. But Pretorius wouldn't have known that when he discovered the tracker. He would simply have seen proof that the guy was spying on him. Bald stood perfectly still. Didn't move a muscle. He was done. No way out. The pistol muzzle glowered at him. Eight inches from his face, Pretorius poised to pull the trigger. Bald felt his entire body constrict with fear – and hate. Grealish had fucked him, again. Belfast, twenty years ago. Now this.

The migraine exploded. A jarring pain tore through his head. As if someone had buried an axe in his skull and was now trying to jerk it free. Bald dropped the bottle and its base disintegrated in a hail of shards, like someone had fed a block of ice into a log splitter. Whisky darkened the wooden floor. Bald lost his grip on the bar and fell to his knees.

Above him Pretorius rasped, 'Get up, you miserable fuck – and die like a man.'

Bald experienced a moment of clarity through the searing pain. The glass. A dagger-like fragment seized his attention, the point splashed with whisky. Pretorius was still above him, confused by the sudden onset of the migraine. In a flash Bald grabbed the shard of glass and stabbed him just above the knee. Pretorius howled in agony, clamping his free hand to his leg. Bald yanked out the piece of glass. Blood pumped steadily from the wound, impairing Pretorius's movement and forcing him to stoop forward for a moment as he bit back on the pain. Bald lunged at him, slapping his left hand around the guy's right wrist and thrusting his arm towards the ceiling. At the same time he balled his right hand into a fist and delivered a sharp dig to the ribs. Pretorius grunted loudly. His reflexes automatically depressed the trigger and he loosed off a round that tore into the beamed ceiling, showering both men in a hail of crisp splinters of wood.

Then Deet rushed through the door, eyes wide with alarm, bellowing with rage as he charged towards Bald with the shovel in both hands. The Scot gave Pretorius another quick jab to the guts and followed up with a sharp elbow to the jaw. The Beretta tumbled from his loose grip as he fell away. In a rapid motion Bald grabbed the pistol and arced it towards Deet when he was no more than two steps away. The bodyguard was swinging the shovel down past his shoulder like an axe. Bald fired twice. Deet stopped. Like he'd run into a pane of glass. His head snapped back and his brains spat out of the back of his head, painting the hunting trophies a dark shade of red. The lodge shuddered as his giant frame hit the floor. Bald spun away from Deet and saw Pretorius scrambling out of the back door. He shaped to give chase when a roar of pain sounded from the yard. Bald raced outside. Saw Pretorius prostrate on the ground, the rusted jaws of a hunting trap fastened around his ankle, digging savagely into his flesh. The

PMC chief clenched fistfuls of dry earth as he fought the pain.

'Bastard,' he said. 'Get it over with.' He glanced up. 'Do it!'

Bald said nothing. He was gripped by a sudden fury. Twice Pretorius had put a gun to his face. No one did that to him and lived to tell the tale. A sinister image of Charles Grealish flashed across his mind: the man who had almost terminated his career in the Regiment. Pretorius had been working with Grealish. Both of them had taken him for a ride, screwed with his brain to the point where he couldn't see straight any more. Now he saw clearly. As if on cue, the migraine started to dissipate. There was only the sound of his breathing, the steady pulse of blood between his ears. This ends now, Bald told himself.

He knew exactly what he had to do.

He slipped into the utility room and seized a length of rope. Then he hurried outside and bent down beside Pretorius. With both hands gripping the trap, Bald wrenched the savage jaws apart, releasing Pretorius. He hauled him to his feet. The guy was groggy, delusional from the heavy blood loss. He mouthed words that remained silent on his lips as Bald slung the rope over his shoulder. Then, at gunpoint, Bald shoved Pretorius south towards the national park two hundred metres away. He could hear the incoherent mumbling of the President as he lay slumped next to the mound of earth. In the distance to the east, Bald glimpsed a pair of white smudges on the horizon, shimmering in the heat of the savannah. Eight or nine hundred metres away. They looked like Jeeps.

Company.

Better hurry it up.

Bald swivelled his gaze back to Pretorius. The guy was totally out of it – could hardly stand up. They reached the perimeter of the national park with the Jeeps four hundred metres distant. The park was bordered by a crude wooden fence reinforced with barbed wire. A sign on a metal post next to the fence read: 'DANGER LIONS.' Bald shoved Pretorius through a gap in the fence. Now they ventured deeper into the jungle. Strange growls and squawks carried through the air. After two hundred metres Bald stopped beside a tree with a trunk as thick as a man's chest. Then he pushed Pretorius against the tree with his back pressed against the hard bark, slipped the rope off his shoulder and began wrapping it around the tree and Pretorius's waist. The wide look in his glazed eyes told Bald that, behind the pain, the man knew exactly what he was doing.

'You can't do this to me,' he croaked.

Bald stayed silent. He continued to bind Pretorius tightly to the tree.

'I don't deserve to die like this. Like a . . . dog.' Pretorius let his head drop. Then he lifted his gaze, anger briefly flickering in his eyes. 'Fuck it, then. Shoot me in the head. Anything but this.'

Bald still said nothing. When he was done wrapping he secured the rope with a double knot. Not that Pretorius was in any fit state to escape. Satisfied with his work, Bald took a step back. Deep growls drifted through the jungle.

'Hear that?' Bald said. 'They can smell your blood. By the time they're finished tearing you to shreds, there won't be anything left except bones and scraps. You're a fucking animal. Now you're going to die like one.'

Pretorius summoned one last iota of strength. Lifted his heavy head and met Bald's eyes. 'You're the same as me. A monster. We're – brothers.'

'No,' said Bald. 'I'm nothing like you.'

Then he gave his back to Pretorius and retraced his steps out of the park, Pretorius shouting at his back that they were the same, that killing him would be like Bald killing himself. The Scot tabbed back towards the lodge with a clear conscious and a pressing weight lifted from his shoulders. He was a hundred metres shy of the lodge when a roar echoed through the jungle, a chorus of animal snarls followed by a piercing howl of very human agony. The lions were getting stuck into Pretorius. Ripping him limb from bloody limb.

Bald reached the lodge with a spring in his step. The Jeeps had stopped out front and several figures were debussing, white men and women in dark suits and shades. Poster boys and girls for the Firm. That made a certain amount of sense. The suits were always waiting in the wings to claim the credit. A woman, fortyish and prim, approached Bald. She wasn't exactly dressed for a safari, wearing a pair of low heels and a black two-piece, her skin pale, her shades blocking out the sun. She gave the impression of a frigid professional – cold and hard-edged – the kind of woman who spoke her mind and seized ruthlessly on the weaknesses in others. But Bald knew her better than that. Knew that once you looked under the hood there was a vulnerability she went to great lengths to disguise. She wasn't a corporate ball-breaker. But a fighter. The kind of woman who, if backed into a corner, would fight like hell. Bald recognized her immediately. His handler. Avery Chance.

'Hello, John,' she said. As she neared Bald he noticed that her hair, usually cropped with a touch of blonde at the fringe, now betrayed strands of grey. She was entering middle age. They all were, thought Bald.

She cast a look at the President, the blood spattered over Bald, and cleared her throat. 'It appears you've been busy.'

Bald looked down at his shirt and hands. He needed a shower. And a drink. And a shave. 'Aye,' he said. And then: 'How did you know where to find me?'

'Grealish,' Chance replied as she ran her eyes over the lodge. 'We've been listening in on our old friend, picking up chatter on GCHQ. Once we knew the President was in danger, we had him tapped up, allowing us to trace his signal here. We were hoping that the President would lead us to Grealish too . . .'

The words drifted silently from her lips. They both knew: sometimes the bad guys slipped through the net. Not everyone paid their dues. That was the way of the world and it didn't need articulating. They both looked across to where two agents were attending to the President. He was a nervous, animated wreck. Then Chance looked back to Bald and frowned.

'Mind telling me what happened to Pretorius?'

'Went for a walk in the park,' Bald replied, jerking his thumb in the direction of the jungle. 'Got a feeling there won't be much left of him by the time your people have secured the scene.'

Chance nodded warily. 'You know, normally, I'd have to launch an internal investigation. There are all sorts of rules and regulations about what we can and can't do to people like Pretorius.'

Bald clamped his lips shut. He watched Chance very closely as she went on, 'But I think we can make an exception in this case.' She stared at him hard. 'If there's no body, then there's no evidence. No evidence means no crime.'

'Don't worry about a thing,' Bald replied, grinning.

She doesn't know any of the dark shit that went on, he thought. He'd covered his tracks thoroughly. Priest was dead. So was Stegman. And Pretorius. He was in the clear. Finally he could look forward again. A new job with the Firm. A clean slate, a decent salary. It wasn't as good as the seventeen-odd million he'd stood to make with Pretorius – wasn't even in the same solar system as 'good' – but under the circumstances he was willing to compromise. He broke out a broad grin.

'I told you, Avery. Back in Poland. Good as my word. I kept my nose clean.'

Chance looked at Bald in a way that troubled him. She wasn't smiling. In fact, she seemed unsure about something. Hesitant. 'If that's the case,' she said carefully, 'do you mind explaining this?'

She passed Bald the iPhone 5s she had been gripping in her right hand. YouTube was already open and a clip was waiting to be played. Three million hits. Curious, Bald tapped Play. There was an ad for some kind of sports drink, which Bald skipped after five seconds. Then the clip started.

The footage was sharp. Crystal clear. A child stood among a group of prisoners. He was five or six years old. There was a white-hot flash and the tinny report of a shot being fired, and the boy jolted as a bullet struck him in the centre of his face. An old man wailed off-screen as the boy slumped to the ground. Then the camera panned across from the dead child to the face of the man who had pulled the trigger. Bald went cold. He recognized the face in an instant. Of course he did.

Bald was looking at himself.